Jackie

J Melvin Smith

MULTIPLES

J MELVIN SMITH

JMelvinSmith.com

Woburn, MA

© All rights reserved.

Printed in the United States of America.

This is a work of fiction. Any resemblance of characters to actual persons, living or dead, is purely coincidental. The Author holds exclusive rights to this work. Unauthorized duplication is prohibited.

Acknowledgments

To the many people who helped this book become a reality through their comments, suggestions, editing, proofreading, designing and other assistance, I am truly grateful. Please forgive me for not mentioning all of you individually.

To my brother, Bernie: Thanks for providing your professional editorial skills and your continuing support.

To Esther Davis, a professional editor and close friend of my daughter: Thanks for going through the final daft with a fine-toothed comb. I highly recommend your services to other writers.

To my son, Christopher Allen, and daughter, Stephanie Lyn: Thanks for developing into better offspring than I deserve, and for allowing me to use your names in the book. I hope that I did justice to them.

To Gale, my wife: You have always encouraged and supported me, regardless of the endeavor. You have been a true companion.

My apology to the town of Winchendon, its council and police department. My sister-in-law lived in Ashburnham. While visiting her, I found the towns in the area, including Winchendon, delightful and friendly.

1

Lori Moore and her husband, Richard, sat in Doctor Walter Force's inner office and watched as he flipped through the chart in front of him. The room was small, stuffy, and devoid of personality.

Several weeks earlier, Lori had noticed her breasts had become sensitive and somewhat different in shape. She immediately scheduled a visit with her physician. The doctor ordered several tests, the results of which he now sat reviewing.

"Lori, I received the results of the tests. As we suspected, they came back positive. They confirm that you have inflammatory breast cancer." Lori had anticipated the news. She was not sure what inflammatory breast cancer was specifically, but she knew what breast cancer meant. Her research made her familiar with her best treatment options.

"I was concerned the biopsy would reveal cancer. I've done some reading about various forms of breast cancer and treatments, but nothing I read referred specifically to inflammatory cancer. What is it, exactly?"

"Inflammatory cancer is a very aggressive cancer. We should schedule you for a radical mastectomy as soon as possible. Then we'll follow up with chemotherapy and radiation therapy, as needed," the doctor answered.

"What's the prognosis?" Lori asked.

"We won't know how invasive the cancer is until the surgery. As I said, this is a particularly aggressive cancer. If it has already spread beyond the point of origin … well, let's discuss the prognosis after we go in and see how extensive an area is involved. The important thing right now is to remove what is already there and start treatment."

Richard sat without emotion, staring out the window behind the doctor. He heard little of the conversation after the doctor said breast cancer. When Lori first told him about the problem, he convinced himself it was nothing more than a mild infection, or some minor problem. He refused to think about the possibility his wife could have cancer. Confronted with reality, his body reacted. His hands became clammy, perspiration formed on his forehead, and his legs started to twitch.

Later that night, Richard and Lori were sitting up in bed. Lori intently read medical information, and occasionally jotting notes in a notebook. Richard was reading a Tom Clancy novel. Lori disliked Clancy's novels. She said they contained too much death and destruction.

Richard turned and looked at his wife and asked, "You all right?" Lori looked at him, reached over, took the book out of his hands, and placed it on the nightstand on her side of the bed. She pulled the covers down and straddled his hips.

"That's the third time this evening you asked me if I'm all right."

"I'm just concerned."

"Yes, I know. And I appreciate it. If I could do anything to eliminate your concern and spare you the emotional roller coaster we are about to ride, I would. But listen carefully … this cancer is just a challenge. We will beat this. The day after tomorrow, I'm going to have surgery. Then chemotherapy, radiation therapy, and whatever else is needed to make sure the cancer's gone. Then we will go on with our lives." She pulled her nightgown over her head, and placing her hands under her breasts, and said, "I know you love these. I'm rather fond of them myself. But, they've become the enemy, and they have to go. The plastic surgeon will perform reconstructive surgery and replace them with implants. As a matter of fact … " She stopped, drifted off into thought, and then continued, "You enjoy giving my breasts so much attention, I think I'll ask the surgeon to double their size." She gave him a sheepish grin. Leaning forward, she kissed him on the neck.

"Cancer is not going to separate us. We have a lot more life and love to share and I'm certainly not leaving you."

She reached down between his legs and guided him into her. As their lovemaking progressed, he felt the eruption building in his groin. He closed his eyes and concentrated on holding back just awhile longer. He wanted this to last forever. Just before he exploded, he opened his eyes and gazed at her face.

A combination of fear and panic twisted Lori's features. She was screaming, but Richard could no longer hear her. She was pointing frantically at him. Not in bed, she was suddenly sitting in the driver's seat of her car, and he was watching her from behind the glass door that led from the kitchen to the garage. He fixed his eyes on Lori's face as she screamed and pointed, screamed and pointed. He tried to open the door but it would not move. Frantically he drove his shoulder into the door. Nothing happened. He watched her as she finally stopped screaming, then she stopped pointing, and settled back in the seat. He never knew what she was saying. She relaxed, tilted her head back against the headrest, and closed her eyes.

2

Richard Moore picked up the phone that had nagged him into wakefulness. "Chief Moore," he said.

"Chief, Lieutenant Allen, I'm on River Street at the bend just before Miles River. Shirley Robinson went off the westbound side of the road. She'd been heading east. The EMT says she's been dead for a couple of hours. A trucker found the wreck."

"Shirley Robinson, the most cautious driver in Winchendon?" Richard asked in disbelief.

"That's her."

"What's the situation?"

"Her car is in the woods on the west side. She apparently bounced off a couple of trees, then came to rest about thirty-feet from the shoulder of the road."

"Okay, Chris. Keep a tight wrap on everything. I'll be there as quickly as possible ... Chris, have you notified Pete yet?"

Pete Robinson was Shirley's husband. He was the third generation owner of the local hardware store and an influential member of the town council.

"No, but he should be calling me soon. He called at eleven o'clock and reported his wife overdue. He's been calling every half-hour since."

"Have a car meet me at his house. I'll call his sister and have her get someone over there so he can go to the hospital."

"Right, Chief. By the way, I called Doc Fenton. He's on his way to the hospital now."

Chris was referring to the town's oldest, and, until a few years before, its only resident physician. Calling him "Doc Fenton" rather than "Doctor," was a sign of respect and affection.

"I'll see you shortly," Richard said, hanging up the phone and raising his five foot, eleven--inch body off the bed. Twenty minutes later, he was showered, shaved, and dressed in his uniform.

Richard maintained the personal discipline he had developed in the military. Now forty-three, he stayed in excellent condition with a daily physical exercise program. His uniform and white shirts were always clean and pressed. He had them tailored to help project a command presence. They were never tight enough to exhibit his fit physic or loose enough to look shapeless. A meticulous man with high personal standards, there were few gray areas in his life. He saw the world as black and white, good or bad, positive or negative. This approach provided order to his life, order that did he did not have while growing up.

Before leaving, he called Diane Simms, Pete Robinson's sister. The Robinson family had been in Winchendon since its incorporation. The elder Robinsons, Katherine and David, were born and raised in the town of sixty-eight hundred residents and still lived in the house they had bought forty years earlier. A sleepy male voice answered after five rings.

"Hello?"

"Alex, this is Chief Moore."

"Who? What? Chief Moore?"

"Alex, I know it's late, but I need to speak to Diane."

"Chief, is everything all right? What's happened?"

"I need to speak to Diane."

"Okay, here she is."

"Chief, what's wrong?"

"Diane, Shirley has been involved in an accident."

"Oh, no! Is she badly hurt?"

"I can't give you any details until I talk to your brother."

"Chief, this sounds bad."

"Diane, Pete will need someone to be with the kids. I'm sure he will want to go to the hospital. Please meet you at your brother's house."

He arrived at the Robinson's house before Diane. Officer Peggy Butler had arrived five minutes earlier and was waiting down the street out of sight. When Richard pulled his car in front of the Robinson's house, she pulled her cruiser up behind it.

The Robinsons lived on Jamison Way, a cul-de-sac off Baldwinville State Road. The house was part of a twenty-five-year-old development that was new by town standards. Richard had been in the house several times, always while attending some function hosted by the councilman. A brick front garrison, the house had two floors, a full basement, and an attic. Four bedrooms occupied the second floor. The first floor had a kitchen, dining room, study, and living room.

The lights were ablaze in the room to the right of the front door. Richard remembered that this brightly lit room was the living room. The lights cast a shadow of Pete pacing back and forth in front of the windows. Before going up to the front door, Richard stopped and talked with Officer Butler.

"Hi, Peggy."

"Chief. Tough night. You want me to go in with you?"

"No, stay out front here until Diane Sims arrives. That'll give me some time alone with Pete."

"Okay. Will I be transporting Mr. Robinson to the hospital?"

"I think so. We'll know after his sister Diane shows up."

Richard then went to the front door and rang the bell. Pete Robinson answered the door almost before the bell finished sounding. His face, full of hope, changed quickly to an expression of terror as he looked at Richard standing in the doorway.

"Oh my God, Chief, what are you doing here?"

"May I come in, Pete?"

"No, wait … Where's Shirley? What happened?"

"Let's go inside."

Without hesitation, Richard stepped purposely into the hall, encouraging Pete to move with him. He guided Pete back into the living room, where both sat.

"Pete, Shirley had an accident. She drove off River Street at the bend near Miles River. I'm on my way to the scene from here."

"Shirley? Is she all right? Is she on her way home?"

"The accident was very serious, Pete." Richard paused, and then continued, "I'm sorry to have to tell you this … Lieutenant Allen told me she died at the scene."

Richard watched and listened as Pete Robinson went through a series of emotional changes after hearing the news. At first, he denied that it was Shirley.

"Chief … someone must have made a mistake in identification. Shirley just went to visit her mother in Royalston. She isn't dead. She couldn't be. I just talked to her on the phone. She was on her way home. She isn't dead. It's just a short drive from her mother's. She'll be home soon. She just got delayed, that's all." Then he felt the loss and the reality of the news and broke down.

Diane Sims came rushing into the house followed by Officer Butler and Pete's parents. From his seat, Pete looked at his sister.

"Shirley's dead. What are we going to do?"

Diane moved quickly to her brother's side and wrapped her arms around him. The news shocked both Katherine and David. Pete's mother let out a shriek. The color drained from her face. She almost fainted. Her husband helped steady her and sat her in a chair. He then went to his son, pulled him out of the chair and hugged him. The elder Robinson felt helpless.

Turning to Richard, he said, "Chief, are you sure it was Shirley?"

"I'm afraid so. Lieutenant Allen responded to the report of an accident. He has confirmed the identity."

"Is the doctor there? Wasn't there anything that he could do for her?"

"Mr. Robinson, when the EMTs arrived, they tended to Shirley. They did what they could, but she was gone before they arrived. When I get to the scene, I'll release the body. The EMTs will transport Shirley's body to the hospital. Doc Fenton is waiting to examine it."

"You mean to tell us the doctor hasn't seen Shirley yet?" This time the question came from Katherine Robinson.

"I can only tell you the EMTs arrived within minutes after receiving the call. They examined Shirley and said that she had been dead for a while. I am going to the scene from here."

"We're going with you," Diane said, and Peter agreed.

"Shirley is being transported to the hospital. You don't want to go to the accident scene. I suggest that Pete and Diane go to the hospital. Officer Butler will take you if you prefer not to drive. Mr. and Mrs. Robinson, you can go with them if you want, but someone has to stay here with the children."

They all agreed, Officer Butler would take Pete and Diane to the hospital, and the elder Robinsons would stay with the children, Richard left the house.

When he got in his car, Richard just sat there. His heart raced slightly, his palms were wet, beads of sweat formed on his forehead. When Pete started to react to the news about his wife's death, Richard started reliving the similar response he had to the news of his own wife's death.

Richard had met Lori Clement nine years earlier at Suffolk Law School. Both had previous careers; both were serious students; both were committed professionals. They also found that they enjoyed each other's company, and soon, they were dating each other exclusively. After graduation, Lori joined the Boston District Attorney's office, and Richard joined the Boston Police Department. They married a short time later.

For Richard, their life together was beyond anything that he had dreamed about before meeting Lori. Then, suddenly one day, the dream became a nightmare and Lori was dead.

Richard pulled himself back to the present, and willed his body to regain control. Slowly, he brought his heart rate and his respiration back to normal, pulled his car from the curb, and headed for River Street.

3

Richard approached the accident scene from the east on River Street toward Royalston. Ahead of him, where the road bent to his left, a Winchendon fire truck, Chris Allen's cruiser, and Jake's tow truck sat with their large assortment of warning lights in full operation. He noticed a tractor-trailer parked on the east side of the road. Yellow and red marker lights outlined the trailer and cab. Its warning lights were flashing and three triangular reflective signs were positioned at various intervals behind it. On the opposite side of the road was a hearse.

Richard parked behind the tow truck and got out of this car. He walked past Jake who was leaning against the left front fender of his truck smoking a cigarette.

Jake was a beefy man in his sixties, with a full beard, and tattoos on both arms. His barrel stomach protruded well beyond his chest, causing his jeans to angle down in front. His voice was gruff from decades of chain smoking. His personality and manner were hardened from a life of drinking and carousing. He owned an assortment of businesses including: Jake's Gas, Jake's Transmission, Jake's Auto Repair, Jake's Used Auto, and Jake's Towing. Richard was not sure Jake had a last name.

"It's about time you got here," Jake barked as Richard passed. "I could've pulled that wreck out and been back in bed by now. Tell them to get the equipment moved so I can hook it up and be on my way."

As Jake started moving toward the driver's door of his truck, Richard turned toward him and said, "I'll be finished in a couple of minutes, Jake. I'll tell you when it's okay to hook up."

Richard spotted Lieutenant Joel Simpson. Sampson was directing his fire crew as they stowed their equipment.

"Hi, Joel."

"Chief. What a tragedy."

"Yeah. What can you tell me?"

"Not much. We were right behind the ambulance, and the EMTs went right to work. Carla asked us to cut open the driver's door. The force of the impact drove the door in twelve to eighteen inches and shattered the windows. We cut the door, and the EMTs pulled her out. They had to pry her right hand from the steering wheel."

"You've been through this before. Did you notice anything unusual?"

"We usually get to the scene of an auto accident earlier. The driver was already showing signs that she was dead. That means that she must have been here for some time. Another thing, she was facing the driver's door window. Her eyes were wide open, and she didn't look peaceful."

"What do you mean?"

"The first thing I thought of when I saw her face was terror."

"It must have been a terrifying experience for someone who hated driving as much as she did."

"Yeah, well it was more like the terror set in after the accident. She must have been busy while the car traveled through the brush and bounced off the trees. It was the damnedest expression I ever saw on an accident victim."

"Okay, Joel. Anything else?"

"No. We're waiting for the body to be removed so we can get our cardiac board. I'll get my report to you this morning. I know the Council will be requesting your presence as usual."

Richard thanked him, then took time examining Shirley's body. When he was through, he motioned to the hearse attendant and told him he could take the body.

Richard walked around Shirley Robinson's minivan, now a wrecked heap. It had traveled thirty feet off the westbound side of the road. It had been traveling northeast, and, given the distance and the amount of damage caused by the impact, more than seventy miles per hour. The speed limit on this section of road was thirty miles per hour.

Leaving the minivan, he walked along the center of the road a short distance east and west of the accident site, and found that the car was not visible from either direction.

After looking over the wreck, the path of travel, and the impact marks on the trees, Richard called Phil Brice over. Phil, a young man in his mid-twenties, worked as a photographer for the <u>Winchendon Times</u>. His pictures of the wreck would be on the front page of that day's edition. Phil was also the unofficial photographer for the Winchendon Police Department.

"Phil, make sure you get some shots from the eastbound side showing the travel path. Get all sides of the vehicle, including a couple of the driver's-side door."

"I got most of them already, Chief, including the standard shots of the body."

"Thanks. You're learning fast."

Chris was talking with Lieutenant Simpson as Richard approached him to get the remainder of his report.

"Chris, I hope you have some useful information for me, because right now I don't understand how this happened."

"Unfortunately, Chief, I don't know that we ever will." Lieutenant Allen flipped through the pocket notebook he had been using.

"A truck driver was driving east around 12:45 A.M. and spotted a reflection of light in the woods. The driver stopped and went in to investigate. After finding the car, the driver called it in. Dispatch received the call at 12:51. I was on scene at 12:58, followed by the EMTs and fire crew.

"Shirley was traveling east, I assume, coming home from her mother's place in Royalston. She crossed the westbound lane and went through the brush. After traveling off the road surface, she hit several trees. From the looks of the driver's door before the fire department cut it open, according to Simpson, she must have hit a tree broadside. The EMTs went right to work. They told me that she had probably been dead for some time. I called you when I realized who the driver was.

"Shirley's face was dotted with blood from small cuts caused by glass splinters from the shattered windshield. Blood smears ran across her forehead. Her face was pale and her lips purplish. After the ambulance left, I looked around but didn't find any debris on the road. I don't think she hit anyone as she crossed the road. I also didn't find any debris west of where she went off the road, so it doesn't look as if she hit or was hit by other vehicle."

"What do you think?"

"Chief, it's hard to believe Shirley could have fallen asleep, but it's a logical explanation. If I didn't know her, that would have been my first guess. She could have fallen asleep, accelerated to seventy-plus and missed the turn. The jolt caused by leaving the pavement may have woken her. From then on, she becomes terrified as the car bounces off several trees. This section of the road is dark and isolated. No one driving by sees the wreck for several hours, and Shirley dies of untreated injuries."

"You said a truck driver found the wreck. I saw a tractor-trailer, but didn't see the driver. Where is he?"

"She."

"She?"

"Yeah, she ... The driver is that woman over there." Chris waved the woman to join them.

"Chief, this is Joan Ripley. She's the driver of that eighteen-wheeler. She found the wreck. Here's her commercial driver's license."

Richard reviewed the license and mentally added his observation: *Joan Ripley, five feet, six inches tall, age forty-four, one hundred and thirty-five pounds, shoulder length, auburn hair, and hazel eyes. Not like any tractor-trailer driver I've ever met.*

"Chief Moore," he said, as they shook hands.

"You don't look like the typical small-town police chief," she said. She looked him right in the eyes, and an impish grin played around the corners of her mouth.

Richard's face colored, as he thought, *Good-looking and smart, definitely not the typical truck driver.*

"Miss, Ripley, tell me how you happened to find the wreck."

"Joan, please, Chief."

"Okay, Joan. Tell me."

"I make a nightly run hauling fruits and vegetables to supermarkets. I'd just left Royalston, headed for Route 202. I'd had a couple of good crews at the last two stops, and was running ahead of schedule. Coming up the straightaway toward the bend, something reflected my headlights back to me. I've traveled this stretch of road enough to know that accidents are all too common here. I pulled over to check it out. I don't think I'll ever do that again. As I walked off the shoulder into the woods, I saw the car and called out. No one answered and I didn't see any movement, so I went to the driver's door. I ... she ... her eyes ... She was staring straight at me. Her eyes were wide open and a look of confusion and terror was frozen on her face. The eyes were slightly sunken and her skin was a funny color under the light from my flashlight. The combination of all that nearly made me scream. I've stopped at accidents before, even found a dead driver, but this … this scared the shit out of me. I went back to my truck and called the locals."

"Did you see anyone or any other vehicle in the vicinity?"

"Not a soul."

"How about earlier? Anyone come westbound driving erratically?"

"Chief, I got on Winchendon Road in Royalston, traveled along as it changed to River Street, and all I saw between there and here were ghosts in the shadows of my headlights.

"Look, I know it's important for you to get information, Chief, but the lieutenant asked me these same questions. Right now, I need to get on my way. I'm an owner-operator, and this contract is my bread and butter. I can lose the contract without notice if any of the clients complain, and they always complain if I run late. You guys have my contact information. I come through here every night, Sunday through Friday. Can we arrange a more convenient time to go over this?"

"Lieutenant, you have any questions for the lady?"

"No, Chief. I have all I need for now."

"Okay, Joan. Thank you for the information. I don't want you to lose your income, but I will want to talk to you again."

"That's good, Chief, because I sure would like to talk to you again." Joan smiled and gave him a wink of her eye as she turned to head back to her rig. When she got there, she turned her head back over her left shoulder to look at Richard again before climbing into the cab and driving off. As she passed him, she flashed him a smile.

Richard turned to his right and almost knocked Jake over.

"If you're finished impressing the attractive lady, I'll tow the wreck out of here now."

"Phil, get a couple pictures of the rear bumper, will you?" Richard said, not letting Jake take control of the situation.

"Once Phil is done, you can have the wreck, Jake," he said as he turned, looking for Chris.

"Chris, I'm going to the hospital. Wrap it up here. As usual, you handled the situation well. I appreciate your patience with me. I don't have much information, but at least I can answer some of the questions the council will throw at me later this morning."

"Chief, you should find a way to have that crap stopped. You spend more time before the council than in your apartment."

"I know, Chris, but it's the price I pay for the privilege of serving the town." The two had a lighthearted laugh. Richard added, "I want you to have that trucker stopped tomorrow night. Ask the same questions, and see if she remembers anything new."

"Right, Chief thanks. See you at the office."

4

The emergency room was quiet. The intense activity usually associated with a severe motor vehicle accident had evaporated. The nurse on duty sat at the nurses' station, casually reviewing reports. Richard spotted Carla Evans, the senior EMT who had been at the accident scene, sitting on one of the waiting room chairs, sipping coffee.

In her late Twenties, Carla was slightly overweight with long, sandy, blond hair tied back in a ponytail. Her smooth complexion needed no makeup and her deep-blue eyes added to her perpetual smile. She saw Richard as he was walking toward her and stood.

"Chief, Mrs. Robinson was the last person I would have expected to be involved in a car accident. A single car fatal accident with her as the driver is beyond comprehension."

"I know what you mean. She never drove more than thirty. How much damage can you do under thirty miles per hour?"

"Well, she was traveling a whole lot faster than thirty to go that far into the woods."

"What did you find when you arrived there?"

"As I said, the vehicle was so far into the woods, you couldn't see it from the road. Lieutenant Allen showed us where it was. Shirley was alone in the driver's seat, facing the driver's door window. She had contusions on her face, hands, and arms. Her face was a purplish-blue color, as was the rest of her skin, and her skin was cold. Her eyes were sunken into her skull. Dark, purple-black lividity stains, were present in her earlobes, folds of her neck, and extremities. Fingernails were white. She was unresponsive, had no pulse, no respiration … I'd say she was dead for an hour or two."

"You're sure she was dead when you got there?"

"Jeff, my partner, got in the passenger side and checked her heart. He got nothing. As I said, she was absent of any spontaneous respiratory or cardiac function. Her heart had not been pumping for a while and the blood had drained to her lower extremities, causing unfixed blanch lividity. When we finally got her out, we only put her on the fire department's cardiac board so she wouldn't be on the wet grass. Don't worry, Chief, we followed protocol to the letter. The physician backing us up here agreed with the call at the time."

"How long did it take to get her out of the vehicle?"

"The fire crew cut the driver-side door open ... we had her out fifteen minutes after we arrived. We had to forcefully break the grip she had on the steering wheel."

"How long did you wait for the fire department?"

"They were right behind us."

"Okay, Carla. Get a copy of your report to me later this morning. The town council will to want to know every detail."

Richard asked the nurse on duty where Doc Fenton was, and she directed him to the physicians' lounge. When he entered the small room on the second floor of the Winchendon Health Center, he found Doc Fenton sitting at a small table. He was concentrating on a cup of coffee in front of him.

Fenton looked up and said, "Grab yourself some coffee and sit down, Chief. As I'm sure you already know she was dead at the scene. I just had to officially confirm the fact and pronounce death."

The coffeepot was half-full. Richard picked it up and held it to his nose. The coffee smelt fresh not burnt so he decided the liquid was worth drinking. He filled a cup and sat next to the doctor.

"Chief, I'm getting too old for this, you know. Hell, I'm retired."

"You retired so you could slow down to fifty hours a week. You'll never be too old to do what you love."

"Well, it's times like this I'd rather be pumping gas. Shirley Robinson, dead in a car accident." He shook his head, then continued, "You know, she lost both parents in a car accident. She was just fifteen when it happened. She said she would never get behind the wheel of a car." He brought his cup of coffee to his lips and sipped the liquid as he thought about Shirley

"I didn't know about her parents," Richard confessed. "That explains why she was so cautious. She frustrated every other driver on the road because she always drove under the speed limit. Any idea what caused her death?"

Fenton thought a moment, and then said, "There's a good question. She had a broken right forearm, broken right leg, broken left foot, and cuts in her face and hands from the shattered glass." He paused to let these facts take root in Richard's mind, and then added, "No major bruises, no internal damage, or bleeding. She should have survived, except … she broke her neck."

"What?"

"She died of a broken neck. Technically, it was spinal shock caused by broken cervical vertebrae, neck bones, cutting into her spinal cord. I'd say she was out there for at least several hours. I'll know more after I finish the post." He picked up his coffee cup and stared into it for a few seconds, then placed the cup back on the table.

"Right now, Pete's with her. I'll have to pry him away from the body soon."

"Doc, have you seen many accidents where the driver died due to a broken neck?"

"I've seen too many car accidents in my day, and, yes, some of them resulted in broken necks. Statistically, however, it's not a common cause of death. In most of the traffic fatalities I've seen, the body is usually in much worse condition than Shirley's. If the driver or occupants of a crash sustained the limited amount of injury and trauma Shirley sustained, the accident is usually not fatal."

He drained his coffee and rose from his chair saying, "I have to get Pete out of the emergency room and headed home. I'll have a preliminary post for you in a couple of days. Take a week or so for the final report with toxicology. Won't change anything though, she died of a broken neck sustained in a car accident."

As he opened the door to exit, he stopped, and then said, almost to himself, "I don't know if this was a tragedy or a blessing."

"What do you mean, Doc?" Richard asked.

"Shirley. She had a brain tumor. Her specialist scheduled all kinds of treatments, but in the end, a couple of years, if she were lucky … It was inoperable. If the treatments didn't work, she wouldn't have lasted long."

For the second time that night, Richard broke out with clammy palms, beads of sweat on his forehead, and his heart rate picked up. He hesitated for a moment, not sure he wanted to ask the next question.

"Doc, is it possible that Shirley intentionally drove off the road?"

"Drove off the road?" Fenton stood in the doorway, looking at Richard. "You mean, could she have committed suicide?"

"Well, so far there's nothing to explain the accident. Maybe she fell asleep, but she was always so nervous about driving that I doubt her system would have allowed her to fall asleep. Now you tell me she had a terminal illness. What's your take?"

"Chief, we never really know what anyone is capable of doing. Psychiatrists often get it wrong and their patients kill themselves. Shirley asked many questions about the impact her illness and treatment would have on her family. She was concerned about becoming a burden to her husband. She worried about the potential disruption to her children's normal routine."

Richard closed his eyes and saw Lori's handwriting in her notebook. She had written questions about her illness and treatment, and many focused on the effects these would have on her family, on him.

Fenton stood quietly for a while, and then said, "I would bet against Shirley trying to commit suicide, at least not by driving off the road. She couldn't have expected that she would break her neck. I also know she wanted to tell her children about her family. She was the last survivor. Her brother died in an accident several years ago. It was just before you moved out here."

"What happened to her brother?" Richard asked.

"He was an electrical inspector for the town of Andover. He was in the basement of a new building when it blew up. I think they said that they found a gas leak." Fenton drifted off into thought, then looked at Richard and added, "You know, it's ironic. Shirley's brother had the same type brain tumor." He then turned and left Richard to his thoughts.

5

Richard spent the rest of the early morning in his office at the police station. At six forty-five, his phone rang. "Chief Moore."

"Moore, what a terrible incident last night. A councilmember's wife killed in an auto accident. I hope you have a report for us." The caller was Theo Reuben, a member of the Town Council.

"Morning, Theo. You're up early."

"Most of us have been up all night. We've been with Pete. I hope I haven't disturbed your rest."

"I've been up all night as well. You reached me at the office."

"Good. The Council will be in chambers at eight. I'll see you then." Theo hung up, and Richard prepared to face him and the rest of the Town Council.

Seven elected members made up the town's council. Except for Pete Robinson, all the other members were present when Richard arrived punctually at eight o'clock.

"Chief Moore has arrived. Maybe now we can get started," said Theo.

"Chief Moore, will you give this council an explanation how the wife of a council member was killed on one of our own streets? A very cautious and safe driving member of the community, I might add."

"There isn't much information to go on yet. Shirley was traveling east on River Street. She crossed the westbound side of the road, and went into the trees. Preliminary reports from Doc Fenton indicate that death was almost instantaneous."

"Almost instantaneous, but you didn't know that when you denied her immediate medical attention. Did you?" Theo asked.

"Theo, I am not sure what you are asking. I don't appreciate the suggestion that I somehow denied anyone medical attention."

"You know full well what I mean. You rested comfortably for almost an hour after the report of the accident. Then you instructed everyone to stop what he or she was doing until you arrived. You delayed treatment for almost two hours. Your conduct was a gross abuse of power, position, and authority. We should terminate you right here and now."

The rest of the council members were as shocked and bewildered by Theo's irrational accusation as Richard was. They began to shift uncomfortably in their chairs. No one knew what to say.

"Theo, how long it took me to arrive at the scene had nothing to with Shirley's treatment or the lack of it. The EMTs made that decision based on criteria set by the law. If you have a problem with their decision, then you need to speak with them and their physician backup. As for the rest of it, this unfortunate and tragic accident is still under investigation and any assumptions about the cause, outcome, or actions of anyone involved are premature."

Theo quickly changed tack. "Well, our assessment of your actions is not premature. You're not even conducting a proper investigation. Why did you let that truck driver go this morning? She was a prime suspect and you let her continue with her job as if nothing happened."

"The truck driver was a concerned and helpful citizen. She stopped to investigate something unusual. She called for help when she realized what she had discovered. When questioned, she was cooperative and gave us a detailed description of what she found. Her identification was in order, and there was no indication she or her vehicle was involved in the accident. We learned where and how to contact her, and there was no need to detain her longer."

"You kept Jake waiting while you flirted with this woman. Your unprofessional behavior allowed a possible perpetrator of a fatal accident to walk away. Have you any comments to offer that might keep us from terminating you?"

Richard replied evenly, "The investigation into Shirley Robinson's accident is not complete. I have given you all the information available. As for the actions the Council decides to take at its meetings, I am not a member, nor have I a vote, so you will have to handle that on your own."

He then stood saying, "I will leave you to decide what actions are necessary."

After Richard left and went back to his office, all but one of the other council members excused themselves, staying they had to get to work. Without a quorum, the meeting was finished.

6

In Ashburnham, the small town to Winchendon's east, firefighter Paul Kenney rose at six thirty in the morning, put on a sweatshirt and sneakers, and went downstairs to the kitchen. After setting the coffeepot to start at six forty-five, he went out for his daily run.

Paul's exercise routine included a five-mile run followed by a workout with weights at the fire station if time permitted. He concentrated on his muscle tone and endurance, not muscle bulk. He believed it was important to be in top physical shape in case he had to carry someone larger than himself to safety.

Now in his early thirties, Paul had been involved in firefighting since joining the auxiliary fire department. As a teenager, he sat in on training sessions about equipment and its use, and most important for him, he learned emergency health techniques. After graduating from high school, he earned his EMT certificate and joined the volunteer fire department. As Ashburnham grew, so did the need for full-time firefighters, and it was not long before Paul received an appointment to the regular fire department.

Early in his training, he learned fighting fires was only one part of the firefighter's job. They also perform home inspections as part of purchase, sales, and refinancing. They perform inspection of new construction to assure that the construction met fire code, they make informational presentations for various groups and schools, and they continuously clean and inspect equipment. Some of Paul's coworkers got bored with the details and inspections. "Busy work," they often said. None of it was busy work to Paul. He considered it a privilege to work as a firefighter.

His morning run took him through several of the older sections in town where sturdy, old maple trees lined the streets. Their impressive, full branches shielded various parts of the front yards of the houses on this part of his route. Unlike some of the newer sections of town, the homes along these streets were unique wooden structures of various sizes and styles. Front porches, some with pillars and railings decorated with hand carved ornamental designs, greeted visitors. Turning off one of the streets, he headed down the main thoroughfare toward the center of town, waving to familiar shop owners who were opening for the day. Downtown he made a circuit of the four streets that comprised the rough boundary of Winchendon's retail center then retraced his route back to his home.

When he arrived home from his run, his wife, Deanna, stood in the kitchen. "Hi, love," he said, as he gave her a warm hug and kiss.

"Oh, yuck! You're drenched in sweat, and you stink. Go shower, then come back to me," the smile playing at the edges of her mouth belying the harshness of the words.

Paul stepped back quickly, then, seeing her expression, he grinned and ran upstairs to shower and shave.

They lived on the same street growing up, became high school sweethearts, married shortly after Paul joined the fire department, and now had a seven-year-old daughter who idolized her father. Although it was not perfect, Paul and Deanna had a good life. They enjoyed each other's company, and the fact that they were living their lives together.

It was just before seven when he returned to the kitchen. Clean, shaved, and dressed in his uniform, he walked up behind his wife, wrapped his arms around her waist, and kissed her on the neck. "Is this better?"

"I don't know. Let me see." She turned around, still in his arms. Facing him, she yanked his shirt out of his pants and put both her hands under it. Caressing his chest, she kissed him passionately.

"Ohhhhh, much better." She snuggled into his bare chest. "Why don't you stay home today? I'm sure I could make it worth your while."

"I'm sure you could, but you know I can't."

She pulled her head from his chest and looked him in the eyes. "Sure you can. The chief will understand. Just tell him you're not feeling well."

"I can't start doing that now. The time will come when I'll call in, and it'll be the truth."

"Come on, honey, you're taking tomorrow off to visit the doctor and have more tests. The chief will understand if you stay home today."

Paul spun her around and patted her on the behind, encouraging her to move away.

"We've gone through this before. As long as I'm cleared for work and not having a bad day, I go."

Several months earlier, Paul complained of twitching, cramping of muscles, and bouts of fatigue. The first test results indicated he had Amyotrophic Lateral Sclerosis or ALS, also known as Lou Gehrig's disease. ALS, he learned, is a progressive deterioration of the nerve cells that control muscles, resulting in a gradual paralysis. Eventually, the paralysis spreads to the muscles that control breathing, and the victim dies from a lack of oxygen. A battery of tests to determine the current stage and progression of the disease was scheduled.

"Paul, I know we've talked about this, but it's only one day. You have a long day of tests tomorrow, and you should rest today."

He reached out, pulled her to him, and squeezed her tightly. "What you're suggesting we do if I stay home doesn't sound much like rest. I'll get more rest at work. I just won't have as much fun."

"Don't worry! I'll be gentle on you."

"It's getting late. I need coffee and breakfast. I know ... let's have lunch at Kate's."

"Is that the best you can do?" She moved to the kitchen counter and picked up the coffeepot.

"You love Kate's."

"I do, but—"

"I know that's not what you meant. It's the best I can do for now. One o'clock lunch, the regular lunch crowd clears out by then."

Their daughter walked into the kitchen.

"Well, good morning, beautiful," Paul said, as he picked her up, and gave her a big kiss.

"You going to work today?" she asked with a sleepy voice.

"Yes, I am."

"Why can't you stay home with me?"

"Have you been talking to your mother this morning?"

"No, I just got up."

"Well, I'm going to work today, but I'll be home tomorrow morning. How about you and I go to breakfast then?"

"Can I have waffles with whipped cream and strawberries?"

"You sure can."

Her face brightened. The sleepy look disappeared, and she smiled, exclaiming, "Okay!"

Paul put his daughter in a chair at the kitchen table. While Deanna and Paul had coffee and toast, their daughter drank orange juice and toyed with her cereal. She was thinking about waffles with whipped cream and strawberries.

"I have to leave. See you for breakfast tomorrow, beautiful. And I'll see you for lunch." He kissed them, and left for the fire station.

7

Paul arrived at the station, reported to the shift commander, Lieutenant Weiss, and checked the schedule. After an equipment inspection, they had two house inspections, a presentation to the Ashburnham Business Council, and a test of the fire sprinkler system and alarm at a new warehouse. If all went well, he would have a calm morning, a nice relaxing lunch with his wife, and a peaceful afternoon.

Several of the firefighters were loitering near the truck entrance, talking. A slight overlap of shifts built into the schedule allowed the previous crew to bring the incoming crew up to date on any events of interest. Paul joined the casual conversations for a while then decided to begin the inspection of equipment on the pumper truck.

Modern pumpers carry hundreds of feet of fire hose, and an array of gauges that monitor water flow and pressure. The typical pumper carries several hose types and sizes, all designed to lay flat when not in use. Flat hose takes up less space, and, if stored properly, deploys easier and more quickly when needed. Fire hoses used to be made of cotton, and the pressure generated by pumpers often caused hoses to rupture. Over time, improvements in the manufacturing process and materials have significantly reduced the incidence of hose failure. However, although modern hoses last longer and endure higher pressures, they require regular inspection to ensure that the material has not tattered or weaken in spots. Like everything about the job, Paul took the inspection of the hoses serious. Although he sometimes caught grief from those who called it busy work, even they had a grudging admiration for his knowledge and commitment.

Finding a fold of hose that needed work, he dropped it over the side of the truck. When it hit the garage floor with a loud thud, all conversation stopped, and the men looked around. Paul noticed the silence and stood up on the truck. His station mates, who were all aware of and concerned about his condition looked fretfully in his direction.

"Hey, guys, I threw a fold of hose over the side. Lighten up. I'm not going to drop dead on you."

The conversation got back to normal and Paul resumed his equipment checks, running a pressure and flow rate test of the hoses as well as a detailed visual inspection of the hoses and connectors. Following the equipment checks and tests, the crew set out to complete the morning's scheduled.

The big pumper pulled in front Kate's Diner at one o'clock, and Paul jumped out. He told the driver, Jessie, that Deanna would drop him off back at the station after lunch. Paul then entered the eatery and found Deanna already seated at a table. They took their time and had an enjoyable and relaxing lunch. When lunch was finished, they ordered coffee.

As Paul sipped his coffee he said, "I talked with the chief this morning. I asked him for a week's vacation, and he said it was okay."

A sense of relief filled Deanna. Firefighting was a dangerous profession, and she was used to an ever-present sense of anxiety when Paul was at work. Since his diagnosis, however, that anxiety had grown into a conscious concern that each day he spent on the job increased his risk of being harmed. It was a concern she chose not share with Paul.

"That's great, honey! Why did they drop you off? You should have driven your car here, then we could have gone straight home."

"Oh … no, I start my vacation tomorrow morning after my shift."

Deanna was disappointed, but at least she would have a week to work on him about finding a way to leave his work on permanent disability. After they finished their coffee and paid the bill, she drove him to the station.

Promising to call later, he gave her a hug and a kiss, said, "I love you," and left the car.

8

At 9:38 that evening, a motorist reported seeing flames inside the building at Riley's Service Station at the junction of Route 12 and Depot Road. .

Lieutenant Weiss, Jessie, CJ, and Paul were rolling in minutes. When they reached the scene, Paul jumped off the rear of the slowing truck with a feeder hose end in one hand and hydrant wrench in the other. He quickly attached the hose to the hydrant and opened the valve, sending a steady flow of water coursing through the hose to the pumper. As he was doing this, Jessie pulled the pumper to the side of the road in front of the service station. CJ got out, opened a tool cabinet on the truck, took out a pickax, and headed for the front door of the service station. The lieutenant went to the control panel of the pumper and prepared to operate the valves that supplied water to the crosslays.

Two sets of one and one-half inch hose, each two-hundred feet long, lay in bins, one on each side of the pumper. Firefighters call these hoses as crosslays. One end is connected to a fitting controlled by valves at the control panel, and the other end is positioned so one man can grab it, and run toward a working fire. Jessie got down from the driver's seat, moved around to the passenger side of the truck, grabbed a crosslay, and headed toward the front door right behind CJ.

Riley's pumps stood in front of small storefront with two large glass windows framing a door to the interior. Inside, on the left wall, another door led to the two-bay cinder block service garage next to the storefront. The rear of the garage opened on to a wooden building attached to the rear of the garage and the storefront. This addition had a dirt floor, no interior walls, a flat tarpaper roof, and two roll up doors facing Depot Road.

When they reached the front door, Jessie and CJ looked through the windows and saw active flames on the back wall. When Jessie's hose came to life a moment later, CJ hit the door handle with the pickax, and the door flew open. The fire on the back wall became more active as a fresh supply of oxygen entered with the opening of the front door. Jessie opened the nozzle of the hose and moved into the building with a wide spray of water clearing the way. The flames retreated in defeat from the onslaught of the water. Once extinguished, Jessie signaled CJ to hit the wall with the pickax. Fire can travel in the space between walls and come out elsewhere in a building. Opening the wall allowed the firefighters to see if the fire had traveled.

Paul walked up to the lieutenant.

"Paul, they have it knocked down. Take a line and go through the service bays to the back building. Make sure there are no hot spots. I'll go around the right side and check the building from the parking area."

"Okay, Lieutenant."

"Hold on," the lieutenant said. Over the truck's loudspeaker, they could hear that a call had come in for the ambulance. Dispatch was notifying them the ambulance was on its way to aid a possible heart attack victim.

"Okay, Paul, let's get this wrapped up and get back to the station."

Paul grabbed a crosslay and moved into the storefront.

"Hey, Jessie, you didn't leave any for me."

"We can start it up again if you need the practice."

"Not tonight, I got a date with a nice warm cot."

Paul went through the door into the two-bay service area and looked around. He then went through the opening at the back of the first bay into the back building and looked for flames or hot spots. To his right was a room and door constructed of plywood. A toilet and utility sink were inside, although Paul did not know that. He was on the backside of the storefront wall and could hear the banging of the pickax pulling the plaster down from the other side. Paul put his hand on the door and found that it was not hot. Before he opened the door, he flipped up the shield of his hat to wipe his face. A spot in the upper right corner of the room caught his eye and he stared at it. Then he pulled open the rest room door. As the door opened, he thought he heard a hissing sound then he felt a light mist hit his face.

He saw the pickaxe open a hole in his side of the wall directly across from where he was standing. Suddenly, a tongue of flame raced across the ceiling of the restroom. When it hit the wall just above the door, it streaked down the wall and out the door. It puffed into a ball and hit Paul's face so hard that it knocked him down. The space within the back building ignited all at once. The ignition raised the temperature inside the building so quickly that the expanding air blew out the windows.

Lieutenant Weiss, who had been examining the wooden building from the parking lot in front of the roll-up doors, had just turned to walk back to the front of the main building when a shower of glass flew at him. Small, razor-like fragments of glass peppered his face and neck, and a large wedge of glass pierced his right thigh like a dagger. The dramatic change in air pressure blew CJ and Jessie back from the hole in the wall. They were up quickly and screamed into their radios for Paul. They moved out of the storefront through the service bay toward the rear building. The heat was intense and flames were crawling through the opening, hindering their progress. Jessie, hose in hand, sprayed the opening hoping that it would give Paul a chance to walk out. CJ reached down, grabbed Paul's line, and started pulling. Paul did not walk out and was not holding the other end of the hose.

The lieutenant called on the radio, asking what happened. They told him that Paul was inside the inferno. The news prompted the lieutenant to call for assistance and an ambulance. With a hose each, CJ and Jessie battled their way into the back to look for Paul. When they found him, he was lying on the ground, face up and motionless. CJ shut off his hose, grabbed Paul, threw his limp body over his shoulder and he and Jessie refought their way out of the fire. They emerged a little battered and burned. They made it to the parking area near the fire truck.

The two firefighters laid Paul on the ground. Jessie looked at Paul's face and involuntarily vomited. Paul's flesh had been rolled back on the sides of his head, and his hair, ears, and nose were all gone. Several of his fingers were smoldering. His arms, shoulders, neck, and part of his chest were black and charred.

With a report of injured firefighters, nearby firefighting and ambulance teams from Winchendon and the town of Gardner were dispatched to the scene. Ashburnham's own ambulance was still helping the heart attack victim. The Winchendon ambulance arrived. Carla was on duty and, while her partner treated the lieutenant, she began working on Paul.

She discovered that his heart was still beating, and he was still breathing. However, Paul not only had severe burns of the nose and mouth, but also signs of burning in his upper throat. His body was quickly rushing fluids to fix the damage, and, as a result, the tissues of the upper airways were swelling and beginning to block his airflow. With CJ holding Paul's head at the proper angle, she inserted a tube deep into Paul's throat, struggling to get it past the swelling so it could provide a passage to his lungs for air. Once the tube was in and secure, she connected an oxygen line to it.

Because of the extent of the tissue damage she saw in his throat, Carla was certain that the damage to his lungs would inhibit him from absorbing enough oxygen to prevent brain damage or even death. She had to get him to the Winchendon Medical Center as quickly as possible. If the emergency crew there could stabilize him, the State Police helicopter might get him to the University of Massachusetts Medical Center in Worcester in time to save him. She called her dispatcher, who alerted both the medical center and the State Police. Satisfied that CJ and Jessie could look after the lieutenant until the ambulance from Gardner arrived, she and her partner put Paul in the ambulance and headed for Winchendon.

John O'Malley, Chief of the Ashburnham Fire Department, arrived just after the Winchendon ambulance left. O'Malley spoke with Lieutenant Weis for a moment before the Gardner ambulance took the lieutenant away. A firefighting crew from Winchendon arrived and, with firefighters from Winchendon, was hard at work on the fire. The Winchendon chief, David Cromwell, had come with his men, and, after seeing that his lieutenant had taken command, approached O'Malley.

"John, this is going to be under control shortly. Why don't you go to the hospital and check on your men? I'll finish here."

"Thanks, David. I appreciate that. I'm going to talk with the other two men involved, first. If you don't mind, I'll send them back to quarters."

"Go right ahead John, we've got more people than we need here anyway. I'll be sending most of them out of here soon."

Chief O'Malley went directly to his men.

"CJ, Jessie, you guys okay?"

CJ responded, "We're fine but Paul … Paul … Chief, I have never seen anyone alive look like that."

"What happened here?"

"Damned if I know, Chief. It was a small fire in the storefront. We put it down. We opened the wall. It was clear. Paul went around back into the rear building. He opened the door to the head. We looked right at him. Then the place exploded. It was like something ignited the air."

"All right, you two stow the gear and go back to the station. Some of the guys from the next shift are already on the way there to give you a hand. I'll be at the hospital"

Before leaving for the medical center, O'Malley called Father Bernardo, the pastor of Ashburnham's only Catholic Church. Among his many other duties, Father Bernardo was the chaplain for the fire and police departments. O'Malley and the priest had been friends since high school, and O'Malley still called the priest by his nickname, Bernie.

"Bernie, it's Jack. We have a serious situation."

"What's happened, Jack? Are you alright?"

O'Malley assured his friend that he was fine then told him about Paul and Lieutenant Weiss.

"Bernie, it doesn't sound good for Paul."

"Indeed, it doesn't. I'll call Mary Cunningham and ask her to go see Paul's wife. Mary's a former nun, and still active in the Church. She and Deanna know each other well."

"Thanks, Bernie. Deanna will want to go to the hospital. Can Mary handle that?"

"Yes, I'll have her take care of it."

"They have a little girl. I think she's seven. Someone will have to stay with her."

"If Deanna doesn't have someone, Mary will get one of the other volunteers."

Paul went into cardiac arrest shortly after the ambulance pulled away from the fire scene, and Carla began a desperate effort to revive him. A doctor and three nurses met the ambulance at the hospital. Carla continued pumping Paul's chest and briefed the doctor as they rushed him into the center.

The second ambulance arrived with Lieutenant Weiss and the emergency room personnel took the lieutenant into another room. Several minutes later, two nurses wheeled Weiss out on a gurney.

"What's happening?" Carla asked.

One of the nurses said, "We're taking him to surgery. The glass cut an artery and he's lost a lot of blood."

Fifteen minutes later, Chief O'Malley arrived. He knew Carla, and when he saw her, he asked, "How are they?"

"They took the lieutenant to surgery to repair the damage to his thigh." Pointing to the treatment area, she said, "They're in there working on Paul. Chief … it's not good. He arrested on the way over."

O'Malley sighed, "How much worse can it get?"

Just then, Richard arrived and greeted O'Malley and the others. Before he could ask about the firefighters, a doctor came out of Paul's room.

Carla spotted the doctor first. "Chief, here comes the doctor who was treating Paul."

"Who's with the firefighter?" the doctor asked. He recognized Richard, but not O'Malley.

"I'm Chief O'Malley. Paul's my man."

"I'm sorry, he didn't make it," the doctor said.

No one said anything for a few moments, and then the doctor asked, "Any family?"

O'Malley replied, "Yeah … yeah, we have someone bringing his wife. She should be here any minute."

"We'll need to prepare her. Her husband is not a pleasant sight. His face was burned beyond recognition."

O'Malley voice cracked as he answered, "Okay. I'll … I'll talk with her … and … ah … go in with her. … Doctor, is there something … you know … something you can give her if she needs it?"

"I'll take care of it."

"Thanks, Doc. We'll let you know when she arrives."

9

Later, after Deanna Kenney had left and Paul's body moved to the morgue, Richard and O'Malley sat quietly in the doctor's lounge. O'Malley had grown silent as the loss of one of his men took hold, and Richard could guess what was going through his friend's mind. Richard had lost his share of men, and notified his share of wives and loved ones.

O'Malley was the first colleague from a surrounding town to welcome Richard after he became chief of police in Winchendon. They developed a friendship and now had lunch or dinner at least once a week. O'Malley had also persuaded Richard to meet him for a round of golf twice a month, something Richard did because he enjoyed O'Malley's company, not because he was fond of golf.

O'Malley was in his early sixties, with a middle-aged spread, thinning, gray hair, and eyes that, though they needed the help of steel-rimed, oval glasses with progressive lenses, looked out on the world with intelligence and wit. Except for the afternoons when he played golf, he worked seven days a week. Work and golf were his life in the four years since his wife died.

John O'Malley married Gloria Dunne when they were both twenty-one. They raised three children, two boys and a girl, all of whom eventually left their small hometown for successful careers in big cities. Four years before, Gloria died of a massive heart attack in her sleep. O'Malley consoled himself with the knowledge that she had not suffered.

"I never want to do that again." O'Malley said. "It was difficult enough looking at Paul in that room by myself, but when his wife came in and saw him … " O'Malley shook his head. "I'll hear her scream for the rest of my life. That poor woman, nothing anyone tells you can prepare you for that."

"How is she now?" Richard asked.

"The doc gave her a sedative. I don't think it did much good. She wanted to go home and hug her daughter but, at the same time, she didn't want to leave her husband. Bernie finally convinced her to go home so her daughter wouldn't hear the news on her own."

"Christ, Paul lived for this job. He was distraught when the doctors told him that he wouldn't be able to work much longer."

Richard did not know Paul, and he never heard O'Malley mention that one of his men was ill.

"What made the doctors tell him that he wouldn't be able to work?" Richard asked.

"He was diagnosed with ALS … you know, Lou Gehrig's disease. Shit, he was going to Worcester tomorrow, or later this morning, for a battery of tests. He asked me if he could have the next week off as vacation. Said his wife wanted him off the job and he wanted to keep working. He wanted them to have time to decide what to do next. Know what I said?"

Richard looked at O'Malley and shrugged.

"I said, 'Go home. Take as much time as you need.'" O'Malley's face tightened in anger. "All Paul could say was, 'Thanks, but this is my shift and I'll finish it.' He finished it all right … why didn't I send that kid home right then and there … .

"You know, Richard, I've lost only one other man in my thirty plus years, and he was careless. Paul wasn't careless. The crew can't explain how that building exploded into flames. What the hell happened out there?"

"John, you can't blame yourself. You couldn't have sent the kid home. He made the decision to work his shift. He did his job. Now it's your job to determine what happened. You said your men told you they put down the fire. Maybe it was a backdraft," Richard suggested.

"From what the crew said, I doubt it. It was an explosive flash of fire, but it burned longer than a backdraft would. Moreover, neither the back building nor the restroom had any sign of fire before the explosion. A backdraft occurs when air enters a contained area that has a fire deficient in oxygen. It doesn't sound like the case in this situation. The area wasn't deprived of air, and the crew didn't open a new source of air after opening the front door."

Trying to keep O'Malley thinking about the events of the fire rather than his guilt over Paul's death, Richard asked, "What about a flashover?"

"No, not a flashover, the wall in the storefront was active when they arrived. That might have caused heat and gases to build up in that room, but not in the restroom. When the crew pulled the wall, they found no evidence that the space between the walls had been involved. I can't imagine how the restroom might have developed enough heat or gases to cause the rear building to explode at once."

"When is the State Fire Marshal's crew coming?"

"They have someone debriefing CJ and Jessie now. A team will be out in the morning. They'll comb through the fire site looking for a cause of the fire, and run through the actions of my men."

"Well, we can't do anymore here. Let's do something constructive. Let's go sit with your men during the debriefing. Your support will be comforting."

"Good idea, but first we should check on Lieutenant Weiss."

They learned that Weiss was out of surgery and stabilized in the recovery room, and, after O'Malley had spoken with the lieutenant's sister in Syracuse, they left the medical center.

10

In the weeks following September 11, 2001, most Americans became familiar with much of the solemn ritual and tradition that attends the funerals of fallen firefighters like Paul Kenney. Contingents from across the state and the nation, comrades in arms hardened in battle against an implacable enemy, came to honor their fallen brother. An Honor Guard stood post by the closed casket during visiting hours at the funeral home. A picture of Paul in dress uniform sat on top of the casket, along with a frame containing his nametag and unit insignia patch. Fire apparatus stood fast outside the funeral home during all viewing hours.

On morning of the funeral, the Honor Guard preceded the flag draped casket as the pallbearers, all firefighters in dress uniform and white gloves, carried the casket out of the funeral home and placed it atop a fire truck. When Father Bernardo finished the funeral mass, fire personnel assembled outside, forming a row on each side of the walkway to the fire truck. After this, the color guard emerged, followed by a firefighter carrying Paul's helmet. The casket came next, carried by the pallbearers, who placed it on the truck. Then, as Father Bernardo, followed by a pipe and drum corps and the color guard, started a solemn journey to the cemetery, the fire truck began moving slowly behind them. Additional fire apparatus followed the cars transporting the immediate family.

When they arrived at their destination, they found a ladder truck standing sentinel on each side of the cemetery entrance. The stars and stripes waved from a line secured to the trucks' extended aerial ladders. The procession passed under the flag and entered the cemetery.

Once inside, the procession stopped, and firefighters moved forward to line either side of the path from the fire truck to the gravesite. This "walk of honor," as it is called, solemnizes the final distance the fallen firefighter will travel. The color guard lined up at the beginning of the walk of honor, followed by Father Bernardo. The pipe and drum corps moved out, and reassembled one hundred yards from the gravesite. A bugler was stationed twenty feet past the gravesite.

When all was ready, the pallbearers removed the casket from the truck, and, when they were ready to proceed with Paul's casket in hand, the honor guard cried out, "Firefighters, attention!"

As all firefighters came to attention, the command, "Firefighters, present arms!" followed, and the pallbearers began their walk toward the gravesite. As the casket passed, each firefighter rendered a hand salute.

When the gravesite service was completed, the honor guard removed the flag from the casket, folded it, and passed it to the guard commander. He then presented the flag to Paul's wife.

The honor guard gave one last command, and after hearing this, the bugler played "Taps." When the last notes died away, loud speakers on the fire apparatus echoed the fire dispatcher's voice, giving the ceremonial announcement of "Last call!" over the radio.

Richard and O'Malley, both wearing their dress uniforms, walked together toward their cars. They talked about Paul's wife Deanna and her daughter, and about the show of support and respect exhibited by the community and the firefighters.

O'Malley turned to Richard and said, "You know, Richard, I'm getting tired of wearing this dress uniform and black ribbon. I have attended a funeral for a comrade almost every month of the last three years. I don't remember it being as frequent years ago."

At first, Richard was surprised at this. As part of the local community of police and firefighters, he had attended as many funerals as O'Malley, and he had not thought about their frequency. As he reflected a bit, however, he remembered that before his wife's death he had sensed a rising frequency of funerals among the ranks. Perhaps after Lori's death, he had been out of touch, and oblivious of the fact.

"What did the State Fire Marshal's Office say about Paul's death?" Richard inquired.

"Inconclusive. That section of the building had a dirt floor. Over the years, the dirt accumulated gasoline, diesel fluid, transmission fluid, grease. You name it. The walls and supports were all made of exposed wood that sucked up fluids over the years. Those fluids helped the fire burn hot and quick. Even so, they still can't explain why the fire erupted the way it did. It was possible that enough fumes had accumulated from the ground and wood, but not probable."

"So, what do you think, John?"

"I don't know. Something was in the air in that building, and something ignited whatever it was. CJ and Jessie were positive that the original fire was out before Paul opened that door."

"What about the increase in deaths that you mentioned? Is there a connection do you think?"

"The detective's mind at work, Richard? No, I don't think there's any connection."

"Okay, then. Do you think that the increase in deaths might be because of changes in procedures?"

"No, they're probably due to changes in lifestyle. Deaths by natural occurrences, accidents, and suicides have all increased.

"I spoke with Don Williams, the director of personnel in the Boston Police Department. He confirmed that their mortality rate had increased during the past couple of years. He said that the insurance companies checked into the increase, and concluded it was an insignificant statistical variance. Insignificant! They don't realize that those insignificant statistics are workingmen and women with families."

"Don Williams, I remember him from my time with the Boston Police Department. He's pretty smart, and an advocate for the force. What made you go to him? He doesn't handle the fire department."

"I go back a long way with him. We went to school together. As you said, Don is an advocate for personnel. I figured that if my feeling about the increase in deaths were right, he would know, or would at least be interested in knowing."

O'Malley paused, then took a deep breath and said, "I have to get to the reception and pay my respects and socialize. Are you coming?"

"No. I have to get back to the office. I'll call you later in the week and we can set up a date to get together."

11

Heading back to the office and the never-ending flow of paperwork on his desk, Richard came to the burned-out service station, and, unexpectedly, pulled into the parking area. He got out of his car and walked into the storefront. That part of the building, and the cinderblock service bay were still standing. As he entered and looked at the far wall, he remembered the report about the firefighter's actions. *The fire started in a wastebasket and climbed the wall. The firefighters had the fire doused then ripped open the wall.*

Walking into the service area, he saw that the walls were black with soot, and the ceiling above the rear opening burned through to the roof. Stepping through the opening, and into the rear working area, he found himself in bright sunlight. Because CJ and Jessie had been busy trying to save Paul, the fire gained the upper hand here, and all that was left of the building was burned rubble.

Walking through the ruins, Richard tried to picture what the place looked like as Paul Kenny entered it that night. He estimated the building measured forty feet by twenty feet. A work counter covered in blackened debris still stood to his left, and the double overhead doors would have been to his right. Turning in that direction, he walked along the rear of the storefront wall until he came to a toilet partly buried in wreckage. This was where CJ had broken through the wall from the storefront side.

As he stood there trying to picture the scene as it was at the moment of the explosion, he was unconsciously moving pieces of wood and ash with his shoe. Suddenly, the sun glinted off something below him, and, looking down, he saw that his shoe had uncovered a short length of wire. Putting on a pair of exam gloves, he reached down and picked it up. The vinyl insulation had melted in spots to reveal the metallic mesh shielding used in coaxial cable. He picked the debris off and found a large lump of melted plastic attached to the other end. He examined it, not sure what he was looking at. Removing a plastic bag from his pocket, he placed the wire and plastic lump into it. After another twenty minutes of walking in the fallen debris, he left.

12

A man, known only as "Ghost," punched the speed dial on a cell phone.

"What?" came the only response.

As always, the scrambled call was rerouted several times and the voice was electronically distorted. Ghost never knew the exact location or identity of the man on the other end of the line. He was not even sure that the "he" was not a "she." It did not matter; he, or she, paid well, and, for several years, had been his major source of income. The money and the reputation the person behind the distorted voice had, made Ghost willing follow the voice's instructions to the letter.

"The police chief from Winchendon was here. He wandered around for a while; spent forty-five minutes. He picked up something and placed it in an evidence bag. He just left."

"Any other activity?"

"State Fire Marshal was out a couple of days ago, and again yesterday. They combed the area taking samples and released the site early this morning. A construction company dropped off a front-end loader shortly after the police chief arrived. They'll start to clean the area tomorrow."

"Any idea what the chief picked up? Did you leave anything behind?"

"I have no idea what he picked up, but I never leave evidence behind, so it isn't important."

"Important or not, I want to know what it was. Stay there until dark. Then find the evidence bag. Check the police station, his car and, if you have to, his home. I'll have information about security systems and his address for you later." With that, the conversation ended.

Ghost put away the cell phone, collected his gear, and eradicate any remaining evidence of his four-day stakeout in the woods across from Riley's service station. Although he had been there continuously since the night of the fire, when he left, there was no indication he had been there. A short time later, he was in his motel room, cleaning up and preparing for his mission in Winchendon, a mission that he knew would bring him face to face with his past.

Born in the hills of West Virginia, Henry Thomas was the only son of indifferent parents, and had had been making his own way in the world almost since he learned to walk. He was a quiet person, although not introspective. Moreover, for someone so quiet, he was prone to getting into confrontations with his peers. In a fight, he would do whatever it took, not just to win, but also to eliminate his opponent as a future threat. Self-preservation motivated his actions. He was devoid of moral scruples. If there was anything he needed or wanted, he would get it by whatever methods, legal or illegal, he saw fit. He also had great cunning and, usually, managed to cover his tracks well enough to avoid getting into serious trouble. In high school, he became the primary suspect in a string of burglaries, but clues were few and never connected directly to him.

Out of high school, he joined the Marines. The Corps refined his fighting skills, introduced him to a variety of weapons, which he quickly mastered, and improved his surveillance and tactical planning knowledge. After completing his basic and advanced training, he joined an elite reconnaissance unit where he proved to be a deadly long-range sharpshooter, making confirmed kills from as far away as eleven hundred meters.

It soon became apparent that he was even deadlier using his large, powerful hands at close range. He learned how to exploit all the vulnerable spots on the human body, and how to move with speed and silence. His ability to appear out of nowhere, make a silent kill, and disappear back into the shadows undetected, caused his peers to nickname him "Ghost." The name reflected his lethality and his stealth: he was as much a ghost maker as he was ghostly. It was also a testament to the fact that he was considered unique in an organization of elite individuals. Ghost was the model surveillance and killing machine.

He was not just a mindless killer, however, but had courage, intelligence, cunning, patience, and initiative. He even, on occasion, displayed a sense of humor, or at least a sense of irony. Once, after more than a week watching a Russian military base in Afghanistan, Ghost decided that he wanted to eat something more appetizing than the military Meals Ready to Eat. He entered the Russian base, getting past the fence, guard dogs, barbed wire, and constant patrols. In the mess hall, he enjoyed hot coffee while he gathered fresh fruits, vegetables, and leftover cooked meat. He then went back to his post and continued his surveillance mission.

Initially, Ghost did well in the Marines, but, over time, his poor team skills, and little disrespect for rules and authority, brought him into increasing conflict with his peers, his superiors, and the highly structured and disciplined culture of the Corps. His old ability to cover up his misdeeds, were less effective in the closed society of the military, and his record began to fill with a succession of disciplinary actions and transfers. Eventually, he found himself facing a dishonorable discharged.

At that point, his latest commanding officer, wanting to rid himself of a problem, but not wanting to mar his unit's record with a disciplinary discharge, referred Ghost to a newly formed CIA quasi-military program. Despite his disciplinary record, or, perhaps because of it, the CIA recruited him into its Special Armed Intelligence Force program.

The Special Armed Intelligence Force program, SAIF, was created to execute covert sensitive intelligence and counterintelligence missions in situations requiring the use of deadly force. SAIF personnel, who were recruited from elite units of all the armed services, were detached from their regular units, but retained their active military status, benefits, and privileges. However, they lived and trained in small groups in CIA facilities, in secret bases, or in areas segregated from other troops. Funds provided by the CIA augmented their regular salaries. When training or deployed on missions, they wore uniforms devoid of insignia or any other identification, local mufti, or, on occasion, the uniforms of other nations. The number of SAIF personnel was never large, and they usually trained and operated in small teams. If necessary, however, local armed forces, guerilla forces, mercenaries, or regular American special ops units provided additional support. In theory, a special department at the CIA headquarters in Langley conceived SAIF missions and special CIA handlers supervised in the field. In fact, however, the program had inadequate oversight and was vulnerable to misuse both by elements at Langley and agents in the field.

Ghost found the SAIF program more to his liking than the Marine Corps. His CIA handler was more interested in his results than in his methods, his ethics, or his social skills. His extraordinary ability at infiltration soon made him a prized assassin.

Over time, he also became known for using unsanctioned techniques when interrogating detainees in the field—techniques that would still be off-limits a few years later at Abu Ghraib and Guantanamo. His methods were often so harsh, and applied so ruthlessly, that they occasionally caused toughened veterans to object.

It was while in SAIF, that Ghost encountered two men who would have a significant impact on his career. One was a CIA officer named Rob Lee, and the other was Captain Richard Moore, then the commander of an Army special operations unit.

13

When the SAIF program began, the CIA made Rob Lee the military liaison. It was his job to select and requisition special operations personnel for all SAIF missions. It was also his responsibility to ensure good communication and coordination between the military unit and the SAIF team. This responsibility required he be present during the mission. Lee was not a coward, but he did plan to lead a long and highly successful life, and was reluctant to enter harm's way without providing for his own security. He decided, therefore, to use someone from the SAIF teams as a personal bodyguard in the field. After an extensive review of the SAIF personnel files, he found a likely candidate, a man with a reputation as a killing machine. Lee took him along on a couple of missions and found that he performed beyond expectation. They did not become friends, neither had the personality to establish close friendships, and Lee was clearly the man in charge, but they did form a type of symbiotic bond based on mutual self-interest. After those first missions, Lee never went into the field without Ghost at his side.

Lee also decided he needed to find an Army special operations commander who was self-structured, self disciplined, and self-informed. His search led him to Captain Richard Moore. Richard had a reputation as a self-contained personality who also enjoyed the respect and admiration of his peers and superiors, and the loyalty of his troops. His extensive combat record showed he was an effective leader, collaborated well with other units, completed his missions, and always brought his people back. Lee arranged to have Richard's unit deployed on a highly sensitive mission and found, like Ghost, Richard performed beyond expectation. Lee began requesting Richard's unit for missions whenever it was available.

Lee and Richard worked well enough together, but the two never developed a bond of any type. As he did with most people, Lee felt superior to Richard, whom he saw as a skilled, but limited and naively idealistic man that he could manipulate to suite his purposes. Lee's attitude was not lost on Richard, but he overlooked it provided it did not interfere with their ability to function together.

After working with Lee and Ghost on a number of missions, Richard learned of Ghost's reputation for using unsanctioned interrogation techniques. Because of the negative reactions he occasionally encountered early on, Ghost had become careful about where, when, and in whose presence he used these techniques. He was also careful to ensure that no victims or victims' bodies were ever able to provide evidence of his work. As a result, neither Richard nor any of his men ever witnessed Ghost using unsanctioned techniques, or seen evidence that he had done so. Even so, Richard had difficulty abiding the man's manner and methods, and Ghost made it plain that the feelings were mutual.

On a SAIF mission in Central America, Richard and some of his men inadvertently came upon Ghost just as he was finishing the interrogation of a young teenage boy. When Richard saw what had been done to the young man, he pounced on Ghost and might have beaten him to death if his men had not pulled him off. Richard had his men bury the boy's mutilated remains. Richard then marched the seething Ghost back to camp under guard.

In camp, Richard demanded Rob Lee have Ghost shipped back to the States to face charges. After a few moments thought, Lee took Richard aside.

"Captain, I'm afraid that you're going to have to release the man. We're not due to be extracted for two weeks, and we damn well can't keep him under guard that long. Besides, he's SAIF, and you know that means he's not subject to your authority. In effect, he's CIA, which means I decide what happens to him, and I haven't seen him commit any wrongdoing ... Look, Richard, I don't want to pull rank on you, but I am in overall command of this mission, and we need everybody we have to complete it, including Ghost. He's not going anywhere, and you can prefer charges against him when we get back to the States, however, I have released him and returned him to duty." Richard tried to argue with Lee, but got nowhere. Eventually, Richard turned on his heel and left.

A few minutes later, Lee talked with Ghost. "I know you. I know how your mind works. I know you're thinking about how you can kill Moore and get away with it. So, before you do anything stupid, remember that every person in Moore's unit knows what happened today. If you kill Moore, you're going to have to kill them all, and before that happens, one of them will kill you. Personally, I don't give a shit if you all kill one another, but I'm not going to let you ruin my life by provoking a court of inquiry. So, let me tell you what's going to happen. We're going to complete this mission and go back to the States. When we get home, Captain Moore is going to file charges against you. The charges will go absolutely nowhere. In fact, the charges will never even appear on your service record. Keep the fuck out of his way, for the next two weeks, and pray he makes it back to the States alive, because I'm making you personally responsible for his safety. If anything happens to him, I'll kill you myself."

Richard did make it back to the States alive, and did file charges against Ghost. A week later, he received official notification that, since the military had relinquished jurisdiction over SAIF personnel, his allegations had been forwarded to the CIA's SAIF group. When he followed up several weeks later, he learned the case had been sealed for reasons of national security. After he filed a written protest, his commanding officer, Colonel Vincent, called him into his office.

When Richard arrived, the Colonel said, "Richard, I've been in the Army for a long time, and I've seen damn few officers as good as you. If you aren't killed or caught in bed with your commanding officer's wife, you have as good a chance of reaching star rank as any man I know. However, if you push this thing, you're going to spend the rest of your career buried so deep in some shithole, all they'll have to do when you die is play "Taps" and throw dirt on you. And, it will all be for nothing, because this case has been buried in a hole shittier and deeper than the one they'll put you in." The Colonel handed the protest letter to Richard. "Carry on, Captain."

Richard came to attention, saluted, turned, and left the office.

After he had gone, Vincent picked up the phone and dialed a number at the CIA. When the party answered, he said, "It's Ernie. Shit, this SAIF program and the assholes running it are a bigger pain in the ass than an elephant's hemorrhoids! You guys at the Agency better get rid of it and them before it bites all of you in the ass. I just talked to our man, and he took it back. I know him, he's not only a good soldier, he's a good man and a true believer. This thing is going to gnaw at him until the Army loses him over it; and when we do, I'll hold you responsible. Better than that, I'll appoint you as one of his guardian angels, or in your case, a guardian demon ... Agreed ... Okay, I hold you to it. See you the next time I get up to that political cesspool we call the nation's Capital."

Colonel Vincent was right about Richard; the image of the boy's body haunted him. Richard was a soldier; maiming and killing his country's enemies was a part of his job; he was good at it, and had no compunction about doing it when it was necessary. He told himself what was done to the boy was different; an aberration his country would repudiate and condemn. Instead, his country, or those tasked with acting in its behalf buried the incident along with the boy. Maybe, he thought, it was not an aberration but a part of his job from which he had just chosen to insulate himself. If so, the horror he had seen lying on the jungle floor had ripped the insulation away, and every nerve was exposed and raw.

He had leave time available and his colonel granted his request to take it. He spent some of his leave on Nantucket Island in Massachusetts, sailing, fishing, and sketching various island scenes. He spent more time, however, in deep thought about his future. Shortly after he returned from his leave, he resigned his commission and left the Army.

Ghost and Lee went on one more mission together, a mission Lee himself proposed to the Langley SAIF group. According to him, a trusted intelligence source had revealed that a small, high-ranking group had splintered off from a large, well-funded international terrorist organization, and established a base camp in Libya. Before making their move, the splinter group made copies of the parent group's most critical computer records, including files detailing the organization's finances, international connections, membership rolls, base locations, and arms suppliers. If the Agency could get these disks, he argued, it could use the information they contained to inflict severe and lasting damage on the entire international terrorist movement. Since the parent organization was planning a strike against the dissident base in an attempt to wipe them out and retrieve or destroy the copies, the Agency would not have time to negotiate a deal with the dissidents. He said, the Agency should immediately attack the dissents, and grab the records before the parent organization made its move. The SAIF group approved the operation, and authorized Lee to procure the necessary resources to carry out the operation.

Forty-eight hours later, a SAIF team, accompanied by a special ops force, flew to Souda Bay in Crete and rendezvoused with a Wasp Class amphibious assault ship. The ship transported them across the Mediterranean to a position just off the coast of the Libyan-Egyptian border, where all but six boarded two of the ship's CH-46 Sea Knight assault helicopters. The remaining half-dozen boarded an armed cargo helicopter loaded with reserve fuel. The Egyptians had agreed to turn a blind eye to the operation, so all three helicopters used Egyptian airspace to fly one hundred and fifty miles south to a point on the Egyptian border seventy-five miles east of the dissident's camp. There, they landed and the Sea Knights refueled from the tanks brought in by the cargo helicopter. The refueling completed, the Sea Knights took off and began to dune hop under the Libyan radar to the dissident's base, while the cargo helicopter and its small force remained behind to guard the refueling area. Shortly after 1:00 A.M., the Sea Knights arrived at the base, and the strike force debarked. The dissidents were expecting an attack from the parent group, and were on the alert, but their defensive strategy had not anticipated an airborne assault coming from the east. Their small force put up a spirited defense, nonetheless, and inflicted several casualties on the strike force before being overcome. Lee, Ghost and the SAIF team then spent the next half-hour searching the camp for the records. When Lee was certain they had found what they were looking for, the small SAIF force still in the camp headed back to the waiting helicopters.

Just as they were about to board, the night was rent with bright flashes and loud explosions. Several men went down, badly wounded and screaming, and someone yelled, "Incoming." Taken by surprise, the door gunners began firing into the night. Rob Lee shouted for everyone to get on the choppers, and people began scrambling into the Sea Knight closest to them. Ghost was the last to board, and had to be dragged into the doorway because a final explosion wounded him just as the helicopter, it door guns still pounding away at the night, became airborne.

As the two blacked out craft streaked through the night to the Egyptian border, the trip was a nightmare. The cabins of both ships were slippery with blood and other body fluids. Dead and wounded soldiers lay where they landed after being pushed or thrown just before takeoff. Empty shell casings littered the deck and rolled around with every movement. All was bathed in the eerie glow of infrared lighting. Medics ministered to the wounded. It was not until the force reached the relative safety and sanity of the refueling point that Rob Lee was missed. He had been left behind, and with him, the disks.

The fruitless operation had cost the Americans several hundred thousand dollars, five dead, fifteen wounded, and one missing in action. It had also inadvertently helped the parent terrorist organization by eliminating the dissidents. It left people at Langley very unhappy. A formal inquiry was held, and since it was well known that Ghost was Lee's unofficial bodyguard, he was grilled extensively about why he did not notice that Lee was absent. He swore that just before the attack Lee had split them up so each of them could go to a separate helicopter and ensure everyone was on board before liftoff. In the confusion, resulting from the attack, he was certain that Lee was on the other helicopter because it took off first, and he was the last one left on the ground when his took off a few moments later. Once they were airborne, the medics had medicated him and he was hazy for most of the trip. His story spawned skepticism, but there was no proof events had not happened as he testified. In the end, the inquiry concluded that Rob Lee was "Missing in action, presumed dead." Shortly after, a little ceremony was held at the CIA, during which Lee was awarded a posthumous medal.

Ghost was not unscathed, however. During the inquiry, the charges preferred by Richard came to the attention of people outside the SAIF program, and added to the skepticism about Ghost's story. The SAIF group received pressure to take action. The SAIF group told Ghost he could take his discharge, or face the charges. He took his discharge, and then disappeared. The SAIF program was discontinued.

If the Agency could no longer use his services, however, Ghost quickly found that others could. He became a freelance operative, and, as his reputation grew, a highly successful one. It was a role that seemed to suit him well. He was his own boss, doing work that was good at and he enjoyed. He was making more money than he thought possible. The money provided him with nice toys and surroundings; the work provided an outlet for his special skills and talents.

14

The Winchendon police station was on Pleasant Street, and was not a typical building for a police station. In 1950, the town purchased a turn-of-the-century Victorian home and converted it to accommodate the needs of the police department.

Except when guests are staying in one of the holding cells, the station remains closed at night. Guests were more likely to be in the holding cells on weekend nights than on other days of the week. The call center, part of the fire station, handled incoming calls and dispatches when the station is closed.

Ghost disconnected the security system and entered the police station through the back door. Once inside, he opened his tool kit and donned a set of night vision goggles. He had memorized the floor plan, and reviewed it mentally as he proceeded. The basement had two entrances, a bulkhead in the back and a stairway leading from the kitchen. The heating system and a locker room for the employees were the only items in the basement. On the first floor, a kitchen lead to the old dining room now converted to a holding area with wire cells. The front room was the main office and reception area. Just inside the front door stairs lead to the second floor. The chief's office was in what had been the front bedroom. The room's closet, now a vault, held tactical weapons and ammunition. Offices occupied two other rooms on the second floor: one for the lieutenant, and one shared by the rest of the force. The third floor had two rooms used for storage.

He started his search in the kitchen, worked his way to the reception area, and then headed to the chief's office.

The chief's desk was clean; his in-basket had only two papers in it. Ghost opened the desk drawers and found them neat and orderly. The bookcase and credenza along the wall behind the desk were clean and polished. The bookcase contained binders with officers' reports, budget reports, staffing rotations, and an evidence log. The last entry in the log was dated several days earlier.

Books on personnel management, time management, and supervisory techniques took up most of the space in the bookcase. A dozen books on criminal psychology took a full shelf. The bookcase also contained several books on military physical fitness, tactical weapons, and military tactical procedures.

The closet had a separate security system and electronic lock. Ghost bypassed both, and stepped inside. On one wall, a gun rack contained a variety of rifles and shotguns. A set of drawers on the other side held ammunition, handguns, teargas grenades, stun guns, and flash bang grenades. The drawer and cabinet marked *EVIDENCE* were empty.

Before moving on to the basement, he did a final visual sweep of the office to assure himself that nothing was out of place. As he did, he spotted the framed picture of an attractive woman. He was startled to recognize her.

For a few moments, he thought seriously of spending more time looking around to see if he could find the reason the woman's picture was in the chief's office. Time was running out, however, and he still had to search the chief's apartment. It was time to leave. If the presence of the woman's picture were related to the mission, he would find out eventually.

Ghost left the police station after resetting the alarm, and went to the chief's residence. Once there, he entered the garage below the chief's apartment through the side door, opened a state of the art infrared scanner and aimed it at the ceiling. After he made a few minor adjustments, a picture of the heat sources in the apartment above appeared. To the untrained eye, it looked like an abstract painting made of fuzzy orange and yellow blobs, but Ghost saw an infrared blueprint of the four rooms above. More important, in one of those rooms he saw the heat signature of a live human body in a horizontal position—the chief was home; he was alone; he was lying down; and he was in a room to the right of the kitchen.

Smiling to himself, he took out a hypersensitive listening device and aimed it at the ceiling underneath the room with the chief. After a few moments, he heard the rhythmic sounds of slowed human breathing—the chief was sleeping.

Putting the device aside and donning his goggles, Ghost searched the garage and the car, stopping periodically to check both the scanner and the listening device. Each time he did, the chief was in the same position, breathing in the same manner.

When he was satisfied that the evidence bag was not in the garage or the car, he checked his instruments again and, finding the situation unchanged, put them in his tool kit.

Leaving the garage as he had found it, he climbed the outside wooden stairs on the rear of the building and entered the apartment through the kitchen. To his right was the entrance to a bedroom and on the bed was the man from the service station, the chief. An open door off the bedroom revealed a small bathroom. Directly across from the main door and entry was the living room. Off the living room toward the back was a small room that appeared to be a home office.

Ghost stuck a motion detector on the wall just inside the bedroom, and pointed it at the sleeping chief. Significant movement, more than just rolling over, would activate the sensor. The sensor would then send a signal to the headset Ghost was wearing, thus alerting him. Entering the bedroom, he put a lightweight pole in a stand, placed it beside the chief's bed, fastened a small tube, and positioned one end of the tube directly in front of the chief's nose. The other end of the tube he attached to a can of nitrous oxide: sleeping gas. Nitrous oxide works best as a fifty-fifty mixture with air. The stream from the tube would deliver the right mixture without filling the room with the gas. Ghost could work efficiently and suffer no effects of the gas, while the chief remained in a deep sleep. Ghost turned a small valve on the can and a stream of gas flowed toward the chief's nostrils. Ghost watched the chief's breathing as it slowed. When he felt confident the gas was working, he began his search.

He found that the apartment just as clean and orderly as the chief's office, a fact that did not surprise him. He did not find the evidence bag, however. Whatever the chief had picked up at Riley's was not in his apartment, his car, or the police station; further searching was not going to find it.

He did find another picture of the woman he recognized at the police station. This one had a dated inscription on it that read, *To Richard, your loving wife, Lori.* When he read the inscription and the date, he was dumbfounded. The woman he knew as Lori Clement had been the chief's wife!

It took him a few moments to process this information, after which he went through the apartment to make sure that he had left no sign of his presence behind him. He dismantled and stowed the nitrous oxide apparatus, and put the rest of his equipment away. When he was through, he looked down at the face of the deeply sleeping man, a man he recognized the moment he saw him at Riley's burned-out service station.

Sleep on, Captain Moore, he thought. *When this assignment is over, I'm going to kill you, but first, I'm going to tell you about Lori Clement and me.*

15

Richard woke with a start. He had a headache, a strange taste in his mouth, and he felt groggy. Looking over at the clock, he realized that he had slept later than he had intended, but when he tried to get out of bed, he had to sit back and shake the cobwebs out of his head before proceeding.

When he emerged from his apartment and came down the stairs, Mrs. Hall was already busy in the kitchen.

"Good morning, Chief. I see you decide to sleep in this morning. Good thing, too—you work too hard and don't sleep enough, if you ask me."

"Good morning to you, Leslie. How are you this morning?"

"Just fine, Chief. The coffee is on, and I made some muffins—the ones you like so much, with cranberries and nuts. Come, join me."

"Sounds like a great way to start the day. Thank you, Leslie."

Leslie Hall was a widow. Her husband died of a massive heart attack six years previously. She was the proud mother of two sons, one deceased, the other a prominent surgeon at Johns Hopkins.

As she got cups and plates, Mrs. Hall said, "You went to the funeral of that poor firefighter in Ashburnham?"

"Yes, I did."

"Such a tragedy. I understand he left a wife and seven-year-old daughter."

"He did. The irony was that it was most likely going to be his last day on the job. His doctor told him he had Lou Gehrig's disease. He was going to Worcester the next day for a battery of tests. His wife had been trying to persuade him to leave the fire department."

"His poor wife, someone needs to get her help coping. When my son Jim died, Sharon, his wife, wouldn't talk with anyone. One day she just picked up and left. I used to get a card occasionally. Haven't seen her or my grandchild in three years. The last time I heard from Sharon, they were in Arizona and planning to move again. That was eighteen months ago. Not a word since." She poured coffee, placed a muffin on Richard's plate, and sat at the table. "It's so much for a young wife to suffer. First the news of a serious illness, then a tragic accident, life can be difficult and, if you're young, with a child, you can have the feeling the world is against you."

"Was your son ill?"

"Yes, he was. The doctors said he had cancer."

"If you don't mind talking about it, would you tell me about him?"

"Talking about it now isn't as difficult as it used to be. I came to terms with the loss of my son. The loss of my daughter-in-law and grandchild still wears on me. I'm losing time with them, time I can't make up."

She fixed her coffee with cream and sugar, cut her muffin, then had a little of each before continuing.

"My husband, Tony, and I, have two sons, Jim our youngest and Tony Junior. Junior, I'm not supposed to call him that. He went to college and then to medical school. He's a physician at Johns Hopkins. Jim must have seen how Tony's school tuition strained our finances. We didn't go into debt. We just put off vacations and kept the car longer than usual. We were happy to do it and were willing to do it again for Jim. When Jim said he didn't want to go to college, we left it at that."

"More coffee, Chief?"

"Yes, please, Leslie."

She poured coffee in Richard's cup, added some to her cup, and then continued.

"Anyway, Jim found a job with the municipal light company after graduating from high school. He enjoyed his work. Winchendon was growing and he was one of the first to meet people new to the town. He met Sharon, his wife, when he went to fix a line that had come down during a storm. She was a senior in high school and five years younger than he was. When they married, I had that apartment you're living in built. Jim and Sharon didn't want to live in this house with me. I understood. Newlyweds don't want to worry about bumping into Mom after waking her with noises from the bedroom. I insisted the apartment be built and they move in. They could save money on rent and have the house and a rental after I was gone. Jim was going to inherit the house. Tony junior wanted his younger brother to have it. As you can see, I won. The apartment was built. Jim and Sharon moved in."

Mrs. Hall served Richard another hot muffin.

"Leslie, these are the best yet."

"Thank you, Chief. You're always so kind."

Leslie checked the stove and turned it off. She again sat at the table.

"Sharon was fond of these muffins also." Mrs. Hall paused as she recalled a time when her daughter-in-law would join her for breakfast.

"My grandchild was born two years later. Oh, what a wonderful day! My first grandchild: I was so happy. Then, four years ago, Jim was working in the yard one day and doubled over with a sudden pain in his gut. It went away quick, but it came back so bad about a week later that he went to the emergency ward. They thought at first that he had some kind of stone, but it turned out he had cancer of the stomach, and they scheduled him for surgery, and radiation.

"Maybe someone else would have gone on sick leave right away, but Jim said he was going to work right up to the day before surgery. Two nights before surgery, he was on call. He received a report about trouble with the transformer on the pole out on Main Street. It was two in the morning. When Sharon awoke at seven, Jim hadn't returned. She just assumed the problem was major and taking a long time to correct. At seven-thirty, she came rushing into the kitchen here. She handed Madeline to me. She told me Jim had had an accident and she was going to the hospital."

Leslie picked up her napkin and wiped her mouth. Richard knew she was buying time to compose herself. As she continued, her voice was softer, with a slight tremor to it.

"Jim had fallen from the bucket, the thing the workers use to get up high and work, while working on the transformer. He broke his neck in the fall." Tears welled up in her eyes. "The doctor said he'd been on the ground for hours before they found him."

Silence filled the kitchen. Leslie busied herself by pouring more coffee and setting the mixing bowl and other dishes in the sink.

When she sat again, she continued, "After the funeral, Sharon withdrew into herself. I tried talking with her, but she didn't want that. I guess I was too insistent about the need to talk, or maybe I was just too strong a reminder of Jim. Whatever the reason, Sharon told me she was leaving. She said she had a friend in Arizona who got her a job. She left the next day."

Silence again filled the room as Mrs. Hall looked longingly into her cup of coffee.

Finally, she said, "You know, Chief, Jim was the most safety-conscious worker in the company. He often gave safety orientations to new and existing employees. No one could understand how he could have fallen out of that bucket."

Richard had a deep-seated need to create order in his life. It was one way he had coped in a childhood dominated by the unpredictability of his mother's emotional illness. His curious and intelligent mind was constantly observing the world around him, storing bits of information, and trying to fit the pieces together and form a coherent whole. Much of the process occurred on a subconscious level. His training and experience in the military and police greatly enhanced the process. Much as Ghost had become a killing machine, Richard's brain had become an investigating machine. During the last few days, it had been gathering and processing data about several apparently unrelated deaths, the latest was that of Mrs. Hall's son. His subconscious was furiously working in the background, prompting Richard to provide it with more data by asking the woman questions. Richard was not a machine, however. He was a man with many admirable human qualities, including empathy. Despite his need to gather more data, he judged Mrs. Hall had been through enough this morning.

He rose from the table and said, "Leslie, thank you for breakfast and for telling me about Jim, I know it was difficult. May I do a favor for you? Would you mind if I try to find your daughter-in-law and grandchild?"

She looked at him in amazement.

"You think you could do that?"

"I don't know but I have resources available to me that can help. Your daughter-in-law isn't hiding, so it shouldn't be difficult to find her. I can't promise anything, but if you agree, I'll try."

She did not know what to say. She wrapped her arms around him and said, "Thank you, Chief."

16

At the office, Richard asked Jill, the clerical staff person, to pull together any information about Jim Hall she could find. After dealing with paperwork and other administrative details, he called Don Williams at the Boston Police Department hoping to set up a luncheon meeting.

"Is this that important chief of police from Winchendon calling to talk to a lowly Boston Police Department director of personnel?" Don asked.

"I suppose I deserve that."

"Only if you think two years between phone calls is a long time."

"Okay, Don, I promise I will be more attentive to staying in touch."

"I'll hold you to that promise. Tell me how you like running your own show."

They made small talk for a while and exchanged information about the whereabouts and assignments of mutual friends. Finally, Don asked, "So, Richard, you didn't call me after all this time to catch up. What can I do for you?"

"Well, I was hoping to get together for lunch later today or tomorrow."

"After all this time you pick now. You have rotten timing. I'm cleaning up a few things this morning and I'm going on vacation. The wife and I are taking a cruise to several European countries. Be gone for about a month. If it's important, I can spend some time with you now on the phone."

Richard agreed, then, after explaining the circumstances of Paul Kenny's accident, said, "Chief O'Malley and I were talking after the funeral. He told me he sensed an increase in the number of deaths of police and fire personnel. He told me you two talked, and you had done some checking. I wanted to hear how you determined the number of deaths was up, and to get your take on any other information you might have."

"Richard, I know you well enough to know that mind of yours is looking for a connection here, but I've already gone down that road, and all the information I have suggests the increase in mortalities within the ranks is just a cyclical occurrence.

"You see, like you and O'Malley, several ranking officers and I were talking after a funeral about four years ago. We crossed notes and concluded funerals for fellow officers were more frequent than we remembered. I was concerned and called our accident and life insurance company. They had already looked at the data, and determined that there had indeed been a spike in the mortality rate, and the rat had leveled out higher than in previous years. However, they didn't find any obvious cause, and didn't make any recommendations for educational or safety programs to mitigate the trend. As I told O'Malley, to them it was just a statistical occurrence."

"How thoroughly did they search for common factors in the increase?"

Don thought for a moment and replied, "I was not privy to the details of their study, but they had a good reason to be thorough: an increase in deaths meant an increase in losses for them. However, the department did review several of the cases involving accidents on and off the job. They looked for evidence that might have indicated they were something other than they seemed. They found a couple of questionable circumstances, but no pattern, if that's what you want to know.

"Look, we're talking about natural causes: accidents, suicides, and job-related deaths. The increase is across the board. It's a hard notion to accept, but the normal occurring percentage of mortalities in our workforce population has increased. The fact that those statistics represent our colleagues and friends, makes them unwelcome, but it doesn't make them sinister."

"Thanks, Don. You're right. It's just that some of those statistics have been hitting close to home, lately."

Don grew silent and thoughtful for a moment then said, "Richard, I know Lori's death hit you very hard. I couldn't understand how it could happen. I still don't. If I were you, I'd be looking for answers too, even in the deaths of others, even when those deaths had nothing to do with Lori, even when others are saying there are no answers. If it helps you any, I know a reporter from the Boston Globe who investigated the increase of police personnel. She wrote a piece on it. Talking to her might help you put it into perspective."

"What's the reporter's name?" Richard asked.

"Stephanie Lynn. Here's her telephone number."

"Thanks, Don. I'll call her."

Before they hung up, they set a date to get together when Don returned from his vacation.

Richard called Stephanie Lynn, and she agreed to meet with him at nine the next day. He then called Charlie White, a longtime friend at the FBI. Richard gave him a run-down on Sharon Hall and her daughter, and asked him to see if he could find information about their whereabouts.

His final call went to a confidential number.

"Hi, Tim, how's business?"

"Any business is more business than I want. How about you?"

"I lost a resident the other night in a car accident. She was the wife of one of the Town Council members."

"Oh? Anyone that might be of interest to me?"

"No. I called to see if you found anything."

"Your people are clean. We double-checked our information, so you can feel confident about them."

"I do. That's why they were involved in the raid."

"Yeah, well, you have more faith than I do. The information you passed on does confirm that the cartel's principal warehouse was missed and suspended operations. You may be right about the identity of the warehouse man, but until the cartel starts moving product in your direction again, we're not going to be able to nail them with the goods."

"Okay, Tim. I appreciate your willingness to hold off on your end until they make their move here. Keep me informed."

"I will, my friend, and, Richard, watch your back. You pissed off some nasty people."

"I will, Tim. Thanks again."

The nasty people Tim Curtin referred to were individuals connected with a Winchendon drug operation Richard had put out of business six months before.

Aggressive law enforcement and prosecutorial action in major American cities has forced many drug dealers to flee to small towns where they find untapped markets, less competition, and law enforcement agencies with less drug-savvy. Winchendon had become one such refuge for dealers from Boston and Worcester. The drug dealers quietly set up distribution centers operated out of several houses in the western part of town. They distributed to other towns in the north-central part of Massachusetts and southern New Hampshire. As the distribution network expanded, and the dealers became more confident, they started selling to children in the Winchendon school system. By the time that the problem was acutely noticeable, the dealers were entrenched in the town. Richard's predecessor had proved inept at dealing with the problem; his inconsistent and uncoordinated raids and arrests were minor inconveniences for the dealers When Richard arrived, he began developing a network of informants, and using other techniques to gather information about the local drug trade and the players in it. He also began an intense training program for his small force, teaching them what they needed to know about the drug trade and modern police techniques for dealing with it. All of this activity, coupled with Richard's reputation, led most dealers to become cautious, and for a while, it looked as though Winchendon's drug problem was going away. Richard knew, however, that this was just a temporary period of adjustment, and that eventually he would have to launch a series of coordinated and well-timed raids to eliminate the major players for good.

When he felt the time was getting ripe, Richard began training his people in the assault tactics they would need to use to carry out the raids successfully. He knew, however, that no amount of training could replace their experience in this type of work, so he quietly deputized twelve former special operations colleagues to beef up his strike force for the week of the intended operations. They started by hitting the three key locations simultaneously in the early morning hours of the first day of the operation. The speed and proficiency of the raids netted Richard valuable information, substantial quantities of illegal drugs, and zero injuries to his combined forces. During the remainder of that day and the next, the strike groups continued to conduct raids, while the rest of the force processed prisoners, intelligence, and evidence. By the end of 48 hours, they had hit every known major dealer, every known distribution center, and the only drug factory in the town. They were so successful; it took the efforts of the combined force to finish the paperwork before the "deputies" were discharged at the end of the week.

The raids appeared to deal a fatal blow to the major players in the Winchendon drug trade Richard's people picked up most of the minor dealers during the next couple of weeks. The others left town. By the time a month had past, the amount of product moving into Winchendon had been reduced to a trickle, and none of it was coming directly from the region's major supplier.

Jill knocked on Richard's door.

"Come in."

"Chief, here's the file on Jim Hall, as you asked." Jill handed the file to him.

"Thank you, Jill."

As Jill turned to walk out of the room, Richard suddenly asked, "Jill, were you here when Jim Hall died?"

She stopped, turned, and said, "Yes, I was. His death really shook this town. Jim was well liked."

"Do you remember anything about the investigation?"

"Not much. It was routine. Because it was a work related accident, the chief did not spend much time having it investigated. Is there a problem?"

"No. I talked with his mother, Leslie Hall, this morning. Our conversation just sparked my curiosity. Thanks again for finding the file."

Jill left as Richard opened the file and started reading. The file was sparse: the responding officer's two-page report, three black-and-white photos, the EMT's report, a copy of the autopsy, and a copy of the death certificate. After looking through it, he knew little more than Mrs. Hall had told him earlier.

Doc Fenton had signed the autopsy report, so Richard decided to call him to see if he could add any information. .

"Hi, Doc."

"Chief Moore, always a pleasure. What can I do for you?"

"I have a few questions about an old case. If you're going to be in your office for a while, I'd like to come by."

"Be my guest. I could use a distraction. I'll be in the pathology lab."

"Thanks, I'll be over shortly."

When he arrived at the medical center pathology lab, Richard found Fenton hunched over a microscope.

"Hey, Doc, I thought you said you were retired. What are you doing in the lab looking through a microscope?"

Fenton lifted his head from the microscope.

"Ah, Richard, I told you the other night that Shirley's brother had a brain tumor. This slide is from Shirley's tumor. I'm sending it to a friend, a specialist in cancer research. Maybe the slide and Shirley's health history will be of help in the research."

After looking through the microscope again, Fenton turned the seat of the stool he was sitting in to the side.

"Do you want to go to my office, or is this okay?"

"Here will do."

"Then pull up a stool and tell me what's on your mind."

Richard grabbed a stool, brought it near Fenton, and sat.

"I was going through the file on Jim Hall's death and noticed that you signed the autopsy report."

"Jim Hall. That was some time ago."

"So you remember the accident and the report?"

"I didn't say that. Jim's mother and I are friends, have been most of our lives. This is a small town remember. I would have to look at my notes if you want to go over any specifics of the post. What makes you interested in Jim's death?"

"Leslie and I were talking over breakfast this morning. She told me about Jim's death. I got curious and looked into the file. It was very thin."

"Breakfast? Does she still make her own muffins?"

"Yeah, she does." Teasing Fenton, he smiled and added, "I enjoyed several this morning."

"I'll have to pay her a call some morning. I haven't had one of her muffins in a long time."

"You really should, Doc. Give her a call. Her daughter-in-law left after her son's death. Leslie hasn't heard from her or her granddaughter for eighteen months. I think she'd like company once in a while."

"Well, I knew they'd gone, but I thought they still kept in touch. I'll be sure to do that. She's a fine woman. So, what do you want to know about the report?"

"Well, I was hoping you still had some notes that didn't make it into the official report."

"It might take some time to find them, but I still have them. Have every note I ever wrote. Let's go to my office. You can help me look."

17

When Fenton opened the door to his office, Richard stood in the doorway and surveyed the room. Stacks of periodicals, books, and files covered every flat surface. Towering, precipitous stacks of files sat in the chairs near the round table. Stacks also occupied two side chairs, and sat on top of the open draws of the lateral files. Books and magazines lined the windowsill behind Fenton's desk. The centermost part of the blotter was the only visible work surface of the top of his desk. Clutter obscured the rest. Richard did not see a computer or telephone anywhere in the office. Moving in the office was limited to the floor space not occupied by more stacks.

As he sank into his desk chair, Fenton asked, "Well, are you coming into help, or are you going to stand there all day?"

"I'm afraid to enter. Aren't you concerned something may be growing in here?"

"Nonsense, this is a typical office of a very busy physician of my status. Grab the pile on that chair near the table over there, and lean it against the wall unit."

Richard moved to the chair and lifted the heap.

"Okay, now take that stack of files under the table, the one with the gray folders. That should have patient files from around the time Jim died. You can look through it. I have a stack with notes over here."

Richard heard a phone ringing and looked at Fenton. Fenton opened the file drawer of his desk and picked up a phone receiver.

"Hello." He listened for a few moments then said, "Tell her to come to the hospital pharmacy. I'll call them and have a prescription ready for her. Tell her not to worry about the cost. They won't charge her." He returned the receiver and closed the drawer.

Seeing Richard's inquisitive look, he said, "That was my service. Mrs. Brown needs a refill for antibiotics. She can't afford to get it at the drug store, so I have her pickup at the hospital pharmacy. She thinks she's getting it free, but they bill me."

"You pay?"

"Don't worry. I get the stuff at a fraction of what a patient is charged. Besides, I'll add the cost to your bill or someone else who can afford it"

"You're a good man, Doc."

"Flattering me won't stop me from overcharging you, young man. Now, let's find that file. Unlike some overpaid public servants I know, my time is valuable. I have to see some patients later."

Fenton started pulling file folders and looking in them, stopping occasionally to mutter a comment on something he saw. While he was doing this, Richard was looking for the file tab for Jim Hall.

Ten minutes later, Fenton said, "Got it. Jim Hall, work related accident and death," and started thumbing through the file. After a few moments, he said, "Hmm, that's interesting," more to himself than to Moore.

"What?"

"My handwritten notes ... hold on ... let me see the final report." He pulled another sheet out of the folder and read it. "I remember this now. How could I have forgotten this? Maybe I am getting old."

"You want to share this with me, Doc?"

"Here, read for yourself. Look at the scratching toward the bottom of this sheet, the part with the large question mark."

He handed Richard a yellow lined paper with handwritten notes on it. In the section he pointed to, Richard read, *Fractured collarbone broke skin in back, little blood evident; lividity evident front of body, the body was face down.* A large question mark was next to the note. Next to the question mark was another note. *Mention to chief and follow up.*

Richard looked up. "Okay, so what were you supposed to follow up?"

"The broken collarbone punctured the skin. The wound should have bled, but there was little blood evident when I first looked at the body. Gravity causes lividity. Postmortem the blood flows, like all fluids, toward gravity. Stand a dead person up and the blood flows toward the feet and hands. Turn him upside down and the blood flows toward the head. Jim was face down, and the blood flowed toward his chest and the front of his body."

"Okay, Doc. I know that, but what did you want to follow up?"

"Think about it, Richard. Alive, the heart pumps blood and produces pressure. Take a water balloon and squeeze it and you simulate the heart pressure. Put a small hole in the balloon and keep squeezing it, what happens?"

"Water squirts out the hole."

"Exactly, stop squeezing the balloon, and keep the hole near the top of the balloon, and what happens?"

"Nothing … the water stays in the balloon."

"Your hesitation tells me you figured it out."

"If there was no blood at the break in the skin caused by the broken bone, Jim was dead when the bone broke the skin. If he wasn't, the heart would have continued to cause pressure and the blood would have been pumped out of the break in the skin."

"Excellent! It's an oversimplification, but essentially correct. If the fall resulted in the broken neck, it should have also caused the broken bone and puncture of the skin. Death would not have relieved the blood pressure, immediately, so a noticeable amount of blood would emerge from the puncture. So, what happened to the blood that should have accompanied the break in the skin? That's what I wanted to follow up about with the chief."

"Did you?"

"I did. The chief told me he did an investigation and found no reason to suspect anything other than an accidental death. I knew he could be slipshod at times, and I thought about pressing the issue. The problem was that Jim had been dead for six hours or so when he was found. Many things can happen to an exposed body in that time. In addition, there was the possibility of an unexplained circumstance, like a sudden crash in blood pressure— no pressure, no bleeding. And, sometimes, Richard, things that are supposed to happen—like blood spurting out of a puncture—for some unknown reason, just don't. I decided that I couldn't state with certainty that the lack of blood was important. Without that certainty, I knew the chief wouldn't pursue it further. I couldn't produce a compelling reason not to affirm it as an accidental death but I sure would like to have known for certain."

"Doc, if someone had broken Jim's neck, took him up in the bucket, and dropped him, would that produce the same physical signs that you noticed?"

"Hmm … maybe. It would be more consistent with that explanation than the assumption that he was alive when he fell. However, he went to that call alone … Why would anyone hurt Jim, anyway? He was well liked. What are you getting at, Richard?"

Richard thought about the question. *What, indeed? Should I tell you I have one of those feelings?*

"Doc, you said that you would have liked to found out why Jim's wound didn't bleed, and you would have pursued it further if the chief had been more cooperative. Well, I'm the chief now, and I'd like to see if we could find the answer to your question."

Fenton leaned forward in his chair. "You know you're implying Jim was murdered?"

Richard gazed off for an instant. Images of Lori, Shirley, and Jim flashed into his mind. *Does all death imply murder to me now?*

He looked at Fenton, "Yes, it does sound like it."

"What're you going to do, Richard?"

"I don't know yet, Doc. Right now, I'm going to let you get to your patients. Thanks for your help. You've given me a lot to think about."

"And you've given me something to think about as well. I may have helped let a murder go uninvestigated. Not a pleasant thought."

"You did what you thought was right, Doc. Let me work on it for a while before you start second-guessing yourself."

"All right, Chief. I'll let you do that, but I'm becoming concerned about you. Here you are suggesting Jim may not have had an accident. You're suggesting someone killed him. Last night you suggested Shirley might have committed suicide. It's a different world you live in. Do you see ghosts in your room at night?"

Richard looked Fenton in the eye and slowly shook his head. "No, Doc, not in my room, just in my dreams."

Richard stopped at the office of the Winchendon Times to talk with Vinnie Esposito, the paper's editor and owner. Vinnie was absorbed in typing up an article on his computer and did not hear Richard enter the office

"Must be an interesting story: Can't be one of yours."

Vinnie jumped, saying, "Christ ... Richard, you startled me. Don't you know better than sneaking up on people?"

"Vinnie, the door was open. Doesn't anyone come in here during the day?"

"Yeah, but they usually cough or make some sound instead of sneaking up on me. Hey, wait minute. Were you trying to imply I don't write interesting stories? I could practice by using you as one of my front page items." Vinnie laughed.

"A story about me would only be interesting to Theo."

"Ah, yes, I know what you mean. Does he still call Council meetings and drag you in for them?"

"You know Theo will never change."

"I know. Next election, I think I'll feature him in a couple of front-page stories. Maybe I can convince the voters it's time for a change."

"Don't waste your ink and paper. He's a fixture in the town's politics. Besides, I always have so much fun during those meetings."

"Okay, Richard, I'll leave him alone, so you can continue to have some fun. What brings you to my humble office besides a desire to criticize my writing?"

"Do you remember the accident that killed Jim Hall?"

"I do. We ran several stories about the accident itself. Then we ran one or two on his family. Leslie Hall, his mother, was active in the community, and we wrote about the contributions she and the Hall family have made to the town over the years. We also did a story about workplace safety."

"Who did the stories?"

"Who do you think? I'm the reporter for this paper."

"Oh, sorry, I thought that you were the janitor."

"I am, and the delivery driver, ad salesperson, and layout designer."

"Okay, so you work hard. Tell me about the accident."

"What's to tell? The police chief at the time gave me a brief report. He told me Jim fell from the bucket of his truck and broke his neck. Apparently, Jim had been on the ground some time. He went out early in the morning, I don't remember exactly what time, but the story will have it. Someone found him about seven in the morning, if I remember correctly. What's your interest?"

"I was having breakfast with Leslie this morning. She told me about Jim's death. I got curious, so I checked the file when I got to the office. It's thin."

"Well, your predecessor wasn't much for recordkeeping or investigative persistence."

"The file had a few pictures in it. I wanted to ask Phil if he had taken any other shots and, if so, if he still had them."

"Phil wasn't with us. However, I think we still have a file with the photos in it. I'll ask Phil to find it and get it to you."

"Thanks, Vinnie, I'd appreciate it."

"No problem, but remember, if you find something of interest, I want the story."

"You'll get it. See you later."

He started to leave, then stopped, turned, and said, "Do you happen to remember a story about Shirley Robinson's brother being killed in an explosion a couple of years back?"

"Sure do. Because her husband is on the Council, most of our town officials went to the funeral, and, because the brother worked for the town, most of that town was there too. It was a big deal, so I covered the story."

"Do you remember his name?"

"Who could forget it? His name was Raymond."

"Well, was that his first name or his last name?"

"Both."

"What do you mean both?"

"Chief, his name was Raymond Raymond."

"You're kidding."

"Cross my heart and hope to die."

"It's diabolical to do that to your kid."

"His parents didn't do it to him. You see, his biological father was Shirley's father. Just after Shirley was born, the old man, who was no good, was murdered. Two years later, Shirley's mom married Tom Raymond, a terrific guy and a successful businessman. He insisted on adopting Shirley and her brother, Raymond. The young man wound up with the name Raymond Raymond. As far as he was concerned, Tom Raymond was his dad, and even when he was old enough to change his name, he wouldn't out of loyalty to his adoptive father."

"They must have been close."

"From all accounts, I guess they were. Anyway, I'll never forget his name and neither will you, I imagine."

"No, I guess I won't. Thanks again, Vinnie."

Later that night, before going to sleep Richard thought about the four deaths they were all local, all with puzzling features, and all unexpected. Then he thought to himself, *It was not their deaths that were unexpected, it was the manner and timing that was unexpected.* All of them had been recently diagnosed with potentially fatal illnesses, but had died of other causes well before those illnesses could have killed them. Coincidence? Maybe, but, he did not believe in coincidence.

Just like Lori, he thought. *They died just like Lori.* Then sleep overtook him, and with it came the dream.

18

The Boston Globe's offices are in a long brick and glass building on Morrissey Boulevard in the south side of Boston. Massive printing presses anchored several stories below ground run the length of the left side of the building and are visible through tall windows that stretch several stories. Richard found Stephanie Lynn typing away on a computer keyboard in a cubicle office on the second floor. Notepaper, printouts, and copies of various newspapers cluttered her desk.

"Ms. Lynn, I'm Chief—"

Lynn held up two fingers and continued typing. When she finished typing, she scanned the text on the screen, retyped some information, then pressed the *Enter* key. The screen went blank.

"Sorry about that. I had to get the thought down before I lost it." She stood and extended her hand.

As they shook hands, Richard did the usual assessment he does when he meets someone for the first time. *Stephanie Lynn, reporter for the Boston Globe, thirty-five to forty years old, five foot six inches tall, about one hundred and twenty-five pounds, brown shoulder length hair, hazel eyes, firm handshake with a solid grasp, probably works out regularly, Brooks Brothers suit well-tailored, minimal jewelry, nothing flashy, and not wearing a wedding ring.*

"A typical cop," she said. "Let's see if your mental assessment is correct."

"I'm sorry … what?"

"You just did that cop thing as we shook hands; height, weight, and personal assessment. So, let's see how you did with your assessment."

He repeated his list to her.

She studied him for a moment then smiled.

"Very good, Chief Moore, five foot five inches, one hundred and thirty-five pounds, the weight is a bit more than appearances because, as you noted, I work out and muscle has more density producing more weight. I'm not married, never had time for a lasting relationship, and I never confirm my age."

He chuckled to himself. *I wonder if this is her usual reporter's dance.*

She smiled. *Now I throw him off balance.*

"My turn. The obvious; tailored suit well-pressed, five feet eleven inches tall, hundred and eighty-five pounds, brown eyes, forty-six, the handshake is firm, but not meant to impress." A smile crossed her face, "Diplomatic, smart, law degree, widower, about two years, Chief of Winchendon the last two years, seven years with the Boston Police Department as the commander of an antiterrorism unit, military police, and Army Special Forces. Shall I go on?"

"You've done your homework."

"I always do," she said. "You left out highly intelligent."

"What?"

"Your assessment of me. Most men leave out an intelligence rating when they meet and assess a woman. You're typical in that department."

"Every day, I try to learn something new about myself. You just gave me my lesson for the day," Richard said.

"Good." Stephanie sat in her chair and pointed toward the only other chair in her confined space.

"So, what else do you want to learn from me today?"

He presented the facts of Paul Kenney's accident, related the conversation he had with Chief O'Malley, and explained that Dan Williams suggested that he contact her.

"Dan said that you did a story on the increased mortality rate in the police department. I wanted to know more about what you learned."

"You didn't have to come all the way into Boston from Winchendon to see me. I would have sent you a copy of my article."

"I have a copy and read it. I'm more interested in what was not it the article: your thoughts, insights, and how you got the information, and data."

"I never divulge sources."

"I'm not doing a criminal investigation. I'm trying to put an unusual set of circumstances into perspective."

She threw up her hands and waved them briefly. "Chief, even if you don't know that you're conducting a criminal investigation, you are. You're a cop. You investigate everything you see. You suspect that something is not quite right with some of the deaths.

You just don't know whether a crime has been committed. As a reporter on the beat for some years, I'm like you. I see something out of the ordinary and start looking for the bad guy. That's what I did as I researched the story. I didn't find a bad guy, and I'm very good at what I do."

"Okay, no bad guys, no crime, no need to protect sources. Tell me about your research."

"I like you, Chief. You walked me right into that. Okay, we'll talk. I don't have names anyway."

Stephanie explained that she had attended a meeting of local police officers about six months before. She was working on a story about a series of drugstore robberies. One of the robberies ended in the execution of a pharmacist and a high-school-aged clerk. She thought the meeting would give her the opportunity to talk with police officers from a variety of cities in the surrounding area. However, the officers had other things on their minds. Their conversations focused on the recent funeral of a fellow officer. The female officer died of a self-inflicted gunshot wound. Her death was the latest in an increased number of deaths among police officers.

Stephanie's interest was piqued, and she made subtle inquiries about the increases in deaths and the officers' opinion about the causes. Over the next several weeks, she contacted police departments within a thirty-mile radius of Boston. Almost all departments told her the average mortality rate of department personnel was up, but none of the deaths involved questionable circumstances.

Stephanie leaned in and continued, "I investigated six on-the-job accidents and four suicides. I could find no connections. The consensus among the various departments was that the increase in mortality was an unfortunate natural occurrence. I needed to understand how they reached that conclusion, so I decided to find someone who could explain. I wound up talking to an insurance actuary.

"Ann Suthe, a college friend, is the personnel director at City Life Insurance Company. After I told her what I needed, she said I should talk with someone who studies the mathematics of risk, an actuary. She told me about a rising star at Life Advantage

Insurance, named Bryan Hayden. He has several degrees and can run analyses in his head, a 'numbers geek', is how she referred to him. She had tried to recruit him, but lost out to Life Advantage. Anyway, Ann arranged a meeting for me with Bryan at Life Advantage. Bryan was very patient and helpful. He had done a study of police department mortality rates, and walked me though the process so I could understand how the results were determined. His conclusions were the same as everyone else's.

"By the time I was through with Bryan, my head was swimming in statistics. I didn't want that to happen to my readers, so I dressed the story up and gave it a human interest angle."

Richard sat quietly for a while, and then said, "You said you investigated some of the deaths. Did any of them seem unusual?"

"They had to. That was one of my criteria. I had to assume that natural causes such as heart attacks would have been within the statistical norm. As you know, staging accidents or suicides is not uncommon, so, I selected those events."

"And what, if anything, did you find? I mean, did one or two leave you curious?"

"Two left me with questions that are still not answered."

"Care to tell me about them?"

Stephanie rummaged through papers on her desk and pulled out a notebook.

"Here we are. Officer Joe Davenport was a twenty-year veteran of the force. He started with MDC, the Middlesex District Commission. He worked out of the Stoneham Mounted Unit. He was a real horse lover, learned to ride when he was a kid. As a teenager, he competed in equestrian events. Therefore, it was natural that he joined the mounted unit when he got his appointment to the MDC Police. That was before the state merged the MDC Police with the State Police some years ago.

"Officer Davenport, Cowboy Joe, as he was affectionately called by his fellow officers, usually patrolled the Middlesex Fells with his partner. It was one of the reasons for stationing the MDC mounted unit in Stoneham. The merger of the MDC Police with the State Police was the result of tight budgets. The budgets didn't get better for the State Police, especially the mounted unit, so Joe and his partner rotated through several of the state's parks.

"One day, Joe and his partner were patrolling in Bradley Palmer State Park. They came to a fork in the path. The path to their left looped up a hill through dense woods. The path to their right went down and arched around the base of the hill. Both paths rejoined again several hundred yards to the northeast. According to his partner's report, a naked man on a dirt bike appeared on the path to their left. When the man saw the officers, he turned around and headed back up the path. Because there were no other paths for the man on the dirt bike to take, Joe told his partner to go down the path to the right and head the man off. Joe took the left path and followed the man. Joe's partner reached the junction of the two paths, but didn't hear the dirt bike. A few moments later, Joe's horse came galloping down the path without Joe. He stopped Joe's horse, grabbed the reins, and rode up the path. He found Joe lying on the side of the path. His head, covered in blood, was on a boulder. Joe's partner radioed for assistance and an ambulance. By the time they got Joe out and to a hospital, he was dead.

"An investigation determined that the cinch on the saddle had been too loose. The theory was that when Joe got into a gallop chasing the dirt bike, the saddle shifted to the right. The trail Joe was galloping on was narrow and lined with trees with low limbs. A limb of one of the trees hung directly in his route. The investigators theorize that, as Joe slid with the saddle to the right, he didn't see the tree. He must have hit the tree face first. The impact knocked him out of the saddle and he fell to the ground on the side of the path and struck his head again. No one saw the guy on the dirt bike again. Apparent the biker had turned around and headed back in Joe's direction. Either he turned around spooking both the horse and the rider, thus causing the fall, or he looked back and saw Joe on the ground. Despite what happened, he went right past Joe without stopping. That's why the partner never saw him again.

"Here we have one of the department's best riders dying in a freak accident. The horse's training included conditioning so it would ignore crowds, gunshots, and all kinds of noise. Moreover, what about the biker? No one ever found him nor was there ever another report of similar activity."

"Did you talk with Joe's partner?"

"I did, although he wasn't very cooperative. He doesn't trust reporters. He thought that I'd try to discredit his former partner, or his account of the incident."

"You said that there were two incidents. What was the other?"

"Frank Natalie was a twenty-three-year veteran of the Andover Police Department. As a cop, Frank had three principals he worked by. He believed he should maintain physical fitness to be able to respond to any situation the job required. He believed that proficiency in self-defense and some form of martial arts was a key to success on the job. He was adamant that deadly force was never justified.

"In keeping with those principals, Frank was an instructor in self-defense and martial arts. He voluntarily trained and worked with any officer interested in expanding his or her physical capabilities. He also provided workshops on self-defense for civic organizations. He maintained a routine of exercise and martial arts practice. Also, from all accounts, Frank was a deeply religious man. It may have been part of the reason he didn't believe in deadly force.

"Frank and his wife Stacey had two children and two grandchildren. The day they christened their second grandchild, everything changed. Their married daughter and son-in-law lived in an apartment and couldn't have the christening party there, so Frank and Stacey held the affair at their house. It was a very large gathering; Frank was the proud grandfather and invited everyone he could think of. The family went to church in the morning, went back to the house to prepare for the party and, when the time came, they went back to church to christen the child.

"According to the guests, the party was a huge success. Most of Frank's fellow officers attended. Friends and neighbors were in and out, and of course, all the relatives showed up. The officers I talked with said Frank, as was usual at parties at his house, kept everyone involved. He introduced everyone, checked their drinks and food, and posed for pictures with the grandchildren and guests. The last of the guest and family members left about eight.

"Frank started cleaning up. He was in the kitchen and Stacey said she was going upstairs to change before she started working on the dishes. As she left, Frank was consolidating and putting away leftovers.

"When Stacey returned to the kitchen, Frank wasn't there. She assumed he had gone out to the trash containers at the rear corner of the house. She started washing dishes. It took some time to do all of them. When she had finished, she realized Frank had not come back in. His absence was unusual because he always helped Stacey with any cleaning after a party. She called for him as she walked through the house. She didn't find him and there was no response from him. She went outside and checked the yard and the garage. No Frank.

"She went back inside and went to the study. Frank seldom used the study on weekends unless he had something to work on that could not wait until a weekday. It would have been unusual for Frank to be in the study after a party. Finding the door locked, Stacey knocked and called for Frank. No answer. Now she was panicking. She got the spare key to the study and opened the door.

"Frank's study was pretty basic: a desk and high-back chair, bookcase, file cabinets, computer, telephone, those kinds of things. The only non-work related items were an assortment of family photos in frames, and two items he deeply treasured; a Double Katanakake, which is a Samurai sword, and a small dagger called a Bogei Tanto.

"When Stacey opened the door to the study, the family pictures were lined up on the deck opposite the desk chair. Frank was kneeling over in front of the desk as if paying homage to the pictures. Stacy saw the blood on the floor around Frank. She called nine-one-one. The Tanto had pierced his heart and he bled to death. He had a firm grip with both hands around the Tanto. It looked like suicide, in a fashion similar to a samurai warrior, only with a Tanto instead of the Katanakake.

"Frank was inside the locked study. The investigators found both keys, and no evidence of forced entry or exit. Stacy had thoroughly cleaned the whole house, including the study, the day before. The only prints found were those of Frank, Stacey, a neighbor whom Frank had showed the swords to earlier in the day, and two family members who had gone in during the day to make telephone calls away from the noise. Frank's prints were the only ones on the pictures and the Tanto.

"Before you ask, the investigators looked into Frank's life. He had two credit cards with ten-thousand-dollar limits each and no mortgage. The combined balance of the credit cards was six hundred forty-two dollars and thirty-seven cents. Frank hated debt. He had no unexplained cash or securities. His net worth was slightly higher than would have been expected. It was higher because Frank started saving early when he first married. He wanted a comfortable retirement. He was in excellent physical condition, had no financial or family problems, and he did not believe in killing or suicide, yet all the evidence indicates that Frank Natalie took his own life using a samurai dagger. You explain it."

"Ms. Lynn, were Joe, Frank or any of the others that you reviewed forgetful, depressed, under investigation, or did they have any diagnosed health issues?"

"Chief, are you sure that you aren't a prosecutor? And please, call me Stephanie."

"I guess I've been an investigator far too long to realize that my questions come off as direct examination. I'll try to keep that in mind."

"Okay. In answer, there were no notes or comments about any health problems. I reviewed the official investigation reports. I don't remember any notes about health issues."

"Did Bryan have a chance to analyze any factors like age, family status, or health issues of the deceased group?"

"No. He looked at the group compared to the whole population of police officers. That's the second time you asked about health issues. Why do you ask?"

"I don't know. I'm still finding it hard to accept the increase in mortalities as a normal statistical variation. You mentioned geographical area. Did he look at that?"

"No. He just mentioned that the data encompassed a large geographical area. That eliminated environmental factors."

"Would you mind if I contacted Bryan Hayden at Life Advantage? He's not a protected source, is he?" He smiled.

"Sure you can contact him, but he's not at Life Advantage he's with … " she moved papers around her desk, "Let me see. I have a new contact for him … yes, here it is. He's with HISH, Health Insurance Services Holding. It's a health insurance carrier with offices in the John Hancock Tower."

Richard stood to leave. He shook her hand and turned to walk away. He stopped, and then asked, "Did you look into any other employee groups?"

"No, just the police departments. Why?"

"Fire department personnel and municipal employees may be riding the same wave."

Now she had the questions, but Richard said he had to run. He promised to talk to her again.

19

As usual, traffic heading downtown on the Southeast Expressway moved slowly when it was not at a standstill. Richard took advantage of the creeping pace to call Bryan Hayden at HISH.

"Mr. Hayden, my name is Richard Moore. I'm the chief of police in Winchendon. Stephanie Lynn at the Globe gave me your name and number, and suggested that I call."

The mention of Stephanie's name got Bryan's attention.

"How can I help you, Chief?"

"I was following up the article that Ms. Lynn did some time ago. The one about mortality rates in the law enforcement community. She told me you were very helpful in explaining how actuary analysis works to identify norms and variances."

"Yeah, she was a quick learner. What's your interest? I'm a little busy at the moment and can't tell you much over the phone."

"I was calling to see if we could have lunch. I'm in Boston, and not sure when I might get back this way."

"I get an hour for lunch. I was going to pick up a sandwich from the deli and eat at my desk. If you don't mind me eating while we talk, we could use one of the conference rooms."

"Sounds great. I appreciate your taking the time."

They agreed to meet at one o'clock. Richard said he would pick up sandwiches and they could have a working lunch.

Richard parked in the Hancock garage, bought sandwiches and bottled water at nearby deli, then entered the John Hancock Tower. He found the entrance to HISH's fiftieth floor offices was to his right as he exited the elevator. Going through the glass entry doors, he told the receptionist behind a large mahogany reception desk his name and that he had an appointment with Bryan. She called Bryan and, after hanging up the phone, said, "Chief Moore, Bryan will be right out. Would you like some coffee or something to drink?"

"No, thanks, I brought lunch."

"All right, please have a seat. Bryan will be along shortly."

Richard looked around at the expensive decor. Just off the reception area, one wall of a corridor was all glass. In the room on the other side of the glass wall was a twelve-foot long conference table surrounded by high-back leather chairs. A breathtaking view of the Boston skyline was available through the floor-to-ceiling glass exterior wall. The decor and view impressed Richard. He surmised that HISH, like most health insurance companies, was making money for its owners, despite the state of the economy.

"Chief Moore, I'm Bryan Hayden."

"Hello, Mr. Hayden."

"Please call me Bryan," he said as they shook hands.

"And please, call me Richard. I am not on official business," replied Moore.

Hayden led him to a small meeting room where they sat at a four-foot round table. Richard set out the sandwiches and bottled water

"Thanks for bringing lunch, Richard," Bryan said, "The place is crazy. I'm working on a special analysis, and it doesn't leave much spare time."

"I am the one who appreciates the meeting. I didn't give you much notice. Thank you."

"It's a strange place. Don't get me wrong, I love working here. I'm working on interesting stuff, but they are a little overboard on the security stuff."

"What do you mean?"

"Some of the supervisors also work for the security company. They check e-mails and phone messages. The company gives us great benefits and they treat us well, but they keep a closed lid on information so it doesn't get out to the public. I think it has to do with investors. I don't pay much attention to it, but you always know the security is there."

Richard started eating his sandwich and Richard joined him.

"So," Bryan said, pausing in his eating, "you talked with Stephanie about my mortality analysis?"

"Yes, she said that you were very helpful. She told me you spent a lot of time explaining the process and the results."

"She's a very attractive woman. I've never worked with a woman as beautiful, and she followed my analysis as well as most of my coworkers. I didn't want our time together to pass too quickly." His face went flush as he spoke, and he avoided looking directly at Richard.

Bryan was in his late twenties, had a pale complexion, except when he blushed, and was slightly underweight. Richard found his handshake weak and uncertain.

"Yes, Stephanie is attractive. She is also intelligent, as you learned, and as she pointed out to me this morning. I know you don't have much time, so if it is all right with you, I'll get right to my questions. Can you give me a summary of what you did for Stephanie?"

"Sure, if you don't mind if I talk between bites." He took a bite, and after a few moments, continued. "One of the things life insurance actuaries do is assemble and analyze data on death rates in various populations or combinations of populations. In this case, as you know, Stephanie was concerned about a spike in the death rate of police department personnel, and wanted to understand how the various studies of that spike concluded that the spike was a statistical variation. The first thing I did was to review the studies that had already been done. All of them, including mine, confirmed the statistical variation conclusion."

He paused to eat more of his sandwich before continuing. "A death rate for any group, like police officers, is an average of the death rates over a given period, but in that period, the rate fluctuates, and may even plateau above or below the average for an extended period. These studies concluded that the spike was just one of those normal up movements that had plateaued above the norm. The average death rate of the group has gone above the statistical norm: it might eventually come down and go below the norm to balance things. Now, there is a possibility it might not fall far enough, or stay down long enough to balance things. That might cause concern, but there's insufficient data Life insurance actuarial work is like that: The trends move at a snail's pace. In the Health insurance business, everything moves faster."

"How so?"

Bryan took another bite. After a few moments, he said, "Hmm, let me see if I can explain it with an example … Okay, between 1990 and 2000, the average life expectancy increased by one year, while medical advances increased the life expectancy of an HIV patient by four years. That means in one small category, HIV patients, the healthcare actuary had to deal with a larger change in life expectancy than his counterpart in life insurance. A four-hundred percent change. And that doesn't even address the changes in the types and costs of HIV treatment that healthcare actuary had to deal with. Also, unlike the life insurance people, we can't just sit back and wait for trends to develop, we have to know what drugs are in the pipeline, what treatments are—"

"Bryan, what's going on here?"

Two well-dressed authoritative men had entered the room. The one who had interrupted Bryan was glaring at him.

Bryan went pale as he rose from his chair.

"Mr. LeBlanc ... sir, this is Chief—"

"Richard Moore," Richard said as he slowly stood and offered his hand. Neither man accepted.

"Bryan, you know we have strict rules about divulging company information, and no one at your level is permitted to talk with the police."

Bryan just stood there with a blank expression on his blushing face.

"Perhaps I can clear up the misunderstanding."

"No misunderstanding, Chief Moore, except on Bryan's part. Bryan, I'll talk with you later. You can go," said LeBlanc.

"Yes, sir." Bryan left the room.

"I think you overreacted without having all the facts." Richard's pleasant smile and open posture quickly hardened.

The man with LeBlanc sensed the change in Richard, and interceded. "Chief Moore, I am Alex Wells, chief legal counsel for the company." He extended his hand.

This time it was Richard's opportunity to rebuff the handshake. After a moment, and as Alex started to withdraw his hand, Richard extended his.

"Mr. Wells, nice to meet you."

"Everyone calls me Alex."

"Alex, I'm Richard, not Chief. I'm not here as a police officer." Directing his attention to LeBlanc, he added, "And I have no interest in learning anything confidential about your company. Since my presence here is so disturbing, I will bid you a good day and be on my way."

LeBlanc had gotten Alex's message. He needed to soften the situation, or Richard would leave determined to learn why they were so harsh. As Richard move to leave, LeBlanc said, "Chief Moore … Richard, sorry, please let's sit for a moment. I believe you were correct. I may have overreacted without having my facts straight."

Richard looked at LeBlanc and decided to play along. At least he might get Bryan out of a problem with his boss. He sat, and the two men joined him.

"Richard, I'm Pierre LeBlanc, president and founder of HISH. This company is my baby, and like most parents, I nurture it and overprotect it." He smiled, and Alex laughed.

Richard wasn't amused, but he replied, "I did hear that company founders often have feelings for their companies similar to parents with children."

"I'm glad you understand my protective emotions. These are difficult times for the health insurance industry. We're getting a lot of criticism from malicious people who will go to any lengths to dig up information they can distort to suit their own agendas. Some of them want to put us out of business altogether. In addition, HISH itself is at a crucial stage in its development. We're developing strategies for increasing our market share, and the competition knows this. They have been employing every tactic they can to learn our plans. That includes talking with employees at all levels of our organization.

"We have contractual relations with several large employers, unions, and municipalities in the Greater Boston and New England area. We've invested significant resources in obtaining and maintaining contracts with municipalities. It's a highly lucrative, but highly competitive market. Our competition would love to find a way to interfere with or counteract our contractual relationships. That would hurt my baby. I also have to be vigilant about the possibility that one of my own employees may do what the competition can't. If, for example, you came here on official business and dragged Bryan out in cuffs under arrest and it hit the media, it could be a blow from which the company would have a hard time recovering."

Richard watched LeBlanc. *The man is doling this out as if someone might believe him,* he thought. "What makes you think an arrest would be such a problem? With the number of employees you have, I'm sure a couple of them will have a run in with the law."

"In the case of most companies, your assumption would be correct. However, Richard, we employ a security firm that does extensive background checks on all potential hires. Our statistical probability is lower than most companies. It has to be. As I said, we have many municipalities as clients. That means we insure a large number of police officers. Imagine the predicament if one of our employees made a presentation to a police department or the police association union and later ended up on the front page of the local newspaper under arrest. The departments might determine that an association with our personnel is not wise and move to another carrier. I don't want to take that risk.

"I hope you can see why the arrival of a police officer to interview one of our employees got me upset … especially an employee like Brian who has access to highly confidential information, and who is well aware of our security policies."

Richard still was not buying LeBlanc's story, but he decided to play along. If nothing else, it might help Bryan.

"I can assure you, Mr. LeBlanc, that Bryan is not a person of interest in any investigation, and that we were not discussing any proprietary information. I'm the chief of police for Winchendon, a small town in north central Massachusetts, an hour and a half from here. I've been chief for two years. Administrative duties, budgets, scheduling, and employee management, that type of thing, takes up too much of my time. My law enforcement training and experience had not prepared me for all the administrative work. Frankly, I need help understanding how actuarial analysis works in determining life insurance rates.

"The town's been looking at its costs for employee benefits. Our life insurance carrier has hiked the annual premiums substantially. Our carrier said they based the increase on actuarial analysis. They determined that our category of enrollees has a shorter life span than the general population. Now, that might make sense to you, but, to me, it's Greek. I wanted to gain a better understanding of the analysis, so I could do a credible job talking with them about a more reasonable rate.

"A friend told me that Bryan Hayden of Life Advantage, that young man you just threw out of the room, was very good, not only at analysis, but at explaining, in simple terms, how the analysis works and how an insurer determines risk and sets premiums.

"Turns out that Bryan joined your company recently. I called him and told him I was interested in talking with him. I also told him I was in Boston on other business and hoped he could meet with me today. He said he didn't think it would be a problem if we met during lunch. If I didn't mind sitting in one of these conference rooms, he could work until I arrived. He was very clear when he told me he only had an hour for lunch. He didn't want to interfere with his work. He was in the middle of enlightening me when you arrived."

"Well, I do owe you an apology, Richard—"

"You don't owe me an apology, but that young man is probably packing his desk thinking you'll be firing him when you leave this room. The only reason I was in your office was because he was conscientious about completing some project he's working on."

"You're absolutely right, Chief," LeBlanc said as he stood. "I'll apologize to Bryan. I'm a bit late for a conference call. If you don't mind, Alex will walk you out. It's been a pleasure."

20

Bryan entered his cubicle, kicked his chair, then sat on his desk. The noise startled Stuart Scott. Scott and Bryan had been friends since high school, and Stuart had helped HISH recruit Bryan. He had never seen his friend so upset.

"Bryan, what the hell is the matter with you?"

Bryan was almost in tears.

"I really fucked up, Stu. Remember that Globe reporter I told you about?"

"The one you drooled over for several weeks?"

"Yeah, that one. She gave my name to a guy looking for follow-up information. Imagine, Stephanie remembered me, even recommended me to someone looking for additional information. Can you imagine? Anyway, this guy called and we were having lunch and talking in conference room C. Know who came in about ten minutes after we started?"

"No. Who?"

"LeBlanc and Alex!"

"Really?"

"Yeah, and LeBlanc was pissed. He reminded me about company policy then sent me out. I'm going to lose my job, Stu."

"Bryan, that doesn't make sense. Why would LeBlanc and Alex care if you were having lunch with some guy?"

"Oh, I didn't mention his name. Richard Moore, Chief Richard Moore, as in chief of police."

Stuart's manner changed abruptly. "He's a police chief?" He lowered his voice, "Bryan, what were you two talking about?"

"He wanted info on mortality analysis, like Stephanie wanted. He seems to think that there's a problem with the current upturn in the incidence of mortality in the law enforcement population."

Stuart got excited. "He does? Listen, Bryan, did you talk about your analysis of the cost of disease states?"

"Not directly. I only told him how the analysis for life expectancy was similar, but healthcare had more variables."

Stuart began writing on a piece of scratch paper.

His friend's action puzzled Bryan. "Look, Stu, you—"

He stopped because Stuart was out of his chair and heading toward the conference room where Richard, LeBlanc, and Alex were now talking.

Some HISH supervisors also doubled as agents for the firm's security provider. They surreptitiously checked computer screens of other employees as they worked, listened to phone conversations of employees near them, and periodically, after hours, checked e-mail and phone messages. The security company had installed software that scanned for keywords. When the software identified one of these words, the message was stored for closer review. The supervisors also looked for unusual employee behavior. They reported anything of interest to the security firm.

Ulanda Sims, one of several supervisors in Stuart's section, was one of these security firm operatives. She was standing in a cubicle near conference room C speaking with one of the claims processors when Stuart caught her attention. She watched him as he walked past room C several times, turned the corner, and leaned against the wall after each pass. On one occasion, he unfolded a piece of paper that was in his hand. He read whatever was on it, then took out a pen and added to it.

What's he doing? she was thinking, when the door to room C opened, and Alex Wells came out, followed by another man and Pierre LeBlanc. Stuart seemed to take a large breath, and with his eyes on the floor, quickly walked around the corner and bumped into the man.

"I'm terribly sorry. I wasn't watching where I was going." Stuart looked at the three men. Nodding his head as a greeting, he said, "Mr. LeBlanc, Alex, my apologies. Excuse me."

He started to move away, then stopped and asked, "Mr. Moore?"

"Yes."

"I don't believe this. What a small world. I'm Stuart Scott."

Stuart extended both arms to shake hands with Richard. As they shook, he passed the note that he had concealed in his hand.

"You probably don't remember me, but I'll never forget you. You coached my younger brother in youth soccer. He was a shy kid, but you kept encouraging him. You'd be interested in knowing that he stayed with soccer, leading our high school to a state championship. He received a scholarship and played in college. I don't believe I just bumped into you like this. No pun intended. My brother will be surprised when I tell him I saw you. I have to get back to work. Have a good day." Stuart turned and started walking away.

Richard said, "Stuart," and, when the young man turned toward him, continued, "thanks, and say hello to your brother for me."

After the young man had disappeared, Richard and Wells headed for the reception area, where Richard said good–bye to Wells then went to the elevators.

An agitated Pierre LeBlanc went back to his office, picked up his private line, and punched a speed dial number.

"We have an unusual development. A man claiming to be Richard Moore, a police chief, showed up asking questions. Do you know anything about this?" As the other person spoke, LeBlanc looked at his calendar, then said, "Lunch tomorrow at one? Follow the usual procedure? Okay."

The note had read, *Might have info of interest - coffee shop corner of Boylston and Berkeley at 3 p.m.* At three o'clock Richard was sitting at a round metal table outside the coffee shop watching Stuart Scott cross Boylston Street. Scott's head and eyes were in constant motion as he scanned the mix of people around him. Stuart spotted Richard, but did not approach. He headed directly to the door of the shop and entered. After a few moments, Richard got up, went inside the shop, and got in line right behind him.

"You know, I never coached soccer. Don't know a thing about it."

"That's okay, my brother played and he did receive a scholarship." Stuart kept looking around at everyone in the shop.

"You think you have information of interest to me?"

"I'm not sure, and I don't have time to go into it in detail now. Bryan told me you wanted to know more about the increase in police mortality rates. I'm a computer expert. I help manage and control member records. A while ago, I discovered a backdoor access to our computer system." He moved forward and placed his order.

"What's a backdoor access?"

"Normally, the only way to access information in a secure system like ours is by typing in an access code. The access code tells the computer to let you see the information you request. Every time you use the code, however, a record is made of the event. If you don't want access to show on the record, you have to build your own doorway, one that doesn't create a record. Someone has done that to our system. Someone who either isn't authorized to access the information, or who doesn't want anyone to know they're accessing the data."

"You know."

"Yes, that's what I get paid to do, but, truthfully, I only tripped over this backdoor access by accident."

They got their orders and moved to the counter for cream and sugar.

"Look, I don't have much time," Stuart said. "I have to get back, so just let me say what I have to say. It looks like the person using the backdoor access is copying the records of certain HISH policyholders and storing them in a separate database. The database is in our system, but hidden behind a very sophisticated encrypted code. I reported the unauthorized access to LeBlanc. He told me to ignore it. He said that the security firm had been given special access so they could monitor activity. The security firm does have access to monitor general activity, but this is different. The information in the database has nothing to do with general activity. I know; I cracked part of their security code. The other day I isolated the database and tracked some of the information. With luck, I'll break the encrypted code then I'll be able to make a copy."

"Why should that be of interest to me?"

"I helped Bryan with the analysis for the Globe reporter. I think I found a link between the analysis that I helped Bryan work on, and the database I found."

Ulanda Sims had seen Stuart slip the note into Richard's hand outside the conference room. It aroused her suspicions further, and when he left the office, she decided to follow him. After he entered the coffee shop, she waited a few moments then entered.

Before Stuart could continue, Richard said, "There's a young woman standing to the left of the entrance. Turn a little to your right. You should be able to see her."

Stuart did as Richard asked. With a sharp intake of breath, he turned back to Richard and said, "Shit, she's one of the supervisors. She also works for security."

"I thought I recognized her from the office," Richard said.

Stuart became visibly upset. "Do you know where the Sheep Fold is on 28 near Stoneham?"

"I do."

"I take my dog there on Sundays. If you meet me there, I'll explain everything. I'm usually there at noon."

Before Richard could respond, Stuart turned and headed out the door, pretending not to notice the young woman. After a moment, she also left. Richard moved to the window as he sipped his coffee. He spotted her walking behind Stuart, but keeping a distance from him. It was obvious to Richard she was following Stuart, so Richard followed her. She hung back when Stuart entered the John Hancock building then entered after him. Richard broke off the tail and returned to his car.

Once she was back in her office, Ulanda Sims made a phone call and reported what she had seen.

Richard drove back to Winchendon. If he had started the day with many questions, he had made little progress in gathering answers. In fact, his mind was now swimming with more questions. He had hoped to learn if Stephanie Lynn had discovered any relation between the increase in mortality and factors such as age, gender, or health problems. He had found her intelligent, attractive, and unsettlingly intriguing, but unable to shed any light on those issues. She had directed him to a young man with a brilliant mind and an adolescent personality, who might have had answers, but was now probably too frightened to talk to him. Then there was Pierre LeBlanc, a health insurance executive obsessed with information security on the one hand, yet, if Stuart Scott were to be believed, willing to ignore a breach in that security on the other. Richard thought LeBlanc was worried about more than just bad press and competition. Richard, however, was concerned about the way the man would treat Bryan. Finally, there was Stuart Scott. What would possess him to reveal to a perfect stranger, and a law enforcement officer at that, the fact that there was a breach of confidential company and patient files? Stuart was violating his boss's direct order to ignore the breach in computer security. Richard wondered if he were willing to help Stuart violate LeBlanc's order. More important, Richard wondered what, if any, connection existed between that information and the increase in police department deaths.

21

Richard's ambivalence about meeting Stuart Scott was still present when he went for his morning run the following Sunday, however, he was reluctant to pass up the opportunity to see if Stuart had somehow stumbled on information that might be connected to his probe. Stuart might have, he reasoned, the only clue that looked like a lead.

After his run, Richard showered, shaved, and dressed in dark-blue slacks, short sleeve pullover shirt, and comfortable shoes. On his days off, he usually wore an ankle holster with gun. This day, however, he decided to wear his waist holster, so he could carry his 9 mm pistol.

The Sheep Fold is ten acres of open field in the twenty-five-hundred acre Middlesex Fells Reservation, a Massachusetts state park located a few miles north of Boston on land in the towns of Malden, Medford, Melrose, Stoneham and Winchester. In the 1890s, the park's original management brought in about two dozen sheep to graze the field and maintain a pastoral scene, and it has been called the Sheep Fold ever since. Gas-powered, noisy lawnmowers replaced the sheep decades ago. The Sheep Fold and the surrounding woods and trails play host to joggers, bike riders, dog owners, horseback riders, picnickers, and others seeking a temporary escape from the artificial environments in which they spend the rest of their lives. Its access road branches off Route 28, dips under a pedestrian overpass, and climbs a small hill, splitting briefly into inbound and outbound lanes. A small parking area is on the right, where the two lanes meet again at the top of the hill before continuing to the main parking lot.

Richard arrived at the main parking lot few minutes before noon and found that only one of the fifty spots was still open. After parking, he walked along the row of cars toward the low fieldstone wall that separated the parking lot from the Sheep Fold field below. Stopping there, he looked up at the few cotton ball clouds that dotted the otherwise clear blue sky, and felt the therapeutic warmth of the sun. Before him, rich green grass sloped to the diamond-shaped field ahead, and a line of trees and brush on the left. About halfway down the slope, the trees jutted out, partially obscuring his view of the left border of the field.

Beyond them, he knew a running path exited from behind the line of trees and ran along the border of the field until, at the apex of the diamond; it disappeared back into the woods. About thirty yards to his right, a hill rose to a thicket of trees. He knew that just on the other side of the trees was a paved area, the start of a soapbox derby run that traveled four-hundred yards down the opposite slope until it met the running path at the apex, and ended.

Near the base of the hill, a couple lay side by side on a blanket talking and occasionally touching. The sight brought him a rush of memories.

In the morning, Lori and Richard usually ran together on a five-mile route through the streets near their house. On Sundays though, Lori preferred to walk the trails near the Sheep Fold. The last time they were here, she started chasing him as they emerged from the path on the left of the field. When they reached the top of the slight hill, she tackled him, and they fell, laughing as they landed. It was a great ending to a two-hour hike.

"Look, Richard," Lori said, turning and pointing toward the top of the derby run. Two horseback riders were descending the hill and heading their way.

"Come on. Maybe they'll stop and let us pet them." She ran off ahead of him adding, "The horses are beautiful."

The riders did stop, dismounted, and, using twenty-five foot-long lead lines, let the horses graze. Richard and Lori talked with the couple, and Lori was like a schoolgirl, her eyes wide and bright as she watched the horses graze.

You're still here, aren't you Lori? That was a wonderful day, wasn't it love? We always thought we'd have many more like it.

The reverie ended, and he turned his attention back to the scene in front of him. The field was dotted with wooden picnic benches, packs of dogs, and families enjoying a Sunday together. Groups of dogs ran around playing almost as children would, enjoying the freedom and companionship of their friends. The dogs' owners gathered in small groups, standing around chatting while paying varying levels of attention to their playful four-legged charges. A few of the owners and their dogs, however, had paired to follow other pursuits. Some were walking or running together, some were playing games of fetch, and, in at least three cases, the owners were running their pets through obedience training exercises.

Richard spotted Stuart Scott talking with four others in the center of the field, and started walking down toward them on the dirt path that led to the field. Stuart saw him coming, left the group, and walked toward him.

As he approached, Stuart called out, "Bruce, come."

A large dog with heavy, shiny, black fur and drooling jowls came bounding up to the two men. The dog sat next to Stuart, his tail wagging faster than a windmill in a stiff gale.

Stuart knelt on one knee and wrapped his right arm around the dog's neck.

"Chief, this is Bruce. Bruce, shake with the chief."

The dog lifted his right paw until Richard took it and said, "Hello, Bruce."

"Bruce is a three-year-old Newfoundland."

Stuart stood, gave Bruce a treat, and told him to go play. Bruce was off in a flash.

"I love Sunday afternoons here. It's one of the few places where you can let a dog loose. Here, not only do they get to run loose, but they have other dogs to play with."

"With groups of dogs running around here, don't you worry about fights?"

"That's the other nice thing about this place. It's general knowledge that everyone frowns upon mean or overly aggressive dogs. People who come here regularly either train their dog to get along or they take their dog out to one of the walking paths in the woods. Some dogs don't have the temperament to mix with other dogs. The rest of the owners try to group with owners whose dogs do get along."

As they walked along the dirt path, Stuart started talking about his job with HISH. He had joined HISH three and a half years before. The company was growing quickly and the volume of data the system had to handle was immense. He was responsible for the conversion to a large computer system. The primary database contained members' records, member demographics, account numbers, primary care physicians' information, and treatment information, including diagnosis. He set security protocols and maintained access. He was also the HIPAA compliance officer.

"What is HIPAA?" Richard asked.

"In 1996, the Federal Government enacted The American Health Insurance Portability and Accountability Act, or HIPAA for short. It is a set of rules about handling patient records and other information in a way that attempts to protect patient privacy. Health plans, doctors, hospitals, and other healthcare providers had to follow HIPAA rules after April 14, two thousand three. In the healthcare and medical profession, the great challenge that HIPAA had created was the assurance that all patient account handling, billing, and medical records be compliant. The regulations called for the designation of a compliance officer. Since I set up the system and security protocols, the boss elected me. One of my duties is to monitor who accesses patient information and why.

"One night a couple of weeks ago, I was working very late. While reviewing the electronic activity log of the system, I noticed that someone was accessing the member database right then, late at night, when no one else was in the office. As I watched the activity, I checked the login file. No one else from the company was logged in. I tried to identify the access point, but whoever was in the files hadn't accessed them from inside the office. They had to be getting into the computer system from outside even though we had built the system to prevent that type of access. The next day, I reported the breach to Mr. LeBlanc.

"A couple of days later, he said he'd looked into it and it was nothing to worry about, it was just part of routine security activity. I was stunned. The least that could happen is the company could have some serious embarrassing publicity if the unauthorized access ever became public knowledge. Covering it up could lead to worse than that under HIPAA, criminal charges, fines, even jail time. In my spare time, I worked to identify the source and to isolate the file they had created. Turned out whoever was hacking the system was very good and had sophisticated resources."

Richard stopped walking and turned toward Stuart.

"Look, it sounds like you've uncovered a serious breach in company computer records, but I have no experience or interest in corporate espionage."

"Corporate espionage!" Stuart laughed. "No, Chief. I broke into the file. The member records are unique in their grouping."

"Unique? In what way?"

"The members or relatives of members in the file all—"

Bruce had been running large circles around the two men as they walked slowly along the path. He was making a large arc from their left to right, tail wagging, tongue hanging out, and drool flowing from his jowls. The dog gave a loud yelp as he passed out of their right peripheral vision. Stuart stopped in mid-sentence, turned his head, and opened his mouth to call out to the dog.

Richard's reflexes went into overdrive, and events appeared to shift into slow motion, as Stuart's left jaw exploded, spraying him with a cloud of blood, mucous, bone, and flesh. Instinctively, he leaped at Stuart, wrapped his arms around the young man's chest and arms, and fell to his right. The move caused both to roll down the hill toward the tree line. Grass, dirt, and pebbles sprayed Richard's head as a succession of shots dug divots around their rolling bodies.

Richard tried to vary the speed of their role thereby offsetting the shooter's aim and timing. At the same time, he was trying to steer their tumbling bodies to avoid rolling into a couple who seemed oblivious of the situation. As they were about to roll past, however, the woman, who had her back to them stepped to the side. As Richard and Stuart hit the back of her legs, she screamed, tumbled backwards, and landed on top of them. The man started to yell at them and stepped forward, planting his left foot three feet away from Richard's head and between him and the shooter. As he put his foot down, a bullet tore through his calf, shattering the bone, and causing the leg to buckle underneath him. He fell, adding to the rolling pile of wounded flesh, which came to an abrupt halt.

Pinned beneath them, and momentarily protected from the shooter, Richard's training and experience told him that he would have to extricate himself from the people on top of him and attempt to draw the shooter's fire away from them. It also told him that before he exposed himself to the shooter, he would first need to ensure that a massive amount of help would arrive on the scene as quickly as possible. Even as his brain was processing this, he was tapping the nine-one-one speed dial on his cell phone. It was answered on the first ring, and before the operator finished the usual greeting, he said, "I'm an off-duty police officer requesting assistance. Shots fired with multiple severe casualties at the Sheep Fold, Middlesex Fells State Park. Home in on this phone. I repeat: Officer needs assistance, shots fired, multiple severe casualties, Sheep Fold Middlesex Fells State Park, home in on this phone."

Richard knew when any dispatcher heard the words "Shots fired, Officer needs assistance," the response would be immediate and massive, with police and emergency medical response from the state and surrounding communities. Even if he were hit, or the dispatcher did not register the location, they would have a fix on his cell phone in moments. Making the call had taken twenty precious seconds, and he hung up before the startled operator could respond. The fact that he broke the call off, something that was a common occurrence when an officer was in trouble, would actually underscore the urgency of the situation better than anything he could have added anyway. A moment later, he was rolling sideways away from the pile and downward into the tree line.

Shortly after Ulanda Sims had called in to report the meeting between Stuart Scott and Richard in the coffee shop, Ghost received instructions to keep Stuart under surveillance. When Stuart drove to the Sheep Fold that morning, Ghost, thanks to the homing device he had attached to Scott's car, follow him from a safe distance. A few minutes after Stuart parked in the main parking lot; Ghost parked his car in the secondary parking area, walked up a slight hill to the derby starting-pad, and went into the trees just to the left of the pad. After a few moments, he found a spot from which he could watch the entire field without drawing attention, lay prone, and fixed his field glasses on Stuart.

When, a short time later, Richard came into view walking toward Stuart, Ghost grabbed his cell phone and punched the speed dial.

"Yeah," came the distorted response.

"I'm in a state park north of Boston. It looks like the subject is meeting in an open field with the police chief from Winchendon."

"Okay, that changes things. I want both eliminated now. The kid is the priority target. Take him out first. If you can get both together, fine, but make damn sure you get the kid. Understood?"

"It's taken care of."

The call ended.

Ghost looked around to make sure he wouldn't startle anyone, and, when he was sure the way was clear, started back to his car to retrieve a plastic case from the trunk.

On the way back to his car, Ghost felt disappointed that he was getting paid to kill Richard, and that he would not be able to tell Richard about Lori Clement before he killed him. It would have been more satisfying if the thing had been kept very personal. Still, it would be his bullet and his skill that ended the man's life, and he would have to be satisfied with that.

He also thought about the actual hit. If he just took out the kid and Richard in rapid succession, it would look too much like a contract hit. That might start an investigation that would lead back to the connection between Richard and the kid. His client would not be happy with that outcome. He would have to camouflage the hit by spacing his shots, and taking down other people as well. Killing them all, however, would be as stupid as just killing Richard and the kid. He would kill one, wound three more, and fire four misses. The result would look more like the work of a deranged amateur than that of a highly skilled professional.

When he returned to his position in the trees, he opened the case, and then removed and assembled the parts of his eight–thousand–dollar German-made Heckler and Koch MSG 90 sniper rifle, a weapon with an effective range of thirteen hundred yards. After he assembled the weapon, he mounted a fifteen-hundred-dollar Leupold M3A riflescope and made adjustments. Then, he attached a custom-made acoustically tuned cartridge casing catcher that not only collected the spent cartridges, but also, together with the acoustically-tuned suppressor he attached to the end of the barrel, nearly eliminated the noise of firing. His last action was to load the weapon with a ten-round magazine of seven point six two caliber ammunition.

When he was through, he made himself comfortable in a prone shooting position, and poked the suppressor at the end of the barrel just outside the brush that provided his frontal cover. Looking around the field, he selected several targets before flicking the firing selector to semiautomatic and releasing the safety. He then focused the crosshairs of the riflescope on the back of Stuart's head, adjusted for the breeze that crossed the open field, and gently, almost lovingly, squeezed the trigger.

At that precise moment, the young man turned his head and the bullet hit his jaw. Ghost, who was already beginning to aim at Richard, reflexively tried to swing back to fire a coupe-de-grace. It created only a moment of hesitation between shots, but it was in that moment that Richard grabbed Stuart and started rolling down the slope. Suddenly, instead of an easy stationary head shot, Ghost was firing at an erratically moving blur of tumbling torsos and limbs. When the pair tumbled into the woman, the tumbling slowed, and, for one moment, he had Richard's head in his crosshairs, and fired. Instead of the satisfying decapitation he anticipated, however, Ghost watched in dismay as his shot missed Richard and hit the man's leg. When the man fell on top of the woman, he could no longer get a clear shot at Richard or Stuart. It did not matter. The magazine was empty—the shot that crippled the standing man was his last round.

When he saw Richard roll out of the tangle of bodies, he smiled and thought, *No need to take evasive action, my friend, it's getting too hot for me to stick around. You got lucky, this time, but, never fear, the next time, your luck won't hold.*

He pulled back his rifle and broke it down. After placing the parts back in the case, he took out a nine-millimeter, fifteen-round, P226 SIG-Sauer pistol, screwed on a silencer, and headed back to his car.

He stopped a short distance from the parking area and leaned against a tree while a couple left their car and walked down a path. When they were out of sight, he got in his car and drove away. Exiting by the outbound access road, he turned left onto Route 28. A couple of hundred yards on his right was an entrance ramp to Route 93. He made the right turn and accelerated to merge with the southbound traffic. As he approached Roosevelt Circle, he saw a line of local police cars and ambulances racing northward on Route 28. Overhead, a helicopter was flying north along a parallel course with Route 93.

When he had reached the tree line, Richard recalled the nine-one-one line and had the operator put him through to the State Police dispatcher. The dispatcher in turn relayed information from him to the State Police Special Tactics and Operations (STOP) command truck, already headed toward the scene from Logan Airport in Boston. He explained who he was and said that he believed the shots had come from the general area of the bluff between the Sheep Fold path and the Soap Box Derby area.

Moments later, he heard the sirens in the distance, but did not get up. The shooter could be waiting for him to relax at the sound of help coming, waiting to fire off one more deadly shot before leaving. On the other hand, the shooter might move to another spot to lie in wait.

Next, he heard the helicopter coming in from the north. It assumed a stationary position over the soapbox derby start pad, and dropped three lines. Two figures in full tactical gear stepped out on to the helicopter skid and trained their automatic assault rifles on the ground. They were State Troopers from the STOP squad attached to the State Police Air Wing Unit in Lawrence. At their signal, a third STOP trooper stepped out on to the skid, hooked up to one of the lines, stepped off the skid, and quickly rappelled to the ground. Once there, he crouched, positioned his rifle, and swept the area, before giving a thumb up signal. The other troopers rappelled down to join him and, spreading out, headed toward the bluff Richard had indicated. They quickly found the shooting position, and, after ascertaining that the shooter was no longer in the area, informed the newly arrived mobile command post.

The command post deployed a complete STOP platoon at the entrance to the access road. Three men went left, six went up the main road to the parking lot, and three went right, through the trees to the secondary parking area. Finally, a squad of three troopers followed the walking path to a point below and behind the signal coming from Richard's phone. Richard caught movement to his right and turned in that direction as the STOP squad emerged from the woods, and, fanning out with their rifles at the ready, began moving slowly toward his position. Richard told the dispatcher he had eye contact with them and that he was getting up.

All three troopers heard that information in their headsets. However, when the trooper closest to Richard saw the cell phone in Richard's hand and his shoulder holster with the service revolver in it, he yelled, "Freeze! Back on the ground! Move!"

The other two immediately assumed a covering stance and aimed their weapons directly at Richard. He knew there was danger here. The combination of pumping hearts, flowing adrenaline, and uncertainty had produced a potentially deadly situation.

"Okay, okay," he said calmly, "I'm Chief Moore. You were informed there was an officer in civilian clothes present."

"Just get down," the trooper said, closing in on Richard.

"I'm going to my knees, trooper," Richard said. As he braced himself, however, pain shot through his upper left arm, and, looking down, he saw he was wounded, and he stopped. The trooper immediately put his foot on Richard's back forcing him the rest of the way to the ground.

"Hands behind your back," he ordered.

Despite the pain, Richard complied with the order. His reward was a pair of handcuffs securely fastened around his wrists.

After the trooper cuffed Richard and removed his gun from the shoulder holster, he signaled his squad mates to check the wounded civilians a few yards away. They only had to take a quick look to let him know that the situation was very grave. He immediately radioed in his position and said, "Control, we have bad casualties here and a wounded prisoner."

"Roger that. Help is on the way. Hold the prisoner and maintain security."

The officer then rolled Richard over and frisked him. When he found Richard's badge and ID, he helped Richard sit. "Sorry about that, sir," he said to Richard, "Can't be too careful under the circumstances. I'll have to keep the cuffs on and hold your ID and weapon until the lieutenant gets here. In the meantime, I'll put a field dressing on that wound."

The large black STOP truck started rolling down the path, followed by ambulances and police cruisers. When it arrived, several STOP squads formed a defensive perimeter around the wounded, and EMTs rushed to tend to them. At the same time, local police were sent into the meadow to clear the way for the Medevac helicopter that was about to land.

"Jesus, where did his face go?" one of EMTs asked when he rolled Stuart over. "He's lost a lot of blood, and he's in shock. We have to take him to the chopper. Now."

"This guy's leg is all smashed to shit, but at least he's responsive enough to be moaning. He can be evacuated by ambulance."

"The lady looks like both her legs are broken and she's passed out. She can go in an ambulance as well," said a third.

Richard was about to head to the chopper behind Stuart's stretcher, when he heard his name called.

"Chief Moore, I'm Lieutenant Brewer. I'm in charge here. What happened?"

Richard gave Brewer a quick summary of the events then told him he could talk with him at the hospital, as he was going with the young man in the chopper. He also asked that someone take the cuffs off.

"You're not going anywhere yet, Chief. The homicide guys aren't here yet and I'll catch hell if I let you go before they have a chance to talk to you."

"With all due respect, Lieutenant, your homicide guys are taking their own sweet time getting here. I'm tired; I'm filthy; and I'm wounded, so, unless you want to read me my rights, and create grief neither of us wants, I'm going out in the chopper to get medical attention, and your homicide guys can find me in the hospital. Just tell them I pulled rank on you, Lieutenant."

Before the lieutenant could respond, Richard turned and headed for the helicopter. Brewer hesitated a moment, then ordered one of the troopers to remove Richard's cuffs and escort him until further notice

Two men sat in a car not far away listening to the police radio. The driver decided they should report what was happening.

"Mr. Billings, do you copy?"

"I'm here. What's the situation?"

"We followed Moore to Stoneham. He and a couple of others have been shot."

"How bad is he?"

"I haven't received a report. The cops are still securing the area. A chopper is coming in to transport one or more to the hospital. Wait one. Sounds like Moore is going in the chopper."

"Oh, shit! Where are they taking him, and whose operation is it?"

"The State Police are in charge. I'm not sure which hospital. I'll get back to you when I find out."

"All right, get back to me quickly. I want to handle this on the other end."

22

An ambulance transported the man and woman to a nearby hospital, while the Medevac helicopter airlifted Richard and Stuart to the Massachusetts General Hospital. When the helicopter landed at the hospital, emergency personnel took the two men to separate treatment areas. A doctor removed the dressing from Richard's arm and treated a three-inch flesh wound. He stitched it, applied a clean dressing, and had Richard put his arm in a sling.

"It was deep enough to have affected the muscle. It will be painful for some time. I'll give you a prescription for the pain. You'll need to change the dressing daily. See your doctor in seven to ten days to have the stitches removed, or drop by here and we'll take them out for you."

"Thank you, Doctor."

Richard asked about Stuart's condition, and learned that although part of his right upper jaw and most of the left lower jaw were missing, and he had bone fragments embedded in the roof of his mouth, there was no indication of any trauma to his brain. He had been stabilized and taken to the operating room for extensive surgery. Given the situation, he was in better shape than he had a right to be, but it would be at least forty-eight hours before a real prognosis could be made. The doctor added that if Richard wanted to talk with the young man he should make an appointment for next year. If he survived, Stuart would be unable to talk for a very long time.

Blood had soaked through Richard's jacket, shirt, and pants, and his clothes were stuck to his skin. With his escort in tow, he found a linen closet and grabbed clean scrubs, then headed for the doctor's dressing room to shower and change. As he entered the doctor's lounge, two State Police detectives caught up to him.

"Chief Moore, I'm Detective Nelson and this is Detective Kelly. We have some questions."

"Okay, I was just going to take a shower. I'll be with you after I cleaned up."

"Now," Kelly said, "You gave the lieutenant the slip but now you're going to sit and answer some questions."

"I'm just taking a shower. I won't disappear down the drain."

"Look, Small-town, our captain has half a dozen mayors and the governor up his ass looking for answers. You're going to start giving us some right now. So sit down."

Richard sat. He knew what was going through their heads. To them, he was a small-town cop who had somehow created a hornet's nest on their turf, and now they had to deal with the fallout. They were not happy, and he was the cause. Still, he did not like Kelly's attitude, and he decided to be careful about the amount of information he shared with him.

Richard leaned forward in his chair, ran his free hand through his hair, then sat up straight. "I've been doing some administrative work that required research on the mortality rates for police personnel. Scott heard about my interest through an actuary I talked with, and contacted me. He said he might be able to help, and asked me to meet him at the Sheep Fold today to discuss it. We were just beginning to talk when the shooting started. I have no idea what caused the shooting."

"So, Small-town, you just happened to travel sixty-five miles to the Sheep Fold to enjoy the scenery, while you passed the time of day with a guy you hardly know, when he gets hit by a shooter. He gets popped in the head, you and another guy also get hit, some broad breaks both her legs, and for a few minutes there's so much lead flying around it looks like the beginning of Saving Private Ryan, but you have no idea what it's all about. Some kind of convenient if you ask me."

Richard was dirty, sore, and tired. He jumped out of his chair and turned on the smart-mouthed Kelly, going nose to nose.

"No one asked you. If you think it's convenient, go talk to Stuart Scott. He's the one on the surgical table fighting for his life. I know you're getting heat over this, Detective, but coming on to me with a piss poor attitude isn't going to help you. I gave you the facts, as I know them. If they don't make sense to you, try using that gray matter between your ears to do some investigative work instead of looking for someone to hand you answers. I'm taking a shower."

Kelly's face contorted with anger and he spit out, "I'm not finished with you yet."

The door to the lounge opened and a tall, lean, gray-haired man entered.

"Chief Moore, I'm Captain Tomlinson," he said, while extending his hand to Richard. "We have a few things to go over, but, first, I would like to talk with my detectives, if you don't mind."

"That's fine with me, Captain. As I was just telling your men, I'm going to take a shower."

"I understand. You look like shit. Of course that's to be expected, given the day you've had. Take your time, I'll be here when you're finished and I'll not keep you long afterward."

Richard went into the shower and let the hot water relax his tense muscles, while his mind replayed the events and images of the preceding few hours. When he had finished and put on clean scrubs, he felt refreshed and ready to deal with Captain Tomlinson.

Tomlinson was waiting for him alone in the lounge, and Richard asked him where his escort and the two detectives were.

"Oh, they had real police work to do, and I offered to finish questioning you." He paused, then said, "You know, Chief, our Detective Kelly doesn't think much of you or your attitude," softening the criticism with a low chuckle.

"I did react stronger than I should have. I'd like some answers as much, if not more than him."

"Your quick reaction to the shooting probably saved that kid's life. Must have been your military experiences that caused you to react the way you did." Tomlinson let the last statement hang in the air for a few moments. "You saw some unusual action with that special operations unit you commanded. In Columbia for a while, I understand."

"I don't think the United States has a base in Columbia, Captain."

"Well, us common citizens don't know of any military bases in Columbia, officially that is, but we do wonder about the possibility."

"What's your question, Captain?"

"Do you have any enemies from your past service that might have had something to do with this shooting?"

"As you probably already know, I left the military nine years ago. That's a long time for someone to carry a grudge without acting on it."

"So, what's your take?"

As had Lieutenant Kelly's' attitude, Captain Tomlinson's remarks made Richard cautious.

"You don't want to hear it, but it was most likely a random shooting."

"You're right, I don't. What makes you think that?"

"As I said, I've been out of the military for nine years. If someone wanted me, say a bad guy that wants revenge, there were better times and places than now and the Sheep Fold. If someone wanted Stuart, he could have done a drive-by or a snatch and made him disappear. I just met Stuart so there is no connection between us. A shooting out in the open in a public place looks like a desire for publicity."

"I hope you're wrong, because if you're right, we'll have more dead before it's over."

"And, if I'm wrong, you'll only have two dead on your hands, me, and Stuart."

"I didn't intend to trivialize either outcome, Chief."

The news media spent the afternoon and early evening reporting on the shooting. Therefore, it was no surprise when, as Richard waited at the elevator, Stephanie Lynn walked up to him. "Hi, Chief, or is it Doctor?" She was admiring the scrubs Richard was wearing.

This guy is in great shape. Those scrubs look good on him. Muscles, a nice butt, charming, and a potential story: what else could a girl ask for, she thought to herself.

"No comment, Ms. Lynn."

"Is that any way to treat me? I've been sitting on those god-awful plastic waiting room chairs for hours just to see how you are, and, what do I get? 'No comment.' We reporters have a heart, you know."

"Yeah, I know. It's just not made of the same substance that real people's hearts are made of."

Before Stephanie could respond, Richard held up his hand. "I'm tired and hungry. If we keep bantering back and forth like this, I'll say something I'll regret."

"Okay, Hotshot, but I owe you one for that last comment. I haven't eaten either. Let's go. I'll buy."

"Even in my current state, I can't be bought."

"Loosen up. Just dinner. Besides, I have information for you."

"My car is still at the Sheep Fold. One of the troopers was going to give me a ride."

"Forget it. I'll take you. We'll go out the receiving dock entrance. That'll keep you away from the throng of reporters waiting outside for you."

Richard weighed his options for a moment, and decided that dinner with Stephanie was a better deal than interacting with more reporters or a ride with a state trooper. "That would be great, if you don't mind. Do you like Chinese food?"

"Second only to Italian, and no, Chief, I don't mind at all."

"I know a place on Route 28, a couple miles north of the Sheep Fold. We can get my car and you can follow. I also have a change of clothes in the car."

"Oh, but I like your fashion statement," she said with a slight smile.

23

At the restaurant, they ordered drinks and Richard excused himself to go to the men's room to change. Walking back toward the table, Richard paused, his eyes focused on the table where Stephanie sat. The day had started pleasantly enough, with a clear sky, pleasant temperature, and a beautiful field. It had abruptly turned deadly, and now a young man with half a face was fighting for his life on an operating table. *And here I am*, he thought, *about to have dinner with a very attractive woman*. He watched Stephanie as she brushed back her hair with her hand, and thought of Lori brushing her hair back the same way. *Lori, you're always there ... but I miss talking with you. Stephanie is an attractive woman, don't you agree? And in case I forget, highly intelligent.*

As Richard slid into the booth, Stephanie picked up her drink, "Here's to better days," she said as she lifted her glass.

"I'll vote for that."

"How's the arm?"

"Sore, stiff, but okay. I've had worse." The tone of his response told Stephanie that she would get no more on the subject.

After they ordered, they made light getting-to-know-you conversation, but when their food arrived, Stephanie said, "You haven't asked me about the information I told you I have."

"Figured you'd get around to telling me or you'd changed your mind."

"You're not curious?"

"Yes, I am. I was also curious earlier today and that didn't work out too well."

Inwardly, Stephanie winced. "I can see where that might have dampened your curiosity. Well, I did some checking, and you were right. The numbers of mortalities within the fire departments, law-enforcement, and municipal employees in the surrounding cities and towns is up. It was fairly easy to confirm with the police departments and fire departments, but receiving information about the municipal workers was more difficult."

"Why was that?"

"Different work culture. You became aware of a possible increase because you and a fire chief were talking after a funeral.

When a member of the fire or police department dies, coworkers and comrades from other communities turn out and mingle. That's not as likely to happen with a municipal worker. Mostly immediate family, coworkers, and friends attend his or her funeral. So, there's less sharing of information, less speculation, and no one brings the question to the mayor or town manager."

"I see your point."

"Also, remember that we are not talking about a rash of deaths in one city or town, just a statistical increase too small to cause much bureaucratic questioning." She paused, looked down at her plate, and then looked up at him. "I still don't know if there is a question."

After that, they ate in relative silence for a while.

Stephanie got the conversation started again. "Tell me about your meeting with Bryan. Was he of any help?"

Richard related the brief conversation he had with Bryan. He told her how LeBlanc and Alex interrupted and sent Bryan on his way. "The poor kid looked as if he were being sent to the principal's office. Do you know anything about HISH or Pierre LeBlanc?"

"I've read some articles about LeBlanc and his company. I remember reading something about them employing an innovative method for structuring in–network health providers. The info on its president, Pierre LeBlanc, was mostly basic and bland. Why do you ask?"

"You said earlier that you weren't sure if there is a question. Until today, I wasn't sure either, but I was really surprised at how angry LeBlanc was at Bryan for talking to me, and not real convinced by his stated reasons. Now there's this thing with Stuart Scott. Was he just a random target, or is something else going on: something connected to the increase in mortalities, to HISH, or to both? I don't know. I might never know. But I think there are some questions worth asking."

Stephanie briefly considered Richard's comments and responded, "There's nothing to suggest that the increase in mortalities is anything other than a statistical variance. Many competent people have investigated the variance. As for HIRSH, if LeBlanc had been told that you were a cop, it would be quite natural for him to interrupt your meeting with Bryan to see what was going on. How is Stuart Scott connected to any of this? Who is he?"

Richard stared at Stephanie, wondering about her motives. *Is she a reporter sitting there asking these questions for a story, or is she an ally feeling some obligation to help because she made the introduction to Bryan?* He decided to answer carefully.

"I had a connection with his brother years ago. It turns out that he works with Bryan at HIRSH, and when we bumped into each other, we arranged to meet briefly in a coffee shop around the corner from the HISH offices. Stuart knew I had talked with Bryan and offered to help. He's a computer expert of some kind. He told me he that he exercised his dog at the Sheep Fold on Sundays. He suggested that if I wanted more information about statistical analysis and computer modeling, we could talk while his dog got exercise."

"Hmm, talk about your coincidences."

"Well, I don't ordinarily believe in coincidences, but you're right."

They finished their meal, and Stephanie paid the bill over protests from Richard. "I offered to take you to dinner. A bribe, I believe, is how you categorize the offer." Outside, after an awkward moment, Stephanie extended her hand to Richard.

"I'm going to make some inquiries about HISH and LeBlanc, and get back to you. Make sure you change the dressing on the arm."

"Stephanie, it might not be wise of you to make any inquiries about HISH or LeBlanc. Stuart was trying to help me, now he's fighting for his life, and, if he lives, he has a long recovery ahead of him. I wouldn't want anything to happen to you. Getting close to me could be hazardous to your health."

"I appreciate your concern, Chief, but I've been an investigative reporter for some time. I can handle myself."

"Just be careful. Thank you for dinner. I enjoyed your company."

24

Richard's cell phone voicemail system was full. When he got home and checked his home phone voicemail, it also was full. Some of the messages were from other Town Council members, but the majority were from Theo demanding that he return the call immediately. The day had been demanding and draining, he was tired, and, now that the anesthetic had worn off, his arm was aching—Theo and the others could wait; he was going to bed. In a nighttime ritual he had practiced for years, he drank a glass of milk at the kitchen table and reviewed the day, trying to organize the jumble of events into a pattern, a practice that reflected his need for order and predictability. As usual, the exercise calmed him, and, when he got into bed, sleep came quickly.

He saw Lori close her eyes and sprang upright in bed, his heart pounding, his breathing rapid, and his palms and forehead sweaty. After sitting motionless in the dark for several minutes, he swung his legs over the edge of the bed, and, ignoring the pain in his arm, pushed himself up into a standing position. Walking barefoot into the kitchen, he poured himself another glass of milk, sat at the kitchen table, and thought about the day Lori died.

On that day, two and a half years before, Richard, who was then the commander of the Boston Police Department's antiterrorism team, was finishing some paperwork in his office, when his phone rang.

"Moore here."

"Richard, Paul." Paul was the Chief of Police in Stoneham, Richard's home city at the time.

"Hi, Paul, to what do I owe the pleasure?"

"Lori's had an accident. She's in transit to New England Rehab. You had better get up there. I'll meet you."

"Lori, an accident? What happened, Paul? Is she all right?"

"Richard, just get moving. I'll see you at the hospital."

When he arrived, a nurse directed Richard to one of the offices where he met the attending physician.

"Mr. Moore, I'm sorry to have to tell you this, but your wife died of carbon monoxide poisoning."

Richard staggered backward. The doctor's words hit him harder than any force he had ever encountered. The doctor stepped toward him.

"Are you all right, Mr. Moore? Would you like to sit for a minute?"

Still stunned and dazed, Richard said, "What ... No, I'm okay." Disbelief, shock, and questions filled his mind.

"How did this happen?" he mumbled almost to himself.

"I really don't know. I assume that the police are investigating. As the ER physician on duty, I met the ambulance when it arrived. I believe that your wife was dead for some time before she was found."

"I'd like to see her. Tell me where she is."

"I'll take you. Just down the hall."

Richard stood next to the table holding her hand. Except for the tears running down his cheeks, his face was as pale and empty of expression as hers was. Paul came up behind him and put his hand on his shoulder.

"Richard, you talked to the doctor?"

"Yeah," He wiped his cheeks while saying, "Paul, what the hell happened?"

"A neighbor called us. She heard the car running in the garage for a long time. When the responding officer checked it out ... he found Lori in the front seat."

The rest was a blur. Suicide, they said. The medical examiner confirmed the finding after the autopsy. The official records stated: *Lori Moore sat in her car with the windows open and engine running. Medical records indicate that she was being treated for a very aggressive form of breast cancer, and had apparently had been reading information about her treatment and the effects on family members. She drifted off and died peacefully of asphyxiation. In light of her medical condition, the absence of any sign of forced entry, and the lack of any other signs of foul play, a conclusion of suicidal death by carbon monoxide poisoning was reached.*

Richard never believed that Lori committed suicide. He had felt the intensity of her love and her will to live; the investigators had not. On the night of her death, Richard had a nightmare in which he was trapped behind a glass door watching Lori die in panic. He had been having the same dream ever since.

25

Theo Reuben called at six thirty. "Moore, you still work for this town? Why the hell haven't you returned our calls? The Council's been trying to reach you since that fiasco yesterday made the news."

"What can I do for you, Theo?"

"What can you do? Start by answering your calls when we try to reach you. Hell, there could have been an emergency that needed our chief of police."

"Okay, Theo, I'll add that advice to my emergency response protocol. Anything else?"

"Don't get smart with me, Moore. You serve at the pleasure of this town and right now, this town is not pleased with you. The Council wants to see you in its chambers at eight."

"All right, Theo, I'll be there," Richard said, and then he hung up.

Theo had not slept much after hearing about the incident at the Sheep Fold. Right after talking to Richard, he placed another call.

"Carlos, did you try to kill Moore?"

"No entiendo inglés."

"Don't give me that shit. I told you I'd handle him. What were you—" The connection went dead.

When it became known that Richard was under consideration to replace the old chief, Lieutenant Allen, aided by one of his politically connected uncles, began lobbying for the job. Theo Reuben and two other council members quickly endorsed Allen, despite Allen's immaturity and lack of qualifications. "The position should be filled from within the ranks of existing officers," was their reply whenever Richard's appointment came up for discussion.

When, despite this opposition, Richard became the chief, Theo seemed to take it as a personal affront, and started an almost incessant campaign to discredit Richard and replace him with Allen. Whenever there was any event, inconsequential or otherwise, affecting the town or townspeople and the police department, he convinced the Council to call Richard in for a meeting. During the early period of Richard's appointment, he always found a way to have Lieutenant Allen in attendance, and Allen would add information that was unfavorable to Richard whenever possible.

Recently, however, the lieutenant had informed the Council that he would no longer cooperate in these attempts to discredit Richard. Working with Richard, he said, had shown him how much he had to learn before he would be qualified to be chief. He also stated that he regretted the problems he had caused for Richard and the disrespect he had shown toward him. Allen even bluntly told the Council that the town should be thankful it had such a conscientious and dedicated chief of police. "Leave the chief alone, and let him, and us, do the job you pay us to do," he said.

Strangely, although the lieutenant's comments removed the stated reason for Theo's opposition to Richard, they did not deter Theo's antipathy toward Richard in the least. He wanted Richard out and he continued to pursue that objective with unbridled determination.

Richard entered the Council's chambers at precisely eight in the morning. Five of the seven council members and the town manager were already there. Inevitably, these meetings were closed-door affairs, which meant none of the citizens of the town could be present. One exception, however, attended most meetings.

Bill Blackstone could trace his family's lineage to the original settlers of Winchendon. A Blackstone family member has been involved with the town's political history since the beginning. Although Bill himself had never held a political office, he wielded more political power than any other resident of the town. He was the reason for Richard's appointment as chief, and took an interest in the Council's actions related to Richard. Rather than interfering when things got foolish and petty, however, he preferred to watch how Richard handled himself in this small town political arena.

Theo was the first to see Richard enter the chambers. "Chief Moore, it's about time you arrived. Gentlemen, now that the chief has graced us with his presence, let's begin."

Theo Reuben was not the president of the Town Council; that honor belonged to Frank Della Russo. Frank, like all of the council members, had a full-time job. Unlike the other council members, however, Frank, and Mary Cullen, another council member, did not work in the town. Their jobs prevented them from attending meetings conducted during weekdays. The other five members owned small businesses in the town. In Della Russo's absence, Theo acted as the self-appointed president. This meeting was no exception.

"Chief Moore, please explain to this council what happened yesterday and make sure you tell us what you were doing that you got involved in that incident."

Richard was holding a copy of the morning's newspaper. He held it up and asked, "Did any of you read this morning's paper and the account of the incident at the Sheep Fold?"

Everyone nodded their head indicating they had. Theo added, "Yes, Chief, we have read it, as has most of the town."

"Good, then you don't need me to explain what happened. The story covers it in detail. As for how I was involved, it appears the incident was a random shooting. I was a victim. A physician at Mass General treated me for an injury. The treatment included pain medication, which left me quite drowsy. I went to bed when I arrived in town. Since all of you have as much information about the incident as I have, there is no reason to continue this meeting. I have to get to the station." He finished, and got up to leave.

"Chief Moore, this town does not pay you to bring statewide publicity to it. I have information that you were conducting some kind of investigation, an investigation that does not pertain to this town."

"Theo, the only activity I was involved in was my attempt to save the life of a young man who had just had his face blown off by a sniper's bullet. As for an investigation, your information is wrong. If I were involved in an investigation, it would have to pertain to this town and I would only apprise you of it as needed or upon completion. Now, why don't we all go back to work?"

He walked toward the door. The other council members had had enough. This was going nowhere. They stopped Theo from responding, and the meeting was over.

26

Theo owned the oldest pharmacy in Winchendon, and when he returned to it after the council meeting, he was both frightened and furious. Frightened, because he was sure Moore was working on something that he needed to know about, something that had brought unwanted attention to the community. Furious, because, when he asked Moore about it, the man virtually thumbed his nose at him.

"I need this prescription taken care of right away."

Startled, Theo looked up from behind the pharmacy counter. A young man in jeans and a Red Sox T-shirt was standing at the counter with a piece of paper in his hand.

"I'm sorry, but I'm backed up. You'll have to come back for it late this afternoon."

"You don't understand. It is special. You need to take care of it right away."

Theo looked at the prescription form.

"Oh, yes, I'll take care of it. I'll deliver it myself; it will take some time to fill. You don't have to wait."

"Thank you."

As instructed in the young man's coded prescription, Theo left the pharmacy and drove to a prearranged drop site, where he found a small package sealed in a plastic bag. Returning to his car, he opened the package, removed the untraceable cell phone that was inside, and pressed the buttons for the first speed dial number.

The call was answered on the first ring, and without preamble, a voice said, "Theo, you know what I do to people who do not follow security by calling me on an unsecure phone?"

"Carlos, I apologize. I was—"

"I kill them. I can't afford such stupidity." His anger was mounting and his voice was rising. "How many times have I told you to follow security procedures? Are you really so stupid?"

"Carlos, I apologize. I called you earlier because I was just so concerned about the attempt on Moore's life."

"So you call me on an unsecured phone and ask me if I'm the one who tried to kill him and you expect me to answer. Are you fucking crazy?"

"I wasn't thinking, Carlos. I apologize."

"Apologize? You don't understand. This is not like waking me up and then you apologize for the inconvenience. Your stupidity could result in our being discovered and arrested. What then? Do you apologize as we sit in separate cells, you piece of shit?"

"No, Carlos, you're right. It will never happen again."

"If it does, we will not speak of it because I will cut your tongue out before I slit your throat. Now, did you fire Richard yet?"

"We brought him in for a meeting this morning—"

"Another fucking meeting? It's been seven months since he shut down our operation. We're losing money. You're losing money. Money you owe me. I don't want to hear about meetings. Take care of him or I will. You are running out of time." Carlos hung up.

A badly shaken Theo put his arms on the steering wheel and rested his head on them. He knew he had made a major error calling Carlos earlier in the morning, but he had to know if Carlos had been responsible for the attack on Moore. It appeared he had not been, but he made it clear he was close to bypassing Theo and getting rid of the chief. If that happened, Theo knew, he would become an accessory to murder. The thought brought back an overwhelmingly painful memory. *How did I get into this mess?* He asked himself.

Theo's father was not only a good pharmacist; he was also a good businessman, a valuable combination for a young man just starting out in the nineteen thirties. The elder Reuben used that combination to start and grow a successful corner pharmacy and variety store in the small town of Winchendon. He had not become rich, but he had provided his family with a very comfortable living.

Theo recognized the success his father enjoyed, and decided to follow his footsteps. The Longwood College of Pharmacy approved his application and they accepted him as a first–year resident student. He attended the Boston campus on Longwood Avenue, and lived in a nearby dorm.

Living away from home, though he was only an hour's drive away, was not all Theo had envisioned. He was out of his element; classmates seemed more knowledgeable about the world. They certainly knew more about partying and having fun than Theo did.

Theo shunned the party crowd, opting instead to stay in his dorm. He spent Sundays during the fall watching profootball on television with dorm mates, some of whom were die-hard fans. Occasionally, Theo would listen to the banter about point spreads and how some had lost a bet, though the team they bet on won. The explanation for this possibility intrigued Theo. He eventually became a regular participant in the weekly betting pools. It may have been beginners luck, blind luck, or dumb luck, but Theo maintained a winning record through his sophomore year.

Betting on sports and watching the game in anticipation of a payoff was a nice diversion from lonely nights in his dorm. Watching a game he had wagered on filled him with a combination of tension, excitement, and heart pounding thrill. The larger the bet, the more thrill. When his need for the thrill outgrew the capacity of dorm room stakes, he contacted a bookie and started betting serious money on sports games.

Theo's luck held for a while, and, besides the heightened thrills of the bigger bets, he had larger payoffs. Almost as importantly, in the school's gambling fraternity, he was treated with the respect he thought he deserved, but had never experienced. Luck is not a long-term substitute for skill, however, and although he enjoyed watching sports, Theo never developed the passion for researching teams necessary for a skilled handicapper. Over time, he began to lose more often than he won. He barely managed to survive six years of school without losing all he owned and without incurring a large debt, but with a doctorate in pharmacy, he also graduated with an addiction to gambling.

He spent the first two years after graduation working with his dad, learning the business end of the pharmacy and variety store operation. At the end of that time, the elder Reuben sold the business to Theo, and moved to Florida with Theo's mother.

Theo was pleasantly surprised when he learned how much cash remained in the company's bank account. He was also surprised at the volume of cash the operation generated. It did not take him long to start using the company's bank account as his personal piggy bank. The money supported his gambling habit.

Theo's dad had left the funds in the bank account because of the seasonal nature of the business. Changing inventory items on shelves to meet the various seasonal consumer demands required planning and a reserve of cash. Theo paid no attention to this fact until it was too late.

To conserve cash, he reduced the size of orders. This left bare spots on his shelves, which, in turn, caused customers to ask about the health of Theo's business. The questions prompted Theo to borrow to fill in inventory. The debt with the bank and with his bookie mounted. He barely kept the operation afloat. Eventually, the bookie called and told Theo they had to talk. They met at a coffee shop on Longwood Avenue in Boston.

"Theo, you've been a very good customer for many years. I have watched your luck flow from good to bad and back again. Unfortunately, your current string of bad luck has lasted longer than I can support. Your debt has become a concern for my bosses."

"I know. I owe you a lot of money, but I need some time to pay it back. Business has been off, but I'm working on correcting that. Once I fix it, I'll have better cash flow and will be able to repay you."

"Theo, I have to start charging serious interest on the money you owe. At your present rate of payment, you will be lucky to cover the interest. You need to find a way to make larger payments."

"I don't know what else to do right now. Except for my pharmacy, I don't own much."

"You could sell the pharmacy."

"No! No! I couldn't do that. I haven't paid off my father."

"Your father will understand. I'm sure he will be more understanding than my boss."

"I don't know. There must be another way. Give me some time to see if I can come up with another solution."

"Believe me, Theo, if I could give you more time, I would, but it's out of my hands. My bosses want payment now. However, as I said, you've been a good customer and I think I can help another way. A colleague of mine may be able to lend you the money. He has helped other clients of mine. His interest rate is much better than what I charge. I could put you in touch with him."

"I'd be willing to meet with him as long as he's not going to be too demanding."

"Theo, you don't have many options. I have to tell my boss tomorrow that you have paid your debt or that you have given us your pharmacy as collateral."

Ramon, the bookie's colleague, agreed to have dinner with Theo at the Captain's Seafood restaurant. During dinner, Ramon was an amiable and talkative companion, asking Theo about his life and his views, and listening with interest to the answers. Although Theo had apprehensions about the meeting, it felt like so many other business dinners he had attended that he began to relax.

After the waiter had cleaned the table and brought coffee, Ramon stopped the social chat and got down to business. "Theo, I understand you are experiencing some financial difficulties. Your bookie wants payment tomorrow or he wants your pharmacy as collateral. Of course, he only wants the collateral until you sell the business. He does not intend to carry your debt much longer. In anticipation of this meeting, I have purchased your debt from your bookie."

"What did you say? You already paid my bookie?"

"That is correct."

"We haven't even discussed a deal. I don't know anything about you. I don't even know if I want to do business with you."

"I know that there are details to discuss, but the bottom line is this, my deal will be better for you. The interest payments are better, you will not have to sell your business, and you will not have to be concerned about your health."

"My health? Are you threatening me?"

"Me, threaten you? Theo, you seriously mistake me. I'm a businessman, not a thug. The men you owe are not so benevolent. The longer you go without paying, the less benevolent they will become, and the more likely they will inflict physical harm on you to motivate you to pay. If you haven't realized this fact, you are very naive. As a show of good faith, I paid your debt with the understanding that if you decide tonight that you don't want my help, the bookie will return the money to me, and your bookie's boss will look to you for payment. First, I ask you to listen to my terms. So?"

When Theo slowly nodded, Ramon smiled and continued. "It is very simple. I have paid off your bookie. I am prepared to pay off some, not all, but some of your business debt. I want you to put the business back on track. I will require no payments for the first twelve months and you will not be charged interest for the first twenty-four months. This is an interest free loan for twenty-four months with no payments until next year. Kind of like one of those television ads for furniture."

"I don't know what to say except, what's the catch?"

"You can't appreciate the opportunity without looking for a catch? Well, here is the *catch*, as you put it. You will have five years to pay off the debt. Five years from the start of your payments, which, as I have said, will start next year. After twenty-four months, you will pay interest of prime plus ten percent."

"Those sound like reasonable terms. Given my current financial situation, they are more than reasonable. Why would you be willing to do this, and why are you so interested in me keeping the pharmacy in operation?"

"We offer the terms because we do not want to overburden your finances. We want you to be able to get your finances back in order. That reminds me. One other point, you may not resume betting. As of today, you are finished betting on anything. We want you to keep the pharmacy operating, because from time to time we may have need for some of your services."

"Need for some of my services? That sounds very vague."

"Okay, let me be more specific. You have access to prescription drugs. We have clients in need of some of those drugs. Not all of them will have prescriptions. We will ask you to fill the order without proper paperwork. We will, of course, pay you your cost of the product."

"You expect me to sell you controlled substances without proper paperwork? How long do you think I'll be able to stay open or keep my license if I do that?"

"We will help you cover the transactions. You will not lose your license or your pharmacy."

"I'm not sure this is a deal I can agree to. Besides losing my license, I could go to jail."

"Theo, we will not let you go to jail, but it might be better than what your bookie's boss has in store for you."

In the end, Theo had to agree that Ramon was offering him the only way out, and he agreed to the deal.

Ramon contacted him several weeks later and placed an order for some pain medication. Over the next several weeks, Ramon placed several more orders, gradually increasing the quantity, but doing so slowly enough to avoid arousing the suspicion of Theo's drug wholesaler.

A fear of incurring Ramon's wrath made Theo refrain from gambling of any kind. With money in his pocket, however, the gambling demon started calling him again, and he rationalize that Ramon's prohibition only applied to large bets and frequent bets. He had learned his lesson; he was through being a big-time gambler. A small wager on a game was a different story, however. He deserved a little relaxation now and then. Ramon could not object to that, and, besides, if he were careful enough, Ramon would never know.

Three months after his initial meeting with Ramon, Theo arranged to have dinner with one of his old pharmacy-college gambling buddies. Theo told his friend he no longer gambled the way he used to, but he would like to make an occasional small bet without his political opponents learning about it. The friend offered to help him by acting as an intermediary, provided Theo paid him the money up front. Theo agreed, and handed the man a crisp, new fifty-dollar bill and instructions for placing the bet.

The following day, Theo was shocked to learn that his friend had been killed in a freak automobile accident on the way home from the restaurant. When his mail arrived the day after, it contained a secure business envelope with no return address. When he opened it, he found a crisp, new fifty-dollar bill. He never tried to make another bet, and Ramon never mentioned the subject.

MULTIPLES

Nine months after this incident, Ramon asked Theo to meet him for dinner to talk about the payments that were about to come due. At dinner, Ramon introduced Theo to Carlos, saying that Carlos had a business proposition that might benefit all of them.

"Theo, I am sort of Ramon's silent business partner, and I am very impressed with your cooperation with us. You have been very helpful to our clients and you haven't asked many questions. I like that. You're to begin making payments on your loan next month. I'd like to make a proposal. We are starting an import operation soon and need a place to receive the shipments. I'd like to use your store location for that purpose. We will not leave the products with you. Once the shipment arrives, someone will pick it up and distribute it."

"Why do you need to use my location?"

"We don't have a warehouse or other facility yet. We are not sure how successful the import operation will be, so we do not want to incur a lease. We will only be receiving product that we have orders for, and that we can distribute the same day."

"Would you mind telling me what types of product we are talking about?"

"I cannot do that, Theo. The products might compete with some of yours. If we find this to be the case, we will compensate you. And, speaking of compensation, we will credit you with a monthly payment toward your debt for each month we use your services."

"That seems reasonable provided I don't have to hire a staff to unload the shipments and if the shipments don't take up the little space I have in the back room of the store."

"Excellent. I knew I would be able to do business with you, Theo. Here is to a successful import business." Carlos hoisted his glass in a toast. It was the beginning of a long, dead-end journey for Theo.

Theo lifted his head, looked around, and started to drive. He only hoped he could mollify Carlos enough that the man did not attack Chief Moore.

27

Back at his office, Richard started his computer and checked his e-mail. After reviewing a half-dozen, he realized they all concerned yesterday's events. He scrolled down and found a message from Steve Deschenes.

Call me. I have your info, Steve wrote. Since Steve was on the West Coast, Richard would have to wait until late afternoon before calling him.

Lieutenant Allen came into his office. "Morning, Chief. You all right?"

"Hi, Chris. Yeah. Theo didn't draw blood this time."

"I wasn't referring to your meeting with the Council, but about the shooting. Are you okay?"

"Thanks for asking. Just a flesh wound." He pointed to the upper part of his left arm.

"So, Theo was at it again in the Council this morning."

"Yeah, I met with them at eight."

"Think they'll ever stop that foolishness?"

"No way. They're just practicing on me, so they'll be ready for you when you become chief."

They both laughed.

"Chief, are you working on something I should know about?"

Richard thought for a moment, then said, "The simple answer is no, because, until yesterday, I wasn't working on anything that you weren't already up to speed on. Then someone started shooting, and now I'm working to find out who and why."

"Okay, so where do we start?"

"No, no, Chris, we have a town to defend. You know, traffic tickets, parking tickets, and the occasional protective custody. We can't all go looking for a shooter an hour and a half and 65 miles southeast of here."

"After yesterday, you shouldn't be out there without someone covering your back. Maybe you were only lucky."

"Maybe the shooter didn't want me at all. The first shot was aimed at Stuart Scott's head."

"And if you were his second target, the shooter isn't finished. I don't have your background and experience, but you've taught me a lot. I'd like you to be around to keep teaching me. Hell, I might learn enough to take your job." Christopher smiled, then continued, "I figure it's a better-than-average chance the shooter will come after you again."

"That's possible, but I don't know why. Until I know, I want you guys to tend to business. I have to go to Boston later this morning. I'll be back late this afternoon. Maybe I'll have some information then."

At 11:30 A.M., Richard was across the street from the main entrance to the John Hancock Tower, waiting to catch Bryan Hayden when he came out for lunch. He called earlier and confirmed that Bryan was in. If Bryan did not leave for lunch by one thirty, Richard would have to risk visiting him in his office again.

Bryan appeared at 12:20, turned left onto St. James Street, and walked toward Copley Square Park, a large open area just past the Trinity Church. When he neared the water fountain, he found a spot to sit and absorb the heat of the sun. He was deep in thought about his friend, Stuart.

"It's a nice day to be outside for lunch."

Bryan turned and found Richard sitting next to him.

"Jesus, what the hell are you doing here?"

"We need to talk."

"Talk! No way. Get out of here, and leave me alone. Being seen with you is bad for a person's health. Or wasn't what happened to Stuart enough for you?"

"Stuart asked to see me. He said he had information I might find useful. We still don't know who shot him or why."

"Yeah, well I don't want to be your next lead. Just leave me alone."

"Bryan, Stuart said he found an unauthorized file hidden behind an encryption in the company computer. Do you know anything about it?"

"He's my best friend. He got me this job. I'm not going to do anything that might further jeopardize him or me. I don't know about any file, and he never mentioned one to me. If you won't leave, I will."

Bryan got up and started walking.

Richard followed, saying, "I think he knew he was taking a risk in meeting with me, but he was willing. It was that important to him. If it was that important to him, you need to step up and help finish what he started."

Bryan kept walking.

Richard did not pursue him, but returned to his office, arriving at three o'clock. After telling the dispatcher to inform Lieutenant Allen of his return, he called his FBI friend.

"Hi, Charlie. Do you have information for me?"

"First, congratulations for still being alive. That was quite a show you put on up there. I thought you had retired from that sort of thing and were giving out parking tickets and holding up traffic so little old ladies could cross the street. You should have joined the Bureau as I asked you. Hell, the only danger I face these days is the possibility I might fall out of my nice, cushy, government-issued chair. All kidding aside, Richard, I heard you were wounded. What really happened up there? Are you okay?"

Richard gave his friend a condensed version of the shooting, assured him he was all right, and, after thanking him for his concern, asked him again if he had any information.

"I think I've found Sharon Hall. Two women fit your description. Both have daughters and are single parents. Both are from the Boston area originally." He gave Richard contact information about both. One was in Denver, Colorado, and the other one in Medford, Oregon.

"Thanks, Charlie. Listen, I need another favor."

"Hey, Richard, I work for the Federal Government, not you."

"I know, and I wouldn't ask, except something strange came up, and I'm not sure where to go with it."

"Strange, ha? Personal or business?"

"A little of both."

Richard told Charlie about his encounter with Captain Tomlinson after the incident at the Sheep Fold.

"The strange part is, Tomlinson talked as if he had first-hand knowledge that I was in Columbia for a time."

"No shit. You mean you were there too. Where the hell else were you that I don't know about? Never mind; I don't want to know. So, you want me to see if this Tomlinson has an inside track?"

"Right and I want to know whose telling secrets out of school."

"I'll see what I can find out, but it won't be easy or quick."

"Thanks, Charlie, and thanks again for your concern."

Next, he called Steve Deschenes on the West Coast.

"Captain, it's been a while. How are things in ... what the hell is the name of that metropolis you're chief of now?"

"Winchendon."

"Yeah, Winchendon. How are things?"

"Quiet for the most part. Then, maybe you'll tell me differently."

"You mean that hunk of melted plastic you sent me?"

"I was hoping you could tell me more about it."

"First, tell me a little about how you got it."

"I found it in the ashes of a fatal fire in a gas station. It was lying on the floor of what was left of a rest room. I sent it out to you a couple of hours later."

"Wow! The rest room floor in a burned out gas station was maybe one of the last places I was expecting."

"Why, Steve?"

"A really nice piece of optics was surrounded by that melted plastic."

"Optics? You mean a lens?"

"Correct, Captain. The lens is part of a very expensive micro camera that produces high-definition quality images. The camera is generally used with a computer, but you won't find it in your local computer store. In fact, I've only seen cameras of this quality used twice before, and, get this; both times the CIA was using them. You back collaborating with the Agency?"

Richard's special operations unit often provided combat support for covert CIA operations. Occasionally, it operated under the supervision of a CIA operative called a "handler." It was one such situation, which had prompted Richard's resignation from the military. Steve had been a member of Richard's unit. His specialty was computers and high-tech surveillance equipment.

"No, Steve, As far as I know, this doesn't have anything to do with the Agency."

"Well, I can't imagine that it was part of some bathroom freak's peeping tom system, or even part of any security system: This camera is used strictly for facial recognition, and, as I said, very hard to come by. Of course, there's always the remote possibility that some Agency guy was taking a dump there and dropped it."

"I assume your joking, Steve."

"Not entirely, Captain. You see, there's no way in the world this camera should have been where you found it, and no chance it was there as part of a functioning system."

"Why not?"

"If it were part of a functioning system, what was its purpose? Why would anyone want to use an application like facial recognition in a toilet? Did you find anything like a computer nearby?"

"Not unless you count the cash register, the lottery computer, or the diagnostic computer in the service bay."

"No, those wouldn't work. Captain, if this lens were part of an operating facial recognition system, it should've been hard-wired to a nearby computer or attached to a transmitter. If it were using a transmitter, then the receiving computer would have been nearby."

"Why nearby?"

"The software for facial recognition needs an ultrahigh-quality picture to work on. Anything that degrades the quality makes it harder for the software to make an accurate match. The more degradation, the less likely the software will produce an accurate match. Even if you hard-wire the camera to the receiving computer, the quality of the picture deteriorates as the cable gets longer. You have the same problem if you use a transmitter. The closer you go to the maximum edge of the transmission range, the more your image degrades, and most transmitters have limited range. If, for some reason this camera was part of a functioning system, and it wasn't hard-wired to a nearby computer in the building, my guess is that it was transmitting images to a receiver no more than three-hundred yards away."

"Thanks, Steve. Anything else?"
"Nothing more."
"Okay. Thanks again for the information about the camera. Good–bye."

Richard cleaned up the items in his in-box, and then called the Sharon Hall living in Denver. She was the wrong person. The next person on the list, however, the Sharon Hall in Medford, Oregon, was indeed Leslie's daughter-in-law. They talked for half an hour, and Richard discovered that Sharon wanted to return to Winchendon but was not sure she would be welcome. Richard explained that Leslie would like nothing better than to have Sharon and her daughter return home. Sharon said that she needed a day or so to decide what she should do. They agreed to talk again.

Before he closed the station, Richard made a call to Tim Curtin.

"Tim, I got a message you called."
"Hi, Chief. Your hunch may have paid off."
"I could use some good news. What happened?"
"We intercepted a brief phone conversation. Both parties mentioned you, and neither was happy. There may be some infighting. Nothing specific, but my advice remains. You be careful. We'll see where today's developments take us."
"Think you can make a connection that'll stick?"
"Not based on what we heard today, but now we have another number, and another source to track. I'll let you know."
"Okay, Tim. Talk with you soon"

He was about to leave, when Jill knocked on his door.
"Hi, Jill. I thought you'd be gone by now."
"I'm leaving now. I just wanted to give you this envelope. Phil Brice dropped it off earlier today. He said you were expecting it."
"I almost forgot that I asked for some pictures. Thanks, Jill. Have a nice night."
"Good night, Chief."

After Jill left, he took the pictures out of the envelope, spread them over his desk, and studied them. A dozen pictures showed the scene where Jim Hall died, each taken from a different angle.

After a few minutes of moving them around and picking a couple up for closer examination, he separated two of interest and put the others back in the envelope.

Taken from across the street, they showed the scene shortly after the discovery of Jim's body. Richard studied one picture in particular. It showed Jim's company truck and its extended bucket, the power pole, and the lines running up to the transformer near the top of the pole. The truck faced left, and the pole was on the right, close to the truck's rear bumper. From the back of the truck, the bucket arm extended up, and the bucket on its end was just to the right of and just below, the top of the pole.

Richard's subconscious told him something was skewed in the pictures. He just did not see what it was. He knew he had to leave or he would be late for a dinner appointment with Lieutenant Allen. As he slid the pictures into the envelope, however, he stopped and reexamined them. Two items struck him. First, the bucket appeared to be too far from the transformer. He would have to check if the angle of the shot was distorting the distance, but, if what he saw in the picture were correct, Jim would have had to lean dangerously far out of the bucket to get at the transformer. Mrs. Hall claimed Jim was an extremely careful worker. A careful worker would not have positioned the bucket as it appeared in the pictures.

Secondly, Jim's body was lying on the shoulder of the road behind the truck. Unless the body had been moved prior to the officer's arrival, or the officer had moved the body, something that was highly unlikely, Jim had fallen out of the side of the bucket farthest from the street, not the side closest to the transformer. He could not have been reaching toward the transformer when he fell, as everyone had assumed.

Richard decided he would have to go out to the scene and compare the photos to the actual topography, but the evidence in the pictures added to his suspicions rather than alleviating them.

28

Driving toward the restaurant, Richard thought about Lieutenant Allen and the change in their relationship. He had endured a very trying first year with Christopher.

Chris and the other officers under Richard's command were ill prepared to handle anything but routine police work, and were most certainly not up to the task of eliminating the town's drug problem. They had no operational procedures for responding to difficult and potentially dangerous situations. None routinely wore a protective vest or called for backups, and they often stormed head-on into perilous, and, sometimes, lethal, situations. Essentially, they operated as separate, uncoordinated individuals, rather than as members of a cohesive organization.

Others may have been daunted by what he found, but Richard had spent his life creating order out of chaos, whether it was circumstantial chaos, or the chaos created by people in those circumstances. He was a superb organizer and team builder, something he had demonstrated repeatedly in the Army and in the Boston Police Department.

Richard spent time with each officer under his command He assessed each person's strengths and weaknesses, then fashioned an individualized component for that person as part of his overall training program. After working with Chris, Richard decided that the surliness, flippancy, and lack of cooperation he observed in the man were more the result of his immature reaction to being passed over for the chief's position, than incompetence or lack of ability. In fact, Richard believed that Allen had the makings of a good police officer, and actually had the potential to become the chief in Winchendon someday. Richard had seen people who were a lot worse straighten themselves out in the Army.

He quickly learned that Chris did have two problems that had the potential to derail his career. Chris had a reputation as womanizer. Allen routinely stopped attractive woman drivers for minor violations or for no reason at all. He would let attractive woman drivers off with a warning for offenses that caused him to issue tickets to anyone else. Chris bragged openly about his sexual conquests.

Richard also discovered that Allen had a reputation as a boozer. When he was not spending his off-duty time with women, he was spending it drinking with his buddies. As he did on his sexual forays, he took his cruiser on these outings, and it was not unusual for people to see it parked for hours outside one of the local bars.

Richard had dealt with enough immature young men in his day to realize that Chris's reputation undoubtedly exceeded the reality of his exploits. His use of the highly identifiable cruiser, the public nature of his drinking and his boasting were acts of bravado meant to increase his standing with the other immature young men he saw as his peers. Unfortunately, for him, his peers would not determine the future of his career as a police officer, and for those who would make that determination; his reputation was a liability and not an asset.

Richard's strategy with Chris was to admonish the lieutenant promptly, but privately when he saw him getting out of line, and to praise him promptly and publicly when it was warranted. He also made a genuine effort to treat him as a valued colleague, soliciting his input, giving him important assignments, and supporting him whenever possible. Despite all of this, however, while the rest of the officers were shaping up into a well-disciplined, competent, and effective force, Allen continued to act like a recalcitrant adolescent. Then, while Richard was on patrol one Friday night, he saw Chris's cruiser parked outside a bar, and, when he stopped to look it over, discovered that the doors were unlocked. Inside, he found Allen's portable radio, several boxes of pistol and shotgun ammunition, a bulletproof vest, a taser, and several other items all lying around loose. When he checked the Mossberg twelve-gauge shotgun, he discovered that it was not locked into the center console gun rack. He locked the shotgun, put the loose items in the cruiser's trunk, then locked the cruiser itself before going into the bar. Richard found the lieutenant bellied up to the bar, with his friends. A woman was clinging to his shoulder while she rested her head on the nape of his neck. Chris was still in uniform, but his tie hung loose, the top three buttons of his shirt were open, and his service pistol was on the counter.

Richard walked up to the bar and addressed Chris, "Lieutenant, I need a word with you."

"Hi, Dick. Hey bartender, get Dick here a drink. What do you drink, Dick?"

"I don't want a drink, Lieutenant. I want to talk with you."

"Sorry, Dick, I'm off duty. I'll talk with you in the morning."

"I think it would be better if we talked now."

"Look, Dick, I know why you want to talk, and I'm not interested. You can take your rules and book tactics and shove them. Your rules and tactics won't save your sorry ass in a real confrontation or fight, so leave me alone."

Richard realized Allen was too drunk to be reasonable, and pressing the issue further at this stage would result in a confrontation, not a conversation. In addition, the bar was full, and many of the male patrons had formed a circle around Richard and Chris. The last thing he wanted or needed was a public brawl. He decided to address the situation under more private and reasonable circumstances.

He said, "Okay, Lieutenant, we'll continue this discussion later," then he turned and walked slowly to the door.

As he did, he heard Allen say, "Dick, big time chief. That pussy couldn't be a real cop in Boston, so he came here to bother us."

Allen was scheduled to cover the night shift the night following the incident at the bar, so Richard planned to meet with him when that shift ended the following morning. Richard spent much of the day reviewing his notes about Allen's performance and the many conferences he had held with him. Richard realized Allen's behavior had crossed the line from recalcitrant to irresponsible, and he had become more a public safety liability than a public safety guardian. In addition, the rest of the department was shaping up into a cohesive, competent, and effective police force, a force with a growing sense of esprit de corps, and a decreasing tolerance of the lieutenant and his antics. They were beginning to resent the fact that Richard expected so much of them, while apparently expecting so little of the lieutenant. For these and other reasons, Richard decide he had cut the young man enough slack. He would have to tell Allen he already had enough documentation to terminate him, and the next time the lieutenant screwed up, he would convince the Council to approve the termination.

Shortly after Allen's shift began that night, the dispatcher got a call about a disturbance in the parking lot of the Lakeside Arms, the town's last independently owned hotel. The Arms, as it is known locally, is located just off Route 202 on Lake Monomonac, the small, man-made lake the town shares with Rindge, New Hampshire. Originally built as a summer resort hotel that catered to families from nearby Worcester, it is now known more as year-round local eatery and watering hole.

After taking down the information, the dispatcher relayed the disturbance call to Allen's cruiser. "Lieutenant, there's a disturbance at the Arms."

"Okay, Tracy, I'm on my way. What's the situation?"

"The night manager called and said that three guys have been drinking in the parking lot for several hours. They are very noisy and have accosted several of the women patrons. I'll call Sam and have him meet you for backup."

"No need. I'll handle it."

"But the Chief said you're supposed to have backup in situations like this."

"Tracy, I said I'll handle it. I don't need backup."

"Okay, but you explain it to the Chief."

The previous chief was often more concerned with keeping his job than with running his department professionally, and many of the department's problems could be traced to this fact. His unwillingness to make unpopular disciplinary decisions, for instance, created fertile ground for the growth of Lieutenant Allen's maverick behavior. Because he served at the pleasure of the Town Council, the chief was careful not to upset them, and since requests for budget increases always upset them, he avoided making such requests. As the town had grown over the years, the demands on the police department had grown. In consequence, the chief's reluctance to seek funding for increased staffing meant that each officer was answering more calls each year. On an increasing number of occasions, an officer requesting a backup found that none was available because everyone else was also on a call. The chief deflected complaints about the situation by encouraging the notion that calling for a backup was a sign of weakness. In the machismo culture of a police force, no one wants a reputation as a "wimp," and it became commonplace for Winchendon officers to answer trouble calls alone or with inadequate support. Correcting this behavior was very high on Richard's list of priorities, and he used two strategies to do so. First, he completed a staffing and utilization study. The results provided the information needed to implement the second strategy. He rearranged schedules to put more officers on duty during peak utilization periods, reduced paperwork requirements so officers spent less time in the office, reassigned two clerical officers to patrol duty, and increased the annual staffing budget request to cover additional hires. He also began an intensive program to change the culture of the department about the use of backups through training sessions, post incident analysis sessions, and, when necessary, disciplinary action. Gradually, calling for a backup when appropriate became viewed as the smart thing to do. As with many other issues, of course, Lieutenant Allen was the exception to this change.

When the Arms disturbance call came in, Richard was at home reading, the police radio on in the background. As he listened to the call and to Chris's response, his instincts told him that his lieutenant was headed for trouble, so he grabbed his windbreaker and drove out to the hotel. Chris was already in the parking lot of the hotel when Richard arrived and parked across the street.

Three men, each with a can of beer, were standing next to a battered pickup when Lieutenant Allen pulled into the parking area. One was wearing biker leathers and a grimy T-shirt that stopped short of his waistline, revealing an enormous gut hung over his belt. He had a full, pockmarked face that glowered menacingly at the world from atop his imposing six foot, three inch, three hundred pounds frame. The shortest of the three also carried extra weight, all of it confined to the abdomen. Unlike the biker figure, this man had powerful-looking biceps. The third of the group wore his long, graying hair pulled back into a ponytail. He was of medium weight and, if not for the hair and disheveled clothing, might pass for a mid–level executive.

As he was getting out of his car, Lieutenant Allen heard the man with the ponytail say, "Well, boys, looks like the gendarme came to join our party."

"Evening boys. I received a call that you've been a little noisy. Are you staying at the hotel?"

The man with the ponytail straightened up. "What's it to ya?"

"If you are, I think it's time you moved into your rooms."

"And if we don't, what ya gonna to do about it?" The man with the ponytail was clearly the leader of this small group.

By this time, the other two men had positioned themselves around Chris, with Ponytail directly in front of him, the biker four feet from his left shoulder, and Shorty four feet from the right shoulder.

"I'm just here to ask you to take your party inside."

"Yeah, well I don't like cops tellin' me what to do, so fuck off." Ponytail moved forward and pushed Chris in the chest. "I think you might want to turn around and lean against that truck."

"I don't think he does," the biker said as he hit the Lieutenant in the left shoulder.

As Chris turned toward the biker, Ponytail threw a punch at his head. Chris caught the motion and deflected the punch. As he deflected it, he grabbed the man's forearm, and turned it up and behind the man's back.

"Don't move, either of you, or I'll snap his arm. Now, I'm going to cuff him and put him in my car. You two can go to your rooms, or I can call for another car to take you in so all three of you can sleep it off at the station."

As Chris reached back with his left hand to grab his cuffs, Ponytail picked up his foot and drove it down on the lieutenant's right instep. At the same time, the man turned to his right, relieving the pressure on his right arm. A switchblade suddenly appeared in his left hand, and he drove it at the lieutenant. Chris saw the gleam of the blade and moved back. He moved too late, and the blade pierced him just below his left ribcage. Shorty then kicked him behind the right knee, and he went down hard. Ponytail quickly raised the knife, ready to plunge it into the lieutenant's chest.

"That's enough," Richard said. He was standing behind Shorty.

"Fuck off. This ain't none of your business," Ponytail replied.

"But it is," Richard said, "That's my lieutenant, and you guys are going to jail."

Shorty and the biker had taken up positions at Richard's shoulders, just as they had with Chris. Ponytail lunged at Richard, who parried the thrusting arm with his right forearm and drove his left elbow into Ponytail's face. Shorty swung at Richard with a powerful right. Richard ducked and kicked Shorty in the groin.

The biker screamed, "I'm going to break you in two," as he raised his arms to grab Richard. Instead of backing up, Richard stepped forward and drove his right fist onto Biker's throat. In successive moves, Richard then battered both of Biker's ears with open palms, punched his eyes with the knuckles of his right hand, and placed a sidekick on the man's left knee.

Shorty was back at Richard. He jumped on Richard's back, and wrapped his arms around his neck. Ponytail was about to punch Richard in the gut, when Richard leaned forward, reached back over his shoulder, grabbed Shorty by the collar, and tossed him up and over. Shorty landed on Ponytail. The biker, who had partially recovered, went for Richard, throwing a vicious punch. Richard deftly grabbed the swinging arm and pulled it up behind Biker's back. With the arm locked behind the man, Richard drove him headfirst into the pickup.

Richard pulled out his service pistol and said, "That's enough exercise for one night. You two lie flat on the ground and put your hands behind your backs." He handcuffed the biker and forced him to the ground. He then went to the lieutenant.

"Chris, you all right?"

"I think my leg is broken!"

"Stay down while I cuff the other two."

He took handcuffs from the lieutenant and cuffed the other two. Satisfied that they would be no further problem, he went back to Chris and checked the knife wound. It was bleeding badly, so he tore a piece of shirt, then wadded it and placed it over the wound. "Hold this in place and press down on it, Chris."

Then he took the lieutenant's microphone and called dispatch. "Tracy, this is the chief."

"I copy, Chief. Where are you?"

"Tracy, send an ambulance to the hotel and get two squad cars out here."

"The hotel? Lieutenant Allen is out there. Is everything all right?"

"I'm with the lieutenant. I asked for an ambulance and a backup. Lieutenant Allen is down with a knife wound. I need three prisoners transported to the jail. Get busy."

Tracy panicked and overreacted. She dispatched the ambulance, the fire department, all available police personnel, and called the surrounding towns for assistance. Within minutes, the area was flooded with the sound of sirens and the sight of flashing emergency lights.

As the EMTs loaded the lieutenant in the ambulance, Richard walked over and talked with him. "Chris, you relax and do what you're told. I'll finish here and see you later."

He watched his officers handle the prisoners, and, when everything was completed, he got in his car and left. He stopped at the dispatch office before going to the hospital. When he walked inside the office, he saw a red-eyed Tracy sitting at the dispatch panel.

"Oh … hi … Chief," she stammered. "How is Lieutenant Allen?"

"He's fine. I want to talk with you in that office," he said, pointing to one of the open doors. Tracy got up and started toward the door, her mind racing with fear.

Tracy was a single mother who had had a very tough time making ends meet until she landed the dispatcher position. She loved being a dispatcher and the pay and benefits greatly exceeded what she had received in other jobs. Now she was sure that she was about to lose everything.

When she entered the office, she started, "Chief, I can explain—"

"Tracy, have a seat."

Tracy took a seat across from the desk where Richard was sitting.

"I listened to the call. I know what the lieutenant said to you. That's why I was at the hotel. However, you didn't follow operational procedures. You're supposed to send backup in situations like tonight's. In the future, you're to follow procedures to the letter. I don't care what the officer on duty tells you. Is that clear?"

Tracy was confused. She expected to be fired, and the Chief was talking about what to do in the future.

"Yes, Chief, I understand. You're not firing me?"

"No, Tracy, I'm not. You're a very good employee, and I never told you directly how to handle orders that are in conflict with protocol. Now get back to work. I know we won't have to have this conversation again."

"Thank you, Chief. You're right. We won't."

By the time Richard arrived at the hospital, Chris was in a room on the third floor. "Hi, Chris. They tell me that you'll survive your injuries and be out of here tomorrow."

"Hi, Dick ... I mean, Chief. The knife didn't hit anything vital, and the leg isn't broken. I had a bad knee from playing football, and the kick aggravated it."

"That's good information."

"Chief, you saved my ass tonight, and all I've ever been is a pain in yours. I've been thinking. If you decide to fire me, I'll understand. There'll be no complaint from me, but if you'll give me another chance, I'll do whatever you say: training, procedures, no more drinking with my buddies, and no more embarrassing situations. You don't have any reason to believe me, but I give you my word."

Richard was staggered. *Where the hell is this coming from?* He thought. *Did they put Chris on some kind of medication that's making him talk like this? Has he figured out I'm going to throw the book at him?* Whatever was going on, he decided, it was not something he was going to discuss now.

"Let's talk about it after you get back on your feet. All I want you to do is take it easy."

Richard left and went home for a couple of hours of sleep. He would certainly need it if, as he anticipated, Theo demanded his presence at a council meeting in the morning.

Theo's call came as expected, and Richard arrived at the council chamber at five minutes past eight.

"Chief Moore, I understand you allowed Lieutenant Allen to respond to a potentially serious situation without backup. I also understand you knew of the situation and failed to lend assistance until the Lieutenant was in danger of losing his life. Your actions were in direct violation of your own procedures and a gross dereliction of duty. What have you to say for yourself?"

"Theo, members of the council, you're correct. Lieutenant Allen responded to last night's situation without an assigned backup. I knew of the situation and went to the scene to observe. The situation degraded quickly, and I responded once I determined that the lieutenant was in a dangerous situation. Unfortunately, he was injured before I could assist."

"Injured?" Theo scoffed, "My god! He was nearly killed! Your incompetence endangered his life, and you obviously—"

"Theo, you have no idea what you're talking about!"

The comment had come booming from the rear of the council chamber, and the entire startled assembly turned in that direction. There, standing as straight and tall as he could on crutches, was Lieutenant Christopher Allen. Although he was wearing a civilian suit with the right pant leg split to accommodate a cast, he was in command of the group of uniformed officers surrounding him.

"I was there. I was the one who violated procedures. Chief Moore interceded at peril to his own life to keep the attackers from me." He moved further into the chambers. "This man, Chief Moore, took on three very determined and dangerous men by himself. He subdued them and tended to me. I think it's time we recognize that Chief Moore is an excellent commander. This town should be honored to have him as police chief. It's a privilege for me to work for him, and, if he'll allow me, it would be an honor to continue to work for him. As for you, Theo, you need to leave Chief Moore alone and let him continue to do the excellent work he has been doing."

Theo nearly had a stroke.

Richard smiled to himself as he pulled up in front of the restaurant to meet Lieutenant Allen. Chris had been true to his word. He followed every procedure to the letter. He participated in training sessions, stuck to operational protocols, and left his car home whenever he went out with his friends.

During dinner, Richard told Chris his suspicions about Jim Hall's death. He asked Chris if he remembered anything about Jim's death.

"Not a thing, Chief. Everyone was sure Jim had a terrible accident. How do you want to proceed with this?"

"I'm not sure. I mean, there haven't been any other suspicious accidents in the town. If I start investigating Jim's death, I may cause undue tension. I think I'll gather information discreetly. If anything unusual comes up, then I may reopen the file. Until then I—"

A crashing sound from outside interrupted Richard's comments. Both men looked out the window and saw two cars sitting in the middle of an intersection. Apparently, both cars attempted to pass through the intersection from different angles at the same time.

"I better go and help," Chris said, as he got up.

Just as he started for the door, he stopped and said, "Oh, by the way. I stopped that trucker like you asked."

"Any new information?"

"Joan Ripley isn't the owner operator. Turns out she was substituting for the regular driver, who is the owner. He told me he contracted with a temp agency that week because he was on vacation. Apparently, Joan Ripley only drove the route that night. I contacted the agency and asked them to send over the file they have on Joan."

"That's great," Richard replied with an exasperated tone. "Theo will love to hear this. Why don't we see if we can track her down? Check the national databases. She should pop up someplace."

"I started a network search for information about her. Rest assured; Theo won't hear anything about this from me. See you later, Chief."

29

Ghost was relieved by the media coverage of the "Sheep Fold Sniper" story. Citing "an anonymous, highly-placed source close to the investigation," most news outlets reported that the police were proceeding on the theory that the shootings were random. Alternative speculation made the news when the rumor about Richard being the target of a drug cartel hit contract surfaced, however, that speculation quickly withered.

The random shooting theory prevailed, in part, because it gave the media a more sensational story, and they could milk it for a longer time than they might with the other possibilities. The police denial that the leak had come from anyone close to the investigation, helped fuel the media's coverage of the incident.

When he returned to his motel room from the shooting, he made a call on the dedicated cell phone he had been given. When the distorted voice answered, Ghost described what had happened at the Sheep Fold. After he was through, there was a long silence before the person on the other end spoke.

"I am very disappointed with today's efforts. You've left things very untidy Tell me how you are going to clean them up."

"You wanted the kid out of the way first. He may survive the shooting, but he is out of the way for now—"

The voice interrupted, "Okay, you're right. You did your job with the kid, but you can't go after the cop again."

"Not directly, but I have a feeling our meddlesome chief is about to commit suicide."

"Suicide? Why would he do that, and how will you pull it off?"

"I have some details to work out. Once I have the whole plan, I'll fill you in."

"No need, just get him out of the picture without more publicity. What about the other target?"

"Since I couldn't take down as many people as I wanted today, I'll use the other target to provide the police with another random shooting victim. I'll take care of the chief when my plans are complete, and the sniper will strike the next day just in time for the evening news. The media, cops, and politicians will be so concerned about a sniper on the loose; chances are that the chief's death will be ignored."

"Yes. That sounds as though it will work." A pause produce a void in the air, then the voice said, "By the way, you should know better than to keep secrets from me. I know all about your connection to the chief." With that, the line went dead.

He was surprised the client knew about him and Richard. After he left the SAIF program, he had gone to great lengths to erase his past and disappear. How and how much did the client know about him? Why had the client bothered to find out? Was it just to impress him, or was it something else? One thing was for sure: Ghost was impressed, and he'd be watching his back even more carefully in the future.

The day Richard interrupted Bryan Hayden's lunch outside the Trinity Church, Ghost was tailing him. When Richard arrived home at ten that night, Ghost, camouflaged and geared up for night work, was hunkered down behind the building. About a half hour after Richard came out of the garage and climbed the backstairs to his apartment Ghost saw the kitchen lights go out and the bedroom lights come on. A half hour later, the bedroom lights went off.

Ghost waited another thirty minutes then entered the garage through the side door. Inside he took out his out his listening device and pointed it toward Richard's bedroom. Almost immediately, he heard the characteristic sounds of breathing associated with a deep, drug-induced sleep. He smiled; the drug had worked.

In the SAIF program, Ghost had access to many drugs developed by the CIA's Technical Services Staff. One of these, APD-6, is derived from acetylpromazine, a tranquilizer commonly used as an anesthetic in veterinary medicine. In its oral form, APD-6 is a clear, odorless, tasteless liquid capable of inducing a deep coma-like sleep about one-half hour after ingestion. It dissolves in most liquids, and, because it produces the desired effect regardless of dosing, there is little concern over the victim drinking too little or too much. Traces of APD-6 generally disappear from blood and tissue about an hour after it takes effect, so it can be used to immobilize a victim immediately prior to death with little or no chance of postmortem detection. With all of these characteristics, the Agency was optimistic about its potential, but it was very expensive to produce, highly unstable, and ineffective in about fifty percent of the intended victims. For these reasons, it is rarely used, and Ghost himself had only used it successfully once.

Earlier that evening, he had entered Richard's apartment and poured a small container of APD-6 into the carton of milk in the refrigerator. Richard's nightly glass of milk was such a constant in his life, that, during his Army days, he carried powdered milk into the field. His troops had affectionately dubbed him, "The Milkman."

After a few minutes of listening to Richard breath, he put the listening device back in a pocket of his black fatigues, and prepared to leave. Before going, he opened the driver's door on Richard's car, then lowered the back of the driver's seat. Stepping out the side door of the garage, he closed it, unlocked, behind him, then quickly went to the back of the house and climbed the stairs to Richard's apartment. After he let himself in, he checked Richard, and, after reassuring himself Richard was unresponsive but alive, went to the refrigerator and opened the door. Inside, was an open carton of milk that he removed and took to the bathroom along with a fresh carton he had brought with him. In the bathroom, he opened the fresh carton, poured some of its contents into the hopper, and then emptied the other container. After flushing everything down, he folded the empty carton and put it into a plastic bag before stuffing it intone of the pockets of his fatigues. He took the fresh container of milk back to the kitchen, set it on the table, and went to the dishwasher. Opening it, he removed the only glass with a residue of liquid milk, washed the glass, swished a little fresh milk around in it, and put it back into the dishwasher. Finally, he closed the container of fresh milk and put it in the refrigerator.

Having removed all traces of the APD-6, Ghost went into the bedroom, pulled off the covers, and began dressing Richard in the bed. When he was through, he knelt beside the bed, rolled Richard's body onto his arms, and gently lowered him to the floor. He made the bed, carefully smoothing out the bedding to erase any sign that it had been occupied.

Kneeling beside Richard, he rolled him into a face down position, then slid around until he was directly behind Richard's head. Hooking his elbows under Richard's shoulders, he stood, pulling Richard into a standing position facing him. With his right arm between Richard's legs, he lifted Richard's body face down against his shoulders before straightening again. Now, just moments after he had knelt beside Richard, he was standing erect with Richard held firmly in place across his upper back.

Carefully, he maneuvered his way out of the bedroom, across the kitchen and out onto the landing. Closing the door with his free left hand, he quickly headed down the stairs, turned the corner, opened the garage door, stepped inside, and closed the door behind him. After stopping a moment for a breath, he moved to the open car door, knelt down facing the front of the car, and rolled Richard off his back onto the seat. Lifting Richard's legs into the car, he pulled Richard's torso around. Richard was now lying with his back against the semi-reclined back of the driver's seat. When he was through positioning Richard, Ghost took a few moments to straighten the man's clothes and comb his hair. He raised the back of the seat. Richard was sitting as upright as possible without flopping to either side. Next, he slipped the key into the ignition, turned it to the accessory position, and rolled all the windows down. Finally, he took the framed picture out of his fatigues, pressed the glass against Richard's lips, then placed the picture in Richard's hands.

For the next few minutes, he reviewed everything he had done since he had entered the garage the first time, going through a mental checklist to ensure he had made no mistakes. After that, he surveyed the garage one last time, accounted for all his equipment, and removed the booties from his shoes. All he had to do now was finish the job.

Returning to the car, he leaned inside, turned the key, and started the engine. For a moment, he looked down at the sleeping man, then, smiling, said softly, "Have a nice trip," before gently closing the car door and leaving the garage.

Joel Kobb and three other men in their twenties lived in a gray colonial house several streets from Richard. They had been, for the most part, good neighbors. They kept their property well maintained and the three men were generally quiet. Occasionally, at one of their weekly poker games, too many men and too much beer resulted in things getting raucous, and the neighbors called the police.

Officer Tara Lorenzo was on duty that night and responded to the call of a disturbance at the Kobb residence. Kobb and his friends had always heeded the advice of the officers to break up the game and quiet down, so no one expected any trouble. Following procedure, however, when Lieutenant Allen heard the call, he responded as Officer Lorenzo's backup. As Christopher pulled in front of the Kobb house, Tara was walking back to her squad car.

"Hi, Lieutenant. They lost sight of time and didn't realize how loud they had gotten. They're breaking up and going home."

"Okay, Tara, I'll be on my way."

On the day after the Sheep Fold shootings, when Richard declined Allen's offer to watch his back, the young lieutenant decided to go ahead and do it anyway. Allen quietly tracked the chief's whereabouts and checked his safety. After leaving Officer Lorenzo, therefore, he drove to Richard's and swung into the driveway. With his flashlight in hand, he got out of his cruiser intending to check around. Close to the garage, he heard the sound of an automobile engine running inside and, going to the side door, knocked on it. When he got no response, he looked up and saw that there were no lights on anywhere in the house. Making a quick decision, he put his shoulder to the door and shoved several times until the lock broke and the door flew open. A wave of warm noxious air swept over him, and he started to cough. He stopped and pointed his flashlight at the car and saw Richard sitting in the front seat, slightly tilted backward, his eyes shut. Chris went over and shook him and he just slumped over on his side. Reaching inside the car, he shut off the engine and pushed the garage door opener button. Instantly, light filled the garage and the door began to roll up. As it did, he opened the car door, grabbed Richard by the shoulders, pulled him out of the car, and dragged him out to the driveway. When a quick assessment revealed that Richard was still breathing, he turned him on his side, then called dispatch, telling Tracy the Chief was down and needed medical assistance, and he needed backup.

A few minutes later, Tara Lorenzo's cruiser roared up with its lights flashing, followed quickly in succession by another Winchendon cruiser, the fire department rescue truck, a third Winchendon cruiser, the Winchendon ambulance, several police cruisers from nearby towns, the fire chief, and, finally, Phil Brice, the photographer. Chris sent Tara and the other officer to check Mrs. Hall, and stayed with Richard until the firefighter EMT's arrived a few moments later. When the ambulance arrived, he called Tara and told her he was sending an EMT into the house to assess Leslie Hall. As the other police units arrived, he told them he was treating the area as a crime scene, and assigned them to various tasks, including a search of the garage, the car, and Richard's apartment. Phil Brice arrived shortly after Chris had spoken with David Cromwell, the fire chief. Chris told Phil to take pictures of all the areas that were being searched. In the meantime, both Richard, and, as a precautionary measure, Mrs. Hall, were taken to the hospital.

30

Richard awoke to find a tube stuck down his throat, a tube going into his bladder, electrodes stuck to his chest, and an IV in each of his arms. He could not talk; he could not move his limbs; and he had no idea where he was. He could move his head, however, and when he looked to his right, he was surprised to see Doc Fenton asleep in a chair. Turning his head made the tube irritate his throat, and he began to gag, causing the old man's eyes to pop open. Fenton got up, went to the bed, stuck a syringe into a small rubber port in one of the IV's, and, a few seconds later, Richard felt a warmth spreading through his body. The medication must have put him back to sleep, because he was opening his eyes again and his throat was sore. It took a moment to realize that the tube in his throat was gone, but when he tried to speak, the pain in his throat got much worse and all that came out was a croaking noise. A nurse he recognized appeared at the bedside.

She took his hand and said, "Chief, don't try to talk, it'll hurt like the dickens if you do. We had to put a tube down your throat to help you breath for a while. It's out now, but it left your throat pretty raw and sore. You'll be able to talk in a little while, and the pain will go away completely in a day or so. You've had an accident and you're in the Critical Care Unit at the Winchendon Hospital. You got here about two hours ago, and it's three in the morning now. You've had a rough time, but you're going to be okay. I'm right here by your bed, so try to get some more sleep."

Richard had a thousand questions he wanted to ask her, but before he could try to say anything, he faded out again.

The next time he woke, Chris was looking down at him. Richard croaked up at him, "Chris, what happened? How did I get here?"

Allen gave Richard a synopsis of what he had found in the garage, how he had responded, and how he had handled the investigation.

When he was through, Richard said, "Thanks for saving my life. I have no idea how I wound up in that car. The last thing I remember before waking up here is falling asleep in my bed."

"Chief, the only conclusion that makes sense is that someone has you in his sights. You were almost shot and asphyxiated. That someone isn't going to stop until he succeeds. I—"

"Chris, my voice is giving out again. Do you mind if we continue this later?"

"Oh, sure, Chief. I'm sorry. I should have realized—well, anyway, I'll let you get some rest. I have to get back to the station to finish my report and hold the fort for you."

"Thanks, Chris."

After Richard and Mrs. Hall had been taken to the hospital, Chris remained on the scene, directing the investigation. By the time the sun came up, he had released all the officers except one, had Richard's car towed to the police lot, arranged to have Mrs. Hall's garage door fixed, and found an off-duty officer willing to relieve the one he was leaving at the scene. He then left the scene, paid a visit to Richard, and Mrs. Hall, then returned to his office.

Just as he was finishing his preliminary report, the phone rang. When he answered it and heard the voice on the other end, he groaned inwardly; it was Theo Reuben.

"Lieutenant, Allen, I just wanted to be the first to congratulate you on saving the life of the innocent townswoman who was almost killed by the actions of that suicidal maniac. This just proves what I've said all along, you're the one who should be wearing the chief's hat in this town and, by the end of today, come hell or high water, you will be wearing it."

Chris started to protest, but Theo cut him off.

"Your loyalty to your boss does you credit, my boy. I know you're in a difficult position in this matter, but you won't be much longer. Sorry, I have to run. It's going to be a busy day for me." With that, he hung up.

What an asshole, thought Chris. *It's an embarrassment to think that I let him manipulate me the way he used to.*

The day shift was just beginning, so he briefed them, and then asked Sergeant McKenzie, who was the shift commander that day, to bring Mrs. Hall home from the hospital. After McKenzie left on supervisory patrol, Chris briefed Jill Bailey, and then asked if there was anything he needed to do in the chief's absence. She told him that she had everything under control, and she would keep him pointed in the right direction as she did for the chief. Jill was the clerical person Richard had promoted to replace the two clerical officers now assigned to patrol. Since her promotion, she had quietly reorganized and modernized the department's paperwork and clerical procedures, allowing officers to spend more time on patrol and less in the office. She also functioned as the chief's executive secretary. The officers held her in awe, and Chris was relieved rather than annoyed by her response.

Since he had been up all night, and had no idea when he would be off duty again, Chris told that he was going to try to get a couple of hours sleep in one of the cells. She said that was an excellent idea.

An hour later, she called him and told him Ben Carney, the town solicitor, needed to speak with him. When he arrived back from the cells, Carney asked if they could speak in private in Chris's office. It turned out that Ben had a subpoena from Judge Rafferty ordering Chris to provide the Town Council all records and evidence pertaining to his investigation of the incident at the chief's residence.

Chris said, "Can they really make me do this, Ben?"

Carney replied, "Well, since this in an investigation of the chief, himself, Rafferty has the right to keep him from accessing material related to it. I'll admit that handing it to the Council is an odd way of doing it, but Rafferty and Theo Rueben are buddies, and Rueben is the one who persuaded the Council to ask for it. The whole Council has been huddled in closed session since eight, and they dragged me in to get my advice. Now, they have me running around like their messenger boy, first to the judge to get the subpoena, and now here to get the stuff. I have a feeling it's going to be a long day. Anyway, Chris, you do have to give me the stuff."

After Carney left with the subpoenaed material, Chris thought for a few minutes, and then called the hospital and checked the chief's condition. They told him Richard was listed as stable, and had been moved from Critical Care to a private room. It was good news, and he thought about letting Richard know about Theo's call and Ben's visit. In the end, however, he decided the chief needed more time to recuperate from his ordeal.

At 1:00 P.M., however, Carney returned with a memo from the Council that read:

To: Lieutenant Christopher Allen, Winchendon Police Department.
From: The Honorable Franklin Della Russo, President, Winchendon Town Council

In the absence of the chief of the department, you will present yourself before the Council at 3 P.M. today to assist the Council in its investigation into the case of Mr. Richard Moore, as well as its deliberations on the future leadership of the Winchendon Police Department.

The lieutenant looked up from the note.
"Ben, what is this all about?"
"Like it or not, Chris, Moore's suicide attempt has given Theo just the ammunition he needs to dump the chief, and he's been firing it at the other council members all morning. As it stands now, he almost has the majority he needs to do it. Bringing you in is just the move to put him over the top. He's been portraying you as the humble hometown hero who saved a local woman from an arrogant, disturbed outsider. Now he's going to trot you out in the flesh. A vote to retain the chief will be a vote against you, the town hero, standing right there in front of them in the flesh."
"Is he crazy? Doesn't he know I'll defend the chief?"
"Look, Chris, don't underestimate Theo. He's not the slickest guy in the world, but he's nobody's fool, either. He has your appearance before the Council all scripted out. He'll be asking the questions, and the only questions he'll ask are ones with answers that will make the chief look bad. Even if you manage to say something to support the chief, he's been spreading the rumor for months that the chief has somehow forced you to stop criticizing him. He's going to use you to give the chief the coup de grace."

After Ben left, Chris sat at his desk wondering how to beat Theo's plan. After a few minutes, he picked up the note and read it again. Something about what it said, nagged at the edge of his mind. He read it again carefully, and then repeated each word aloud. Six words hit him, and he knew what he was going to do, or, at least, what he would try to do!

Picking up the note and heading out of his office, he thought, *No, Theo, you're not going to use me again. Not if I can help it.*

Chris told Jill the Town Council had summoned him, and he was going home to clean up. He did not go home; however, instead, he went to the hospital and found the chief's room. To his relief, the man looked and sounded better than he had earlier. Quickly, he told Richard everything that had occurred since their earlier meeting, and, when he finished, handed Richard the note. When Richard finished reading it, Chris told him about his idea.

Richard smiled at this young protégé. "Lieutenant Allen, I'm afraid I've been a bad influence on you. That's a very devious idea—a damn good one—but very devious."

"Well, Chief, are you well enough to do this? I mean, you look and sound better, but how do you feel?"

"My throat's still sore from the breathing tube, and my left arm is sore."

"Is the gunshot wound bothering you?"

"The nurse says one of the emergency room docs looked in on me while I was out and discovered the wound had opened. A couple of the stitches had popped, so he took them out and replaced them. However, Lieutenant Allen, if you'll just help me escape from this sanitized cell, I'll promise not to die on you."

It took some persuading and, it almost gave Doc Fenton apoplexy, but, at 3:00 P.M. sharp, Richard walked into the council chamber in full uniform.

His entrance was greeted with stunned silence, and Theo looked as if he had just swallowed his tongue. He recovered it quickly enough, however. "What is the meaning of this? Where is Lieutenant Allen? Why aren't you—"

Frank Della Russo's gaveling cut him off.

"Theo, I'm running this meeting. You will get your chance to ask questions after I ask mine."

Turning his attention to Richard, he said, "Chief, aren't you supposed to be in the hospital? We had been informed you were in the Critical Care Unit."

"Yes, Mr. President, I was taken to the hospital last night, but my condition quickly improved, and I was discharged."

"Well, Chief, I'm glad to hear that, but why are you here? We requested Lieutenant Allen's presence. Where is he?"

Richard reached into his pocket and removed the note that Allen had given him. "Mr. President, your note to the lieutenant requests his presence, 'in the absence of the chief.' As you can see, Mr. President, I am not absent. I have returned to work, and the lieutenant is at the station, executing his duties as my second-in-command. I will be happy to answer any questions you had planned to put to him."

Della Russo hesitated then said, "Chief, would you mind showing me that note?"

Richard handed him the note, which he looked at for a moment before passing it around to the other council members.

When it was returned to him, Della Russo did not seem to know what to do next, then, suddenly, he asked, "Do any of the members have any questions for the chief?"

With a tinge of sarcasm, Theo replied, "If you will permit me, Mr. President, I have some questions."

"Yes, Theo, go right ahead."

"Thank you, Mr. President. Chief Moore, thank you for coming this afternoon. I hope you are feeling well." *You clever bastard,* he thought. *I bet you think you've caught me with my pants down with your little note trick, but I'm not going to let you wriggle out of this one so easy. I've got a few tricks of my own.*

"Thank you for your concern, Councilman Reuben," replied Richard. "As you can hear, my voice is a little hoarse, and my throat is a little sore, but I've been told that will improve quickly."

"Well, I'm glad to hear that, Chief. Tell me, do you know how Mrs. Hall is doing? I understand she was taken to the hospital as well."

"She's back home. She had been admitted as a precaution."

"Oh, so you've seen her, and talked with her, and, hopefully, apologized for endangering her life?"

"I don't understand what you mean about endangering her life."

"Isn't it true that if it wasn't for Lieutenant Allen's prompt and heroic action, both you and Mrs. Hall would have died of carbon monoxide poisoning?"

"It's certainly true that the lieutenant saved my life, and, quite possibly, Mrs. Hall's. Lieutenant Allen is a fine officer, and—"

"You don't need to tell me Lieutenant Allen is a fine officer, Chief. I've been saying that to this Council and anyone who would listen for two years. He's not only a fine officer, he's a fine man. Frankly, Chief, I must say he's a finer officer and a better man than you are. He's not so cowardly that he would run away from his problems by attempting suicide, and he's not so callous that he wouldn't care if he took the life of an innocent victim in the process!"

"I'm not sure where the notion I tried to commit suicide came from, or why you are making that assumption without asking me first, but —"

"I'll tell you why we know, not assume, but know, you attempted suicide. Lieutenant Allen, not only saved you and Mrs. Hall, while you were sleeping off the effects of your own actions, he was up all night, conducting a thorough investigation of the incident and completing his report it time for us to make a thorough study of it." He held a file folder up for emphasis. "That report states you were found in a locked garage, sitting inside your car, unconscious and fully dressed, with the motor running and all the car windows rolled down."

Before Theo could go on, Richard said, "I have no idea how I came to be in the car. The last thing I remember is going to sleep in my bed."

"Oh, come on, Moore! Neither the apartment nor the garage showed any sign of forced entry, and your bed had not been slept in. Do you want us to believe somebody could actually get into your apartment, get you dressed, make your bed, carry you down to the garage, load you in the car start the engine, and leave, all without waking up you, or Mrs. Hall, or half the neighborhood, or leaving a trace? Who was it, a homicidal sandman? Maybe what happened is you were sleepwalking. That's it, isn't it, Chief? You got up sleepwalking, got dressed, made your bed, tiptoed unseen down to the garage, started the engine, rolled down the windows, then fell back into a sound sleep. I know you don't have a very high opinion of us, but do you take us for a bunch of fools?"

Richard's throat was beginning to throb, he had a headache, and he was beginning to feel battered by Theo's assault. He was also running out of patience with the man.

"Theo, I really don't have all the facts. I received a quick briefing this morning while I was still in Critical Care, and another briefing before coming to this meeting. It's too early for anyone to jump to any conclusions about this incident,"

"That's right, Moore, you don't have all the facts, or all the evidence, but, we do." With that, he dramatically held up a large plastic evidence bag, Inside, clearly visible, was the inscribed picture of Lori Moore. "When he found you in the car, Lieutenant Allen found this picture on your lap. It's obvious what happened here, Chief. You're a sick man, sick with grief over your wife's suicide, and last night you decided you would join her by committing suicide in the same sick way she—"

Richard leaped across the table, knocking Theo out of his chair. With his right hand firmly around Theo's throat, Richard picked him up and pinned him against the wall. Theo's feet were dangling several inches off the floor.

"You don't know anything about my wife. If you ever bring her name or memory into one of these meetings again, it will be the last time."

Pandemonium broke loose in the chamber: one of the women screamed, several of the men started yelling, Ben Carney and two councilmen, jumped up and began frantically trying to pry Richard from Theo. The only person not moving, screaming, or yelling was Frank Dell Russo; he was frozen in shock, his eyes glazed, and his mouth agape.

Alerted by Ben Carney about the afternoon meeting, Bill Blackstone had slipped in unobserved earlier and was following the proceedings when Richard launched his attack on Theo. While the others were prying the two apart, Blackstone went to the immobilized Della Russo and spoke to him sharply. Della Russo immediately began banging his gavel loudly. Richard released

Theo and stalked out of the chamber. Blackstone hurried after him. While Ben Carney tended to the dazed Theo, the suddenly energized Della Russo hurriedly gathered the remaining Council members, and adjourned the meeting until the morning.

It took Theo ten minutes to get on his feet, and, as he did, Blackstone returned to the chamber. When Theo saw him, he began shouting, "Where the hell is that lunatic? I'm going to ruin that son-of-a-bitch. He'll never work another day in law enforcement."

"Calm down, Theo," said Bill, quietly.

Theo said, "Screw you, Blackstone. You're the reason that nutcase was hired. He damned near killed Leslie Hall last night and me today, and all you can say is 'Calm down'?" Turning to the remaining Council members, he said, "I move we fire Moore effective immediately. No benefits. No severance. This firing is for cause. I also move that we direct Lieutenant Allen to place Moore under arrest for attempted murder."

Frank Della Russo said, "Ah, Theo, the Council has been adjourned until tomorrow morning at eight."

Theo began to sputter, "You, you can't do that! I had the floor! You can't entertain a motion to adjourn when someone has the floor!"

Della Russo looked as if he wished he were elsewhere else. "Ah, Theo, I'm afraid the parliamentarian has already left, so we'll have to take up your issue in the morning." With that, he hurriedly closed his briefcase and left.

Theo rounded on Blackstone.

"You, you did this, you conniving son of a bitch! Well, you're not going to get away with it. I'm going to the station right now and swear out a complaint against that homicidal maniac. He's going to spend the night in jail, and tomorrow morning we're going to fire his ass."

Had Theo been less upset and more observant, he would have seen Blackstone's body stiffen, and a ghost of anger flit across the man's face. Rather than returning Theo's outburst in kind, however, Blackstone exercised his highly developed self-control and, calmly, said, "That's your privilege, Theo. Allow me to point out, however, that the media interest in the chief caused by the shootings has died down. If he's arrested for the attempted murder of a Town Council member, the press will be all over the story looking for a connection with the shootings. Personally, I'd hate to have some of those investigative reporters from Boston poking their noses into my business looking for that kind of dirt. In the meantime, get that throat looked at. It's getting a little black and blue. Good afternoon, Theo."

Blackstone's matter-of-fact manner and words affected Theo more profoundly than any threats he could have made. By the time the man had said his piece and left, Theo's mood had swung dramatically from fury to fear. The thought of what could happen if a pack of bloodhound reporters descended on the town made him nauseated. He could not shake the image of himself and a furious, lethal Carlos locked together in the same cell. After sitting for some time staring at nothing, he put his papers in his briefcase and left the chamber. Instead of driving to the police station, however, he went home to get himself a stiff drink. When he got there, he found an urgent message waiting for him, and, using the usual procedure, contacted Carlos.

The phone was picked up after two rings, and Carlos immediately began to speak. "Theo, my friend, I heard about last night's incident involving your beloved police chief. I think he has removed himself from office. By tomorrow night, I expect that we will be celebrating that happy event. Please do not disappoint me; I get so grouchy when I expect to go to a party and it is canceled." Before Theo could respond, the line went dead.

Bill Blackstone also went home, but only had one drink, which he nursed through several pre-dinner phone calls. After eating, he spent the rest of the evening making phone calls.

31

At eight, the next morning, when Della Russo opened the Council session, every member was present. Ben Carney was present to provide legal guidance. Council sessions regarding town personnel were closed-door meetings. Bill Blackstone, however, sat in the chamber. When the preliminaries were over, Theo immediately demanded to know why Blackstone was present at a closed session of the Council. Della Russo informed him that another member had requested Blackstone's presence. It was obvious to everyone that Theo did not like the idea, but, considering his usual demeanor and yesterday's events, his protest was subdued and short.

When Theo finished, Della Russo turned to Matt Praxton, another Council member. "Matt, I understand you have a request. The floor is yours."

"Thank you, Mr. President. Since one of our leading citizens, Mr. William Bradford Blackstone was largely responsible for bringing Chief Moore to Winchendon; I thought it was only fair this Council hear what he has to say about the matter of the chief's future. Mr. Blackstone, you have the podium."

As Blackstone walked to the podium, Theo rolled his eyes sarcastically, but said nothing.

"President, Della Russo, Councilman Praxton, and honorable members of the Council, I thank you for the opportunity to say a few words about this matter. Before you resume your deliberations, I would like you to consider Chief Moore's performance—"

"His performance?" Theo interjected, cutting Blackstone off. "His performance is exactly why we ought to fire him!"

His words ushered in a silence that hung in the air like a fog. Blackstone bowed his head slightly, pulled his glasses down on his nose, then stared silently at Theo over their tops. The effect was that of a stern schoolmaster eyeing a recalcitrant child. After several moments, Theo shifted uncomfortably in his chair, made a sound in his throat, and then lowered his gaze to the papers on the table in front of him. After a few more moments, Blackstone slowly pushed his glasses back into place and continued speaking.

MULTIPLES

"As I was saying, I think you should look at his performance. He has done everything you asked of him. When he came here, we were the drug distribution center for the area, drugs were being manufactured here, we had drug dealers all over the place, and drugs were being sold to our schoolchildren on school grounds. He devised a plan to deal with the problem. Under his leadership, the plan was expertly executed. He has vigilantly monitored the situation. Because of that, the drug situation is under control and that problem never made it to the state's news media. As a bonus, other crimes like robbery are at their lowest level in a decade. Even traffic violations are down. In two short years, he has taken an incompetent and ineffective police force and turned it into a model community constabulary, while, at the same time, keeping budgetary increases to a minimum. By every measure we have, he has increased public safety, and with it, public confidence in, and public support for the police. Amazingly, he has done all of this while spending more time here explaining himself to this body, than most of us do explaining ourselves to our spouses."

As he had expected, the members smiled or chuckled, and he paused for a few moments before continuing. "I think it is plain from these facts that the town would have a hard time defending a dismissal based on cause as has been suggested."

At that point, a sound came from Theo, and Blackstone paused expectantly. If Theo was going to say something, however, he thought better of it, and after a few seconds, Blackstone resumed.

"As for the Chief's alleged suicide attempt, I would like to remind the Council that the investigation into that incident is ongoing, and we do not know what really happened at the chief's apartment. Now, some of you may not know it, but the chief made some powerful enemies cleaning up this town's drug problems. Rumors persist that a cartel has put a price on his head. These people know they cannot openly assassinate a police chief here as they do in Mexico, so they might try faking an accident or a suicide. I submit that in the light of these facts, removing the chief on grounds of mental instability or jeopardizing Mrs. Hall's life, would prove indefensible without further investigation."

He adjusted his glasses again, and, stared at Theo over the tops of them, saying, "Actually, to my knowledge, neither Mrs. Hall, nor anyone else, has file charges against Chief Moore."

He paused to readjust his glasses, starring at Theo all the time then continued, "Now, as most of you know, I am not an attorney, but I did discuss this situation with several prominent attorneys last night. They universally agreed that an attempt to dismiss the chief, without more evidence or stronger cause, would most certainly lead to a very messy, very public breach of contract suit. Of course the decision is yours to make, but I hope that you will all take my words under advisement."

"Thank you, Bill. Now if we can get on with the meeting, I make a motion—" Theo had been fidgeting in his seat during this part of Blackstone's presentation, and when Bill had paused for a moment after his last sentence, Theo had jumped into the void. Before he could complete his motion, however, Della Russo's frantic gaveling interrupted him.

"Hold on, Theo," said the exasperated Della Russo. "I'm still president of this Council, and I will decide when it is time to entertain motions."

Turning to Blackstone, he said, "Please excuse the interruption, Bill. Have you anything to add?"

"No, Mr. President. All I wish to do is to thank the Council for its courtesy. Now, I will withdraw and leave you to your deliberations."

Without another word, he left the chamber.

Della Russo watched him go, and then said, "The chair will now entertain motions."

Theo immediately said, "I move that Chief Moore be dismissed for cause without severance or benefits, and that Lieutenant Allen be appointed chief in his place, both actions to be effective immediately"

When the motion was seconded and there was no discussion, Della Russo said, "Theo has moved we fire Chief Moore with cause and appoint Lieutenant Allen in his place. I remind the council we have not met the contractual definition of cause, and we may be breaching the contract we have with Chief Moore. All in favor of Theo's motion?" Three raised their hands.

"All opposed? Three in favor and four opposed. The motion is defeated."

"This is a sham. The chief attempted suicide, while putting Mrs. Hall's life in jeopardy. We can't just let him go back to work as if nothing has happened. He should be fired!" protested Theo.

"Theo, I agree, we shouldn't let this go without some action." Everyone's head swiveled at once toward the end of the council table. Mary Cullen, a tiny woman who seldom attended meetings and seldom spoke up when present, was the speaker.

"Now I don't know whether he tried to kill himself or not, but I don't want that man running around the streets with a gun if there's the slightest possibility he could go off his nut and start shooting people before he kills himself. You hear about stuff like that on the news all the time.

"Here's what I think we should do: We should send him out on administrative leave with full pay and benefits pending the final results of the investigation into the incident at Leslie Hall's. We should also confirm Lieutenant Allen as acting chief in his absence. Now I got three reasons for giving him his pay and benefits: First, I don't want us to get sued for taking away his pay without cause; second, I don't think it's right to take away his pay when we really don't know if he's done something wrong; and third, if he really is a nut case, I don't want him blaming us 'cause he can't pay his bills, and coming in here and blowing us all away.

"Now Theo, I didn't vote with yah the first time around, because I didn't think it was right to dismiss the man without real proof, but if you make a motion to do like I just said, then I'll vote with yah. If the investigation proves he's a loony, I'll vote to have him locked up, and we can be rid of him for good."

For a few moments, everyone just sat and stared at her in wonder. It was the longest speech anyone on the Council had ever heard her make in the chamber. Some of them were wondering how she managed to get it all out. Then, people began to turn their heads toward Theo.

Theo was also staring at her in wonder, only he was wondering how he could have been so fortunate. Moments before, he had been terrified at the prospect of telling Carlos he had failed to remove Richard, and now this little woman was removing the chief for him, and letting him take the credit for it to boot. It wasn't a permanent dismissal, but, until that happy day occurred, Richard would no longer be interfering in Carlos's business, and Theo saw no point in going into the details of Richard's absence with the cartel boss.

"Theo, did you hear me?"

Theo blinked his eyes and came out of his reverie. "Yes Mary, I heard you, and I heard your excellent suggestion. If the rest of the Council will give us a few moments together, I'm sure we can draft a motion that will meet with your approval."

It took about six minutes to draft the motion. After that, there was some discussion, followed by some consultation with Ben Carney, followed by more discussion, but in the end, a motion passed. The motion said what Mary Cullen wanted it to say. The vote, to Theo's great relief, was a comfortable five to one, with one abstention.

A few hours later, Theo was on the phone with Carlos.

"Hello, Theo. What news have you for me today?"

"Moore will no longer be interfering with our business. Lieutenant Allen is now acting chief of the Winchendon Police Department."

"Well done, Theo. We will begin operations soon. I will be back in touch."

Around the same time Theo was being congratulated, Mary Cullen was being praised—by Bill Blackstone.

"I understand that you played your part perfectly, Mary. Theo bought it hook, line and sinker."

"It wasn't that hard to do, Bill. Theo was so hell bent for leather to get rid of the chief, I think he'd have voted to keep paying him his salary for the rest of his life, if he left town and never came back. I've never understood what he's got against the man, especially after what the chief has done for all our little schoolkids, getting rid of those vicious drug dealers and all. It's almost like he didn't care that the little tykes were getting hooked on drugs. You'd think he'd be one of those that'd be happiest that the chief was around, him being a druggist and knowing all about how dangerous all that stuff is. Makes me wonder about him to tell yah the truth. As for the chief doing anything to hurt Leslie, Bill, that's a crock. Leslie and I have been friends since we were kids together, and she adores him. Told me anyone says he would ever do anything to hurt her should have his mouth washed out with Lava soap. I'll tell yah another thing, Bill. I don't think for a minute that man would ever try to kill himself. Anybody can see the man is rock solid—wouldn't know a neurosis if it bit him. Anyway, Bill I didn't do what I did just because you asked me to. I did it because it was the right thing to do for the town. It'll be our loss if he goes someplace else. You take care now, Bill. John'll be coming home any minute and I have to get ready 'cause we're going down to Worcester to see those Shakespeare in the Park people perform As You Like It. Bye."

After Mary hung up, Blackstone thought about how remarkable she was.

Mary Cullen's spoken grammar was often marginally acceptable, yet she wrote exquisite poetry. She was a woman of few words, but when she decided she had something important to say, she was a force of nature and one of the most persuasive people he knew. It was that quality that had won her a place on the Town Council. Mary had been a part of his plan to manipulate Theo from the beginning. He knew he was going to use her to spring the final part of his trap even when he was talking to Richard the previous afternoon.

After Richard had throttled Theo and stalked out of the Council chamber, Bill Blackstone chased him.

"Chief, hold on for a minute."

"What can I do for you, Bill?"

"Just hold on for a minute, and get yourself together."

"Sorry, Bill. I played along with this idiot, but no one, especially Theo, has the right to talk about Lori that way. I cleaned up the town as we agreed, but this is too much. I'm finished."

"Look, Richard, I know you've put up with more than anyone else would have or should have in these meetings, and I appreciate it. Theo was way out of line just now, and I don't blame you for taking a crack at him. I also know that if you hadn't restrained yourself, he'd be dead now. Unfortunately, you played into his hands. If he didn't have the votes to remove you before, you gave them to him when you—"

"Sorry, you think that about me, Bill, but, if that's the case you—"

"Richard, please listen to me! I'm on your side. Let me finish what I was about to say."

"Okay, Bill, go ahead. I'm listening."

"Look, I wasn't inferring that you gave Theo the votes by attempting suicide if that's what you mean. You and I both know some very ugly and very resourceful people want to eliminate you. They have deep pockets, and, with enough money, they can sometimes do what looks like the impossible. I also know you well enough to know that, if you really wanted to commit suicide, you'd volunteer to work deep cover in Pakistan, and take as many terrorists as you could with you. You're not the type to go quietly and certainly not the type to risk taking an innocent woman with you.

"I was referring to the fact that you probably gave him the votes he needs when you collared him—"

Richard started to say something but Blackstone held up his hand and said, "I'm not finished, yet. As I was saying, he probably has the votes he needs, but the Council won't be voting today. Right now, while Theo is still in shock, a motion to adjourn is being passed. By the way, you didn't really hurt him, did you?"

"No. He might have to change his pants, but that's all."

"It'd serve him right if he did. Anyway, do you think Lieutenant Allen is ready to run the department?"

"Well, he's come a long way, and the department is in a hell of a lot better shape than it was when I got here, so he's not going to be running around all day dealing with his subordinate's screw-ups. And, of course, with Jill Bailey as office manager, the office work is practically automated. I'd say, the way things are set up now, he can handle the routine stuff on his own, and, with very little coaching, the little that isn't routine. Why do you ask? Is it your way of breaking it gently that you think the Council is going to cut me loose? If it is, don't worry. I'm more than ready to go."

"No, the Council will not fire you. With a little help, folks will be calmed down by the time the Council reconvenes tomorrow. Theo will make his motion, but it will be defeated. A motion will then be presented to put you on administrative leave pending the outcome of the investigation of your alleged suicide attempt. You'll receive full pay and benefits while on leave."

Richard asked, "And what will Theo be doing while this is happening?"

Blackstone smiled. "If I play my cards right, Theo will be the one who makes the motion. Whether he does or he does not, however, he will not have the votes to defeat it."

"And I called Chris Allen devious! Let me think. You're not just doing this just because you like me, are you? What's the catch?"

Blackstone smiled again. "The catch, I want you to finish the job I brought you here to do. I want you to provide behind the scenes consultation for Lieutenant Allen so, when you leave here, this town will have a good police department and a good chief to lead it, and I want you to spend the rest of your time finishing the other part of the job I brought you here to do. Now you'll have the time to do so unencumbered. I'll make sure Lieutenant Allen and Jill Bailey continue to give you access to all of the department's resources. If you want to work on that other thing you've been working on, you can do that too. Don't look surprised, I know all about your little death rate project."

Blackstone smiled, and then his handsome patrician face grew thoughtful.

"Richard, you did me and the town I love, a great turn by coming here. I'm a man of means, and a man who always pays his debts, but even if you left here now, I would be indebted to you for the rest of my life. Considering what you have endured since I first met you, I don't know how you have accomplished so much in such a short time. It would have broken a lesser man. Maybe it's just because of that, though, because of the kind of man I think you are, that I'm asking you to stay and finish the job we first talked about that day two and a half years ago."

The drug problem that had consumed so much of Richard's efforts when he became chief in Winchendon, was, in fact, the reason he had been recruited for the job.

Owen McDougall, Bill Blackstone's grandson, had been introduced to drugs when the Winchendon dealers started selling to the town's schoolchildren. When the young man died of an overdose, Blackstone vowed he would use all his resources and power to rid the town of drugs and ensure that no other family in the town would suffer a similar tragedy. He quickly found, however, that neither the town's police chief, nor the department he ran, was up to the task. The chief was approaching retirement age and was, for the most part, just putting in his time, and this was reflected in the way the department operated. Bill decided, therefore, that he would persuade the town to give the chief an early retirement and replace him with a commander capable of dealing with the problem.

He asked his network of friends, business associates, and political allies to help him find a suitable candidate, and eventually learned that Richard Moore, the commander of the Boston Police Department Antiterrorism Squad, was looking for a change. After looking closely at Richard's record, and speaking with some of Richard's friends, colleagues, and superiors, he decided that Richard was the best of the candidates that had come to his attention. The only flaw that Blackstone could see was that Moore had left a promising career in the Army after some traumatic event, and was now looking to leave the Boston Police Department after his wife's suicide.

Their first meeting took place at Richard's home. After the usual pleasantries, during which, Blackstone offered Richard condolences on the recent death of his wife, Blackstone described the situation in Winchendon. Then, he outlined the plan to replace the current chief with someone who could revitalize the police department and lead it in a successful campaign to eradicate the town's drug problem, and the crime associated with it.

When Blackstone finished, Richard said, "I don't really think I'm interested in spending the rest of my life as a small-town chief, and I'm certainly not interested in helping you remove your current chief from his job."

Blackstone said, "Captain Moore, do you mind telling me why you're thinking about leaving the Boston Police Department?"

"This is not a recent decision, Mr. Blackstone; it's something I've been thinking about for a while. I enjoy running my own show, and I'm good at it. I'm a very organized person and good at organizing. I've enjoyed the autonomy and challenge involved in building a fully functional antiterrorism squad from an idea sketched on paper to an organization as large and complex as the Department. Now that it's done, however, I'm looking for another challenge."

Blackstone thought for a moment then said, "You said you didn't want to be a small-town chief for the rest of your life. We don't need someone who wants to settle down as a small-town chief. We need someone who wants a challenge. We need someone who can whip our police force into shape, and rid us of our drug problem. Chances are someone who can do that successfully will want to move on once things aren't so challenging.

"You said you need autonomy. I have a great deal of influence in the town. I can guarantee that anyone who becomes chief there will be able to run their show, and will have whatever resources needed to do the job. Hell, I'd give the current chief the same thing, except he says he has all he can handle.

"That brings us to your concern about a fellow officer losing his job. It's his job is to keep the children of our town safe from drugs, and he's not doing it. Maybe he can't keep the drug trade entirely out of the area, but he could at least make it feel unwelcome. State statistics show we have the highest incidence of drug abuse for a town our size, and the lowest drug-related arrest rate. The man's only losing his job. My grandson lost his life, and many more children like him are losing the most important years of their lives.

"Whether you come to Winchendon or not, we are going to replace the current chief, and, considering his performance, he'll be getting a terrific deal: an early retirement incentive package that includes full benefits. He'll be able to get himself a cozy little job as head of security and put his feet up on his desk without harming anyone. We should all be so blessed, Captain.

"I'm sure you have other opportunities to explore, and I have other candidates to talk to, but I think it would be premature for either of us to end the dialogue at this stage. What do you think?"

Richard sat quietly for a few moments, before responding, "I do have other situations to look into, Mr. Blackstone, but I don't have any problem with continuing to discuss the Winchendon situation with you. What do you suggest?"

"Why don't we meet for lunch in two weeks?"

By the time the two men met for lunch, Blackstone had interviewed several other prospects and Richard had looked into several opportunities. The lunch went well, and they were soon on a first name basis. At its conclusion, they agreed to meet for dinner a week later.

During that week, Richard drafted a plan, complete with a list of needs, for assessing the Winchendon problems Blackstone researched deeper into Richard's experiences and became more impressed with him compared to the other prospects. When they met for dinner, they were both ready to begin a serious dialogue.

During the next few weeks, they met several times. Blackstone agreed to provide Richard with information and documentation that would allow Richard to do his own assessment of the situation in Winchendon.

Three weeks later, Richard presented his findings and recommendations to Blackstone.

He said the drug problem and the crime associated with it had reached the stage where cleaning it up quietly using local resources could easily take two years. The police department would have to be retrained and reorganized and provisions made to hire two new officers. Critical equipment needed to be purchased, but, more important, the department needed to do a better job maintaining and utilizing the equipment it already had. Funds would be needed to augment a strike force with temporary personnel when the department was finally ready to launch its comprehensive drug bust.

Finally, he said that with so much local and regional drug activity associated with the town, a cartel might be involved, and if so, they could have an agent in the police department or the town government. Access to critical information would have to be restricted, and patience exercised in attempting to expose that person.

"Do you really believe someone on the inside is working with the drug dealers?" Bill asked.

"Yes, Bill. The chief's incompetence can't be the only explanation for the way the drug dealers are thriving. Another factor is at work, and that's the most likely one."

After further discussing budgetary and administrative issues, Bill and Richard agreed in principle: Richard would become a formal candidate for the job, and Blackstone would lobby for his appointment. The next day, after a private meeting with Bill, Chief Mike Tuttle gave the notice of his intention to resign in eight weeks, and the town began its search for a successor.

Richard interviewed with the Town Council several times over the next few weeks. At first, Theo Reuben was the only member of the Council adamantly opposed to Richard's application. As the weeks passed, however, two other members voiced their opposition. An outside consultant was hired. The consultant reviewed the applicants and recommended Richard as the number one choice. The next day, the Council voted four to three to offer Richard the position. He accepted, handed in his resignation to the Boston Police Department, and became the Winchendon chief.

32

At Theo's insistence, Frank Della Russo informed Richard of the Council's decision. "Richard, the Town Council has voted to place you on administrative leave pending the outcome of the investigation into the incident at your apartment. You will receive full pay and benefits while on administrative leave."

A short time later, Richard was in his office, packing some personal items, when Chris entered. It was an understandably awkward moment for the young man.

"Hi, Chief, I hear that was some scene yesterday at the Council meeting. I wish I had been there to see it. I think I would have broken Theo's neck if I were you."

"Attacking Theo wasn't the smartest move I've ever made, Chris, and breaking his neck would have been a disaster. I just wanted to make sure Theo got my point loud and clear."

"I don't think he got it. He's too arrogant and full of himself."

"As acting chief, you better get used to dealing with him."

"Chief, ah … I … hope you know I didn't want this. If I had known Theo was going to use the incident at your apartment to push you aside, I'd've just dragged you out of that car and waited until you came around."

"If you had done that, you might be chief permanently instead of acting chief. Without the oxygen the medics gave me on the spot, I could have suffered permanent brain damage. Don't forget Mrs. Hall; she was still at risk inside that closed house. I've gotten a complete report on everything you did; including the way you conducted the investigation. I know nothing you did was underhanded. It was all excellent police work.

"Far from playing into Theo's hand, Chris, you nearly beat him at his own game by the clever way you interpreted Della Russo's note. I screwed up by grabbing him. That gave him what he needed to push me aside."

"Thanks for telling me this, Chief; it sure takes a load off my mind to know that Theo didn't really get at you through me."

After Chris left, Richard opened an envelope from Stuart Scott. It was postmarked on the Saturday before the shooting. He pulled out the computer disk it contained and put the disk into his computer. The disk contained a pass-protected Excel file, and there was nothing in or on the envelope that suggested what that password might be.

Richard decided to send the disk to Steve. When he left his office, he went directly to an overnight shipping store.

33

At the beginning of the Cold War, before the development of intercontinental ballistic missiles, most atomic weapons were bombs carried in the bellies of long-range bombers. To defend its population against such bombers, the United States initially surrounded each of its major cities with a ring of antiaircraft batteries on small parcels of land on the city outskirts. In the late nineteen fifties, antiaircraft missiles replaced the conventional guns. Missile launch bases were built in different locations from the guns. The military removed the guns and abandoned the gun locations. To clear the abandoned areas of any buildings and other structures the Army left behind, the federal government sold everything remaining on each site through a winner-take-all bidding process. The successful bidder would then have a set period, usually thirty days, to remove everything and clean the site to the specifications called for in the bid document.

One of the batteries defending Boston was in the Medford section of the Middlesex Fells Reservation, about one and a quarter miles southwest of the Sheep Fold. A winding woodland road, in fact, meanders its way from the Sheep Fold to an exit on South Border Road almost opposite the entrance to the gun site. When its contents were sold, the successful bidder was Don Carlin, a letter carrier who operated a part-time demolition company. Carlin had already successfully bid on and removed several buildings at military locations elsewhere in the state, and had developed a procedure that allowed him to make a small profit on each job.

Working afternoons, evenings, and weekends, Don and his sons, with periodic help from his brothers-in-law, carefully dismantled each building by hand. The buildings and the fixtures were then sold right off the site to do-it-yourselfers responding to advertisements placed in local papers. Solid waste was either buried, or hauled off to a dump. With little or no clean air legislation at the time, most combustible waste was burned on the site.

At the Medford site, Carlin used a three-foot square cement lined grease pit next to the dismantled mess hall for burning combustible debris. Ten-year-old Tom Carlin worked right alongside his father and older brothers. One of Tom's routine assignments was to throw asphalt and tar roofing tiles into the blazing pit. On many nights, Tom returned home covered in black, oily soot that required considerable time and scrubbing to remove.

Now in his early fifties, Tom, who had never smoked, had recently been diagnosed with cancer of the lung, and was about to have surgery followed by radiation and chemotherapy.

When their youngest child graduated from college, Tom, and his wife, Lauren, purchased two horses and learned how to ride. Both soon became avid and frequent riders, and, perhaps because they were both raised in Medford, they particularly enjoyed riding through the Medford section of the Middlesex Fells Reservation. They often parked their horse trailer in some turnoff along South Border Road and rode off into the woods. During one excursion, Tom led the way around and up the hill to the gun site. There, they dismounted, and walked around for a while as Tom explained to his wife what it had once looked like, and what he had once done there.

Several days before Tom's scheduled surgery, the Carlins parked their horse trailer across the road from the old antiaircraft site then rode down the Sheep Fold trail. It was an enjoyable afternoon, and, understandably, one they wanted to prolong. As a result, they stayed on the trails until after five, an hour after the time the horses usually ate, and the hungry animals were letting their riders know it was time for dinner by acting up.

On the night Lieutenant Allen found Richard unconscious in the garage, Ghost was watching from the backyard. When Allen broke into the garage, Ghost knew Richard was probably alive. Not enough time had elapsed for the carbon monoxide to do its job.

An hour after Richard was wheeled into the Critical Care Unit, a technician from the hospital's outside lab service arrived to draw blood samples. Just as he was about to stick a needle into the collection port on Richard's IV, Doc Fenton, who had dozed off in a chair beside the bed, woke and stopped him. When the technician showed the doctor a requisition for a stat carbon monoxide level, Fenton said that he had drawn the sample himself earlier and sent it off to the lab by special messenger. Apologizing for the mix-up, the technician left.

Ghost was not easily dismayed by setbacks; it was one of the traits which accounted for his success. He possessed a dogged, unemotional persistence that spurred him on to the next option. Back in his room, therefore, he did not waste time or energy lamenting the fact that, first, the lieutenant, then, the old doctor, had thwarted his attempts to kill Richard. He resolved to return to the hospital that night and try again to induce a heart attack in Richard—a heart attack that would be attributed to hidden cardiac damage caused by carbon monoxide poisoning. That would delay the staging of the second shooting by one day, but because the expiration date on the subject's contract was still several days away, that was not a problem. When he called the hospital that evening, however, he learned that Richard was no longer there, more checking revealed he had been discharged and was, therefore, still alive. Ghost knew his client would be displeased, but decided he would just have to take his chances with his client's wrath while he devised an alternative plan for disposing of Richard. In the meantime, he would go ahead with the second shooting.

As the Carlins and their fidgeting horses approached the parking area, Ghost waited for them in his hidden position across South Border Road. The tracking device on their vehicle had allowed him to follow them to the parking area earlier in the day, just as he had followed them there several times before. He was prepared, therefore, when they pulled off the road. He pulled into a turnoff about three-quarters of a mile behind them. Twenty minutes later, he drove by the parking area, and, satisfied that they had gone riding in the woods, continued north on South Border Road. In Winchester, he made a hairpin turn on to Highland Avenue and traveled south to Route 38 South, which he took to a neighborhood adjacent to Medford High School. Parking his car, he took a backpack out of the trunk and entered the thick woods that abutted one side of the high school. From there he walked six-tenths of a mile northeast to the hill that was the location of the abandoned antiaircraft gun site. Once there, he entered the

MULTIPLES 181

trees and thick underbrush on the southeast corner of the hill, and found a spot that looked down on the horse trailer parked on the opposite side of South Border Road. Opening his backpack, he removed the parts of the sniper rifle, assembled them, and settled down to wait.

When the Carlins finally appeared, he could see that they were having trouble controlling their mounts, and that the animals became more restive as they approached the road, now busy with evening commuter traffic. Ghost became concerned that the spinning and prancing of the horses would make the shot difficult. The horses were such beautiful creatures, he thought, it would be a shame, to inadvertently injure or kill either of them. Both riders started pulling on one rein, causing their mounts to turn in a tight circle, a maneuver that will generally bring the animal under control. Lauren's horse responded immediately, and she had dismounted and stood, reins in hand, while Tom's horse reluctantly settled and stood.

The moment before he dismounted, Tom was a stationary target caught in the crosshairs of Ghost's riflescope, and the assassin squeezed the trigger. Tom's body went limp, and his head and torso bent forward toward the horse's neck before twisting down the left front leg of the horse. He fell to the pavement, landing on his back and striking the back of his head. Ghost immediately switched targets. In rapid succession, he fired a round at the feet of Lauren Carlin, blew a hole in the right side of the windshield of a southbound car, shattered the left front window of one northbound car and the left rear window of another, and fired the five remaining rounds in the clip at various places in the chassis of five other cars. Satisfied that he had created enough mayhem, he retreated a short distance into the woods, broke down and stowed his weapon, and headed back to his car.

Tom's sudden movement and the sound of the bullet hitting the pavement startled his horse. The animal collected his body by moving his rear legs closer to the front, then bounded out into the traffic. Unaware yet that they were being fired upon, the drivers respond to the sudden appearance of the horse. Horns blared, tires screeched, and brakes squealed as startled drivers desperately tried to avoid hitting the equally startled and desperate horse.

Lauren's horse strained at the reins and pulled her toward the street as he tried to follow his companion. Lauren knew she could never hold a determined horse from running, she released the reins, and her horse galloped across the road in pursuit of his stable mate. Lauren went to her husband. As she bent down to help him, she saw the blood and realized he was not moving.

By this time, the traffic situation was a catastrophe. Cars were slewed all over the road; one was off the pavement; and there had been three fender benders. Several people were injured; some people were screaming in fear and pain; some were frozen in shock; and some were yelling in anger.

People called 911 on their cell phones, and, depending on their state of awareness, reported motor vehicle accidents, injuries or both. One person called the Massachusetts Society for the Prevention of Cruelty to Animals to report that horses had run away from their abusive owners; another called her attorney to start a lawsuit; and someone else had his companion call a Boston television station to negotiate a price for the video footage he was filming with his digital camera. No one reported a shooting.

Several motorists got out of their cars and walked toward Lauren, screaming at her. One yelled, "Are you crazy? Look what these horses have done running loose!"

Lauren screamed, then yelled, "Tom! Someone get help, please. Something has happened to my husband! Oh, Tom!"

The man who had yelled at Lauren saw Tom lying in a pool of blood and called 911 requesting an ambulance. A woman pulled Lauren away from Tom, and a man took off his suit jacket and used it as a pressure bandage on the wound.

The first responders arrived several minutes later. They were immediately besieged by demands for help from every side. The man applying pressure to Tom's wound yelled, "Over here. This man is bleeding."

Two EMTs rushed to Tom's side. A few moments after they started working on Tom, one yelled, "Lieutenant, I think this guy's been shot. We're gona lose him if we don't get him to the hospital now."

They loaded Tom on a stretcher, and hurried through the abandoned cars, EMT crews, firefighters, police officers, and distraught motorists, to an ambulance parked on the fringe of the chaos. While one helped Lauren into the front seat, the rest loaded Tom in the back. When everyone was aboard, the ambulance headed to the nearest hospital, only a mile away.

Ghost was hiking through the woods to his car, when a thundering sound coming down the path near him caused him to crouch, turn, and draw his pistol all in one fluid motion. Instead of the squad of police he expected to see, however, two horses raced toward him in panic, their nostrils flaring as they inhaled large volumes of air.

He came out of the woods and stood on the side of the path, calling out, "Whoa! Whoa!" The horses slowed to a fast walk, and he grabbed the dragging reins and got both animals under control. Their eyes and ears were moving constantly, and he knew they could bolt in a moment. This was new territory for them, and they were alert for sounds that might indicate danger. Ghost spoke quietly and gently to them, reassuring them that they were safe, while tying their reins around a tree. He stood still for a moment, admired the beauty of the two horses, and then, inexplicably, straightened the saddle of the dead man's horse before he left. When he reached his car, he called the local police and reported finding two horses in the woods.

34

It was late in the day when Pierre LeBlanc approached Bryan Hayden's desk and asked, "Bryan, how's the analysis coming?"

"Oh, hi, Mr. LeBlanc. It's finished. I'm starting the narrative."

"Very good. Is it possible for me to have it tonight? I'd like to take it to a breakfast meeting tomorrow."

"It'll take a couple of hours for me to write. I could have it done by six thirty or so."

"Good. I'll be here until seven thirty, then I have to leave. When you finish, bring it to my office, and we'll go over it."

Since the incident with the Winchendon police chief, Bryan's life had been a torture of anxiety. He was sure that, even if he were not fired, his prospects for advancement at HISH were nonexistent. The fact that his friend had been shot and nearly died added greatly to his anxiety.

LeBlanc believed it was less expensive for a health insurance company to keep its members healthy than to pay for their healthcare when they got sick. For that reason, he had HISH purchase several wellness companies. He instituted incentives to encourage policyholders to use the services of these companies, and requested an analysis of the results. For several weeks, Bryan had been working on the analysis to determine which of the incentives were working, and whether the money saved by any reduction in illness was worth the expense of purchasing the programs and paying the incentives. Bryan was now preparing a report on the analysis and his recommendations for future action.

Using the guidelines set by LeBlanc, Bryan's analysis showed the pilot program was a success and should be expanded. He was concerned, however, that the guidelines did not include all the necessary variables. If there were factors other than the wellness program contributing to the reduction in claims costs, the results of the analysis would not only be inaccurate, they could lead the company into severe financial difficulty. These concerns weighed heavily on his mind when he entered LeBlanc's office with the report.

"Mr. LeBlanc, I have the report for your review."

"Have a seat at the table. I'll be right with you."

LeBlanc's office was always clean and orderly. His desk was polished and, except for material he was currently working, was never cluttered with papers. An oval conference table with eight chairs was off to one corner. Bryan took a seat at the table and waited.

"Okay, that's done. Bryan, I hate to rush you, but I have to leave in forty-five minutes," LeBlanc said.

"No problem, Mr. LeBlanc. I have two copies." He handed one to LeBlanc. "I'll make notes on mine as we go along. If you're going to share this with others in the morning, I would suggest you give them copies of the first packet. It has copies of your slide presentation highlighting the most important information. There's enough white space for them to write any comments without going to another sheet.

"The second package is your narrative. I entered the bullets at the beginning of each section in case someone loses his place. That way, you won't have to look back and forth between your notes and the slides to guide them."

"Good. I hate long interruptions from people who can't follow a simple presentation. I like your approach. Let me read this narrative."

LeBlanc took only ten minutes to read the narrative. Bryan thought he must be a speed-reader to have gone through the narrative so quickly.

"Bryan, you have some tables here showing the claims reduction trend. I think it would be more impressive if you replace the tables with graphs. I like to have positive data presented visually. Stays with them longer and is easier to find later. Let them dig for the negative data."

"Okay, I'll give you a five-year trend of actual costs and a five-year trend as a percentage of total members."

"This report is good, Bryan. It'll work well with the people I'm meeting tomorrow."

"Mr. LeBlanc, please keep in mind this report attributes the entire reduction in cost to the implementation of the wellness pilot program. It doesn't factor other variables."

LeBlanc asked, "Anything else, Bryan?" His tone and manner indicated he was not concerned about other variables.

Because of the way LeBlanc had responded, Bryan hesitated, a moment before continuing.

"My projections of funds available to spend expanding the program do not include the effects of drug therapies currently in the pipeline. Some of them could dramatically increase the costs of certain therapies, and prolong those costs by prolonging the lifespan of people using those therapies. In that event, there would be less money available to spend expanding the wellness program."

"I share your concern about the drug therapy analysis. I asked two analysts to develop a model to calculate the long-term impact."

Bryan felt a sickening sensation rush through his body. He had been lobbying to develop that model since he arrived at HISH. Now LeBlanc was giving the project to two others. It was a sure sign his future at HISH was on very shaky ground.

"I want you to manage the project for me," LeBlanc said.

"You do?"

"Of course, you brought up the idea, and I'm sure you already have a plan for developing the model. You're the best choice."

"Thank you, Mr. LeBlanc."

"No thanks necessary, Brian. Now, going back to your concern that factors other than the wellness program contributed to the reduction in our healthcare costs, excluding the variables my guidelines accounted for, what else of relevance should we have looked at?"

"Well, I'd want to look at the mortality rates and see if—"

"I don't want you or anyone else talking about mortality rates reducing our expenses. Have you any idea the impact that type of data could have on investors or the public? We're in the healthcare business, not the funeral business. End of discussion."

Bryan cringed at the dramatic change in LeBlanc from one topic to the other. He wanted out of LeBlanc's office immediately.

Realizing he had sounded harsh, LeBlanc backtracked.

"Sorry, Bryan, I'm a little sensitive about negative data, and I think data highlighting the effects of mortality rates on our earnings can only be interpreted as negative data. We probably should do the analysis for internal verification of the assumptions, but let's put it on hold for a while. Anything else?"

After a few more minutes of discussion that led to two other changes in the slide package, LeBlanc said, "Okay, Bryan, make the changes, and put together five presentation folders."

"Sure, Mr. LeBlanc. I could have the folders done by eight."

"Thanks. I have to leave. You can put the folders on my desk. I'll pick them up in the morning."

As Bryan prepared to leave, LeBlanc added, "Bryan, I like your work. You did a great job on this analysis. It'll be very useful at my meeting."

"Thank you, Mr. LeBlanc."

"There's a favor I'd like you to do for me."

"Sure, what is it?"

"I know you and Stuart are close friends. Take the rest of the week off, with pay. Spend some time with Stuart and his wife. Find out what they need: medical, personal, financial, anything. Then let me know Monday. I want to provide them any help they need."

"That's very considerate of you, Mr. LeBlanc. I'll take care of it. Thank you."

Bryan went back to his desk, stunned, but happy at the unexpected turn of events. LeBlanc was not going to fire him, he liked his work, and he was giving him a plum assignment! He was getting a few days off, and LeBlanc was going to help take care of Stuart!

Bryan quickly made the changes, prepared the folders, and put them on LeBlanc's desk.

As he was about to leave, he heard a loud shattering sound, someone screamed, and his eardrums felt a sudden pressure change. Among his many anxieties, Bryan was slightly uneasy about the floor–to-ceiling windows in the John Hancock Tower. The originals had a tendency to pop out during high winds. Those were replaced with single-pane, one-half inch, tempered glass panels. The panels had remarkable flexible strength, and large objects bounced off them, but they can be shattered if stuck hard enough by a hammer or similar object. Bryan ran down the hall toward the area where the sound had originated, and turned into the only office there. What he saw made him stop in disbelief. A large desk had been pushed against a window frame, and the window itself had disappeared. Pebble-sized shards of glass covered the desk, and papers were swirling in the breeze above and around it. The office, however, was vacant.

Who screamed? He wondered.

As if in answer to his question, someone grabbed him by the back of his collar and belt, and thrust him toward the desk that separated him from the gaping window frame.

"What the fuck? Let me go," he screamed, as he was thrust forward until he was bent over the desk, looking fifty stories down to the street below.

"Hey, let go of me. This isn't funny." Panicking, he kicked at the figure behind him while his hands searched the surface of the desk for anything to use as a weapon. He grabbed the telephone and swung it backward only to have the cord snag on the corner of the desk. He threw a pencil holder full of pens, pencils, and paper clips over his shoulder with no effect. His arms and legs were flying in all directions trying to break free while the unknown attacker held his torso motionless.

Bryan twisted his head right and left frantically looking for another object to use as a weapon. Hope surged through him as he caught sight of a heavy hammer on the far end of the desk. He stretched for it, but it was just out of his reach.

"Let me go! Let me go! What the fuck are you doing?"

He kicked and bucked, trying to reposition himself for another try at the hammer. A fingertip brushed the end of the hammer's wooden handle. On the next try, several fingers slid down the smooth handle.

Screaming, "Get off me and let me go!" he bucked and kicked with every ounce of energy, and, in one last desperate effort, reached out and grabbed the hammer.

As he gripped the hammer firmly in his hand, his unknown attacker propelled him forward across the desk into the abyss.

Terror twisted his face; his eyes bulged in their sockets; and, screaming, he tumbled into the cool evening air, the hammer held firmly in his hand.

35

The attack on South Border Road left one dead, two wounded, and a half-dozen injured. The shooting was the lead story on both the local and the national news.

Richard listened to a report on the incident as he was shaving the following morning. At its end, when the announcer moved to the next item, Richard heard him say, "And, in a bizarre twist, Bryan Hayden, a friend and coworker of sniper victim Stuart Scott, fell to his death last night from an office on the fiftieth floor of the John Hancock Tower. Sources close to the investigation told me they believe the young man used a hammer found, at the scene, to smash a window in the office before leaping to his doom. We have been attempting to locate a spokesperson for Health Insurance Services Holding, the firm both young men work for, but their offices are closed until nine this morning. Reports suggest Hayden was having problems at work, and was distraught about the condition of his friend."

Richard was stunned and filled with guilt. One young man he had spoken to had nearly been killed, and another was dead. Had Bryan Hayden really killed himself, or was the young man right when he said that being seen with him was hazardous to a person's health? Had his need to follow his investigative instincts killed one man and wounded another? If so, over what? Some statistics that wouldn't fit into his neat and orderly universe? Was that worth the life of another human being?

That was John O'Malley's point, wasn't it? Too many people had treated this as a statistical trend. No one looked at the human lives behind those statistics. No one, that is, except Richard.

He picked up the phone and called Captain Tomlinson.

"Chief Moore, you're up early. Are you calling to tell me, 'I told you so,' or is this a personal call?"

"Captain, I've been a law enforcement officer too long to say, 'I told you so,' or to take credit for any theory, proven or not."

"I apologize. It's been a busy night, and anyone who thinks it's their duty has given me shit. You saved me a call. I was about to phone you. I have some news you might be interested in. A preliminary ballistics report indicates that yesterday's shooter used the same seven point six two NATO rounds used at the Sheep Fold. We may be dealing with a random sniper after all."

"That was quick work."

"Yeah, we had to run ballistics last night. The governor wanted an answer before reporters surround him this morning. It was the same point six two NATO round. Markings suggest that it was the same weapon. We have more testing to do to positively confirm."

"So, you really do think you have a random shooting on your hands?"

"Unless you can tell me differently, Chief." He paused expectantly, but when Richard remained silent, he went on. "All indications are that we have a shooter who's turning the Middlesex Fells into a personal shooting gallery. We're bringing in all our mounted units. We'll have sharpshooters in Wright's Tower and Bear Hill Tower, and we'll have plain-clothes personnel jogging and walking throughout the area. We'll get him, but I wager there will be more casualties before we do."

"How many shots were fired this time?"

"Ten that we could count. Only one found a victim"

"Thanks, Captain. If I come up with anything that might help, I'll call you."

After his conversation with Chief Tomlinson, Richard was certain the shootings were not the work of a random sniper. One young man was badly wounded while speaking with him and another was found dead after speaking with him. Both young men were friends; both worked together; both had worked on a project related to his inquiry; and both had been observed speaking with him. In addition, after speaking with men, he, himself had been the victim of a bizarre, nearly fatal, event. In Richard's mind, all those connections meant the wounding, the death, and the bizarre event were connected.

Richard was certain that the shooting at the Sheep Fold and this recent shooting had different objectives. They may have been the work of the same shooter using the same weapon, but the shootings were different. At the Sheep Fold, the shooter was trying for multiple kills. That was obvious to Richard because of the number of rounds fired and the length of time the shooter spent on the killing field. He also figured the shooter was a professional, because he or she stayed as long as prudent and then disappeared—Stuart had been a premeditated target, and he may have been as well.

It all fits together, he thought. *Except for one piece—the second shooting. If it turned out, as it seemed it would, that the same shooter did both the Sheep Fold and South Border Road, what was South Border Road all about? Did the man killed on South Border Road have a connection to Stuart Scott, Bryan Hayden, himself, or HISH? Was that why he was killed? Why kill him in such a spectacular way? Why shoot up everything in sight and bring down more heat than you have to? And why do it in a location and in a manner that begs people to connect the two shootings?* Richard's mind was running through the questions, then paused. *Unless, of course, that's exactly what the shooter wanted to do!*

Of course! Tomlinson's people had pretty much dumped the idea he, Stuart, or both were the real targets at the Sheep Fold, exactly because of South Border Road. It was a diversion designed to downgrade the deliberate hit theory and promote the random shooter concept. It was intended to draw as much heat as possible. Tomlinson and his officers were now under considerable pressure to find the "Sheep Fold Sniper." No one was left to work on any other theory. Any evidence that didn't point to a random shooter would be ignored.

The shooter wanted a shocking scene, maximum coverage, and extreme heat. That's why he made sure his first shot killed someone.

Richard suddenly felt chilled. He knew evil when he saw it, and this was evil! He was also sure this evil had something to do with Pierre LeBlanc.

36

When Richard called Sharon Hall, She expressed her joy at the prospect of returning to Winchendon, but it would take some time. She was barely making ends meet as a single parent, and funding a move was not in her budget.

"Sharon, I owe your mother-in-law a great deal. She has been very kind. I'd hate to have your return delayed due to finances. I'll make arrangements to cover your expenses."

"Chief Moore, I can't let you do that. I don't know if I could ever repay you."

"Don't worry about the money. We'll work something out. Let's just get you back home."

It took more discussion, but Sharon finally agreed, and said she would contact a moving company to ship her few household belongings back East. She promised to call him back, so he could book a flight to Boston for her and her daughter.

That evening he had dinner with Leslie Hall. She had insisted on cooking for him, and he knew it was her way of telling him she didn't believe for a moment he had tried to commit suicide, especially in a way that could hurt her. He waited until after dinner to tell her that her daughter-in-law and grandchild were coming back. The next five or ten minutes were a blur of Leslie crying and hugging him and thanking him, and scolding him for not telling her earlier. When she finally settled down, he told her he was staying with friends for the next several nights and moving his things out of the apartment so she could get it ready for her daughter-in-law. She protested, saying the house was big enough for her daughter-in-law to stay with her, but he convinced her it would be wiser to give the young woman her own space. He did not tell her that he no longer felt it safe for her to have him in the house. He also did not think it was safe to stay with friends, and went to a motel.

37

It was late afternoon the next day when Steve called Richard's cell phone. "Captain, whoever sent you that disk didn't want the file opened."

"You mean you couldn't get into it?" Richard felt his frustration building. Maybe he should have sent the disk to his contact at the FBI.

"No, no, I opened the file. It was just one of the more interesting codes to break. You might not appreciate it even if I tell you what the code was, but I impressed even myself."

"So, what was the code?"

"Odysseus Laërtiadês"

"Odysseus Laërti ... What?"

"Laërtiadês. Odysseus Laërtiadês, a character in Greek mythology, also known as Ulysses in Roman mythology. He's the hero of the Odyssey, and a major player in the Iliad."

Richard was no academic scholar, but he was a fair student of military history. Steve's mention of the Odyssey triggered knowledge gained in a long-ago study of the Trojan War. Odysseus was the king of Ithaca who, among other things, masterminded the building of the Trojan Horse and led the Greek warriors hidden in it.

"Odysseus Laërtiadês," he said. "He led the warriors in the Trojan Horse. I was one of his officers—at least I was at the War College, one day."

"With all due respect, Captain, it wouldn't surprise me if you'd been one of his officers at the real Trojan War."

"I think I'll take that as a compliment, Sergeant Deschenes."

"Oh, absolutely, sir. You'll remember the rest of the Greek Army appeared to leave, and the Trojans accepted the horse as a peace offering. After the Trojans had partied themselves into a drunken stupor, the Greeks emerged from the horse and opened the city gates for the rest of their army. The Trojan men were killed, the women taken into slavery, and a good time was had by all. Thus was born the legend of the Trojan Horse."

"I know all that, Steve," said Richard. "But, aside from supplying the access code to the disk I sent you, does the story have another connection with it?"

"It does. In the computer world, the term Trojan Horse referrers to a program or something similar you download to your computer because it looks like something useful or desirable, like a game. Hidden inside it, however, is a computer virus that allows a hacker to break into your computer to read, copy, alter, or destroy files. From what you told me in the note you sent with the disk, I gather the person who sent you the disk believed someone was hacking a computer database from an unauthorized backdoor access. Creating that backdoor is precisely what a Trojan Horse virus would do. So, he used the mythological name of the mastermind behind the original Trojan Horse as his access code."

"And you figured that out?"

"Not actually, I have sophisticated software for breaking codes. The problem with this one was the two Greek letters in the name. The software couldn't identify them. When I saw the pieces, I put two and two together and came up with a horse."

"I am impressed. Now, what's in the file?"

"Well, it's from some company called HISH, which, I assume, from the information it contains, has something to do with healthcare."

"Yes, it's a health insurance company. What made you think about healthcare?"

"Well, it's a list of people who are sick, the list calls them 'members', along with each person's address, dependants, primary care physician, and diagnosis. A few of the names are highlighted, some in yellow, and some in red. I am … recognized one of the names, Captain."

"Who?"

"Lori's name … her maiden name actually, but with your Stoneham contact information, is in the file. She's one of the names highlighted in red."

Richard was silent.

"Captain, are you okay?"

"What? Yeah. Does the file have a diagnosis next to her name?"

"Breast cancer."

Richard sat quietly with the phone next to his ear.

"Captain, still with me?"

"Yeah, Steve."

Images of Lori's face flashed through Richard's mind ... a large smile, twinkling eyes, and a flushed complexion as she rubbed her nose against his; fear and panic stretched across her colorless skin, and her eyes glossed over with tears. Finally, her lifeless expression, complexion, and eyes closed as she lay on the gurney.

Suddenly, he was jolted back to the present and something that Steve had said. "Steve, what did you say about Lori's contact information?"

"It is your Stoneham address."

"No, something else you said."

"Her name, it's her maiden name."

"That's it. We each had our own health insurance, so we had different carriers. HISH is the common denominator."

"What the hell are you talking about, and what the hell is going on, Captain? What is this file?"

"I really don't know." He paused for a few moments, and then asked, "Is the file in front of you?"

"I'll pull it up now ... Okay, got it."

"See if you can find four names for me: Shirley Robinson, Raymond Raymond, Paul Kenny, and Jim Hall."

"Hold for a minute. I'll do a find. Shirley ... what's the last name?"

"Robinson, Shirley Robinson."

"Robinson, I found one Shirley Robinson. Hey, she's from Winchendon. Let me copy this and paste it in another sheet. What were the other names?"

"Raymond Raymond, Paul Kenny, and Jim Hall."

"Did you say Raymond Raymond?"

"I know it's odd, Steve, but that is the man's name."

"Okay. Find Raymond ... Hey, here he is, Raymond Raymond ... copy ... paste. Find Kenny ... copy ... paste. Find Hall ... copy ... paste. Okay, I got all four. How did you know they were on the list?"

"I didn't. Try two others, Joe Davenport and Frank Natalie."

Richard heard Steve talking under his breath and typing. "They're here, too, and, Captain, all the names you gave me are highlighted in red. Who are they?"

"They're all dead, but none of them died of their illnesses."

"Holy shit! What have you gotten into?"

"I'm not sure. Listen, do me a favor. Can you check out Health Insurance Services Holding? They're located in Boston. President's name is Pierre LeBlanc."

"Okay, but it may take some time. I'll call you when I have some information."

"Okay. In the meantime, will you encrypt the file and send it to me?"

"No problem. I'll send it right after we hang up."

"Thanks, Steve. Excellent work on that password."

"I'm glad I could help, Captain."

After the call, he thought for a while. Something about the conversation did not seem complete, as if he had not done or said something important, however, whatever it was stayed just out of reach on the periphery of his mind. It nagged at him for a while as he finished packing for the day, but it was gone by the time he returned to his motel.

38

Stephanie's connection with Bryan Hayden put her on the radar of Ghost's client before she began her inquiries about HISH. When it became known those inquiries had led her to France, the client judged her a threat and needed to be eliminated quickly. Ghost was the only readily available resource, and, for the moment, at least, the client's anger at Ghost's failures superseded the need to eliminate the reporter.

Ghost was thumping his fingers on the steering wheel as he waited. His fingers were always in constant motion when he was frustrated and had to wait.

Stephanie cleared through customs at Logan airport and called Richard.

"Moore here."

"Chief, this is Stephanie Lynn. I'd like to meet with you."

"I'm sorry, Ms. Lynn, but I have nothing to say to the press."

"No, Chief, please believe me, I don't want an interview. If I'd wanted to do a story about you, I would have done it already."

"What is it you do want, Ms. Lynn?"

"I have important information about Pierre LeBlanc you should know."

"I have my own sources of information, Ms. Lynn. I'm sure there is nothing you can tell me about the man I don't know now or won't know soon."

"Really, Chief? Then, I assume you know Pierre LeBlanc is dead?"

Richard paused before he asked, "What is this all about, Ms Lynn?"

"That's why I want to meet with you: to explain what I found. Now, are you willing to meet with me, or should I just take my information elsewhere?"

Again, there was silence for a few moments. Finally, Richard said, "I'm going to see Lieutenant Allen later this evening. There's a restaurant called Maiffe's on Main Street in the center of Winchendon, and I was planning to eat dinner there at nine. Can you meet me there?"

"Sounds good, Chief. I'll be there."

Darkness settled in by the time Stephanie reached Route 2, and headed northwest. Shortly after she picked up Route 140 near Gardner, Ghost switched off his headlights and closed the gap separating him from her.

The plan was simple. The bumper on his pickup truck was the oversized kind used for pushing. He would ram the back of her car. The contact and pushing would elicit panic and cause her to accelerate. Added contact and pushing would trigger increased panic and acceleration. When they came to a bend in the road, he would push again on a corner of the woman's car, causing her to spin off the road and into the trees. He would then stop and go back to check on the woman in the car, and if necessary, snap her neck.

The first jolt startled Stephanie. As she reacted to the car's fishtailing motion, anxiety and confusion quickly began to consume her. Anxiety, because a wrong move in countering the car's fishtailing motion could cause her to lose control and go off the road. She had not seen another car behind her, and that confused her. A second jolt and she fought to maintain control of her car. She had unconsciously accelerated after the first jolt. Stephanie looked in the rearview mirror, but saw no sign of another vehicle. Ahead, the road disappeared just beyond the glow of her headlights.

What the hell is going on? I can't see another car, and I sure as hell can't stop.

The reflection of her taillights in the rearview mirror caught her attention just as she felt the third jolt. This one had more force, and she fought desperately to keep the car on the road. She accelerated, ordered her cell phone to call nine-one-one, and struggled to keep the car on the road.

When the operator answered, she gave her location, and explained the situation. Precious seconds passed before the operator responded. "A State Police officer on patrol is headed your way. Can you maintain a distance from the other vehicle for a couple of minutes?"

"No," she screamed, "Now that I know he's there, I can see him just before impact. The glow from my rear lights reflect off his bumper. I can't go faster on this highway without risking losing control, and, if he hits me at high speed, I may not be able to counteract the fishtailing motion. My only hope is to make a U-turn."

"You can't do that. If you stop, he'll drive you into the trees."

"I'm not stopping. I'm making an evasive U-turn. If I'm successful, it will buy a little time, but I'll be heading away from the state trooper. I have about thirty seconds before he hits me again."

"All right, stay on the line, and keep telling me what's happening. I have another officer coming in from the other direction, but she's further away."

"Here he comes, closing in."

Stephanie could not just turn into a U-turn; she would rollover. She had to break first then turn. If she waited too long, her breaking would intensify the force of the impact from the pickup, and it would all be over. She positioned her left hand at eight o'clock on the steering wheel, near her left leg. She then grabbed the emergency brake lever, located in the center console. She waited. Her action had to surprise the other driver.

"I'm making the turn."

She pulled hard on the emergency brake, and spun the steering wheel counterclockwise. The brake locked the rear wheels, which began to skid to the right as the vehicle pivoted around the counterclockwise-facing front wheels. For a moment, all Stephanie saw was a blur, all she heard was a squeal, and all she felt was the centrifugal force of her body pressed against her seat. Almost before her senses could register these facts, however, all movement, sound, and sensation abruptly ceased. The car had skidded to a stop on the opposite side of the road and was now facing in the direction from which it had come. Stephanie instantly spun the steering wheel back to its original position and released the emergency brake. Now headed in the opposite direction from her assailant, she stepped hard on the accelerator and sped away.

As Ghost shot by, he was impressed and angry. With his truck's higher center of gravity, he could not duplicate Stephanie's maneuver without rolling over. He hit the brakes hard and came to a complete stop before he could turn around and renew the chase. The turn cost him a few seconds: they turned out to be a few seconds too many. Just as he was about to step on the accelerator, he heard the wail of a siren, and looking in his rearview mirror, in the distance behind him he could see the blue lights of the cruiser. He didn't know if they were after him or if it was a coincidence. Either way, the chase was over. It was time to disappear.

Stephanie also saw the flashing lights of the police cruiser in the distance behind her. Not knowing if the pickup that had sped past her was still behind her, she did not slow down until the cruiser got closer. Stephanie watched as the pickup that had nearly killed her shoot by her. She told the dispatcher, and then pulled to the side of the road.

Ten minutes later, at Stephanie's request, one of the state troopers on the scene called Richard and gave him a summary of the incident.

"I listened to her talking to the dispatcher. She was cool, kept her emotions in check, and concentrated on keeping her car under control. When she was finally able to pull over and stop, she lost her composure. She's all right now. We'll finish the report then she'll meet you. I'll follow her all the way."

Half an hour later, Stephanie pulled to the curb in front of the restaurant where Richard was waiting outside. He greeted Stephanie and waved to the trooper, and she waved back and drove off. As they sat down at the table, Stephanie asked, "Do they serve drinks in this place?"

"I think they do."

"Good." Stephanie stopped the passing server and said, "I'll have a Scotch on the rocks please. Actually, make it a double. Then again, bring a water glass full."

The server looked at Richard with a confused look on her face.

"She just had a terrifying drive. A double will do for now. If she needs more, we'll order again."

He looked deep into Stephanie's eyes.

"You all right?"

"Oh, sure. Some nut just tried to push me off the road. I spent an eternity fighting to keep the car and me steady then had to perform an evasive U-turn. Just kicks for an evening drive."

"Well, you impressed the hell out of the troopers. How did you manage to keep control and make a U-turn?"

"Antiterrorist training."

"What?"

"I took an evasive driving course that was part of an antiterrorist training program. I was writing an article about high-profile kidnappings and went through the course. The trainers stress getting help, keeping calm, and controlling the car. They taught us how to get out of some sticky situations. I liked the course so much I go back regularly for a refresher."

"I'll be damned. I wonder what the odds were that you'd have to use what you learned."

"I don't know, but I hope they're much higher for a second round. I don't want to go through anything like that again."

After her drink arrived, she was quiet for a while, and then said she would like to eat. Richard was surprised she could have an appetite, but when the meal came, she devoured the meal and had little time for conversation as she did.

When she was through, she said, "I was upset about Bryan. I'll tell you, Chief, Bryan might've been quiet and shy, but suicide was not in his nature."

"We never really know who's capable of suicide, or murder, for that matter, but, I agree, Bryan didn't commit suicide. Besides, he was hoping to get another chance to impress you. I think he was infatuated with you."

"Oh? You think so. Why?"

"He all but told me so during our first meeting. He may have been shy, but he had excellent taste in women."

"Why, Chief, I do believe you just paid me a compliment."

Richard looked directly into her eyes. As he broke off the eye contact, he let the corners of his mouth rise in a slight smile. "Well, Ms. Lynn, I can assure you that the fact that you are an attractive woman won't distract me from the purpose of our meeting. You said Pierre LeBlanc was dead. What were you talking about?"

"Pierre LeBlanc of HISH is supposedly from Metz, France. Pierre LeBlanc of Metz, France died in an accident the year our Mr. LeBlanc of Metz, France arrived in the States."

"I'm sure there is more than one Pierre LeBlanc in Metz."

"There certainly aren't two born on the same day in the same year to the same parents. The birth information given by our Pierre LeBlanc when he applied for entry into the United States is exactly the same as the information on the birth certificate of the dead Pierre LeBlanc."

"And just how did you come by this information, Ms. Lynn?"

"I'm an investigative reporter, Chief. I've been at it for a while, and I'm good at it. I have my sources, just like any good investigator."

"Has it occurred to you that those sources might be wrong?"

"When I got the information, I flew to France to verify for myself. My boss had a fit, so I could only spend a day there, but I got an official copy of the birth and death documents. I also talked to a well-known Metz reporter who covered the accident. What he told me is a matter of public record, so I can share it with you without violating any confidences. It appears Pierre LeBlanc was the last surviving member of a family of local winemakers. He went to pick up a new winepress and somehow, as the crane was lifting the crate toward his truck, it broke loose from the holding straps and crushed him. His death meant the end of the family business, and, as it was a story of some local interest during a slow news week, my friend covered it quite thoroughly. He had no doubt that the man killed was the Pierre LeBlanc in the records I had. He had the same records in his own files, and he showed them to me. Finally, Chief, nobody was trying to kill me until I got this information; that's proof enough for me!"

Richard considered for a moment, then said, "All right, Ms. Lynn, let's assume, for the moment, that your information is correct. What do you propose to do about it? As you know, I'm on administrative leave pending an investigation into my fitness for duty."

"Well, Richard, the first thing you can do is to stop calling me Ms. Lynn, and treating me like a not-too-bright regional edition gossip columnist. I'm not here to do a story on you. There's a lot more story here than some filler about a small town police chief and his alleged personal problems, and I'm going to find out what it is. Furthermore, I don't believe for a moment that being on administrative leave has slowed down your little investigation a bit. Now, we can join forces, coordinate our activities, and watch each other's backs, or go our separate ways, duplicate our efforts, and risk the possibility of being picked off separately. What do you say?"

"I'd say that I think I've you've just tried to put me in my place, Ms. Ly—ah, Stephanie."

"Well, I'm sure you'll get over it. Now, what's the deal? Are you in?"

"Give me some time to think about it. I need to visit Mr. LeBlanc tomorrow. I'll have a better idea after that."

"We."

"What?"

"We need to visit him."

"Stephanie, I don't think—"

"I got the information. I would've gone straight to him instead of here if it weren't for you. If we do form a partnership, we're not going to start by you keeping me out of a meeting with him."

"All right. We'll discuss it more in the morning. It's getting late. We should be leaving."

"There's nothing to discuss. I'm going with you, or I'm going alone. Either way, I will see LeBlanc tomorrow. But, you're right, we should be going; I have a long drive."

"No. No. You're not driving back. We'll get you a room at my motel. Let's get whatever you need from your car."

Stephanie looked at him suspiciously for a moment before saying, "Why?"

"Because, I'm not letting you drive. You're obviously overtired and I just watched you consume alcohol. I would be violating my sworn oath to uphold the law if I allow you to drive."

"What oath? You're on administrative leave, suspended, because you're suicidal." They laughed.

While Stephanie was getting her overnight bag, briefcase, and other items from the car, Richard inspected the car's rear bumper. The marks left by the night's encounter looked familiar. He called Chris Allen.

"Chris, Stephanie Lynn's car is parked in front of Bell's. I suggested she not drive tonight."

"Chief, you didn't get her drunk, did you?"

"Not really, but she did have more to drink than I would approve of for a driver. Someone tried to push her off the road on her way here."

"What happened?"

"We can go over that later. I'm taking her to the motel. Ask Phil to take pictures of Stephanie's car. Make sure he includes the rear bumper."

"I'll take care of it, Chief. You need anything else?"

"That will do it. I'll see you in the morning."

Back in his motel room, Ghost knew that his failed attempt to eliminate Stephanie meant that his own remaining lifespan was apt to be very short unless he took drastic action. The time for subtlety was over. He decided to use direct action to eliminate Moore and the reporter, and tidy up whatever mess remained afterward. He usually worked alone; however, he could enlist skilled help when he needed it, people the client did not control. Now was one of those times, he decided. He got on the phone, and began to assemble his team.

39

After his morning run, Richard poured himself a cup of coffee and began the arduous process of making a relationship map. Many tools are available for unearthing the patterns and connections hidden in the often-formless mass of information encountered in any investigation, Richard chose to use pen and paper.

He started by listing all the people he felt were significant factors in what he was now thinking of as a case. Beginning with Shirley Robinson, and ending with the unknown assailant or assailants, he listed sixteen names. Next, he listed the relevant things he knew about each person: dead or living, on the HISH list or not, yellow highlight, red highlight, and other items as they occurred to him. Having done this, he created a master list of all the characteristics he had written down, and, under each characteristic, listed the people who shared them. From this, for instance, he developed a list of all the deceased. He cross-matched the lists to create groupings of individuals with multiple characteristics in common, such as all the deceased who were also highlighted on the HISH list. Finally, in his mind, he moved the groups and people around as if they were the parts of a puzzle, trying to find which pieces fitted together, and, where possible, figuring out why they did.

In effect, he broke down the mass of information he had into its components, then reconstruct it. He did the reconstruction until it made sense to him. It was an inexact process, dependent on training; experience; his ordered and order-seeking mind; and, sometimes, luck. From it, however, emerged an incomplete but organized picture of the case that both answered some questions and posed others.

He might repeat this process, either on paper or in his head, many times during the course of an investigation. It produced results, but it was time consuming, and, to some, it appeared ponderous and plodding. Due to this, people sometimes thought him less intelligent than most—a judgment the truly wise soon realized was a mistake.

The shooter murdered Tom Carlin, Richard assumed, for maximum shock effect and the murder had no connection to the case. Once it was in front of him on paper, the man's isolation from the others jarred him. He tried pushing it aside, but his eyes kept wandering back to the man's name. Suddenly, he remembered why he had felt the nagging sense his conversation with Steve had been incomplete: he had not checked his assumption about Carlin by asking Steve if the man was on the HISH list. It was a loose thread and needed attention. He opened his laptop and pulled up the copy of the HISH file that Steve had sent him.

The combined effects of international travel, the previous night's adrenaline rush, and alcohol, helped Stephanie sleep long past her usual hour. By the time she and Richard met for breakfast, it was ten in the morning.

After they ordered, Richard said, "I called Pierre LeBlanc and told him I needed to see him today."

"We. We need to see him," Stephanie reminded him.

"Yes. Well, he tried to put me off until next week. Said he was in the middle of a major business deal and could not spare the time. I finally convinced him it was in his own best interest to meet today."

Richard focused on Stephanie's eyes, looking for a hint of doubt or apprehension. When he did, he seemed to lose focus for a few moments before going on. "It's set for six thirty tonight."

"Okay, so, how do we handle it?"

"Look, Stephanie, this morning, I reviewed all of the facts in this case, as I know them. I have no doubt that Bryan Hayden was murdered. It's also obvious his murder and the attempts on you, Stuart, and me are all connected to something going on at HISH. The evidence suggests a highly skilled and determined professional made those attempts. Last night you got lucky; the next time you might not be so fortunate. It's too dangerous for you to confront LeBlanc. Let me handle it."

"Lucky? Lucky? I got lucky? You're the one who would be dead if your lieutenant hadn't shown up in time to drag your cute but sorry butt out of your car. I'm the one who's alive because I kept my head and followed my training. No. This is my information. I have to hear his response, and I have to hear it firsthand. There's a story here, and I'm going to write it. Hell, in the middle of a national healthcare debate, a story about a health insurance executive who's living under an assumed name could be my ticket to a Pulitzer. I'm going. So, how do we handle it?"

Richard's relationship with Lori was most satisfying because they were true equals and partners. Lori was beautiful, feminine, and loving, and she could hold her own with him or anyone else when she needed to. When she died, she was developing a reputation as a fierce courtroom opponent. *This woman*, he thought, *is a lot like Lori*. The thought brought pain, and he had to struggle to regain focus. When he did, he realized there was no sense in arguing with her. He would have to accept the idea of working with her.

"You can tell him what you found out. You have copies of the birth and death documents, so you can give him a set. We'll see how he responds."

"You think he'll actually tell us who he really is?"

"No, he won't tell us, but you might shake him enough with the information and documents to have him say or do something useful."

"How will we find out his true identity?"

"I've been thinking about that. Fingerprints would be helpful. They might match the FBI or Interpol files."

"How do we get the prints? Should we try to take something off his desk?"

"No. I'll use surgical gloves."

"What are you going to do, cut off one of his fingers?" She smiled.

"Nothing like that. I'll put a bandage around my right hand and cover it with the glove. When we shake hands, his prints will stay on the glove. I'll apologize for the glove and explain that I gashed my hand at the Sheep Fold and when the wound became infected, I had to start wearing the glove to keep from infecting others."

Stephanie sat there thinking for a while. "You know we could be walking into the lion's den, never to return."

"That's why you should not come."

"No!"

"Okay. Okay. If we're lucky, it might not be as risky as it seems. They can't have another accident linked to HISH, especially one involving a police chief and a reporter. They could kidnap us and kill us elsewhere, but that's not likely. They won't know if we have backup. LeBlanc and whoever he's working with wants to know what we know. They also want to know whom we've included in the information. They'll probably assess the information and develop a response plan."

"I hope you're right, because I'm coming with you."

"You could always stay here and wait for me."

"No, thanks."

"All right, let's go over to my office … former office. I have to arrange to fly a woman and her daughter to Boston. I also want to look at the pictures of your bumper. I think I know what was familiar about the marks."

"A woman and daughter to Boston? Did you track down a long-lost love?"

"No, not a long-lost love, just my former landlady's daughter-in-law. I'll tell you about it during the drive."

Lieutenant Allen was in his own office when Richard and Stephanie arrived. "Chief Allen, what are you doing in this office? You should be in my old office."

"Hi, Chief," Chris replied, "I don't want your office. I'm only acting chief. You'll be back soon."

"Have it your way, but you could try out the seat and desk for a while."

"No, thanks. I'm comfortable where I am."

"I need to make a few phone calls. Mind if I use the vacant office?"

"Go right ahead Chief, but remember to leave some change to pay for the calls. I don't want to break your budget."

They laughed as Chris stood. "I have those pictures of Ms. Lynn's car you asked for. I'll get them and bring them in."

Richard introduced Stephanie to Jill Bailey, and asked Jill to brief Stephanie on the daily operation of the department. He half-jokingly told Stephanie the briefing would allow her to gather background material for her story while he finalized the arrangements for Sharon Hall.

Thirty minutes later, he asked Stephanie to join him. "Sharon and her daughter are all set. They leave Oregon at seven, day after tomorrow, and arrive at Logan at three. I hired a car to pick them up and deliver them to Mrs. Hall's house. I really want to be there when they arrive. Now, let me get that file."

He pulled the file on Shirley Robinson's accident. It contained, among other things, photos of the accident scene and of all sides of the car.

On his desk, he placed two photos of the back of Shirley's minivan; next, he placed two of the right rear of Stephanie's car.

"Here, look at this," he said.

He explained that the minivan belonged to the wife of a councilmember who had died in a strange accident. "See, the marks on your bumper and Shirley's are very similar, and both are on the right rear. Shirley went across the road into a left bend. Someone had probably been bumping her to make her speed up. When she reached the bend, he used his left front bumper on her right rear to send her spinning across the road. That's why the car sustained so much damage. Spinning, she bounced off several trees. This guy knows what he's doing, Stephanie, you were lucky."

"You keep forgetting; I was smart and well-prepared."

"I stand corrected."

"It's a bit of a reach to conclude the woman was murdered just because we both had similar marks on our bumpers."

Richard realized it was crunch time. He had to clear his distracted mind, and decide whether he were going to share what he had discovered that morning or keep the information to himself.

After a few moments, he said, "You're right, of course, but there's more to it than just marks on bumpers."

He told her about the HISH file, what it contained, and what he thought it meant.

"Shirley Robinson was terminally ill, and insured by HISH. Her name is on the HISH list, highlighted in red. Her brother, who worked for a nearby town, died in a gas explosion around two years ago. He had the same diagnosis she had, was insured by HISH, and is highlighted in red on the list. Paul Kenny, a firefighter, and Jim Hall, who worked for the city power company, both with serious illness, both insured by HISH, and both killed in strange accidents, are highlighted in red. The two guys you thought died mysteriously, Joe Davenport and Frank Natalie: both HISH insured and highlighted in red. In fact, I'm convinced that if we checked out every name highlighted in red, we'd find similar stories for each one." It was too painful to tell her that Lori was on the list.

Stephanie was silent for a few moments, then said, "Okay, I'll admit it sounds suspicious, but what if someone at HISH is just tracking clients with a serious diagnosis who don't die of their diseases? What if it's someone unrelated to HISH? After all, you said that Stuart Scott told you someone broke into the HISH database to create the file. Why would someone inside the firm do that?"

"Those are excellent questions, Stephanie. It's possible no one at HISH has anything to do with this, but I'd say the facts strongly implicate HISH. LeBlanc goes ballistic at the thought Bryan was disclosing company secrets, then Bryan dies under mysterious circumstances. A company supervisor sees Stuart talking to me, and someone tries to take his life. I'm seen talking to both Bryan and Stuart, and someone tries to kill me. You start poking around in LeBlanc's background, and someone tries to kill you. Finally, if what you found out is true, the president of the company is using an assumed name. Too many facts point at HISH in general and Pierre LeBlanc in particular. That's why I'm ... er ... we, are going to rattle his cage a little."

Stephanie suppressed a chuckle, then said, "I have to agree it sure looks like someone at HISH is murderously intent on hiding something, but whatever it is might not have anything to do directly with the mysterious file."

"I would have agreed with you until this morning. You see, this morning I discovered that Tom Carlin, the man killed on South Border Road, was also insured by HISH. He too had a serious disease, advanced lung cancer, and he is on the HISH list, but he isn't highlighted in red."

"Well, but wouldn't that make sense if someone was just tracking unusual deaths? You said there were many people on the list who weren't highlighted. Scott made his copy before Carlin was killed, so his name wouldn't be highlighted on Scott's copy."

"I said his name wasn't highlighted in red, but it was highlighted ... in yellow. Stephanie, after I found Carlin's name, I checked the names of the other people who are highlighted in yellow. Every one of them has a potentially fatal or seriously debilitating disease, just like the people highlighted in red. I think whoever highlighted Tom Carlson's name knew he was going to die in an unusual manner, because, that person was either going to kill him, or going to have someone else kill him. Stephanie, the file isn't just tracking people who've died; it's predicting who's going to die. It's a hit list."

As her mind wrestled with the implications of Richard's words, Stephanie was shocked into silence for a few moments. Finally, she said, "Are you saying there's some sort of psycho mercy-killer at HISH running around knocking off terminally-ill people?"

Richard could understand Stephanie's question. He had seen people, some of them close friends, die in unspeakable agony, screaming for someone to end their torment. Earlier in the morning, after he completed his review f the case, he wondered if Lori's killer, in some twisted way, mercifully spared her such an end. Yet, that was not what Lori wanted. She wanted the chance to live out her life to its natural end. Realizing a killer had robbed her and him of that opportunity filled him with an overwhelming sense of injustice, anger, and, most of all, loss. Where there should have been memories, good and bad, of the most important part of their life together, there was nothing but an enormously painful void. In the end, it was tempting, as Stephanie had suggested, to attribute all this human misery to some inexplicable insanity. He knew, however, her view was misguided.

"I almost wish that were the case, Stephanie, but I'm afraid the real reason, whatever it is, it's more sinister and monstrous."

"I'm having a hard time getting my head around this. Tell me why."

"Well, for one thing, some of these deaths were hardly merciful: One firefighter had his face burned off. An explosion tore another man apart. EMTs described the look on the face of a woman, killed in an auto crash, as one of horror.

"For another, there're indications a highly skilled professional or professionals using state-of-the art equipment and techniques are involved. Such people kill for money, and can charge twenty-five thousand dollars or more per hit. Anyone capable of and willing to spend that kind of money expects some kind of return on their investment.

"Finally, the preliminary ballistic evidence shows the same shooter did both the Sheep Fold and South Border Road shootings. The bumper marks in the photos suggests one person killed Shirley Robinson and tried to kill you. That links the hit list killings and the HISH cover-up. The same person is behind both, Stephanie, and, for my money, that person is Pierre LeBlanc."

"But why, Richard? Why is he doing this?"

"I don't know why, but I'm sure as hell going to find out and stop him."

"In the meantime, what happens to the people on the hit list? We can't just go running around looking for clues while some homicidal machine keeps knocking them off. We have to warn them, get them protected somehow. We have to call in the FBI or somebody."

"I've thought about that. Given the information we have, the only course anyone else could take is to open an investigation, and we're already doing that. I believe we have a better chance of getting results, because we can move quicker and in more directions, than someone burdened with other cases and bureaucratic red tape. Just in case, however, I've let other people know what we're doing, and, when necessary, I have outside resources I can draw on.

"As for warning the people on the list, what would it do except alarm them? To protect them from LeBlanc's killer, we'd have to lock them all up in a guarded compound, and nobody is going to do that. Besides, I don't think it's necessary right now. Somehow, LeBlanc knows, or strongly suspects, that you know about him. After we meet with him, he'll have no doubt, and he'll know you've shared the information with me. It will be too dangerous for him to continue the killings until he determines who else we've told, and how he's going to respond. Everybody, and, hopefully, that includes us, gets a reprieve until he's sure it's safe to move again. I don't imagine we have very long, so we need to get as much information as we can, as quickly as we can."

"I can see your point about people having a temporary reprieve. I see the wisdom in getting as much information about HISH quickly. I already have people working on it. I'll tell them to speed up their research."

"Well, that might not be necessary. I have a source checking on HISH."

"Great. When do you expect to hear from your source?"

"I'm not sure. He said it would take some time."

Stephanie gave him a look that was part disgust and part amusement. "To hell with that. I'm not going to sit around waiting for your guy to do his stuff while LeBlanc finds a tank to use to run me off the road. I'll talk with my people. Go do something useful, and let me use your phone."

Stephanie checked in with her office, and then made several other phone calls.

While she was working the phones, Richard had a closed-door meeting with Lieutenant Allen. When Richard returned, Stephanie was just getting off the phone.

"My dad is well connected in the Boston business community. He's made some inquiries about HISH for me. I called him and he said I should talk with Jonathan Bartman, an investment banker we both know. I just got off the phone with Jonathan and, he agreed to meet with us tomorrow morning at ten."

40

When Richard and Stephanie arrived at the police station, not far away, Theo was on the phone getting a tongue-lashing from Carlos.

"Theo, you think that I am a fool? You want me to invest my money and set up my operation again even though Moore might return?"

"What are you talking about, Moore might return?"

"You know what I'm talking about. The information you forgot to tell me. You did not have Moore fired, you had him put on administrative leave. You think I am a fool? That I would not find out. I would lose everything if he comes back and mounts another raid like the last one."

"He will not return, Carlos. I can assure you of that."

"You cannot assure me of anything, but I will assure you of this: I am going to take care of him permanently. Do you understand me, Theo?"

"Yes, Carlos. I understand."

41

Before they left the police station, Stephanie bandaged Richard's right hand, and he pocketed the exam glove he would use at the meeting. Richard wanted to visit Stuart at Massachusetts General Hospital before he and Stephanie met with LeBlanc, so they left Winchendon early. A few moments after they got in the car and drove away, a white van followed.

Stephanie and Richard arrived at Massachusetts General Hospital around four-thirty. They checked at the reception desk and learned Stuart was out of intensive care and in a private room on the eighth floor. When they entered the room, a woman sitting in a vinyl, rust-colored chair lowered the book she had been reading.

"May I help you? This is a private room."

Richard noticed a sense of concern, even fear, when the woman looked at him. "Mrs. Scott? I'm Richard Moore. I was with your husband when he was shot." Richard walked toward the woman.

"I'm sorry, but I don't know you. May I see your identification?"

Richard stopped, realizing the woman was indeed frightened. "Yes I do. I apologize for not offering it first." He put his hand slowly into the left inside breast pocket of his suit coat, and removed his police ID. "I'm the Chief of Police of Winchendon." He handed her the ID.

Richard looked at Stuart, while Mrs. Scott examined the ID. Clear plastic bags hung on poles dripped fluids into tubes connected to each of Scott's arms. Another plastic bag connected to a machine was pumping a milky substance through a tube that disappeared into his right nostril. Bandages covered Stuart's head and face. Lying on his back, his one visible eye closed, he appeared to be sleeping.

Richard noticed a change in Mrs. Scott as she reviewed the ID. Her tough expression softened to reveal the pretty but weary and concerned face of a woman approximately thirty-two years old. Straight blond hair outlined her head and face and curled slightly at her shoulders. Her denim vest, worn over a gray long-sleeve T-shirt, matched her worn, blue, denim jeans. Reebok sneakers covered her feet. She wore no jewelry or nail polish. Her face needed no makeup. The circles under her eyes suggested to Richard that she had spent little time at home since her husband was admitted to the hospital.

"Thank you, Chief Moore," Mrs. Scott said, as she handed back the ID. "I'm Kim, Stu's wife." She extended her hand.

"Kim, it's a pleasure to meet you, although I wish it were under different circumstances. This is Stephanie Lynn."

"Mrs. Scott, I'm sorry about your husband. How is he doing?"

"Please, call me Kim. I don't feel old enough to be Mrs. Scott. He's doing fine, if you can say someone who just had his jaw blown out is fine. Let's move out to the waiting area. I don't want to disturb him."

They walked down the corridor to an area near the elevators. A row of plastic chairs lined the wall across from the elevator doors.

"Chief Moore, you said you were with my husband when he was shot. Can you explain to me what happened and why?"

Richard knew his conjectures about the reasons for the shooting would be of no comfort, and decided there was little point in burdening the young woman further with them.

"Kim, I can tell you the events as I remember them, but why Stuart was shot … I really don't know. Stuart and I were talking when Bruce gave out a yelp. As Stuart turned to look at the dog, his jaw exploded. Other than that, there's nothing else to tell. I know it isn't much, but I really don't know much."

"What were you doing there with him?" Kim inquired.

"I was going to ask you about that. Earlier in the week, Stuart bumped into me at the office where he works. He told me he had information he believed would be of interest to me. Do you know anything about what he was working on, or anything about a file he found on the company computer system?"

"No. He seldom talked about his work. We tried to keep work and family life separate."

"How was he during the past couple of months? Did he appear to be nervous or distracted?"

"Now that you ask, he did seem distant at times. I asked him about it, but he said that he was working on a challenging project at work. Why do you ask?"

"As I said, he thought he had information I might be interested in. Unfortunately, we never had a chance to discuss it. I was hoping he might have mentioned something to you."

"No, he didn't. I just had a feeling something was on his mind. He was preoccupied."

"I couldn't help but notice you were concerned or maybe a little frightened when we came into Stuart's room. Do you feel threatened here?"

"When Stuart was in intensive care, a police officer was always on duty guarding his room. The guard left after they moved Stu to this room. I asked about the change. They told me they had determined Stu was a victim of a random shooting, and he was in no danger. So, they removed the guard."

"You don't agree with the decision?"

"Chief Moore, for some reason, they initially felt a guard was prudent. I don't know of anything happening that would have changed that reasoning." Her eyes began to water, and, as she continued to talk, her voice quavered.

"My husband has been shot. I can only assume Stu is still in danger or he might be until the person responsible for the shooting is captured. I've been staying here with him twenty-four hours a day except when a family member comes and relieves me, so I can go home, get clean, and change. Unfortunately as you saw, I don't have the skills to identify a danger if it came in the room." She bent forward, tears now streaming down her cheeks. Stephanie put her around Kim and held her. For several moments, the only sound was from Kim as she attempted to gain control of her emotions.

"I'm all right, just a little tired. Even when I have time at home, I don't sleep."

"Would you feel more comfortable if a guard was here?"

"I'd be more comfortable, and it would allow me to take care of other business. Stuart will need long-term care, and I have no idea what that will entail, nor have I investigated how to set it up."

"Excuse me for a minute while I make a phone call. You and Stephanie can chat until I come back." Richard left to make his call. When he returned, he found Stephanie and Kim in Stuart's room.

"How is he?"

Stephanie responded, "He was awake for a while but drifted off. He's heavily medicated."

"Kim, former colleagues operate a specialized security firm. I spoke with them, and they will provide around the clock guards for as long as Stuart is here."

"Chief Moore, Stuart and I do well, but I can't afford a security detail. I don't even know when Stuart will be able to return to work. We may not have an income for some time."

"Don't worry about the cost. These men are close friends. They agreed to do it as a favor to me. All you need to do is relax and concentrate on Stuart's health. The men are very good at what they do. They are notifying the Boston PD and hospital security. The first man will be on duty by six. His name is Jan Pulaski, but everyone calls him Bear."

"Are you sure this is the right thing to do?"

"Kim, I'm confident Stuart is in no danger. However, you need to feel safe enough to leave and take care of other matters. A guard will give you the security you need right now. I feel I owe Stuart and you that much. Stephanie and I have a meeting to attend at six-thirty, so we'll stay with you and Stuart until Bear arrives"

At 5:45, a tall, handsome, broad shouldered, African-American arrived. He hugged Richard in the European fashion, saying something that sounded like "Vee tie, Kapitan."

Richard introduced him to the two women as Jan Pulaski. Pulaski kissed each of the women on the back of the hand saying, "Please, call me Bear."

Richard spoke with Bear for a few minutes, then turned to Kim and said, "I'll leave you and Stuart in the capable hands of Mr. Pulaski. I'll check in on you and Stuart later."

"Thank you, Chief Moore."

"Please call me Richard. No need for thanks."

42

On their way to the car, Stephanie asked Richard, "What was it Bear said when he first came in? It sounded like 'we tie' or 'vee tie.'"

"Oh, that was Polish. He was saying 'Greetings, Captain' in Polish."

"You both speak Polish?"

"I don't, but Bear does. He should, his grandparents lived on a farm in Poland, and he spent most of his summers there as a child. His dad is Polish-American, and his mother is African-American. She was an orphan, so all of Bear's relatives are Polish."

"He sounds like a very interesting person."

"Oh, he is and a very good person as well. He'll be shooing Kim out of there to get some rest when he's certain she feels comfortable leaving Stuart in his care."

"Well, it was very nice of you to provide security for Stuart, but was it necessary? Doesn't Stuart get a reprieve like everyone else? If not, why not have a police detail?" She paused before adding, "And just who are you really, Richard Moore, that you can make a phone call and arrange all this?"

"Yes, I'm fairly certain Stuart isn't in any immediate danger, but it's better to err on the side of caution until we know more. More important, Kim is exhausted and afraid. This way, she can relax and, possibly, rest. As for a police detail, the case belongs to Detectives Nelson and Kelly, and I'd have to tell them a lot more than I'm willing to right now to get them to act. Besides, if there is real danger, Stuart has a better chance with Bear's people on the scene than with a standard police detail. They have the training and experience to deal with the type of killer I think we're facing. What's more, they'll go out of their way to reassure Kim; she'll find them more user-friendly. As for who I am, I'm just a cop who's made some good friends over the years." It was a signal for her to stop probing, a signal she wisely heeded.

Back in the hospital, a woman dressed in a white lab coat was talking on the phone in a small alcove near Stuart's room. "They're just leaving the hospital now, but they left behind a guard. He's big, and he moves like a pro. What do you want to do? ... Okay, I understand. Will do." She hung up, made a small adjustment to her concealed weapon, and started walking down the hall.

When Richard and Stephanie arrived at the HISH offices, a receptionist escorted them to Pierre LeBlanc's office, where they found LeBlanc and Alex Wells waiting.

"Mr. LeBlanc." Richard and LeBlanc shook hands.

"What's the matter with your hand?" LeBlanc asked as he released Richard's hand.

"Oh, sorry about that. I injured it, and it became infected. I was told to keep it covered. This is Stephanie Lynn she's—"

"You're a reporter for the Globe." LeBlanc shook her hand.

"You know Alex," Le Blanc said to Richard.

"Yes. Hi, Alex," Richard said, shaking Wells' hand with his ungloved hand, then introduced him to Stephanie.

"Alex, don't take this the wrong way, but, Mr. LeBlanc, you might want to hear what Stephanie has to say in private."

"Alex is not only corporate council he is also my private attorney. Whatever you have to say, he can hear. I assume, Chief, once again, this is not an official visit."

"That's correct."

"Good, then, Ms. Lynn, please say whatever it is you believe is so important. I don't have a lot of time. I'm late for a meeting."

"Okay, Mr. LeBlanc. While doing some background checks for a story on Boston area insurers, I came upon personal information about you. Company records indicate you are originally from Metz, France. Is that correct?"

"It is. What's your point?"

"Information I received shows Pierre LeBlanc of Metz, France, died shortly before you emigrated from France."

Neither LeBlanc nor Wells showed any reaction to the information, and Stephanie continued, "I confirmed the information myself by traveling to France the other day. I obtained this death certificate." She handed a copy of the document to LeBlanc. He scanned it, then gave it to Wells, who placed it on the desk without reviewing it.

"So, why are you here?" Wells asked.

Stephanie looked at him, somewhat surprised. "I'm doing a story. My information suggests that Mr. LeBlanc is not who he claims. I'm giving him a chance to respond."

LeBlanc said, "Both Pierre and LeBlanc are very common names in France. This document is meaningless."

"You're correct. They are common names in France. However, I found only one birth certificate in Metz matching the information you provided when you applied for your immigration visa." She handed him a copy of the certificate she had procured in Metz. "I have been assured by the people in the public records office and by a reporter who covered Mr. LeBlanc's death, that the document I just gave you is the birth certificate of the deceased Pierre LeBlanc. Do you wish to comment?"

LeBlanc responded, "Ms. Lynn, you spent one day in Metz, whereas I lived there all of my life before coming here. Had you spent as much experience dealing with the city's bureaucracy as I have, you would be more skeptical of their ability to keep their records straight. They have obviously mixed up the records. I appreciate your bringing the situation to my attention. I will personally contact the mayor, and have the records corrected. Now, if there is nothing else, I must be on my way."

"Are you telling me the death was recorded incorrectly?"

"No, I'm telling you I am who I say I am, Pierre LeBlanc of Metz, France. If your information indicates otherwise, your information and that document," he pointed to the paper on his desk, "are in error."

Wells added, "And should you print a story indicating or suggesting Mr. LeBlanc is not who he claims, the Globe will be facing a defamation lawsuit. Now, I believe this meeting is over." Wells opened the office door, and two security guards entered. "Please escort Ms. Lynn and Chief Moore to the elevator."

Stephanie looked as if she were going to say something, but Richard caught her eye, and she remained silent as they allowed the guards to lead them out.

After Wells returned to his own office, LeBlanc made a call from his private line. "Moore and the reporter were here. They questioned my identity. You need to do something before it's too late."

Wells also made a short phone call. "That chief and the reporter were here. I think you need to handle them soon."

Outside, Stephanie said, "Well, that was interesting. I thought I had anticipated all the possible replies LeBlanc might give, but I was wrong. He really surprised me."

"I'm surprised he's still alive. I'm surprised I didn't kill the son-of-a-bitch," Richard said, then quickly added, "Sorry. Let's talk about it over dinner. If I remember correctly, next to Chinese, you prefer Italian food. I know a nice little place in the North End."

Following his lead, Stephanie replied, "In the middle of all of this, you remembered I like Italian food? I'm impressed."

Richard smiled, but did not respond.

They made a detour to an overnight shipping office at Logan Airport, where Richard carefully packed the glove that now, he hoped, had a clean set of LeBlanc's prints on it. Charlie White would have it by eight o'clock the next morning.

An hour after Richard left the shipping office, Charlie White, Richard's contact in the FBI, who had been working late and was preparing to leave, looked up as the door to his office opened.

"Charlie, I'm Claude Billings. We have a mutual acquaintance named Richard Moore."

"Mr. Billings, how did you get in my office? This is a secured floor and visitors are not allowed." Charlie's voice betrayed his concern and apprehension. He moved his hands from his desk and slid his right hand under his suit jacket to his pistol.

"No need for alarm, Charlie, and I'd appreciate it if you take your hand off your weapon. You can call your director and he will confirm my identity. May I sit?"

Charlie nodded, but remained standing as Claude sat in a chair in front of the desk.

"As I said, we both know Richard Moore. He's been in touch with you recently. He just sent you a package that you will receive tomorrow. In the package, you will find an exam glove and a note.

The note will ask you to check the glove for prints and to run the prints."

"How do you know that, and what's your relationship to Richard Moore?"

"How I know is not important. It is important you inform Mr. Moore the prints are not on file in any of your databases."

"Why would I tell him that? What if I do get a match?"

"You won't get a match because you're not going to receive the package. You'll tell him you did receive it and the prints did not match, and you will do it because you have been instructed to do so."

"That brings me back to my original question. Who are you?"

"I'm authorized to instruct you to make the call to Mr. Moore tomorrow and to tell him exactly what I have instructed you to tell him, and that's all you need to know. As for this conversation and my presence here, it never happened. Call your director when I leave." Claude stood and walked to the office door. Before exiting, he turned toward Charles and said, "One other thing. If events progress the way we believe they will, you might have to take a trip to Boston soon." He opened the office door and said, "I'll be in touch."

Charles sat at his desk wondering what had just happened.

43

The streets of Boston's North End are narrow, well traveled, and usually lined with parked cars. The densely populated area is home to the finest Italian cuisine outside Italy, and Mama's Kitchen sets the standard. Mama's is located in a converted two-family wooden structure near the corner of Sheafe Street and Margaret Street. Renovation had eliminated the first-floor rooms to provide as much open space as possible for the dining area. The second floor has two rooms for private parties or, on busy nights, the overflow from the main dining area. As usual, there were no parking spaces available when Richard and Stephanie arrived. The restaurant had a valet service with one space always cleared directly in front of the restaurant. The valet opened the door for Stephanie, gave Richard a receipt, and drove Richard's car away. As Richard and Stephanie entered the restaurant, a white van drove slowly by.

The host immediately recognized Richard. "Ah, Richard, welcome. It has been a long time, my friend. How is Lori?"

"Alfonse, good to see you again." Richard shook the man's hand. "I thought you might have heard ... Lori passed away two years ago."

The news stunned Alfonse. Richard and Lori had been regular customers. He admired the very visible and genuine love they shared. "I am so sorry for your loss, Richard. A more loving couple has never graced this restaurant."

"Thank you, Alfonse. May I introduce Ms.—"

"The beautiful and lovely Ms. Stephanie," he said, as he took her hand and kissed it. "As always, it is such a pleasure to see you."

Alfonse escorted them to their table. When he left, Richard said, "So much for impressing you with my choice of restaurants."

"I am impressed. Alfonse thinks so highly of you ... and the love you and your wife had for each other," she replied softly. Stephanie ordered a bottle of wine. After the wine steward poured them both a glass, she raised hers, "Chief, here's to a quick conclusion for this maddening situation."

"I'll drink to that, but only if you stop calling me Chief, and treating me like a not-too-bright, small-town cop."

Stephanie chuckled. "That was good, Richard. That was very good. Let's drink to that as well."

They tapped their glasses together and sipped their wine.

"All right, Richard, so, what does your investigative mind think of Mr. LeBlanc after our meeting?"

"LeBlanc was very cool. He had his emotions in check. He's been coached, or has been practicing. He had no hesitation in presenting a plausible explanation for the death certificate. I'm sure that, as we suspected, he knew what the meeting was about before we arrived. That shores up our suspicions that he is not who he says he is, and that your discovery of that fact is behind the attempt on your life."

"Okay, so we know he is not who he says he is, and he tried to knock me off. That, plus the file from his computer system tells us he's behind Bryan's death and the attacks on Stuart, you, and me. Why not arrest him?"

"Because, we're still in investigative limbo between what we know and what we can prove. Remember, we began searching for an answer to a completely different question, and we don't know if our original question has anything to do with murder."

"What original question?" Stephanie interjected.

"What's causing the statistical variances in mortality rates?" "But why is that important now? That's about numbers. This is about murder and mayhem!"

"No, Stephanie, it really wasn't about the numbers. It's always been about the people behind the numbers. Yet, the numbers are important. They're what triggered this investigation, and they may lead us to its conclusion."

"How's that?"

"Well, what if the statistical variance isn't just a byproduct of the murders? What if it's the reason for them, or, if it's not, some other set of statistics? What if these people are being killed because some statistician somewhere has deliberately or unknowingly signed their death warrants?"

"Oh, come on, Richard, you're not buying into the secret government death panel crap, are you?"

"Stephanie, I've seen our government do or condone some awful things, but, no, I don't think it's behind this. This, whatever it is, is strictly a private enterprise operation involving LeBlanc and HISH, not government statisticians. Unfortunately, Bryan, the one statistician who might have been involved, has become a murder statistic himself. Anyway, we might know more after we talk with your investment banker friend tomorrow. For now, let's talk about something else. It will help me clear my mind. You seem to know more about me than I do about you. Are you originally from this area?"

Before Stephanie could answer, the server brought their meals and they started eating. After awhile, she said, "I guess I can divulge some information about myself. Dad owns a VC, a venture capital firm. He provides funding for start-up businesses. Growing up, he was always interested in business, so, when he finished high school, he went to Babson College. After graduation, he started a pet shop."

"A pet shop?"

"Yeah, hard-nosed businessman had a soft spot for puppies and kittens." She let out a laugh. Richard noticed that, as she talked about her father, her eyes sparkled.

"His first location did very well, and he soon expanded and continued to do well. After awhile, though, he became bored and wanted a new challenge. He sold the pet shop business at a nice profit, and opened a ground-delivery service company. He started with one van, handling local day deliveries. The business grew, and he gradually expanded coverage to all of New England and parts of New York. He sold the delivery business and received a substantial price. That's when he decided that what he really liked doing was starting up businesses, so, he became a founding partner in a venture capital firm. For many years now he has been providing funds and managerial assistance to business start-ups."

"I'd like to meet your dad someday. He sounds like a bright businessman, and I can always use some advice about my investments. What about your mother?"

"Mom graduated with a degree in psychology. She also earned a teaching certificate. She taught grade school for a few years. When I was born, she took time off and never went back to work. She really should have been an artist. That's where her love was, and she's still very good at it. I'm an only child, as you can probably tell, self-centered and spoiled to the core."

"You? Self-centered? I would never have guessed." Richard teased.

"Wait until you get to know me. If you had taken me for beer and pizza, you'd be dining by yourself."

"Oh, and here I thought you'd go anywhere to have dinner with me."

"No way, I had to join you. I needed a bodyguard, and you were available."

They watched each other, each waiting for the other to show some expression, and then they burst into laughter.

Stephanie continued, "Mom and I are close. Dad was always complaining that mom was spoiling me. He wanted me to grow up self-sufficient, and he made sure I did, but, in actuality, dad was the one who spoiled me. What dad sends his eleven-year-old daughter a dozen roses on her birthday when he's out of town for the occasion? I had friends over that day for a party. They couldn't believe it when the delivery arrived. 'My dad loves me,' I told them.

"I went to prep school then to Simmons College, planning to earn an MBA and join dad's firm. However, I joined the school paper, and ran it during my senior year. The newspaper-business bug bit me and I couldn't get enough of it. Instead of grad school, I went to work as a reporter for a weekly rag, and the rest is history."

"If you don't mind my asking, have you ever been married?"

"No. I was engaged once, but I was more successful than he was and he couldn't handle it. End of story. So, Richard, what about you?"

Richard had never been comfortable talking about himself, so the history he gave her was sketchy at best. Instead of badgering him with questions to fill in the gaps, however, Stephanie was sensitive to his natural reticence, and simply listened without comment. She had already done sufficient research on him to be able to fill in many of those gaps for herself. As for the rest, she sensed she would have other occasions to learn more about Richard; at least that was her plan.

When they finished dinner, Richard took care of the bill, and they made their good–byes to Alfonse before stepping outside. The valet was standing just inside the entrance, sheltered from the light drizzle. Richard gave him the parking ticket and he disappeared into the night.

After he had gone, Stephanie put her arm through Richard's and said, "I like you, Richard. You could be fun to get to know if we survive this."

Richard looked down at her upturned face, and flashed back to a time when Lori had looked at him the same way in this very doorway. To his surprise, the experience felt more familiar and comfortable than distant and painful. He responded by lightly brushing back a wisp of her hair from her forehead. Wisely, she said and did nothing more.

When Richard spotted his car rounding the corner and heading up the street toward them, he led Stephanie to the curb. As he did, a voice behind him said, "Chief Moore! Chief, I think you dropped this."

Richard turned around and almost collided with a man about his own height and build who was wearing a well-tailored suit and carrying an overcoat draped over his right arm.

Pushing the end of the arm gently but firmly into Richard's stomach, the man said, "That's a silenced, nine-millimeter Browning automatic in your gut, so don't make any false moves."

At the same time that Richard was turning around, a second man, who was bald and somewhat heavier than the first man, grabbed Stephanie from behind by the left arm, pinned her against his body, and pressed a gun into her back. As the men made their moves, a black Lincoln Town Car, which had been idling in the street a short distance away, lurched forward and attempted to pull into the open space in front of the restaurant. Just as it did, however, the valet arrived with Richard's car.

Valet attendants are notoriously protective of their reserved parking spaces, and can become quite ill tempered if someone attempts to interfere with their territorial rights. In addition, this particular valet had recently emigrated from Rome, where driving has replaced gladiatorial combat as the national blood sport. When he saw what the Lincoln was attempting to do, he blasted the horn of Richard's car. Twisting the wheel to the left and stepping on the gas, he zoomed past the Town Car. With a hard right, a squeal of brakes, and a string of Italian, he cut off the Lincoln in the middle of the street.

The speed, noise, and unexpected nature of this move startled everyone and caused the man facing Richard to divert his attention for a split-second. It was all the time Richard needed. He pivoted on the heel of his right foot while swinging his right forearm up and away from his body. As his right forearm hit the attacker's right arm, the coat went flying, the gun went off, and a bullet hit the Town Car, further distracting the already flustered driver.

Richard grabbed the man's hand and the gun, swung them around toward the Lincoln, and squeezing the man's trigger finger, forced off two shots, one of which hit the car's driver and put him out of commission. Then, holding the attacker's hand and gun in both hands, Richard ducked down to his right, positioned the man's extended arm over his left shoulder, and sprang upward with his left shoulder while pulling the attacker's arm down with both hands. The attacker's shoulder dislocated with an audible pop, the man screamed, his arm went limp, and Richard gained full control of the gun.

The bald man holding Stephanie was taken completely by surprise, and when he did begin to swing toward Richard, Stephanie drove her right elbow into his solar plexus. This did not disable him, but it did cause him to turn toward her and raise his gun. Before he could fire, Richard shot him in the leg, breaking his femur and causing him to drop his gun, grab his leg, and topple over, screaming in pain.

Richard kicked the gun away, and did a rapid assessment. The two attackers were writhing on the ground in pain, posing no immediate threat; and the Lincoln was slewed sideways in the street, the driver slumped over in the seat. Stephanie appeared unhurt, and though frightened, did not seem panicked or frozen in place. The visibly shaken valet was just beginning to peer over the top of Richard's car, and was muttering a prayer in Italian.

Richard made a quick decision, seeing that the situation was, for the moment, nonthreatening and stable, but lacking any other information, he took Stephanie firmly by the arm, and headed for his car. Going around to the driver's door, he handed the still muttering valet a twenty-dollar bill, got in, and drove rapidly away.

After they had been driving for a while, Stephanie said, "Don't you think we should have stayed for the police?"

"Too risky, those guys may have had backup."

"You know, this is why I don't date."

"You don't date? What are you talking about?"

"This is why I don't date. I can't stand guys fighting over me." She smiled, but the attempt at humor didn't help. "Richard, look at me, I'm trembling uncontrollably. Is this business ever going to stop?"

Richard was silent and deep in thought. He did not want to say, *I told you so*, but he had tried to convince her to stay in Winchendon. He was more concerned that they were alone facing an adversary willing to react in force to every move. He needed more information and time to develop a plan. He needed more resources. He then felt the pain in his arm and the warmth of blood under his shirt. During the attack, he had ripped several stitches.

"The attack was a possibility we discussed before we met with LeBlanc. The speed of their reaction to the meeting and their daring concerns me. We must be closer than we realize."

"What does that mean?"

"It means we need to get you safe, then I play the hand we have. The endgame must be near."

Stephanie was trembling, dazed and frightened, but still, she said, "We, Richard. We have to play the hand. Remember?" Then, without another word, she leaned to her left, put her head on his shoulder, and closed her eyes.

By the time they were on Route 2, heading toward the motel in Ashburnham, Stephanie was asleep. The feel of Stephanie against him, her body-heat, and the contours of her body, made him uncomfortable. Yet, it felt good to have her so close. It had been a long time since he held a woman so close. Not since his wife died, and that is why he was uncomfortable.

44

When they reached the motel, Richard led Stephanie to his room intending to call Chief Mullrenin of the Ashburnham police department to arrange for security for the night. Stephanie was seated on the end of one of the beds, and Richard was calling Chris when the door burst open, and two men stormed in. One tackled Richard, pinning him to the bed, and pointed a silenced weapon at his head. The other man pushed Stephanie backward onto the bed, turned her around, and held her firmly with a silenced weapon at her head. Richard knew any move would be fatal to Stephanie. Without a word, his man rolled him over and secured his hands behind him with plastic ties. The man holding Richard down said, "Clear!" The man holding Stephanie repeated the "clear" order. A third man walked into the room and said, "Let them up."

Pulled up to a sitting position on the bed, Richard found himself looking directly at a face from his past.

"Ghost, I haven't seen you in a long time."

"I know, Captain, but I've seen you several times recently," Ghost said, a twisted smile on his face. "I saw you at the burned-out gas station, and I searched your apartment while you were asleep that night. If you don't mind me asking, what did you pick up, and what did you do with it? I never found it."

"You mean the camera lens? I stopped on my way to the office and sent it to Steve Deschenes."

"Ah, that explains it. And Steve told you it was a camera lens?"

"Yeah, he said it's commonly used for high-definition images like those needed for facial recognition."

"Steve was always good. He hasn't lost his touch."

"So, why the camera?"

"Had to make sure I had the right firefighter. I don't get paid for hitting the wrong guy."

"So, you're wasting people. Why?"

"For the same reasons I've always done it: I get paid, and it's what I do best."

"And the faked suicide attempt, and the Sheep Fold and Ms. Lynn, that was you?" Richard asked with a hint of sarcasm in his voice.

He wanted to ask about Lori. He wanted to shout, *Did you kill my wife too, you miserable piece of shit?* But he was afraid to, afraid not for himself, but for Stephanie. For her sake, he needed to stay in control, and keep them both alive for a while.

"I'll admit they weren't my best work, but yes, it was me. But we're being rude, leaving Ms. Lynn out of the conversation and without a proper introduction."

Turning his head, Ghost continued, "Ms. Lynn, the man standing next to you is John. I wouldn't upset him if I were you. He can be very nasty when he's upset."

"Stephanie," Richard began, "let me introduce you to Henry Thomas, Ghost to you, me, and the rest of the world. It's the only name he's had for so long, I wonder if he remembers he has another. He earned the nickname in recognition of his unique abilities. Despite his recent lapses, he's very good. Actually, he's probably the best there is at completing a mission without detection or leaving any traces except the bodies of the people he's killed. That's why he's called Ghost, he moves like a ghost and he leaves only ghosts behind. We worked together once upon a time."

"Thank you, Captain. You always made sure you complimented the people you worked with, an admirable but useless trait. By the way, Captain, you're bleeding. What happened?"

"Your men at the restaurant, earlier. I pulled some stitches during the attack."

"My men? I had no one attack you earlier. You must have a line of men trying to get rid of you."

The motel was a square, two-story structure surrounded on all four sides by a parking lot onto which the room doors opened. A slight knoll with four-foot tall shrubs separated the front parking lot from the street. The office was a freestanding building located closer to the street and just to the right of the parking lot. It was on the side of this building that Officer Peggy Butler had parked

Winchendon's only unmarked cruiser, a vantage point from which she could watch, unobserved, the entrance to Richard's room. When the three intruders broke into the room she saw them, as did Lieutenant Allen, who was sitting in the front seat with her. A fourth man stayed outside leaning against a car parked directly in front of the room's entrance door.

"That guy against the car," Chris said, pointing at a tall well built man, "must be their lookout. We'll have to remove him without alerting the others."

"I have an idea," Peggy said. "Slip out of the car and work your way behind the cars parked on this side of the lot until you're opposite the Chief's room. Wait for my move, and when the man is down, come over."

Chris started to protest, saying something about additional help, but Butler cut him off. "Respectfully, Lieutenant, we don't have time for that shit. Just trust me on this and get your butt out that door."

Chris looked surprised for a moment, then shrugged and left the vehicle. Butler pulled the trunk release, opened her door, and crept to the back of the car. When Chris was in position, he pulled a silencer out of his pocket, and attached it to his 9mm service pistol. Richard had trained his officers to use them in high-risk entry operations. A few minutes later, Chris watched as a woman in tight jeans and a revealing halter-top came walking from the right end of the building, her ample breasts bouncing and swaying with every step. As she passed each of the hotel doors, she peered at the numbers in the dim light then looked at her hand.

The lookout also saw her and stood up straight. He could not see her face very well, but his eyes took in the rest of her body and the sensuous way it moved. When the woman saw him, she stepped off the walk and approached him, the move revealed a face that complimented the rest of her ample charms. The man grinned and relaxed his grip on his concealed weapon.

"Can you help me? I don't see my room number here," the woman said, showing him her key while leaning forward slightly and showing him a little more.

"Two fourteen ... upstairs, not down here."

"Oh, they didn't tell me the second floor. Do you know where the elevator is?"

His smile widened as he said, "I don't think they have an elevator. You want the stairs there at the other end of the building."

"You're so kind. Are you staying here?"

"No, just waiting to pick up some friends."

"Too bad, I'm traveling alone. I thought if you were available, we could have had a bite to eat together. Bye." As she turned to go, her key slipped out of her hand and landed on the pavement with a clink.

"Let me get that for you," said the lookout.

As he bent to pick up the key from the pavement, the woman brought her knee up with speed and force. It struck him in the jaw propelling him upright and backward. He instinctively reached for his weapon and started to draw it, when the woman delivered a sidekick into his solar plexus that knocked the wind out of him, and sent him stumbling back a step or two before he lost his balance and started to fall, his hand still grasping the weapon. His head and right elbow hit the pavement simultaneously. The blow to his head caused him to spasm for a microsecond before passing out, at the same moment the blow to the elbow forced the muzzle of his silenced pistol against his chest. He never heard the muffled report that sent the 9mm slug from his own gun tearing through his chest wall to stop his heart.

When he saw the woman approaching the lookout, it took Chris a moment to recognize Peggy Butler. He had worked with Peggy for a couple of years, and considered her passably attractive, but had no idea she could look so stunning. Once he got over his surprise, he creep between two cars toward the open space that separated the cars parked against the shrubs from those parked directly in front of the motel rooms. When Peggy began speaking to the man, Chris slipped across the open space to the back of the car outside Richard's door, and, when Peggy dropped the man, Chris sprinted to the door itself, his weapon at the ready. After taking several large breaths to settle himself, he slammed open the door and went in low with his gun held out in shooting position.

Almost reflexively, Chris's eyes sent his mind a panoramic snapshot of the room and everything in it. Two beds were to the right of the door, and Richard sat on the end of the farthest with a man standing in front of and facing him. That man was not holding a weapon. A second man was standing between the two beds, facing the door, and aiming his weapon at Stephanie. The third man was in the corner of the room to his right, a weapon in his right hand by his side.

Outnumbered, outgunned, and with hostages in imminent danger, Chris did not wait for anyone to react. He shot the man with Stephanie once in the chest. The man standing in the corner raised his gun and fired just as Chris's second shot struck him in the throat. The impact of Chris's shot caused the man's shot to go wide.

Ghost had not moved a muscle. It was as though nothing at all was happening around him. However, when he heard Chris's second muffled gunshot, he grabbed the weapon from his belt, turned slightly to his right while raising his right arm, and shot Chris in the chest, all in one fluid motion. Richard exploded. He drove both feet into Ghost's left leg just behind the kneecap. The force of the blow turned Ghost more to his right and buckled his left knee. Richard then drove both feet into Ghost's ass causing him to crash head first into the credenza. His head shattered the water glasses that were on top. Lifting himself slightly off the bed, Richard moved his bound hands under his butt. He brought his legs up tight to his chest and moved his hands past the legs. His arms were now in front of him and more useful. As he started to leap toward Ghost, the man turned around, and pointed his weapon directly at him.

Richard heard the muffled sound, and it left him temporarily confused. He believed you never hear the shot that kills you. Then Ghost fell against his legs, blood spurting from a hole in the back of his head. Richard looked from Ghost to the door. Peggy Butler, in a revealing outfit, was standing there in a shooter's stance, her eyes and weapon sweeping the room.

After the man in the parking lot went down, Peggy had moved in, kicked his weapon away, and kicked him in the ribs to see if he responded. He did not. She saw the spreading crimson stain on his chest. Reaching behind herself, she pulled her own silenced weapon from her waistband and moved to the open doorway with the weapon held out in both hands. She saw only one person standing, and, as he was taking aim at Richard's head, she shot him.

After he realized what happened, Richard said, "Stephanie, don't move. Officer Butler, cut me out of these things then check the other two perps." Richard knew this was Peggy's first shooting incident, and it was important to keep her moving so she did not lock up.

Peggy grabbed a piece of broken glass and cut open the plastic tie binding Richard's wrists. She went to the two bodies on the floor, checked them for weapons, and then checked their pulses. While she was doing this, Richard followed the same procedure with Ghost.

"These guys are both gone, Chief," Peggy said.

"So's this one. Check Ms. Lynn. I'll check Lieutenant Allen."

While Peggy checked to see if Stephanie was unhurt, Richard went to where Chris was lying, and saw at once that Chris was not bleeding. When he tore open Chris's shirt, he discovered the lieutenant was wearing a bulletproof vest. Richard let out a large sigh of relief, and the lieutenant opened his eyes.

"Chief. How did I get on the floor? I feel like somebody punched me in the chest."

As Chris talked, Richard opened the vest and the lieutenant's shirt. He found a reddened area, but no other injuries.

"You're okay, Lieutenant. You just stopped a slug with your bulletproof vest. It knocked the wind out of you. You're going to be sore as hell and have a wicked bruise, but you'll live. Get yourself buttoned up; we've got to get a move on."

Leaving Chris rubbing his sore chest Richard went over to Stephanie and Peggy.

"She's okay, Chief, at least she's not injured."

"How are you feeling, Stephanie?"

"I don't really know, Richard. I'm a little numb right now ... No, that's not right. I'm shook up, but don't worry, I'm not going to wimp out and go to pieces on you. I—" Startled, she looked up, and said, "You're not dead!"

Chris Allen stood behind Richard. He was buttoning his shirt, as he gawk at Peggy.

"No, he's certainly not," said Peggy. "Uh, Chief Allen, when you're finished getting dressed, do you think you could stop staring at my boobs and give us a hand here?"

Chris flushed red, Stephanie turned her face and bit her lip, and Richard thought to himself that Peggy, at least, was going to be all right. Traumatized or not, she had just made a typical cop wisecrack, and it did what it was supposed to do: popped the bubble of tension for them all.

"How did you two happen to be here to help?" Richard asked.

"After our little talk this morning I was more concerned than ever about your safety. I couldn't go chasing you all around the countryside, but I wanted to make damn sure you were safe in your own hotel. I assign Officer Butler to keep an eye on your motel room. We saw the guys go in your room," Chris explained.

Peggy Butler added, "Excuse me, Chief, but we can go into all of that later. We've got three dead perps in here, and I think the one outside is gone as well. We have to call the State Police before we do anything else."

"Yes, of course, Officer Butler, but first I have to thank you both for saving our lives. I owe you both a great deal, and I'll express my appreciation properly when this is all over. When Captain Tomlinson and his men arrive, they'll want answers to questions I'm not prepared to give right now. When his detective Kelly hears I'm involved, and once he gets a hold of me, I'll lose any freedom of action. So, Chris, Peggy, I'm afraid I'm going to have to ask you to delay making the call to the State Police until Ms. Lynn and I have had enough time to put a little distance between us and the scene. Just tell Tomlinson this all happened because you were providing security for me and saw these guys break in. I'm positive that the man you shot, Peggy, Henry Thomas, AKA Ghost, was the sniper at the Sheep Fold and responsible for the shooting the other day in Medford. He's an ex-military sniper, and may be wanted. I wouldn't be surprised if the weapon is in whatever vehicle they came in. Tell Tomlinson I told you that and then took off with Ms. Lynn. If they find the weapon, they'll be too happy and busy to make life miserable for you. In the meantime, Ms. Lynn and I have things we have to do to clean this all up. Stephanie, please grab your things."

As Stephanie and Richard left the parking lot, two figures in a white van watched them. When Richard's car was out of sight, several armed men appeared from the rear of the van, and quickly ran to Richard's room, and the unsuspecting Winchendon officers.

Once he turned on to the main road, Richard said, "Thanks for not asking any questions. How are you doing?"
Stephanie paused, and then said, "Richard, I have to know something before I go any further with this. You said you worked with that man. He was evil. Why did you work with him?"
Richard considered the question, and then responded, "I was a soldier fighting a war against my country's enemies. Ghost was supposed to be fighting the same war. My job was to help him do his. I began to see that his enemy was anyone he decided was his enemy. He fought his war with methods I couldn't support. He finally did something was so horrendous, that I almost killed him for it. I was sure my country would punish him. When it didn't, I couldn't fight for my country anymore, not in the way I had. I left the Army, and found a new way to fight."
Stephanie was silent for a while, and then said, "You asked me how I was doing. Well, I'm very frightened, but I also feel okay. I saw how you acted tonight, and I watched how your people, the people you lead, acted. You all did what you had to do, and you did it well. I also saw how your people acted around you. They were willing to risk their lives for you. Not many people inspire that kind of loyalty. They respect you. They know they can count on you. When you and Lieutenant Allen went outside, I asked Peggy how she could do what she did. She said she just remembered everything you taught her, and she knew that with you and Lieutenant Allen there, she was part of a team, not alone. I think I feel the same way. I think I can count on you, so, it's not so bad being afraid."

Richard didn't respond for a while, then he said, "We have to find a place to stay for the night. We both need to rest."

"We do need to rest. Since we have to be in Boston tomorrow, let's get a room somewhere between here and there. Someplace where the doors open on a hallway, not the parking lot."

45

Stephanie and Richard spent the night in a motel near the junction of Route 128 and the Massachusetts Turnpike. When they left for their meeting the next morning, the white van trailed behind.

En route, Richard called the Winchendon police station. Stephanie, who was driving, could tell from his tone and from his questions that something was wrong.

As he ended the call, he turned to her with a bewildered look and said, "Sometime after we left the motel last night, Lieutenant Allen called dispatch to say he and Officer Butler were on an assignment and would be out of contact for an unknown period of time. He never mentioned the shootings at the motel."

"How can that be? The shootings should be all over the news by now."

"That's just it; there was nothing on the news about shootings in Ashburnham this morning. That's why I called the station."

"What do you think is going on?"

"I don't know. The only thing I have to assume Tomlinson is keeping Chris and Peggy and the whole incident under wraps until he can find out why he has four dead bodies instead of one dead sniper."

"Would he be able to do that?"

"Since the State Police investigate all homicides in Massachusetts that don't take place in Boston or Springfield, he could keep it under wraps for a few hours: Longer than that would be almost impossible. If I haven't heard something by the time this meeting is over, I'm going to call him."

When they entered the State Street offices of Beacon Investment Banking, Jonathan Bartman was waiting for them in his office.

"Jonathan, so good to see you."

"Hi, Stephanie. You look great as always."

"You fast talker. You say that to all the women. Jonathan, this is Richard Moore. Richard is helping me complete some research on a story. Richard, this is Jonathan Bartman."

Jonathan and Richard shook hands, then Bartman said to Stephanie, "You with a helper? I've known you a long time and

I've never seen you with a helper. Since when did you start asking for help researching a story?"

"Jonathan, I'm not sure there is a story, and, if there isn't, I can blame the lack of progress on him. Besides, he kind of likes tagging along with me."

"Stephanie, I know a few dozen men who would love to tag along with you."

"I love you, Jonathan. You always make me feel so desirable."

"Now, whose being a fast talker? So, you're looking for information about HISH?"

"Yes, I am. Dad said you might be able to help."

"I can. Sidney Chang, one of our analysts has been tracking HISH. I asked him to give you a briefing. Let me get him."

Sidney Chang entered the office a few moments later, and Jonathan made the introductions. They all sat around Jonathan's desk.

Jonathan said, "Before we start, Stephanie, you should understand that although HISH is not a client of ours, some of the information we're going to share with you, might have come from confidential sources. Sidney told me HISH is very protective. They employ a security firm to monitor all communications and publications. They're very aggressive in tracking down leaks of confidential information. They might not be able to hinder you much, but they could hurt our reputation. Remember, as an investment banker, my reputation for maintaining confidential information is critical to my business. Therefore, I'm telling you, this interview is off the record. Do you agree?"

"Not a problem. I understand."

"Thank you for your understanding. Sidney, will you proceed, please."

"Sure. As an investment bank, our primary business is the pricing and selling of corporate stocks, so I'll be talking mostly about HISH as it relates to the stock market. Like any other corporation, the ownership of HISH is divided into shares called stock. Because of Pierre LeBlanc's obsessive secrecy, we don't know how many shares of stock there are, who owns them, or what they paid per share."

Stephanie interrupted. "Do you think LeBlanc owns the shares?"

"I would guess ownership is still restricted to a few of the original investors. LeBlanc could be one of them. It's even possible that he owns the majority of the stock, but, as I say, no one knows for sure.

"You see, it's a privately held company. Unlike a listed, or publicly traded company, there is no market for its stock. Privately held or unlisted companies have no obligation to disclose information.

"However, it also means that, unlike a publicly traded company, HISH does not have ready access to millions of investors in the stock market who might want to buy shares in the company, and who, by bidding against one another, could push up the price of its shares. That means that if the company wants to raise money by selling more stock, or the investors want to sell the stock they own, they have a smaller group of buyers and would receive less per share than they would if HISH were publicly traded. So, five years ago, HISH decided to go public."

"But, I thought you said they weren't publicly traded," Stephanie said.

"They aren't. They ultimately decided the multiples were too low, and they backed out."

"Excuse me," Richard said, "but what are multiples, and why did HISH think they were low?"

"Well, Mr. Moore, for our purposes, a multiple is a number that represents the relationship between the price of a stock and the performance of a company. The most well known multiple is the Price-Earnings Ratio, the PE multiple, so I'll use that to illustrate what happened at HISH. The PE multiple, describes the relationship between the price of a company's stock and the company's profit. For reasons we don't have to go in to, generally speaking, the higher a stock's PE the more money the company makes from the sale of the stock. When HISH decided to go public, it followed the usual procedure and asked an investment bank to help it set the price of the stock to be sold in its initial public offering. The bank did an analysis of HISH's past performance and future potential, then recommended the

MULTIPLES

multiples HISH should use in setting its price. After some deliberation, HISH decided they needed better multiples to make going public profitable enough, so they backed out."

"That's not the end of the story, though, is it, Sidney," Stephanie said.

"No, indeed, Ms. Lynn. What they've done in the last five years to improve their position has been very impressive. They've been extremely aggressive in improving their bottom line by reducing their costs. They've instituted a program to pay healthcare providers three times faster than other health insurance companies. The expedited payment is only available to providers willing to accept eighty percent of the fee Medicare pays for the same services. Recently, they purchased hospitals, home healthcare agencies, clinics and other healthcare provider facilities, and are using them to provide services to their members for cost. They also have a long-term drug therapy program that greatly reduces the amount they pay for their members prescriptions. Finally, they've really made an effort to reduce the amount of sickness in their membership by instituting a wellness-program pilot study. We think the pilot study has been completed, and they're getting ready to go public again."

"How do you think they'll do this time around? Stephanie asked.

"Well, their secrecy makes it hard to know exactly, and unlisted companies tend to underreport their profits for tax purposes, but from what I can tell, their real earnings are well above the industry average. I'd say HISH will command a very high multiple this time. In exchange for their initial investment Pierre LeBlanc and his investors are about to receive an impressive return on their investment, and a great deal more than they would have five years ago. I'd say they were about to make a killing."

Richard could see Chang was trying to keep his presentation of complex financial concepts as simple as possible, but he had still found himself playing mental catch up during parts of it. It was a few moments, therefore, before Chang's last statement registered fully and triggered an association in his mind.

"Sidney, you said that HISH's profits were surprisingly above the industry average. In the light of what you've told us about their aggressive approach to cost cutting, why are you surprised?"

Chang thought for a few moments, not sure whether he should answer the question. He looked at Bartman, who stared back blankly, as if to say, *It's your call.*

After another moment, he took a deep breath, and then said, "Few companies go public each year, so there's a lot of competition among investment banks to represent the ones that do. HISH is practically around the corner from us, so we've kept a close eye on them and recently decided to solicit their business. Jonathan asked me to collect as much data as I could find on them and run the numbers as best I could. When I did, the numbers didn't add up. I concluded that, given the data I had, they had to be doing something else to achieve their level of cost reduction, something we didn't know about. Since we knew my conclusions might be based on insufficient data, we approached them and asked if they would mind filling in some of the blanks. They not only refused, but, using very polite language, they basically told us to stop sticking our noses in their business, and not to let the door hit us in the ass on the way out."

Quite suddenly, all the dominoes fell into place for Richard, and he began to feel an immense rage. Before he could say or do anything, however, he felt the vibrator of his cell phone signaling a phone call coming in. He pulled the phone off his belt, and looked at the display. He needed to take the call.

"Could you excuse me for a minute? I have a call I have to take."

"Sure," Jonathan said, "You can use the office on the other side of that door. I'll have my secretary bring in some coffee." Richard left to take the call.

Stephanie was updating Jonathan about the status of her father's venture capital firm when they heard Richard's voice bellowing through the wall. "I don't want to hear that shit. He murdered my wife, and he's going to pay. If someone in the Agency wants to protect him, you better tell them to rethink their decision because I'm going to make him and anyone in my way, pay dearly."

Richard burst through the door of Jonathan's office. His face flushed, his eyes intense, he proceeded out the other door and headed toward the reception area.

Stephanie got up quickly, her face reddened from embarrassment. "I'm sorry Jonathan, Sidney. I can't imagine what that was all about. I better catch up to him." She left without shaking their proffered hands.

When she got to the elevators, Richard was just stepping into one. "Wait, Richard, hold the door." She thrust her hand between the doors as they were about to close.

"Well, thanks for holding the door for me. And what was that all about? You left Jonathan and Sidney very perplexed."

Richard just stared at the elevator floor indicator while he tapped his foot on the floor. "Come on, what's taking this thing so long?"

Stephanie grabbed Richard by the arm and turned him. "What is the matter with you? What was that phone call about? You owe me an explanation."

"Do you believe that asshole LeBlanc?" Richard just started blurting out. "What he did to raise the multiples was control member costs for treating disease states by having them all killed. He killed my wife, so he could earn more on his investment. That greedy son-of-a-bitch thinks no one can touch him."

"What do you mean no one can touch him? What are you talking about?"

"The phone call I got. It was Charlie, my contact at the FBI. He ran the prints. He said there was no match in any of the databases. Charlie told me he thought I was treading into something very big and to let it go."

"Something big! Like what?"

"Charlie didn't say. He did say the fingerprints did not belong to Pierre LeBlanc. He suggested the CIA was somehow involved."

"The CIA?"

"Yeah. I used to work with the Agency. I still have some good contacts. I'll find out who Pierre LeBlanc really is, then he'll be mine."

46

Richard and Stephanie exited the building and turned left, hurrying toward the parking garage through streets congested with people and traffic. Although Richard's eyes were in constant motion looking for signs of threats, he was so preoccupied he did not recognize the danger until it was too late.

"Stephanie, we have to get out of here."

"What?"

"Let's go back, quickly," he said urgently, as he started to turn. A man blocked his way.

"Mr. Moore, you have probably already noticed my men in long tan coats on each of the corners. Underneath their coats, they're holding automatic weapons. If you try anything foolish, they have orders to open fire. You, Ms. Lynn, and many innocent bystanders will die."

A white van pulled up and the side door opened.

"The van is not bulletproof. If you do anything stupid going in, I'll give the word, and my men will open fire. Please get in, and take a seat."

Inside the van, Stephanie and Richard were made to sit in two captain's chairs bolted to the floor of the van and facing forward. An armed man sitting in a jump seat behind the driver faced them. The man who had been talking got in and took another jump seat attached to the rear of the front passenger seat.

"The ride will be a little bumpy, so please fasten your seat belts," he said.

The seat belts were four point harnesses that fastened at the chest.

"Good. Now, the locking mechanism on your safety belts is electronically controlled. You cannot release them unless the driver allows it. Please try to unfasten your belts. I want you to see I am telling the truth." Richard did not move; he just stared at the speaker. Stephanie tried releasing her belt, to no avail. After waiting a few moments, the man said to Richard, "As you wish." He turned to the driver and said, "We're clear." The van pulled away from the curb.

"What do you want, and where are you taking us?" Richard demanded.

"My instructions are simple, Mr. Moore. Someone wants to talk with you. However, if you attempt to resist, my orders are to eliminate you. My briefing indicated you are resourceful, with little fear of personal harm, and because of that, I am to take no chances. At the first hint of resistance or trouble, you and the lady will be killed."

"Who wants to talk with me?"

"You'll have to wait until we arrive at our destination. First, we have a few detours to make. We want to make sure no one else is following."

They made their way through downtown Boston and entered the Callahan tunnel, emerging a few minutes later on Route 1A headed north. As the van approached Boardman Street, it slowed until the main traffic light turned red. The driver stopped in the middle lane of the three lanes and waited. When the light turned green, instead of proceeding straight, the driver made a quick left turn against the red left arrow, and cut across the two lanes of oncoming traffic on the other side of the road. On Boardman Street, just past the intersection, he turned right into a drive-thru lane, went around the far side of a coffee shop, and came to an abrupt stop. A duplicate white panel van that was waiting there lurched forward and, accelerating rapidly, continued around the building, made a left turn onto Boardman Street, then turned left again on to the Northbound side of Route 1A.

The van with Richard sat for two minutes then proceeded slowly around the building and on to Boardman Street. At the intersection of Route 1A, they turned right and headed back the way they had come.

When they reached the tunnel, traffic was heavy, and all open tollbooths had long lines. At the tollbooth, the driver told the attendant he was headed to the airport and needed to turn around. The attendant instructed him to go through and make a U-turn.

Driving slowly the driver checked his rearview side mirrors to see if anyone else made a U-turn or got out of line. No one did. He took the loop around the airport and proceeded out 1A northbound again. The driver made several more U-turns, always returning to a northbound direction. Several miles north of

Boston, he made one last U-turn, crossing the median strip on the Lynnway.

Satisfied they were clear of any tail, they proceeded south over the Tobin Bridge back into Boston. They took the Massachusetts Turnpike west past Framingham and Natick. They exited the Turnpike, and, after they passed through the tollbooth, the man in the back gave Richard and Stephanie each a black hood.

"Please put these on," he said.

After they put on the hoods, Richard sensed they retraced their route several times for twenty minutes. The man in back spoke again.

"Mr. Moore, when we reach our destination, the driver will release the seat belt for the lady. My companion, here, will help her out of the van, and will wait close to the van door for you and me to exit. I'll have your seat belt released and assist you out. The men you saw earlier in Boston have already arrived. They'll be watching for any problems. Their orders are the same: any overt movement by you, they will shoot everyone. If they open fire, we all die. I do not tell you this to intimidate you. I'm telling you only what your trained eyes would tell you if you were not wearing a hood."

The van travelled a cobblestone drive through a long tunnel of tall red pine trees before winding its way across acres of immaculately manicured lawn to the front door of a sprawling, sixteen-room, brick Georgian Colonial home. The van stopped at the front door and everyone got out using the procedure described. Inside the house, Stephanie, and Richard were told to remove their hoods.

They found themselves standing in a formal reception hall whose stained-glass skylight sprayed colored light down upon them. A regal staircase in front of them curved its way to a second-floor hall, which overlooked the reception area. The men with the overcoats stayed outside. The three men from the van led Stephanie and Richard through a door to their right and into a dining room with a built-in, cherry-stained china cabinet and fireplace along the inner wall. Heavy velour drapes framed the outer wall windows. Velour ropes tied the drapes back allowing the sun in. Murals depicting a New England landscape covered both of the sidewalls.

A dining table occupied the center of the room surrounded by French antique high back chairs, three on each of the long sides, and one on either end. A white embossed linen cloth covered the table. Place settings of bone china with sterling silver flatware and crystal water glasses adorned the table along with dishes containing a variety of foods. Alex Wells sat near the head of the table at the far end.

"Chief Moore, Ms. Lynn," Wells greeted, "so nice to see you again."

"You might want to tell Mr. LeBlanc, or whatever his name is, if he comes in here, I won't allow him to leave alive."

"Our host will be with us momentarily. In the meantime, look around, Richard." Wells spread his arm in a circular motion and pointed at the armed men. Then in a quiet, contemptuous voice added, "You are in no position to make threats."

"No threat, Alex," Richard smiled confidently, "I never threaten. It's a promise, and I always keep my promises."

A man came in through the door behind Richard.

"Richard, so good of you to come," he said walking purposefully toward Richard. "And you've brought company. Excellent! Welcome, Ms. Lynn."

Richard turned to face the man behind him and just stared, his body frozen in shocked recognition and disbelief.

"Richard, you haven't said a word. After all this time, can't you at least say hello or inquire how I've been?"

"Rob Lee. I heard you were dead."

"Oh, but I am, Richard. I'm quite dead, and I intend to stay that way. As you can see by looking around you, I'm actually finding it quite an enjoyable experience. I highly recommend it." He let out a large laugh.

"You've both met Alex, of course."

"I'm not interested in Alex, where the fuck is LeBlanc?"

"Please, Richard, not in front of the lady. Besides, what do you want with LeBlanc? Do you ... Oh, Richard, you disappoint me. Do you really believe LeBlanc is responsible for all of this? If you do, you are very much mistaken. Pierre LeBlanc is nothing more than a pawn. A pawn I placed in the game.

"But we will get to him in due course. Please sit, Ms. Lynn, over here, and Richard, on the other side, over there. I was about to have lunch. I hope you'll join me."

As they seated themselves, the three men from the van moved, and stood along the wall holding their automatic weapons by their sides. A woman came in, picked up one of the plates of food, and served Rob Lee. She went in turn to, Stephanie, and Richard, but they declined.

"This is Allison," said Lee, "She runs the house staff. She's been with me for years. I can assure you the food is excellent, so please join me, we have much to talk about."

When no one moved, he said, "Richard, at least have some coffee while I eat."

Richard was still having a hard time controlling his rage. Only his need for answers was keeping him from leaping across the table and throttling Lee. He had worked with Lee enough to know how the man's mind worked. Lee had a specific purpose in bringing them here. If the man were going to harm them, he wouldn't do it until he had accomplished that purpose. Richard decided he would play along with Lee's game for a while. Maybe the man would overplay his hand. He told Allison he would like coffee. The air in the room seemed to lighten and Stephanie decided to follow Richard's lead.

"After the Libyan operation, you were reported missing and presumed dead. Was that another Agency hoax? Is this all some weird Agency operation cooked up by the lunatics who ran the SAIF program? Is that why Ghost was involved and Le Blanc is being protected?"

"Ha! An Agency operation run by the SAIF group. Now, that's quite amusing No one at the Agency has the brains to make what I have done happen, especially not those delusional cretins in the SAIF group. I made money under their noses almost faster than I could put it in the bank. Practically every SAIF mission I went on, I turned into a government financed business trip. I made deals with drug cartels in Central America, arms runners in the Balkans, poppy growers in Afghanistan … Sorry, what a poor host I am being. I'm neglecting your charming companion. Ms. Lynn, please allow me to say that I find you as beautiful in person as I have found you brilliant in print. Are you sure you won't partake of this excellent repast, my dear?"

"No, thank you. I'm choosy about the type of people I eat with."

Lee stopped eating and put on a pained expression. "Ms. Lynn, you've cut me to the quick. Why would you hold me in such poor esteem?" He paused for a moment, and then with a quizzical look, he turned to Richard. "Have you been telling Ms. Lynn bad things about me?"

"I don't talk to people about that part of my life very often or in much detail."

"Oh, yes, forgive me, national security, and all that. Such a burden to carry around." Gesturing to the armed men standing against the wall, he added, "I can assure you these gentlemen are highly discreet. So, Ms. Lynn, just in case you've been misinformed, let me tell you about Richard and me and our friend Ghost, and our wonderful adventures in the world of covert operations."

For the next half hour, he talked about the SAIF program, his relationship with Richard and Ghost, the missions they had been on together and the various ways he had made money on those missions.

After he had described the last mission they shared, the one which caused Richard to resign, he said, "Because of his little tiff with Ghost, I am afraid Richard missed my greatest coup, the Libyan operation. That little junket netted me a tidy bundle of cash, and the start of the new life I'm now living."

"Is that the mission Richard mentioned earlier, the one in which you were supposedly killed? I'd be fascinated to hear all about it."

"Oh, yes, Ms. Lynn, it was quite fascinating. But, I hesitate to talk further about my brilliant exploits, lest you think me boorish."

"Whatever I think about you, Mr. Lee, boorish is not the first thing that comes to mind. Please, go on."

"If you insist, my dear. If you insist."

He had contacts with terrorist groups, he said, and, through one of them, heard that a small group of leaders had defected. These dissidents, who, because of their knowledge, were considered a security risk by the parent organization, fled to Libya, where, for political reasons, the parent group could not get at them. Remaining anonymous, he contacted the parent group through intermediaries. For several million dollars, he said, someone could arrange a CIA mission that would eliminate the dissidents. The security threat would be gone, and the Americans blamed. After negotiations that worked out safeguards that ensured that neither party could be double-crossed, the terrorists agreed to the deal, and revealed the exact location of the dissident camp.

Lee then convinced the SAIF group at Langley that the dissidents had copies of vital terrorist records. The SAIF group authorized his plan to snatch the records, a plan with no provisions for taking prisoners. When the strike group was returning to the helicopters, he hung back and sent Ghost ahead. Just as the last people were about to board, he started lobbing grenades, creating the panic and confusion that allowed his absence to go unnoticed. After the helicopters departed, he collected the evidence he needed to prove the dissidents were dead, commandeered one of their vehicles, and, with help from some bribed officials, made his way to the coast, where he was smuggled out of the country on a fishing boat.

"So you see, Ms. Lynn that is how I became officially dead. Even Ghost thinks I'm dead, despite the fact that I've been sending contracts his way for years."

When Lee was through, Richard said, bitterly, "How can you sit there and talk about that as though it was just some other business project? Good men died on that operation. You may even have killed some of them with those grenades. You damn near killed your own bodyguard. And for what? Just for the sake of putting more money in your offshore bank account."

"Richard, you really can be short-sighted at times. You talk as if the mission was a failure. I have always determined the success or failure of an operation based on the attainment of goals, not lives lost. Those dissidents weren't holding a revival meeting in that camp. They were plotting to unleash death and destruction on innocent, helpless victims. If we hadn't put an end to them out in the Libyan Desert, they might have taken more lives on the streets of Boston, than we lost on the mission. So what if I made a little profit out of it? So did the companies that made the ship, the helicopters, the guns, the ammunition, and the gas we used. Come to think of it, Captain Moore, I never saw you refuse your paycheck just because someone was killed on a mission, even when you were the one who killed them. We both killed for money, Richard, only you did it for a lot less. Put another spangle on your shoulder or another bauble on your chest, and off you marched, gun in hand, ready to kill for God and country! They bought you cheap, and cheapness is not a virtue, Captain, so don't get all virtuous on me. No, Richard. The mission was not a failure, not for the country or for me. It was a spectacular success!"

Richard was subdued and silent for a few moments before asking, "So, why have you come back now? Aren't you afraid the Agency or the FBI will find you ... or have you cut some kind of deal with them?"

"Richard, I'm dead, remember? No one is looking for me. Besides, they're all very busy right now chasing terrorists. No, I returned to the States shortly after Libya, and have been here ever since. I've directed my operations right from here undetected for years. I only leave from time to time on vacation or business. This is my country, Richard. You should know that better than anyone; we fought for it side by side."

"Am I supposed to be impressed?"

"You should be."

"So, you going to tell me about LeBlanc or whatever his name is, or did you bring us here for another reason?"

"I had several reasons for bringing you here, but I'll start by telling you about LeBlanc. As the redoubtable and charming Ms. Lynn has already ascertained, Pierre LeBlanc is not his real name. It's Robert Fournier. He's a French Canadian. I met him at UCLA Davis when I was recruiting for the Agency. Even in those early years, I knew what I wanted, and was looking for talent that could help me achieve it. When I interviewed Robert, I found he possessed a hard-driving ambition and an uncanny ability to identify business opportunities. During his freshman year, he began buying obsolete medical equipment from American hospitals and selling it at a profit to the Indian Health Ministry.

"The Health Minister asked Robert if he could supply inexpensive prescription drugs. In his research, Robert found a suppressed U. S. Food and Drug Administration study that showed ninety percent of drugs are effective for years past their expiration date. With this evidence, he talked the minister into buying short-dated medications from him.

"When I found out what he was doing, I made a deal with him to use my Agency contacts to expand the business in exchange for an ownership interest. With my help, by the time he graduated, he had contracts with health ministers in a dozen different countries, and a network of student buyers around the States providing him with short-dated drugs. One of his student suppliers acquired a carload of IV fluids that were not short-dated. It turned out to be a very lucrative deal. Robert sold the stuff for full price here in the States. Unfortunately, patients started getting sick and a few died, and the problem was traced to the IV solutions. The student, in collusion with the drug wholesaler, had sold us a carload of counterfeit IV fluids, some of which contained toxic contaminants.

"A federal grand jury issued an indictment against Robert for criminal manslaughter. The Feds were going to throw him in jail, and he turned to me for help."

Rob Lee looked up and saw Allison standing in the doorway.

"Would anyone like more coffee?" he asked, as he beckoned Allison to freshen his cup.

"I got him out of the country," he continued, "and settled him in France. As fortune would have it, Pierre LeBlanc, a man of Robert's age and physical characteristics, died in an unfortunate accident shortly after Robert took up residence in France."

"How convenient. I don't suppose you had anything to do with the accident?" asked Richard.

"Don't be tiresome, Richard, the specifics of his demise are irrelevant. Robert spent the next year putting together his plan for Health Insurance Services Holding. I helped secure funding, and voila, Monsieur Pierre LeBlanc arrived in Boston with a solid business plan and plenty of capital.

"HISH was added to my growing list of business interests. Robert, now Pierre, sends me reports and financial information regularly. About five years ago, he sent me a prospectus for an initial public offering. I looked the deal over, then I took the prospectus to some investment advisers. Two of them determined the multiples would be higher if HISH did a better job of managing costs. I told Robert to hold off until he could lower expenses enough to increase the multiples."

"Then, you instituted a plan for murdering members who were sick just to increase the amount of money you would receive." Richard's anger was beginning to bubble up again, and it showed in the tone of his voice.

"Richard, that sounds so cold. I hope you're not going to get self-righteous on me again. We're not just talking about putting a few more dollars in the pocket of some stockholder. We're talking about families that might have been left with hundreds of thousands of dollars in medical bills. That's right, hundreds of thousands of dollars. These illnesses account for two thirds of all personal bankruptcies, and eighty percent of those people have health insurance. The same diseases also cost the healthy members hundreds of thousands of dollars in premiums. They're the ones who really pay the company's bills, after all. What's more, most of these poor unfortunates would have suffered slow excruciating, deaths filled with physical torture and mental agony, and their families would have suffered right along with them. No, this isn't all as black and white as it seems."

Stephanie said, "You can't possibly believe that. What you were doing was monstrous."

"I can assure you, Ms. Lynn that I am not a monster: A pragmatist, yes, but not a monster. In fact, like any other person, I have my sensibilities." Turning to Richard, he said, "This brings me to the main reason I wanted to talk with you, Richard. I want you to know I do not select the candidates for the HISH program, that is done by a person with utilization review experience. I merely pass the information along to Ghost, who, because he is the most exposed element of the program, is never told any more than he needs to know to do his job. When I became aware that you were investigating HISH, I had some people research your life since leaving the service. It wasn't until yesterday I discovered your wife was one of the participants in the program.

"We may not have been best friends, you and I, but I felt an obligation to express my sympathy for your loss and offer my sincere apology. If I had known who she was, I would never have passed her name along to Ghost. If it's any final consolation to you, his bungled attempts on your life have convinced me to replace him permanently."

Richard was surprised Lee did not already know that Ghost was dead, but was not in the mood to enlighten the man. It was taking every ounce of his control to keep from leaping at Rob Lee and killing him with his bare hands. He did not care what happened to himself.

"Richard, Ms. Lynn, I must be leaving, but please enjoy lunch together. When you finish, my men will clean up. Of course, we will not see each other again, Richard, and I hope you know your investigation has ended."

As Lee spoke, Richard became aware of the faint sound of an approaching helicopter. Lee's face assumed a puzzled expression, then, quite suddenly, the faint sound escalated into a deafening roar. Lee's pushed back from the table. At that instant, the windows behind him shattered, and there was an instantaneous series of blinding light flashes accompanied by loud explosions. Instinctively, Richard leaped across the table, grabbed Stephanie, and drove her to the floor.

"Don't move until the shooting stops!"

The words were no sooner out of his mouth when the room erupted in automatic gunfire. Immediately after the light flashes and explosions, armed men in black uniforms, their heads covered with black ski masks, swung through the shattered windows at the end of rappelling ropes. Too stunned, or too foolish to know better, Rob Lee's men pointed their automatic weapons at the intruders, who cut them down without hesitation.

When the shooting stopped, Richard turned his head to his right, expecting to see Rob Lee lying on the floor spouting blood.

Instead he saw Rob Lee's head at floor level staring directly at him for a moment before it disappeared downward.

"Stay here, and don't move around until you're told to." Richard started crawling toward the hole into which Lee had disappeared.

"Richard, where are you going?" Fear and confusion were evident in Stephanie's voice.

"Rob Lee is getting away. I have to stop him."

Richard got to the hole in the floor where Rob Lee's chair had been and cautiously spied over the edge into the semidarkness below. A shot rang out and the floorboard next to Richard splintered, sending pieces of wood in all directions. One piece lodged in his right shoulder; another stuck in the side of his neck a half-inch from his carotid artery.

Hearing a door slam below him, he swung his legs into the hole, and lowered himself. His feet landed on the chair Rob Lee had been sitting in.

Richard found he was in a small, square, musty, room with doors in each wall. Without the light from the dining room above, he would have been standing in complete darkness.

He noticed a damp spot in front of one of the doors, so he pulled the door open and looked into a black void. He held his breath, and, listening carefully, heard the sound of footsteps somewhere down the passageway. Whoever was down there was in no hurry.

Richard entered the dark corridor and let the door close behind him. He flattened himself against the left wall and paced his breathing to calm his body. He proceeded down the corridor in a controlled trot, careful not to allow his footsteps to announce his advance, and kept one hand in contact with a wall. His eyes had nothing on which to focus. It was too dark. He had to rely on sound and touch, and the sixth sense he developed in combat.

The corridor seemed to widen, and he stopped. Reaching out in front of him, he discovered he had stopped just short of running into a door. Then, his hands found three more doors. He was about to open one when, in the distance behind him, he heard movement. The people who had smashed into the dining room were now hunting in the basement. *I hope they're friendly and that they know I'm here,* he thought to himself. He opened the door to his left and listened. No sound. The corridor behind the door in the center was also void of any sound. He opened the third door and stepped forward. He saw the muzzle flash as the door closed behind him, then came searing pain as a bullet pierced his side.

While Richard followed Rob Lee into the basement, the noise and fast-paced activity of the raid on the estate ended as quickly as it had started. In the dining room, the men in black checked the three dead guards, and ordered Stephanie to stay put. After a few moments of checking the area, one of them yelled, "Clear!" and two men in business suits entered the room.

One of them approached Stephanie and said, "Ms. Lynn, it's safe to get up now."

"Who the hell are you?" Stephanie demanded.

"I am Charlie White, FBI. Where is Richard? He was with you, wasn't he?"

"He went down that hole. Rob Lee got away."

The other man turned to one of the men in black. "Sergeant, notify the perimeter, we have one friendly and an unknown number of hostiles on the move. Leave one man here, and the rest of you get down there and find Rob Lee. I want him."

"Yes, sir, we're moving."

"Remember, I want Rob Lee. He does not get away. Richard is a friendly, but not one of us."

"Roger that," the sergeant replied.

"Not one of you?" Stephanie yelled. "What the hell does that mean? You stay the hell out of that basement while Richard is down there!"

No one acknowledged Stephanie or her remarks. The sergeant spoke into his head set and notified the perimeter guards. He turned and ordered, "Sticks, you stay here. The rest of you follow me." Four men followed the sergeant into the hole and began to spread out. It had been a daylight raid, so no one was equipped with night vision goggles or flashlights.

Two of the four doors opened into corridors. The other two were dead-ends. The team split up; three men entered the left side door, while the sergeant and one other entered the door Richard had entered earlier. They moved quickly, one man on each side of the corridor, their backs pressed against the wall to provide a minimal target.

Ten minutes later, Charlie White said into his radio, "All right, they have to come out somewhere. Keep me posted."

"What's going on?" Stephanie asked, as Charlie began to pace.

"The perimeter men haven't seen a thing. We lost communications with the men in the basement."

"Lost communications, what the hell does that mean?" Stephanie yelled. Her frustration with the apparent lack of progress and her concern for Richard were mounting.

"The construction of the basement, or some equipment in the house, must be interfering with the communication signals."

"You don't know do you?" she said defiantly.

"Ms. Lynn, these men are the best professionals—"

"Yeah, Duce, I copy." Sticks held up his left hand to stop the talk in the room, while his right hand went to his earpiece.

"Sticks, we need night vision goggles or some light."

"No NVGs this trip, Duce. I'll get some light."

Sticks went out the front door to a van. Duce popped his head above the floor.

"Damn, it's dark down there."

"What's the status?" Charlie asked.

"It's so dark you can't see your hand in front of your face. Some of the doors lead to dead-end rooms. The doors in those rooms have no handles on the inside. It's set up to trap or delay. The sarge and me are working one of two corridors, but we need light so we don't get trapped. Coms are scrambled. There must be a low power signal-jam working."

Sticks entered the room and tossed two lights to Duce. Duce disappeared back into the basement.

In the blackened corridor, Richard's heart was pounding, he was breathing heavily, and adrenalin was coursing through his system. The bullet had ricocheted off the wall and pierced his right side just under his armpit. *So much for controlling my body,* he thought to himself. He sprinted toward the muzzle flash. Two seconds later, light flooded in from the left just ahead of him. The light caused momentary blindness, but he kept moving.

He reached the left turn, peered around the corner, and saw light streaming in through a door that was closing. The door did not have a latch or handle on it. He made the ten-foot distance in three strides and planted his foot in the door jam. His dress shoes provided little protection as someone on the other side of the door threw his body against it to force it closed.

In response, Richard repeatedly pounded his right shoulder into the metal door trying to force it open further. His foot, still in the jam, was squeezed more as the man on the other side countered Richard's thrusts with his own.

On the other side of the door, Rob Lee threw the man pushing on the door a long-handled axe.

"Jam it, and let's move."

Lee jumped into a late model red Jeep Wrangler and started the engine as the man dropped the axe and, with his foot, wedged the axe under the door. When the man jumped into the back of the Jeep, Lee pushed the accelerator to the floor. The vehicle lurched ahead with a squeal of its tires, and the smell of burning rubber.

Richard's third thrust against the axe-wedged door caused the axe to slide along the concrete floor. The door popped open and Richard stumbled uncontrollably through the opening and across the garage. A stack of wooden crates stopped his momentum. The impact knocked the wind out of him and caused pain to shoot through his side and abdomen. He recovered just in time to see the Jeep disappear down a tree-lined path.

47

Assisted by a masked man in tactical gear, Richard made his way across the three hundred yards of manicured lawn and into the house. He noted an armored assault vehicle disguised as an armored bank truck, several white vans parked around the house, and heavily armed men in tactical gear and ski masks patrolling the grounds. An MH-6H Little Bird assault helicopter sat on the lawn. He said to himself that whoever mounted this operation had to have plenty of influence to requisition this kind of equipment and muscle.

When he entered the dining room, Stephanie jumped out of her chair and ran up to him. Putting her arms around him, she said, "Thank God, you're okay" When he grunted in pain, she backed off, and saw the blood under his right arm. "Oh, Richard you're hurt."

"It's not bad," he said, as he surveyed the scene around him.

"Charles?"

"Hi, Richard."

"I thought you were in Washington when we talked this morning."

"Actually, I was on a small jet headed to Boston. They wanted a face familiar to you if the raid went well. You don't know any of these people."

The other man in a suit walked over and stood near Charles. "Richard, this is Claude Billings. He's not with the Bureau."

Claude extended his hand, and Richard shook it with his left, saying, "I assume you came here looking for Rob Lee. Did you get my report that I saw him take off with one of his men in a red Jeep? I didn't get a look at the license plate, but it was a topless Wrangler. If we get roadblocks set up, we have a good chance of catching him."

"Yes, Chief Moore, the man you told radioed me and we have the situation under control. Please sit down while one of my men looks at that wound."

Richard did as requested, and one of the hooded men began to clean and dress the wound. Stephanie, sat beside him and, reaching out, took him by the left hand.

"I assume if you're not with the Bureau, your real name isn't Claude," Richard said.

Billings smiled, and then answered, "You may use any name you'd like. It's not important." Then, his expression turned serious, and he said, "Chief, Ms. Lynn, I'm sure you both have a lot of questions, and I'll try to answer them as well as I can, but first, please tell me everything you can remember about what's been said and done since you were picked up in the van."

Richard looked at Stephanie, who nodded to him, and he began. As he talked, Stephanie interjected additional details, and from time to time Billings interrupted with questions.

When Richard was through, Billings thought for a few moments, then, looking intently at Richard, said, "Chief, are you absolutely convinced the man you met here today was the same man you served with on those SAIF missions, absolutely sure it was Rob Lee?"

"Absolutely. He looked, acted and talked like him, and knew about things that happened on missions that only Rob Lee and I knew."

Billings seemed to digest the information for a few moments.

Turning toward Charlie, Richard asked, "How'd you find us? The driver was good at eliminating any tails."

Charlie did not reply. "He was very good, but his efforts actually helped us out, by giving us time to mobilize our assault team. We've been monitoring your movements through satellite GPS and a small drone controlled by a specially equipped van," Billings answered.

"The van was tagged?"

"No, you are."

"Me? How?"

"You have a miniature GPS tracking unit embedded in your left arm."

"The stitches! The nurse said a doctor replaced the stitches in my arm the night Ghost tried to kill me in the garage! How did you pull that off?"

"The details aren't important, but, yes, that's when it was done. The whole unit is a little smaller than the nail of your smallest finger, and will broadcast for about eighteen months. We saw the snatch this morning through the drone's camera, and mobilized the assault team while your driver was wasting his time making U-turns. By the time he arrived here, our air assault team was airborne, and a convoy of vans was only a few miles away. The GPS tracker pinpointed the room you were in, and, when all our units were in place, we launched our assault."

"Wait, you were tracking me? You had a doctor put a tracking device in me so you could find Rob Lee. You knew what was going on, and you never contacted me? Don't you know Ghost almost killed Stephanie and me twice last night, and Rob Lee was undoubtedly about to finishing the job when you arrived? We could have been killed just so you could use us as bait!"

Billings seemed to think this over for a few moments before he looked intently at Richard and said, "Tell me, Richard, did you notify anyone on that HISH list that they were at risk of being killed? Didn't you take a calculated risk with their lives for the sake of your investigation?"

Richard was silent for a few moments, then, in a far less indignant voice, asked, "How did you know about Rob Lee, the HISH list and my investigation anyway?"

"Robert Fournier, AKA Pierre Leblanc," said Billings.

"LeBlanc, Lee's partner in murder?" Richard asked, incredulously.

"Yes, LeBlanc. Lee managed his deception this long because he was smart and careful, but, from what I've learned about him, he also has an enormous ego, and a dismissive contempt for those he considers his inferiors. I think he let that contempt cloud his judgment when he brought Fournier back into the country under an assumed name. He probably figured everyone was too dumb to discover that a foreign national running a multimillion-dollar health insurance company was a phony. I'll admit it worked for a long time, but, still, it was an arrogant and stupid move. A recent routine Homeland Security check discovered Pierre LeBlanc was a phony, and, because of the man's position, he was paid a discreet visit at his home on a weekend. Realizing he was in serious shit, he convinced them to contact Langley. He told Langley who he really was, and said if they cut him a deal, he could give them a rogue agent they thought was dead. When he told them it was Rob Lee, they ran a check and found an old reference connecting Fournier and Lee. Knowing they could take Fournier anytime they wanted, they left him in place at HISH with the understanding there would be a deal only if his story checked out. They started an investigation, and, now that we're all doing a better job of sharing information, they uncovered information buried in the files of Interpol, the FBI, the Pentagon, Treasury and other places. The more they dug, they more stuff they uncovered, and, when they put all the pieces together, there was little doubt left that Lee had been lining his pockets at Agency expense for most of his career. When this was all presented to the director, he ordered the Lee case reopened, and restricted access to the file. They decided that if Lee really was alive, the possibility existed that he had somehow cut a deal with the terrorists, so a secret warrant was issued for him under the antiterrorism statutes. This allowed Homeland Security to take nominal command over the search as a top-secret antiterrorist operation. I know it's a bit of a stretch, but as you know, technically the Agency can't operate on American soil, and Homeland Security elite units and operatives can. So, while the Agency has been looking for him overseas, we've been looking for him here."

Richard noticed that, when Billings stopped talking about the CIA and started talking about Homeland Security, he switched from they to we. Maybe he was not Agency after all.

"Okay, so that's how you got on to Lee, but how did LeBlanc, I mean, Fournier, connect me and my investigation to Lee?"

"After a few weeks passed, Fournier's nerves were getting progressively frayed. When someone claiming to be a police officer showed up asking questions, it spooked him badly, and he called us right away to find out if we had sent you, or if Lee had. Of course, when we ran you through the computers, we found your connection to Lee. At first, we thought you were working for Lee, and, when Scott was hit at the Sheep Fold, we were sure you had set him up. Realizing you were no good to us if the State Police put you in the slammer, we asked an old friend to intervene."

Richard interrupted. "Tomlinson. I wondered why he knew so much and why he called his hounds off and hasn't let them bother me despite all the heat he was taking over the shootings."

"It's not my place to say who we talked to, or what they did. Anyway, we posted a watch on Scott, and started keeping tabs on your movements."

"But, Mrs. Scott said the security detail was discontinued," Stephanie said. "Richard had to get some friends in to watch him last night."

"Yes, we know all about that. We replaced the uniformed officers with our own operatives dressed as hospital personnel. They were there when you visited last evening."

"Why didn't you tell Mrs. Scott? She was sick with worry about—" Stephanie stopped as the answer dawned on her. "You miserable bastards were using him as bait too, and you wanted the trap to look as real as possible. How do you people sleep at night?"

For the first time, Billings let his cool façade slip, and there was just a hint of anger in his voice as he said, "Some of us don't sleep very well, at all, Ms. Lynn, I can assure you. We're awake making sure you can."

An awkward pause heightened the tension in the room. Richard decided to change the subject. He then said, "I didn't spy a tail; your people must be very good."

"After we checked your record, we figured you might spot any close surveillance and go to ground. We were also afraid you'd be sweeping your home, office, and car for bugs, so we laid off those as well. In the end, we had to be content with watching you from a distance, and using the drone as a visual spotter when we could. Of course, when we got the chance to do the implant, we took it. Our surveillance crew was down the street watching the front of your house from a distance the night Ghost set up your fake suicide. Before they figured out what he was doing, the lieutenant pulled up and all hell broke loose. We were monitoring the police and other emergency radios, so we had plenty of time to get our person in place in the hospital. By that time, we'd dropped the idea that you were working with Lee. In fact, it was beginning to look like your little investigation stood a better chance of causing him to tip his hand, and doing it a lot sooner than anything we were doing."

"What about the list? If Fournier told you about the list, then he must have known about the murders. He's an accomplice to murder, at the least."

"Fournier didn't know about the list until Scott told him someone was using a backdoor access to the files. When he notified us, we told him to tell Scott it was part of the HISH security routine. We hoped that would satisfy Scott's curiosity, and keep him from doing something to jeopardize our investigation. Of course, we had our own people break into the system to see if they could figure out what the backdoor was all about and if it could help lead us to Lee. As it turned out, Scott wasn't satisfied, and managed to crack open the file and send you a copy of it. We also think he managed to figure out who had created the backdoor. My people say they want to hire him when he gets well, because it took them longer to open the file, and they didn't figure out who was using the backdoor until the day before yesterday. Unfortunately, the man they named will never stand trial for murder."

"He will, if I have anything to say about it," Richard said with emotion.

"I can understand your feelings, Chief, but the man who created the file and selected the murder victims, the man who fingered you, Scott, Hayden and Ms. Lynn, is that gentleman." He pointed to the corner of the room where someone had dumped the bullet-ridden body of Alex Wells.

By now, Richard's wound had been cleansed and dressed. He gently disengaged his hand from Stephanie's, got out of his chair, and walked over to Wells' body. After a few moments staring down at the dead man, he rubbed his tearing eyes, while slowly shaking his head back and forth. He felt no anger, or satisfaction, just sadness.

As Richard returned to the table, Billings received a message on his radio. After listening to it, he said, "Okay, sweep the area again, just in case, and bring the Jeep back here."

"What's this about the Jeep?" Richard asked.

Billings looked exasperated as he answered, "Several late-model, topless, red Jeep Wranglers, abandoned with the engine running, Chief. All found about five miles from here, and about five miles from heavily travelled highways. Now we don't know what the son of a bitch is using for transportation, or where he's headed! Just marvelous!"

"Maybe somebody here knows where he's headed and is willing to make a deal. After all, he's left them all holding the bag," Richard said.

Billings looked at Richard strangely, then realization seemed to dawn on the man. "That's right Chief; you were below when we wrapped up this little fracas, so you don't know the outcome. The four men in the overcoats were muscle rented just for the snatch. We grabbed them on their way home, but we expect there's nothing important they can tell us. As far as we can tell, there were six people on the staff here, and whatever their domestic duties were, they were all well-trained and well-paid security personnel. The three from the van, as you know, are lying there with Wells. A security man at the gate thought his assault rifle could stop our assault vehicle. He's dead. A woman trying to escape into the tunnels wounded one of the assault team when he told her to stop. She didn't survive. The only one left alive is the man you saw escaping with Lee."

"So, where does that leave us?" asked Richard.

"In many ways, it leaves us better off than we were. We now know that Lee is alive. Knowing he cut a deal with a terrorist organization means we can continue with this operation under its present mandate. We've eliminated the HISH murder program. We'll access Lee's interest in the company to help offset the cost of looking for him. We just don't have him in custody, and may have to resign ourselves to the fact that getting him into custody could take us awhile."

Stephanie said, "Well, I'm sure my story will help make it easier. This time tomorrow, his name and picture will be on every news outlet in the country."

Claude asked, "What story, Ms. Lynn?"

"The one about a dead CIA agent and his connection to terrorists, the HISH murders, and a dozen other illegal schemes, to say nothing about attempting to murder a police officer, and a journalist. This story could play for weeks. Hell, this could be the biggest story of my life!"

"And just how are you going to verify the story Ms. Lynn?"

"What the hell are you talking about?"

"Any story implying people were murdered by or for HISH will go unsubstantiated. Law enforcement agencies, insurance investigators, even your own newspaper, have investigated all the deaths with no finding of wrongdoing."

"You're forgetting the HISH file."

"The file has been removed from the HISH database, and all copies, including Steve Deschenes' and Chief Moore's, have been confiscated."

When Richard looked surprised, Billings permitted himself a wisp of a smile. "You really shouldn't leave your laptop lying around, Chief. Don't worry; we're only interested in the HISH file. Nothing else will be disturbed and the machine will be returned."

Then he continued, "The only other direct link between HISH and the murders was our dear, departed friend, Mr. Wells. As for any connection between Lee and HISH, Lee does all his business through a convoluted series of untraceable transactions and aliases. Besides, Ms. Lynne, Rob Lee is officially dead. The search for him, and any activity associated with the search, including this operation, is highly classified. The only people who could corroborate that part of your story know they would go to jail for a very long time if they did. Don't look at Chief Moore, Ms. Lynn; local police are obligated to protect classified Homeland Security information. He and his officers are just as liable to prosecution as I am. In short, Miss Lynn, you don't have a corroborated news story here, at least, not a news story that a competent journalist like you would try to publish."

"You seem to have tied everything up into a nice neat little bow, Mr. Billings, or whatever the hell your name is, but there's the little loose string of four dead bodies at a motel in Winchendon you seem to have forgotten, and my own documentation about Pierre LeBlanc."

"No, Ms. Lynn, I haven't forgotten the four dead bodies. If you'd been listening to the news today, you wouldn't have heard anything about them. After you and Chief Moore left the motel last night, the team that had been following you secured the scene before the two Winchendon officers could call it in."

Richard looked alarmed, so Billings said, "Not to worry, Chief, you're officers are fine. In fact, they're on their way here right now, and should be arriving shortly."

"Before they get here, and before we talk about Fournier, alias LeBlanc, I'd like to clear up a few things, Ms. Lynn. Some people at the CIA would like nothing better than for Rob Lee to stay dead. His story is not only an embarrassment; it has the potential to wreck the careers of people who have great power. Fortunately, some equally powerful people want to bring Lee to justice. It's only because if their efforts that there is any real search for Lee taking place at all. If the Lee story becomes public before we catch him, however, the fallout could lead to a circling of the wagons that would leave the good guys on the outside. The search for Lee might turn into a public-relations circus designed more for show than for success.

"That's one point. The other is that we are dealing with a very intelligent, resourceful, and deadly adversary here. You've seen that for yourself. The less he knows about our operation, the safer it is for all of us, and the greater our chances of success. If the press is telegraphing our every move to him, he's the only one who'll benefit; it'll allow him to keep one-step ahead of us.

"I'm not a fool, Ms. Lynn, and I don't think you're one either. If you're determined to publish this story, I might be able to slow you down, but I won't be able to stop you. In the end, though, I hope that the knowledge that you might be helping Lee get away will stop you. A little while ago, you chastised me for causing Mrs. Scott anguish by attempting to catch her husband's assailant. How will your story comfort her if it helps her husband's assailant go free? How will it comfort Bryan Hayden's mother and father? How will it comfort all those connected with the HISH murder victims? How will it comfort Chief Moore?"

Stephanie didn't answer him. She wanted this story, wanted to shout, *I was almost killed several times! I aided in the discovery of the murder! I paid my dues. I deserve this story!* The more she said the words to herself, however, the less convincing they sounded.

When she looked at Richard, they didn't sound very convincing at all.

"Ms. Lynn … Ms. Lynn."

She realized that Billings was trying to get her attention, and looked up at him.

"Ms. Lynn, I realize you have risked your life and done a lot of research to get this story. I have risked your life to try to catch Rob Lee. I owe you. I owe both you and Chief Moore. The two officers from Winchendon are just arriving, and I have some propositions to make to all of you that might help me pay that debt."

A few moments later, Peggy Butler and Chris Allen both arrived in uniform, and, while the two women hugged, the men shook hands.

After the greetings were over, Billings said he had to check on the state of the operation, and make some arrangements. Before he left, however, Chris talked to him privately for a few minutes.

After a brief discussion with Billings, Chris returned to the table and related what had happened to him and Peggy after Stephanie and Richard left them.

The assault team caught them unawares, and they were quickly disarmed and taken away. They met Billings at another motel. He explained who he was and told them the men they had killed were subjects of a classified operation. He told Peggy and Christopher they were now part of the operation. Chris was instructed to call dispatch, and tell Tracy that he and Peggy would be temporarily out of reach on assignment. Their cruisers arrived; they retrieved their belongings, and were given rooms. Around midmorning, there was a flurry of activity, and Billings summoned them. He told them the operation had a sudden crisis to deal with, and they should go back to Winchendon to stand by for further orders. Both of them spent time catching up on paperwork in the office until they received a call giving them directions to Lee's mansion and orders to meet there with Mr. Billings and Chief Moore.

When he was through, Allen said, "Okay, so now you know what we've been doing, what have you guys been up to?"

With frequent interjections from Stephanie, Richard brought them up to date.

When he was through, Peggy Butler said, "Wow, Chief, this sounds like something you'd read in a spy novel!"

Before he could respond, Billings returned.

"Ms. Lynn, I'd like to start with you. Robert Fournier did not participate in, had no knowledge of, and will not benefit from the HISH murders. He is, however, a fugitive from justice because of the IV fluid fiasco. He's also a prominent business figure. Even without the HISH list, he's a hell of a story, and will be a hell of a story for quite awhile. He may eventually deal his way into the witness protection program, but nobody, not even he, thinks he'll slip quietly away. Federal agents will arrest him in two days. If some sharp reporter who has been digging around in France breaks the story before then, it will be a hell of a scoop, more so if Fournier grants the reporter exclusive access for interviews during the ensuing legal process. Think about it Ms. Lynn."

"The next issue involves everyone at the table. I need to address the unfortunate incident in the motel room last night. The State Police are looking for a single shooter to solve the so-called Sheep Fold Sniper case. Unfortunately, due to the excellent work of Officers Butler and Allen, we have three bodies too many to give them. With everyone's cooperation, I can arrange to reduce the excess body count, and give the State Police one dead sniper. That will end the sniper case, and the sniper scare."

Peggy said, "He was killed with my gun. The ballistics will show it was my gun."

"Trust me, Officer Butler; the slug they find in his head will not match your weapon."

"And just where will this body be found, and how will they know it's the sniper?"

"The details will be convincing and irrefutable. I can assure you."

"What about Stuart Scott? What about the other people wounded by Ghost? What do they get out of all of this, besides your gratitude?" asked Stephanie.

"An anonymous philanthropist will set up a trust fund for the sniper victims. None of the people wounded by Ghost will ever receive a medical bill for any acute or long-term care associated with their wounds. As for Scott in particular, our geeks are so impressed with the skill he demonstrated in finding and decoding the HISH file that they can't wait to talk to him about coming to work with them."

Stephanie gave him a begrudging look then said, "I assume if we don't go along with the story, no one gets anything."

Billings shifted in his chair. "If it were up to me, Ms Lynn, no, it wouldn't make a difference. However, yes, it would make it a lot harder for me to convince those involved to go through with the deal."

Thirty minutes later, Richard was in another room talking on the phone with Tim Curtin. While Chris and Peggy were being given a tour of the assault helicopter, Charlie White was talking to Stephanie.

"I can see where keeping a lid on this would be a hard thing for you to do, Ms. Lynn. Billings, Richard, and I have spent so much of our lives keeping secrets that it almost comes naturally to us. I'll have to admit, we err on the side of being too secretive."

"Please call me Stephanie, Charlie. You're right, it is difficult. My job is exposing secrets. However, a good reporter also knows how to keep a secret until it's the right time to tell it. I'm in on the ground floor on this Rob Lee hunt, Charlie, and Billings knows I can blow the lid off anytime I want to. He'll make sure I'll be the first to get the story when the time comes. In the meantime, I'm leaving here with a story that's a bombshell in its own right. I'll be knocking on LeBlanc's door tomorrow morning, and knocking the socks off my readers in the next edition. Peggy's statement about this seeming like a novel has me thinking. I have enough material for a terrific novel. All things considered, I'd say this was a good day for me."

She paused, as though hesitant to go on. Finally, she said, "Charlie, you and Richard have been close for a long time, so I'm going to ask you a very personal question, and I won't be offended if you choose not to answer."

"Go ahead."

"Did you know Richard's wife and what their relationship was like?"

The question caught White off guard, and it took him a few moments to answer. "Yes, I knew Lori. I knew her as Richard's wife, and I knew her as a colleague. I was with the Bureau's Boston office at the same time she was with the DA. She was beautiful and smart and, as a prosecutor, hell on wheels. I think you'd have liked her, most people did ... They were really in love, and if you knew Richard before Lori, you'd know how remarkable that was. Richard has always been a likeable guy, and a good friend, but, before Lori, he held back a large part of himself from others. She opened him up, and inside was another Richard no one knew even existed. When she died, that part of him was in so much pain, that after a while, all he could do was try to close it all back up again. I'm a cop, not a psychiatrist, but I think that's why he keeps having the dream."

"What dream is that, Charlie?"

Stephanie saw Charlie become very uncomfortable, so she said, "Sorry, Charlie, I'm acting too much like a reporter. Forget I asked."

Charlie looked at Stephanie intently for a few moments, then said, "No, Stephanie, I don't think you're asking because you're a reporter, so, I'll tell you. Richard has a recurring dream about Lori being diagnosed with cancer and the dream ends with Lori trapped in a car suffocating, and Richard tries desperately to save her, but he can't. I'm the only other person who knows about the dream. Shit, maybe I'm not as good at keeping secrets as I think I am. Just chalk it up to the kind of day we've had." He was clearly embarrassed.

"Thanks, Charlie," Stephanie said, and gave him a hug, which made him even more embarrassed.

Richard appeared, and Charlie quickly said, "Richard, I feel like the fifth wheel here. I'm heading back to Washington. You should drop down sometime. I'll give you the nickel tour."

"Thanks, Charles, I've had and given that tour. But I'll come down to see you and we'll have dinner."

"I'd like that. The same invitation goes for you, Stephanie. Come down with or without our friend, here. By the way, I think you've made the right decision to go along with Billings. I know he's going to take a lot of heat for letting Lee slip through the net.

Anyway, I think I'm trying to say that you have a friend at the Bureau, Stephanie, anytime you need one."

"Thanks, I'll remember that, Charlie, and you have a friend at the Boston Globe."

Clearly embarrassed again, Charlie said, "I have to run. Stephanie, it was nice to have met you. I hope we can meet again under better circumstances."

After Charlie left, Richard said, "What was that all about?"

"Maybe I'll tell you someday. In the meantime, let's blow this joint. We both need to get some clean clothes and freshen up, and then, you can take me to dinner. Being almost killed gives me a big appetite."

They found Chris and Peggy, and they all said good–bye to Billings. Peggy said she would ride back to Winchendon with Chris in his cruiser, so Richard and Stephanie could take the unmarked car. After they had agreed on a time and place to meet in the morning, they got into their cars and left.

Peggy and Chris did not say much to each other until they were approaching Winchendon. Then Peggy turned to Chris and said, "Lieutenant, I need to decompress for a while and take a shower. Why don't we have dinner tonight, and we can discuss exactly what we're going to put in our report?"

"Officer Butler, are you asking me for a date?"

"Well, that depends. If we're in uniform, I'm suggesting a working dinner. If we're less formal, say a tank top and hair down, then you can classify the dinner anyway you want." Peggy had a broad smile on her face.

"I think we can go in civvies."

Billings called in a team to sanitize the house, and then debriefed the assault team before dismissing them. Later, sitting in the back of the van bringing him to Boston, he opened his laptop and began writing a report that would not make anyone happy.

Later that evening, Stephanie and Richard were lying in bed, her head on his shoulder, her right palm stroking his bare chest.

"Is it safe to assume no one will be kicking in our door and throwing me out of bed?"

"I can assure you, no one will be crashing through the door. I may kick you out of bed when the dream comes, though." He had told her about his nightly dream.

"I thrash about sometimes."

She kissed him on the ear.

"Then, I'll just have to keep you awake and busy." It had been more than two years since Richard last made love to a woman. He had never experienced as many emotional changes as he did this time; love, lust, doubt, and guilt swept through him before he drifted off to sleep.

The dream came back. Richard was looking at his wife in the car. She was smiling with her right-hand thumb up. Then she laid her head back and closed her eyes. He screamed, "No!" as he pushed hard against the door, expecting it to remain firmly close. It popped open. He rushed to the car and grabbed the door handle. He found it locked. Lori turned her head toward him. "I love you," she said as she laid her head back and closed her eyes again. The dream faded to black. It never came back.

48

Midway through the following morning, Theo was in his storeroom arranging the first of Carlos's new shipments, when his clerk entered and said the chief of police was there to see him. He thought that maybe young Allen had finally seen which way the wind was blowing, and had come to eat a little humble pie. It made him feel more in control, a sensation that had been sorely lacking recently. He wiped his hands, put on his suit coat, assumed his most official manner, and opened the storeroom door.

He was confounded by the scene that greeted him. Young Allen was there all right, but he hardly had the humbled look Theo expected to see. Moreover, he was accompanied by Officer Butler, and several men in suits. Standing apart from them was Bill Blackstone. Most confounding of all, the man who seemed to be leading this little invasion force was Richard Moore, armed, and attired in his police uniform.

It took Theo several moments to find his voice, but, when he did, he ignored Richard and spoke to Chris. "Chief Allen," he said indignantly, "what are all these people doing here and why are you allowing this suicidal mental case to parade around town with a gun?"

It was not Allen, but Moore, who answered. "Theo, the Town Council held an emergency session a short while ago, and reinstated me. As chief of police, I'm required to be armed and clearly identifiable as a police officer when executing my duties."

Theo gave a little laugh and said, "You really have gone around the bend, Moore. The Council can't meet without me." Turning to Allen, he said, "Chief Allen, I don't know what this lunatic has told you, but this emergency Council meeting of his is a figment of his increasingly deranged mind. I order you to arrest him immediately and take that gun away from him before he hurts someone!"

Again, it was Moore, not Allen, who responded. "The meeting was held at Lieutenant Allen's request, Theo, and he was present for part of it. It was also his request that you not be notified."

Theo turned red and blustered, "But, but, that's preposterous! That ... that's illegal! What the hell do you people think you're playing at?"

Moore said, "Unfortunately for you, Theo, we're not playing at anything. These gentlemen behind me are narcotics agents." Reaching into his pocket, he pulled out some documents. "Theo, these are warrants to search these premises for illegal drugs, and an arrest warrant. You are under arrest for possession, possession with intent to distribute, possession with intent to distribute within a school zone, trafficking, and conspiracy to commit murder. You have the right to remain—"

When Richard said the men with him were narcotics agents, Theo felt a sudden sense of fear, his pulse rate rose, the veins in his neck swelled, his breathing became increasingly more rapid and shallow, his hands got cold, his stomach began to flutter, and his gut began to clench. As Richard continued speaking, Theo's fear intensified, and his symptoms worsened. In a matter of moments, his head was pounding and he felt as if he were suffocating. When Richard said, "conspiracy to commit murder," Theo experienced a great crescendo of terror, then, sudden blackness.

Richard had just started to read Theo his rights, when the man went limp and fell to the floor, unconscious. Peggy gasped, Chris said, "Oh, shit!" and Richard quickly knelt down and pressed his fingers against the man's neck. After Richard was sure Theo had a pulse and was breathing, he looked up to find a circle of concerned faces looking down at him.

"Did he have a heart attack?" someone asked.

Richard made a wry face and said, "Believe it or not, I think he fainted. Chris, call an ambulance. Oh, and Chris, have them bring some toilet paper with them—he's messed his pants."

A short time later, Richard received a call from Tim Curtin. "How did you make out, Richard? Was my intelligence accurate?"

"Yeah, Tim, the stuff was there, and we bagged our man. Murray and Williams from your team are going over the goods right now. Cramer and Henshaw are with the prisoner. How did you do on your end?"

"We got Carlos and most of his crew, and we've whisked them quietly away. They're illegals, so, after they serve their sentences, they'll be deported to the waiting arms of the Mexican police. Our friend Carlos and his pal Ramon will probably spend the rest of their lives behind bars here.

"Hey, buddy, I want to apologize again for not being able to warn you about the goons Carlos sent to the restaurant. The guy that screwed up is now on administrative leave."

"Stop worrying about it, Tim. I'm just glad you intervened with the Boston people about my leaving the scene. Thanks for waiting all that time for Carlos to start his operations again. I know you could have taken him long before this."

"Trust me, Richard; I wanted your guy too. I'm greedy that way. Give me a callback in the next few days, and we'll go eat."

"You got it, Tim, and I'll buy."

Chris and Peggy were talking with Bill Blackstone when Richard finished his call.

Looking at Blackstone, Richard said, "It's time, Bill."

"Go right ahead, Chief."

Addressing Peggy and Chris, Richard ordered, "Officer, Butler, Lieutenant Allen, come to attention."

Chris looked perplexed and said, "What?"

"I said to come to attention, Lieutenant, and I don't like to repeat myself."

Both police officers sprang to attention.

Richard stepped in front of Peggy, reached in his pocket and pulled out a set of sergeant's stripes. Holding them out, he said, "Officer Butler, upon my recommendation, the Town Council has approved your promotion to sergeant, effective immediately. Congratulations, Sergeant Butler."

Speechless, Peggy took the stripes, and, when Richard raised his hand in salute, saluted him back.

Stepping smartly to stand in front of Chris, Richard unpinned the chief's badge from his own uniform and held it out to the Lieutenant. "Lieutenant Allen, after you left the meeting this morning, the Town Council, accepted my resignation as chief, effective this hour, and, upon my recommendation approved your promotion to the position of chief to become effective at the same time."

Chris started to protest.

"No, no. You're the chief."

"Not anymore, I resigned."

"Chief, you know I didn't like it when you were brought in. I thought I deserved the position then. I have since realized that I wasn't ready. I'm still not ready, and I don't want your job away."

"Lieutenant Allen, nobody wants to hear you whine. If I told the Council you were ready, then you are ready. Now, return to attention and take this badge or I'm going to unclasp it and pin it directly to the flesh of your chest the same way I had my jump wings pinned to mine."

Allen hesitated a moment, then, repressing a grin, braced himself, and held out his hand.

Richard placed the badge in it, and said, "Congratulations, Chief Allen." He raised his hand in salute, and held it until Allen returned the salute.

Bill Blackstone congratulated them both, and told them there would be a more official ceremony in a few days. He also extended them both an invitation to dine with him.

Richard said he had other business to finish and left the three standing as he hurried off.

Richard arrived at Lesley Hall's house as a limo pulled up. When Sharon Hall and Leslie's granddaughter stepped out of the limo, Leslie shrieked with joy. The women ran toward each other and hugged. Sharon started to offer apologies for leaving, but Leslie stopped her.

"You're here now. That's all that matters, and for as long as you stay, I'm going to help you raise my granddaughter."

Leslie walked Sharon and her granddaughter to Richard and made the introductions, and then she kissed him on the cheek saying, "How can I ever thank you?"

"No thanks needed. Just seeing that little girl's face when she hugged you was enough."

"And what will you do now Richard?" Leslie asked.

"I bought a condominium in Boston. I don't know what I'm going to do long term, however, Stephanie and I are taking a vacation, and then I have some unpacking ahead of me."

Richard got in his car and drove off.

Epilogue

Cardboard boxes cluttered the counters and floor of his condominium. The furniture had arrived the day before. Coordinating the delivery from three different retailers was a two-day project. A handyman and his helper delivered the cardboard boxes that morning. Unpacking had proceeded well until he came across the pictures. Richard was sitting at the kitchen table as he picked them out of the box and focused on the smiling face. Images of joyful times filled his head.

He wiped the pictures and stood them on the kitchen table, so he could look at them as he continued his work.

"I finally took a vacation. It wasn't all it should have been," he said, halfway to himself and halfway to the long dead woman in the picture.

"I had that feeling every night. You remember the one I got whenever I felt justice had not been served. Any ideas about what might be troubling me?" He reached into the box and took out more items, wiping each one carefully before placing it on a towel at his feet. The final item in the box was a picture of his special operations team. Ghost was standing at the far right of the group of ten. As Richard looked at the image of Ghost, the feeling came back. He turned toward Lori's picture, and softly said, "It's not over, is it? That's the feeling. It won't be over until I deal with Rob Lee." With grim determination, he wiped his dust-stained hands, got up from his chair, walked to the rear door, picked up the wall phone receiver, and called Charlie.

"Tell Claude Billings I'm flying down tomorrow to talk with him about finding Rob Lee."

The hunt was on.

Made in the USA
Middletown, DE
02 December 2015